BAD MEDICINE

First Edition
Designed by Paulo Flores
Specialized Publications Company

ISBN 0-9639960-2-9

Composed and printed in the United States of America.

Specialized Publications Company
201 Main Street
Parkville, MO 64152

BAD MEDICINE

by paul s. auerbach m.d.

INTRODUCTION

Something was wrong. Everyone was drinking too much, smoking too much, touching too much. The young professionals hung up their white coats, looking for a little creative recreation. The party was thrown under the transparent guise of continuing education, but the latest advances in medicine were the furthest things from anyone's mind. First came the liquor. Then the marijuana and Valium. Then the recklessness of cocaine.

The youngest woman opened her blouse and escalated the group's excitement. One man was offered her breast to fondle. He stroked as the others waited their turns. She was eager at first, then drew back, as their touching grew rough. She asked to leave, then threatened to tell. Another woman tried to intervene, but was held back by arms much stronger than hers. The men dragged her companion away, against her will.

"Where are they taking her?" The drugs made it hard to focus, harder not to slur. "Let me *go*. I need to find her."

How did it get so out of hand? At midnight, nothing made sense. It was a crazy suggestion — just to frighten her. They were feeling so good. They couldn't stop. She struggled, then lay still. Everything seemed to move in slow motion.

Then it was over.

Later, looking back, they wondered how everything could have gone so wrong...

CHAPTER 1

"Hold this clamp for me. That's right, hang it over the drape. Easy! If you pull on it, you'll tear the vessel, and then we'll have blood all over the place. Attaboy. That's better."

Colonel Frank Klawitter extracted a triangular chunk of glass from deep inside a gash on the bottom of a young soldier's foot. He held it up for his patient to see. "How'd you jam this up so far? Didn't you feel pain? Were you drinking?" As he talked, the doctor deftly looped an absorbable suture around the curved tip of the stainless steel clamp held by Corporal medic Sam Anderson. With lightning speed, Colonel Klawitter threw two surgical knots and cinched shut the tiny bleeding artery pinched between the serrated metal teeth.

"OK, take it off," Klawitter instructed. Sam released the clamp. No bleeding now. The open wound stayed dry.

"Nice job. We'll just clean up a bit, and then I'll show you how to close."

"You mean *me*?" Sam stammered.

The colonel glanced at his rookie medic. The kid looked pale. Straight from college and ROTC, no chance to toughen up. He'd seen them the same way in Vietnam, yanked out of school and sent to basic training, then shipped off to war, all in a matter of months. They were the ones who got killed first.

This war was different. No front lines, no ground fighting. It was a sky war. In the Persian Gulf, a soldier was as likely to be felled by a scorpion as by a bullet. Frank wondered if this were progress, and then decided that right now, he didn't give a damn. "Yes, you. You've got to start somewhere. Unless, of course, this patient has any objection. Private, do you mind if I teach this future medical student how to properly repair your skin?"

"No, sir. And no, sir. And thank you again, sir. I don't know why that other doctor sewed my foot up and left the glass in there. Seems pretty sloppy to me."

"What's the second no for?"

"Your first question, sir. You asked if I was drinking. I wasn't drinking. Maybe the other doc was drinking. I don't understand the mistake."

"What mistake?" Klawitter asked.

"The piece of glass in my foot mistake. How could anybody who knew what he was doing leave a piece of glass in my foot like that? Wouldn't you be able to feel it with the needle or see it with an x-ray or something?"

"You have a pretty good mind for medicine, Private. As to your concern about how the surgeon missed that piece of glass, it was tucked way up in a corner, out of the way of where the light would fall."

"But *you* found it, Colonel."

"That's right. It's always easier to go second."

Klawitter showed Sam how to pull the skin together and insert symmetrical mattress sutures through the wound edges. Twenty minutes and ten stitches later, Sam was sweating as if he had run a mile. The repair was finished.

"Fantastic. Couldn't have done better myself." After filling out some paperwork, Frank led Sam out of the room toward the next patient.

"Uh, sir, I don't understand why you covered up for that other doctor. My grandmother would've found that piece of glass. That was malpractice."

"Don't talk foolishness!" Klawitter spun around intending a tonguelashing, but Sam's troubled expression made him hold back. "Corporal, there's a difference between being lazy or stupid and having something go wrong. What we had there was an honest mistake."

"Sir, how do you know?"

"I know, Sam, because the doctor who took care of that soldier is a good friend of mine. He works his tail off. He just plain old missed the glass. Hell, we *all* miss the glass from time to time."

"Will you tell your friend?"

"Of course I will. He needs to know. Maybe some day he'll have an opportunity to return the favor."

"Yes, sir. But there have to be times when doctors are incompetent. What do you do then?"

He's very young and earnest, thought Frank. "I do what everybody else does. I deal with what I can and be sensible about the rest. Most patients will accept explanations, if you're honest and straightforward with them."

"What if it's a real bad error? Do you discipline each other?"

"It's difficult, but it's done. There are committees and review boards. For the most part, they work pretty well. But there's always politics. You need more proof than the Justice Department on a spy ring. And let me tell you, doctors don't take kindly to a snitch."

"But sir, are you telling me..."

Frank shook his head. "Drop it. We have more work to do." Frank beckoned Sam to follow him, then turned with an afterthought. "Sometimes, the hospital can be like an airport. You know, things probably happen every day that are nearly unbelievable, but nobody ever finds out. We don't hear about every psycho that poses as a pilot or all the bombs found in the luggage. It's the same in medicine. It probably has to be."

"Why?"

"For lots of reasons. Mostly political. An unwritten code of honor. To avoid lawsuits. To preserve reputations. To keep the public from getting scared. To hold onto business. If people knew everything that went wrong, then the *good* doctors would suffer as well. We'd all get lumped in together. It's just human nature. C'mon, let's go."

In another makeshift cubicle, Frank examined a soldier with food poisoning who was severely dehydrated. The doctor ordered a nurse to wrap a hot towel around the soldier's arm in preparation for an intravenous line to return salt and water to the soldier's fluid-starved body.

"Can I help with the IV, sir?" Sam was jazzed after sewing up the foot.

"Nope."

"Why not? I've seen a zillion of these. You could walk me through it just like we did with the foot."

"Sorry, but not this time."

The soldier was leaning over the edge of the cot trying to throw up. He was as green as the canvas. "Oh man, I don't feel good. Can you give me something? My gut's killing me."

"That's why we're here. Let me see what you've got." Frank gently straightened the patient back out and inspected his forearms. He tied a tourniquet around the man's upper arm and poked and prodded in search of a vein below the constriction band. Nothing. He rolled up the soldier's pant cuffs and searched around his ankles. No luck. Sensing the inevitable, he positioned the young man flat on his back and put a stack of blankets under his feet. He asked him to hold his breath and strain, hoping that a vein would pop out on his neck. Zero.

"That's too bad. He's dry as a bone."

"What are you going to do?" Sam asked.

"We've got a few tricks left. Let me show you how to attempt a deep brachial vein. Most people don't know this one. I'll need your help."

Frank felt with the index and middle fingers of his left hand just above the inside crease of the soldier's right elbow. After a few seconds of searching, he found what he was looking for.

"Put your fingers right here. Can you feel it? Good. That's the brachial artery. Just below and inside that pulsation is the brachial vein. You can't see it. You just know it's there. Whatever you do, you try not to hit the artery." Frank painted the skin with an iodine solution, then relocated the brachial artery. "OK, put the tourniquet up, but not so tight that I lose his pulse. Hold still, son. You'll feel a little stick right... now." Frank jabbed the needle through the skin. He advanced it slowly. A sudden yelp from the patient startled the healers.

"Yow! My fingers!"

Frank pulled the needle back a few millimeters. He kept his stare fixed on the target. "Sorry about that. The median nerve runs alongside the vein, so if the patient feels an electric shock, you know you're close. Now that I know where it is, I'll try to stay away from it." Frank made an imperceptible angle adjustment and pushed forward. Blood ran back into the catheter. Frank slid the plastic over the needle, taped it in place, and connected it to a bag of normal saline. He admired his work.

"There. It's done. Now we can get you fixed up. Nurse, please give him two liters as fast as possible, then run in Ringer's at five hundred an hour. Keep that going until he has to pee every ten minutes. If he keeps vomiting, give him five of Compazine IV. Call me if you have any problems. We'll check on him at 2100."

As they walked outside into the daylight, Sam was full of admiration.

"Why'd you become a doctor?"

"What did you say?"

"I said, why'd you become a doctor? I'm just curious. Beg your pardon, sir," Sam added, embarrassed by his own question.

"It's been a long time since anybody asked me that." Frank Klawitter was Professor of Gynecology and Obstetrics at Branscomb University Medical School. This was a voluntary tour of duty for the Vietnam veteran, who entered college after the war. Now he was renowned in his field. The beginning of his medical career was as far away as his youth. "I started as a religion major. I was a junior by the time I realized that the only thing I could do was become a priest or teach religion. I played football, and the team doctor was a great guy. He let me tag along with him at the hospital. At the last minute, I swung all my courses around to pre-med. I loved it right from the start, so it was a good decision."

"Never a second thought?"

"Very few." Frank stared hard at Sam. "I can't think of any profession where you pay your dues as hard. But when you deliver a baby with your own hands, you'll have experienced a miracle that nothing can duplicate. When you save that first little kid, and somebody's mother or father comes up and blesses you, all the nights on call and pain and torture'll vanish like smoke. And you may not believe this now, but when you hold someone's hand and help them die without a tube down their throat and fifteen people pounding on their chest, it'll hurt, but that's good too."

"Yes, sir." Sam stared at his commanding officer. The medic's adulation was visible. It was Frank's turn to be embarrassed. What had compelled him to be so open with this lad? Maybe he sensed that Sam Anderson had the right qualities. Maybe Sam reminded Frank of himself in his own pre-med days. Maybe he was just hungry.

"C'mon. Let's go eat."

CHAPTER 2

...I've been watching the news every night, but I haven't spotted you yet. I'm so glad that this craziness is almost over. PLEASE BE CAREFUL! The girls ask about you constantly. They want to be certain that you'll be home soon. Don't forget that you promised you'd bring them each a camel...

Klawitter grinned as he stuffed his cousin's letter back into the envelope. Eleanor had seen some hard times, and it was good that she was coming out of it. His cousin and her kids were Frank's only family. Since Eleanor's divorce a few years ago, Frank was a substitute father for her children. He'd already ordered their camels. Big, purple, and fuzzy, just the sort of stuffed animals they'd love.

Frank had never married. He became engaged as a medical student to a nurse, but she got cold feet watching some of his classmates' marriages break up. After that, his timing was off; his career always interfered. He enjoyed dating, but a few fantastic ladies got tired of waiting. When Frank was feeling lonely, he sometimes regretted the lost opportunities. A wife and children, a home full of voices and warmth. But the cries of the newborns usually made up for that. Frank Klawitter, ex-college linebacker, a big man with a gentle touch, was as content as any man can be, which is to say, more so than not.

Although this tour in Kuwait was his patriotic duty, as well as a chance to get his hands in on some general surgery again, Frank was very glad that it was almost over. The action was waning, and he was ready to get back to his practice. The physician closed his eyes, intending to rest just a few minutes, and fell sound asleep.

Only a few skeleton crews were left to man the field hospitals. The war was winding down.

Because of the demobilization, Corporal Sam Anderson was assigned double duty as the night watch at the medical tent. It was an isolated and dismal chore. After five weeks of stultifying, vacant nights, Sam was notified that he would be released from duty and transferred back to the States in two days.

The message was delivered at noon. Sam was so excited that he couldn't fall asleep before his final 12 hour shift, and arrived at 1800 hours intoxicated by the thought of his impending freedom.

Six hours breezed by. Sam relaxed his attention and dozed. He was forbidden to leave the vicinity of the medical unit. On this peaceful night, he saw no harm in stepping away to get a breath of fresh air and have a peek at the stars. Sam quietly slipped out the door and strolled off fifteen yards into the desert. He jammed the door latch, leaving the unit unlocked.

The celestial light show was unusually brilliant and filled the entire sky. There was only a sliver of new moon, so the stars never seemed more incandescent. With no sound save the rustle of canvas generated by a brisk desert wind, the landscape was lunar, as Sam imagined the surface of the moon to be. Centuries of war buried under layers of eroded rubble and stone were obscured by Sam's romantic vision of nomads, mountains of sand, and oases populated by scantily-clad and nubile goddesses. He hadn't touched a woman in months. He dreamed on. Sam's reverie was suddenly interrupted by the muffled sound of a man crying out.

Sam rushed back into the medical tent. A soldier was slumped against a box of surgical supplies next to the locked safe where the narcotics were stored. How had he gotten in without Sam's notice? The man's head had fallen forward against his chest and he wasn't moving. A stream of viscous spittle hung from his mouth and chin. He must have yelled before he went down.

Sam flipped on the overhead lights. The collapsed man didn't budge. His left shirt sleeve was rolled up to the shoulder. There was a length of thin yellow rubber tubing cinched tightly around his biceps, which caused the veins in his forearm and hand to bulge. A thin stream of blood ran from a puncture wound on the inner area of the soldiers elbow and dripped large crimson globules onto the floor. The man's right hand lay across his lap with fingers curled around a half-full syringe with a long thin needle. His face was ashen, and his chest moved erratically to achieve weakening gasps in what was an agonizing last ditch attempt to breathe. The soldier's jaw was slack and his eyes were open in a blank stare. A huge multi-dose vial of Demerol lay at his side. The unconscious intruder had discovered the pharmacy of his dreams.

"Holy Jesus! A fucking junkie on my last night." There were telltale needle tracks all over his arm.

Sam reached underneath the angle of the man's jaw and felt in his neck for a pulse, as he'd seen done over and over in his job as a medical assistant. To his surprise, he felt a weak beating under his fingertips. "You son of a bitch, I oughta let you die. Goddamn it!"

The man was still alive, but he looked as though he would undoubtedly die without immediate assistance. There was no one around to help. Sam was his only chance, but the young sentry faced a real predicament.

There was no way Sam could cover up the incident. If the soldier was found dead, Sam would be in huge trouble for not guarding his station properly, and it would cost him his honorable discharge and imminent exit back to college. If he saved the man's life, he would still have to hand him over to someone. Where would he say he had been when the soldier entered the tent? How could he account for the incident, except to say that he hadn't paid attention to his post?

His ass was grass, and now there was no time to waste dreaming up some story that might get him off the hook. He couldn't just stand there and let the bastard die. He had to do something.

All of the soldiers had been trained to self-administer atropine from a pen-shaped auto-injector as an antidote to nerve gas poisoning. He remembered that one of the major effects of the medication was to increase heart rate. Sam hoped that atropine would wake the soldier up. He ran quickly to a stockpile of small field first aid kits. Sam tore one open and pulled out an atropine injector. He popped the safety cap and thrust the green business end with the retracted needle against the stricken soldier's thigh. After he flipped off the yellow safety cap at the opposite end, he pushed hard against the man's leg. With velocity sufficient to fling a dart through a leather boot, the spring-loaded needle shot through his pants into the collapsed soldier's thigh and the medication was discharged. The recipient should have felt pain like a carpet tack being driven into his flesh. He didn't flinch. The drug began to be absorbed.

Sam grabbed the unconscious man by the throat, feeling for his pulse. He found the carotid artery with the tip of his index finger and held on for dear life, squeezing nearly hard enough to choke the man whose life he was trying to save. Over the next two minutes, which seemed like an eternity, the junkie's heart rate increased to 40 beats per minute, which was sufficient to keep him alive. But he didn't wake up. To reverse the lethal central nervous system effects of the narcotic, a specific antidote would be required.

Sam had observed enough to have a basic understanding of what most drugs were used for. He knew that naloxone was a narcotic antagonist, but he didn't have any idea about the dose. Furthermore, he'd never personally given an injection into a vein.

He let go of his patient and looked around, then ripped into a large medical duffel. It was filled with innumerable pouches and plastic canisters stocked with medication vials, pills and capsules. Sam knew that one of them contained both the narcotic morphine and its antidote, naloxone. As he searched containers and didn't find what he was looking for, he flung them away. Frantic, he turned the bag upside down and shook the entire contents out onto the floor. He rummaged roughly through the pile, scattering what he couldn't use. Once again, the junkie's heart and lungs began to labor. He breathed coarsely, and clear fluid ran from the corner of his mouth. Time was running out. Sam examined his pupils and saw that they had gone from pinpoint to dilated. He didn't recognize the side effect of the atropine. He thought the man was about to drop dead.

"Aw Christ, where the fuck is this stuff? Think, man, think. Put the rockets where you can find them. Don't bury the candy in a hole. Look for the markers. Climb on the hard boxes. Give 'em the orange fix." By reciting the phrases he'd heard over the past few months, he was trying to remind himself where the narcotics were kept. He spotted a bright orange plastic soap case sealed with silver duct tape. Sam ripped off the tape and opened the box to reveal neatly arranged rows of medication vials bound into position by a serpentine elastic strap. There was the morphine! He also recognized four red-labeled vials of naloxone, each of which contained enough medication to reverse well over ten times the amount of any narcotic that a human might inject in an overdose. He figured if one was good, four would be better.

"Son of a bitch, it would be easier to frag your butt. This better work."

Sam flipped the plastic cap off a vial. He stabbed a needle-tipped syringe through the soft rubber top and drew out the entire contents. He repeated the process with the others. With half that amount of naloxone, he could arouse an entire busload of junkies.

Just as he had seen a hundred times before, Sam pointed the needle straight up at the ceiling and squirted out the air, leaving only the precious clear antidote within the plastic plunger. As he worked, he continued to talk to the unconscious victim.

"Oh man, this is real trouble for me. If I let you croak, then they're gonna reassign me to some place like the Sudan or Siberia or Kentucky and make me stay in the goddamn army for the next ten years doing time for being such a stupid moron. If I save your life and you get up and leave this place, then I have to explain why it looks like a fuckin' tornado came through here. It's no good. If you ever do this again, I'm just gonna let you go."

He picked up another rubber tubing, which lay on the floor next to the man slumped against the counter, and tied it tightly around the soldier's biceps right next to the one that was already there. Despite the man's condition, one vein popped up like a blue lightning bolt against the porcelain pallor of profound shock.

Sam was sweating profusely. As he leaned over, drops of sweat showered onto the man's elbow and the two tourniquets. With moisture pouring off his forehead, Sam began to grow lightheaded. He shook his head repeatedly and took deep breaths to keep from panicking.

What would Colonel Klawitter do? He'd be cool. Stay calm. Work this like it happens every day. "OK, buddy, here's your medicine." Sam dropped his voice to a whisper. "It doesn't taste too bad. Take it like a good boy." Sam's hands were shaking horribly. He held the syringe with one hand and the needle with the other. He placed the tip of the needle on top of the only visible vein on the inside of the junkie's elbow. With a jerk, Sam thrust the needle through the skin. A large drop of blood squirted out next to the puncture and there was a small flash of dark red blood back into the clear fluid within the syringe. Miraculously, Sam had gotten the needle into the man's vein.

"Ha! First stick! How about that?" Sam pushed the plunger and emptied the contents of the syringe directly into the man's bloodstream. Even though he forgot to undo the rubber tourniquets, Sam was able to inject the medication, which caused the vein to distend tortuously under the pressure head of the fluid bolus. Since the constriction bands remained in place, very little medication flowed past into the general circulation. Sam neglected to notice that the man's forearm was turning blue. Because most of the medicine was confined, there was no immediate dramatic effect. An expanding knotty blood bruise formed around the vein within the skin of the man's elbow, caused by the back pressure of a blocked venous river downstream.

Once again, Sam felt underneath the man's jaw for a pulse. He noticed that his heart was beating slightly faster and that his general color was a tiny bit better. The sweat which had moistened the rubber tourniquets caused them to lose friction and loosen. A minuscule amount of the naloxone immediately coursed directly to the soldier's heart and was circulated throughout his body. The effect was dramatic. He began to breathe more rapidly and deeply. He started to pink up and moaned softly. Sam appreciated a bounding pulse in his neck. However, since the man had been unconscious and with extremely low blood pressure for fifteen minutes, his brain had been stunned from a prolonged period of diminished oxygen. He wouldn't open his eyes, even when Sam shook him. Sam mistakenly thought that this was to be the extent of the soldier's immediate recovery.

"That should do 'er, buddy. I'll check on you as soon as I get this mess cleaned up."

Sam turned his back to the man. He knelt down on the floor and started to gather up the intruder's paraphernalia and all of the supplies thrown around the room.

The rubber tubing continued to slip until it finally popped free. The remainder of the naloxone was released from the victim's forearm and sped up to the right side of his heart, through his lungs, back into the left side of his heart, and out to his body and brain within a matter of seconds. It was a cerebral explosion. As if awakened from a deep sleep by a cymbal crash, the addict was jolted back into the land of the living. Instantaneously, he acquired the confusion and fury of a man brutally scorched by extremely intense pain. He roared out of the refuge of narcotic-induced slumber. With a terrifying bellow of agony, he leaped up and threw himself at Sam.

The junkie soldier grabbed Sam by the throat and slammed his head down against a metal cot. The impact split open the flesh on Sam's forehead like the skin of an overripe peach. Blood gushed into Sam's eyes as he tried to pry the crazed man's fingers from his throat. The addict held onto Sam's scalp and bashed his head repeatedly. Blinded by blood, pain and fear, Sam clasped his hands together and threw them back up over his head in a two-handed karate chop. He knocked his assailant backwards over a pallet of trash barrels.

The psycho withdrawing from narcotics charged out from the barrels and pulled his commando knife. In desperation, and nearly sightless from the blood in his eyes, Sam drew his service revolver and pointed it up at the ceiling to fire a warning shot. Simultaneously, the feral addict sprang in a savage attempt to drive his weapon into Sam's chest. Sam pulled the trigger. A bullet slammed into the right shoulder of his assailant, who fell on top of Sam as he dropped the knife. They crashed to the ground and began to wrestle.

Colonel Frank Klawitter was still snoozing when he heard the gunshot. He ran to the medical tent and bolted through the open door. He separated the combatants and threw the struggling addict into a corner. Sam Anderson pointed his gun at the fallen soldier while he tried to wipe the blood from his face.

"What's going on here, son?"

Frank moved quickly to the wounded intruder and inspected his shoulder. He was growing weak from his ordeal and didn't resist. "My

God, Sam. Put the gun down. You've probably blown out half his scapula. What the hell happened in here? The war's out *there!*"

Sam lowered his weapon. He had just fired upon an American soldier. There was nothing that he could ever do that would have more serious repercussions.

"Are you all right? Let me see that cut on your head." Klawitter spread the margins. "Nasty. This needs to be cleaned out. There's some bone showing."

"Mind if I sit down? I don't feel so hot," Sam said.

"Sure. Tell me what happened." Frank prayed that Sam had good cause for what he had done.

Sam told him everything; that he had been gone from his post and allowed the man to get into the narcotics. He also explained how he had been attacked and that the shooting had been in self defense. He put his head between his hands and began to weep.

Klawitter was faced with a tough decision. Abandoning his post? Shooting a fellow soldier? Frank knew what a hearing would do to Sam's career in the military, and even beyond that. A dishonorable discharge would be part of Sam's record forever. Lesser flaws had kept applicants out of medical school.

In the end, there was no other satisfactory choice. He decided to protect his young friend. Frank couldn't see Sam taking the blame for the overt criminal act of a drug addict. The soldier would be court-martialed and probably sent to prison. Telling the complete truth wouldn't prevent that. On the other hand, Frank could keep a decent young man from sharing an outlaw's disgrace. Knowing that his negligence had contributed to this tragedy would be punishment enough for someone like Sam.

The investigation was kept confidential. Frank conspired with Sam to filter the sequence of events into the barest essentials. The official story was that Sam had left his post briefly and legitimately at Klawitter's specific request to assist him with paperwork in his quarters. When Sam returned, he encountered the addict. The intruder turned out to have a prodigious drug abuse record, so the report passed without so much as a raised eyebrow.

The day before Sam was shipped home, he called on Klawitter to say his last goodbye.

"How can I ever thank you? You saved my life. I'll never forget what you did."

"Hell, you risked your own life to help someone who wouldn't have ever done the same for you. It didn't make any sense to let him ruin your life. Believe me, it won't be the last time I have to do the right thing. I've thought about it a lot, and the decisions get clearer and clearer. The good people have to stick together. Now go home and try to forget about it."

"I'll *never* forget about it. If I can ever do anything for you..."

Frank cuffed Sam on the shoulder. "Here's what I want. The military part's over now. I want you to go back to school and work your butt off. Then I want you to get into medical school. If you really want to impress me, get yourself accepted at Branscomb. If you can keep your nose clean, maybe I'll even consider writing you a letter of recommendation. Now get out of here, before I change my mind."

Sam received an honorable discharge and returned to college. With a renewed zeal for his studies, he consistently scored in the top ten percent on all of his exams. The hard work paid off. Sam did more than pass his MCATs — he crushed them. Supported by a glowing letter of recommendation to the Admissions Committee from Dr. Frank Klawitter, he got a highly coveted early acceptance into Branscomb. Sam requested Frank as his freshman advisor. As if Sam had been a long lost relative coming home, Frank anxiously awaited the arrival of his young protege.

CHAPTER 3

By all measures, Professor Frederick Spencer, M.D. was a genius. As one science writer noted, "Branscomb is among the best hospitals in America because of the power of investigators like Frederick Spencer. And his discoveries have only just begun."

When an undergraduate at MIT, the prodigious Spencer was recognized as a computer impresario. He turned his senior project into a thesis worthy of a doctorate in nuclear medicine. The budding scientist theorized correctly that if a person could overlap consecutive panoramic images of a person's facial bones, then the precise internal location of central nervous system structures could be calculated. His discovery was a dramatic breakthrough for the field of radiation oncology. In an unheard of gesture, the mathematician-engineer was actually recruited into medical school. Medical education at Harvard was followed by a residency in radiology at Thomas Jefferson and a fellowship in nuclear medicine and advanced imaging at the Mayo Clinic. Every major teaching hospital competed for him. Fred Spencer chose Branscomb.

The young doctor became a prominent clinician and a favorite of the Dean, Wiley Waterhouse, who awarded him space and seed funds for any research project he wanted to pursue. It was a good bet. Spencer was able to leverage the start-up money into enormous grants that rained overhead dollars on the Dean's office.

Basking in the limelight of Spencer's achievements, Waterhouse repeatedly offered him a Department Chair; at first Spencer refused, preferring to stay in his lab. "I'll let you know when I'm ready to move on."

The academic leader of the medical center was therefore not completely surprised when Fred Spencer walked into his office one afternoon and told him that he needed to discuss his future. The Dean motioned to Spencer to have a seat. Spencer remained standing.

"Wiley, I have a request to make." Spencer eyed the Dean. Short, rotund, and semi-bald, Waterhouse sported an anomalous thin handlebar moustache that drew attention to his crooked bleached teeth and bulbous lower lip. A gold Rolex hung loosely at his wrist. Wiley Waterhouse was Wiley Waterhouse's favorite subject. If you told him that you were a tennis player, then he had once played doubles with Bjorn Borg. If you liked to backpack, Waterhouse had climbed Kilimanjaro with Peter Hackett. By his account, he had explained the theories of nucleotides to Watson and Crick, who were lucky enough, afterwards, to discover the secrets of DNA.

"By all means, Fred. What's on your mind?" *Why the formality?* thought Waterhouse. They always addressed each other by their first names.

"I want to be Dean."

Waterhouse chuckled, than slapped his knee. "C'mon Fred, I'm busy. What do you want? Another lab? Name the space."

"I want to be the Dean. Look at me, Wiley."

There was no humor in his voice. For the first time since Waterhouse had known him, Spencer seemed nervous. There was sweat on his upper lip. "What do you mean, the Dean? The Dean at Branscomb? You want my job? What's the matter, Fred? Did you lose a grant?"

The radiologist leaned forward. Spencer's prematurely silver hair, his steel-blue eyes, and slender face tapering into an aquiline nose could easily have morphed into the face of a racing greyhound. He was intent.

"It's coming up soon. Early retirement. You always say you want to do it. You *could* do it," Spencer emphasized. Waterhouse was always moaning that he couldn't wait until he was 63.

"Fred. That's just trash talk. Nobody takes me seriously. I have no intention of stepping down early."

"You can't be the Dean forever. At some point, you'll need a replacement. Your Assistant Dean'll never be the one, and you know it."

"Well, uh, of course she won't. But really, Fred, why be a Dean? And why now? You have an unbelievable future as a researcher. And what about your patients?" Waterhouse wanted to keep Fred Spencer happy. His personal clinical radiology practice generated more income than the entire Division of General Internal Medicine. Twice a year, like clock-work, Spencer won some sort of award. American Radiological Society Investigator of the Year. Harold Branscomb Medal of Merit. National Cancer Foundation Outstanding Scholar. Waterhouse needed Spencer to stay right where he was. "What about Chairman of Radiology?"

"No. That's too much the same. I'm getting bored with what I'm doing. I want to have a bigger impact. I see what you do. Nobody gets to call the shots like the Dean. You're the most important person at Branscomb."

"You're right and you're wrong. I'm a bureaucrat, that's for sure, and so what I do is necessary, but people like you are the glue that hold this place together."

"Well, I want to get unstuck. Look, let me explain how strongly I feel about this. I'm thinking about putting my research on hold. My heart's not in it. I can't continue unless I know what will come next. I want to be the Dean at Branscomb. I want to make a difference. The energy is here, right now, inside me. I want to reinvent medical education. Change lives. So, I think I should stop our project."

"You can't."

"Of course I can. It's logical. Look — I love Branscomb. For the last ten years, this place has been my life. You know everything that's happened, what I've sacrificed." Spencer's wife had left him to move back to Toledo, where she had grown up. Their marriage had fallen apart when Fred didn't come home for dinner for weeks at a stretch and they stopped having sex because he was either too tired or up all night in the lab, obsessed with his research. She was a wife and mother first and wanted him to be a husband and father first. He was a scientist first and wanted a cook, housecleaner, and personal secretary. When she filed for divorce, he was completely surprised, so little had he been paying attention. The children were now in junior high and loved their new stepfather very much.

The Dean stood from his chair to protest, then quickly sat back down. Spencer was playing for high stakes. Unknown to anyone except the Dean, Spencer had devised a way to recompute conventional two-dimensional magnetic resonance image (MRI) data to allow construction of 3-D images in a way that could reveal a person in virtual reality. He was on the verge of being able to adjust the human holograms for density, which would hopefully allow him to perform radiological dissections. The impact on radiology would be greater than anything since the discoveries of Marie Curie and would lead directly to Stockholm, and to unbelievable fame and fortune. When Spencer had proposed the expensive project to Waterhouse, the Dean had been quick to offer complete funding in exchange for co-investigator status. He had convinced Fred that doing it all internally was the only way to control confidentiality. Wanting some modicum of secrecy in the early phases of investigation, Spencer agreed to the arrangement and accepted complete responsibility for the work. He was nearly ready to go to an open preliminary clinical trial. Stopping now would be disastrous for the project, and if it transferred to someone else, would likely cut Wiley out of the action. Spencer held all the data. He had to continue his research. The Dean changed tactics.

"Fred, how could I be so blind? I should have come up with your suggestion myself. Up until now, I didn't have a logical successor for my job. You're right about Valerie, of course. But this isn't a situation where I have the only say."

"Wiley..."

"No, hear me out. I don't disagree that you'd make a terrific Dean and that you've earned the right to follow in my footsteps. But before I make a commitment that I can't keep, let me float the idea a little. You know how things work around here. A tiny bit of politics now can save us a lot of hassle later on."

"So, what are you saying?"

"I'm saying that nothing would make me happier than to see you become the next Dean at Branscomb. I'll make you a deal. If you keep on with the project, I promise that as long as I have anything to say about it, you'll be the number one candidate. It'll probably take a transition strategy, but I'll retire to make room for you if it comes to that."

"And the timing?"

"It shouldn't be sudden, and you understand that I have to go through the motions of a search for a successor. So, don't make your announcement quite yet. I wasn't planning on dropping dead any time soon."

"I wouldn't want you to. Look, you know how I feel. When you made me all those offers, I just assumed that this is what you really had in mind."

"Of course it is. I was going to wait a bit, but if you're ready now, then we just get the ball rolling early." Not exactly, thought Waterhouse after Spencer shook his hand and walked from the room. This would blow over. Like all the others before him, Fred Spencer would grow tired of waiting for the Dean to keep his promises, and forget about the whole thing. Waterhouse just had to keep stringing him along.

CHAPTER 4

"Dr. Snell, you have a phone call. It's the Dean. He said he has a question he'd like to ask you. Do you want to take the call?"

"Of course. Put it through. Oh, and close the door, will you please? Thanks."

Valerie Snell was the Assistant Dean for Student Affairs. She waited until her secretary pulled the door shut to pick up the phone. "Hi, Wiley. It's always nice to hear from you. What can I do you for?" Valerie put on her cheeriest voice. This was her boss, the man who would make her career. At least so he promised.

"Hello, Valerie. I apologize for doing this by phone, but I'm out of the office and it can't wait until I get in. I've got meetings all morning. Pay close attention now. There's something I want you to take care of for me."

"Sure. Whadja need?"

"Well, I feel kind of funny asking you to do this, so please keep everything confidential. I want you to arrange to put a young woman into the first year class for this fall. I know that we've already taken most of our admissions, but I hope we still have a spot in the final group. If we do, I need you to enroll her for the fall quarter." Branscomb had a rolling admissions policy, which meant that they sent out letters of acceptance on an irregular schedule. Until the last spot in the medical school class was filled, there could be an adjustment.

This was a strange request, even more so coming from the Dean. He knew the rules and regulations of the Admissions Committee. Valerie couldn't just "put" someone in the class. He couldn't possibly expect her to arbitrarily accept someone into medical school. Particularly at this late date. Everyone had to submit a complete application, write an essay and undergo a laborious round of interviews. The ratio of applications to acceptances was over fifty to one. Nobody got in solely on a phone call or a personal recommendation. Maybe the Dean was tired.

She answered him politely. "Pretty funny, Wiley. Just testing me to see if I know the rules, huh?"

"This isn't a test. I mean it."

"I'd love to help you, but it's already August. The new class shows up in ten days. I think it's a little too late for this year. But if you send me the kid's stuff, I'd be happy to look at her for next year."

The Dean had anticipated that Valerie wouldn't comply, so he was prepared to try a number of different approaches. He wanted to keep this low key if possible.

"Let me ask another way. It's very important to me to have this particular student start with this year's class. I owe her family a personal favor. It was something they did for the school when we badly needed their help. An *enormous* donation. Having this woman come to Branscomb is all they really want. She's highly qualified, but a little intimidated by the process."

Valerie didn't respond. This was all wrong. The Dean noted her silence and notched it up a bit.

"I really must insist on this, Valerie. Find a way."

Snell was in a terrible bind. The man was her boss, but what he was asking was going to be nearly impossible. She had to dissuade him.

"Wiley, you know that I'd do anything in the world for you, but this one just won't fly. Please understand."

"That's not the right answer."

"Please," she implored. "Be reasonable. What if somebody finds out?"

"See that nobody does. Her name is Malinda Dwyer. I'll have her file delivered to you. There are certain deficiencies in her application. Fix them."

Valerie was defeated. "OK, I'll do it. I have an idea that might work. But if anyone ever finds out, it was an innocent exchange of professional courtesy. By the way, I know I'll need some money for another student. Standard application fee, tuition and so forth. Not a penny more."

"Of course. You'll get it. Thanks, Val. This means a lot to me."

"Wiley Waterhouse, if it was anybody else but you..." She heard a soft chuckle, and then a dial tone.

The Assistant Dean opened up a drawer and leafed through the folders of the entering freshmen, looking for the ones stamped "Financial Aid." She found what she was looking for, an outstanding but financially strapped student who planned to support her education with loans totaling over $150,000. Valerie called the student with good news. Because of her academic record and her need for financial assistance, Branscomb Medical School had awarded her a full scholarship from an anonymous donor, with one stipulation. She would have to wait a year before entering medical school. Because of arcane budgetary reasons, Valerie explained vaguely, the scholarship could not be applied in the coming academic year. Was she willing to wait?

The stunned young collegian could hardly believe her luck. She was delighted — of course she'd be glad to sit out for a year. The deal was done. One entering student swept aside to make room for Wiley's request. At least, thought Valerie with a somewhat bitter satisfaction, it's going to cost him.

Valerie's secretary poked her head through the door. She held out a manila envelope.

"This is from the Dean. He said you'd know what it was about."

Valerie opened the envelope and pulled out a folder marked "Dwyer, Malinda." Taped inside the front cover was a waist-length photograph of an attractive woman with dark brown hair and a determined expression. She looked older than most college graduates. Valerie checked her age. It was 37. There was no age limitation on entering students, but she was close to the informal cutoff. Her biography was perfunctory, and the essay section was blank. At least the test scores were decent. Valerie picked up her pen and began to write an essay entitled "Why I Want to Go to Medical School."

The Dean lifted and replaced the receiver three times. This was the biggest risk he'd ever taken. If anyone but Valerie ever found out what he'd done, even the Dean couldn't defend himself. He lifted the receiver again and dialed. *Get it over with.*

"Theresa? It's Wiley."

"Get it right, damn it! My name's Malinda now, not Theresa. It's legal. Don't *ever* call me Theresa again."

Waterhouse grimaced. "It wasn't as easy as I thought it would be. I hope you're satisfied now."

"Wiley, you're breakin' my heart. Spare me the theatrics. You can do whatever you want. We're partners, remember?"

Waterhouse was choking. She would be living in his backyard. Her mockery enraged him.

"This has got to stop!"

"Sure — we made a deal. But I need twenty thousand right now. I just bought a Mercedes. A *used* one, Wiley."

It would never end. He felt a panic rush over him. She was a parasite, a virus feasting on his life. "I can't keep sending you money. That's nearly two hundred thousand dollars in the last year and a half."

Malinda's tone changed to conciliatory. "Come on, Wiley. After I'm a doctor, you'll never hear from me again. But first I have to get into a good medical school. And you know my grades are awesome." Her purr made him tremble.

"You'll have the check in a few days."

"Good."

"Goodbye, Malinda."

"*Doctor* Dwyer. I love it."

Waterhouse slammed down the phone. He reached into the huge candy jar on his desk, threw a handful of jellybeans into his mouth, and munched ferociously.

"D-W-Y-E-R. Malinda. Malinda Dwyer. I'm calling long distance from home about the roommate service. I'll be a first-year medical student. I know it may be kind of late, but it would be great if there was someone available to room with."

"It shouldn't be a problem. I need you to answer a few questions."

"Fine. Ask me anything you want."

"Do you want to live in a house, an apartment or the graduate student housing?"

"It doesn't matter."

"Do you have any pets? They're not allowed, you know."

"No pets. No loud music. No swearing. No violent behavior. I have no current convictions and I can tolerate any religion so long as nobody expects me to practice it. I like to cook, hate to clean and expect my roommate to do her share of the housework. I like my privacy, so we have to have two phone lines."

Malinda began to doubt whether this was such a smart move. She was all set to cancel the inquiry when the woman in the housing office sprang back on the line.

"I think I may have the perfect match. Her name is Lauren Jane Doopleheimer. I spoke with her yesterday. Lauren graduated from the University of Virginia. She just decided to look for a roommate."

"What do I need to do?"

"I'll give you Miss Doopleheimer's phone number so that you can talk and work things out between you."

Malinda took the information. After she put the phone down, she wondered whether she was making a good decision. Her ambivalence reflected her anxiety. She was lonely. A pleasant roommate could certainly be an asset in this difficult first year. But the wrong one could be a living hell. And dangerous.

CHAPTER 5

Fred Spencer was in his element working at the computer console. As nimble as a pinball wizard, his feel for the keyboard and dials allowed the images on the screen to leap to life. Thousands of hours refining the software he had developed to create visions of people and body parts in three dimensions had rendered him a virtuoso of lasers and holograms.

His talents in clinical radiology were nearly as profound, and uniquely diverse. Spencer could read a barium swallow or a pancreatic echo with the best of them, and his interpretations were the gold standard against which all of the other radiologists measured their proficiency. Uncharacteristically, his fellow faculty revered him without envy — such were his talents. The students had voted him the Golden Apple for Best Clinical Teacher four times already. He thrived on the attention and respect. To do outstanding work in the eyes of one's peers was a source of constant satisfaction.

Spencer's laboratory was entirely his own design, more like the command center of a spaceship than a traditional suite for a radiologist. Sitting at his workstation, he faced three large computer screens and a transparent window into the MRI room with its sliding examination table surrounded by the enormous circular magnet. Behind him was a circular pedestal upon which he could project intersecting laser images from an overhanging device that looked like it belonged in a planetarium. A series of baffles separated the mainframe computer and its elaborate cooling mechanism from the work area, and an enormous, locked tape-backup where confidential medical records and image files could be stored. Traditional x-rays and reference materials were arranged in bookshelves nearby. A reference human skeleton dangled from a wire stand in the corner.

By posting for student volunteers, he was able to collect hundreds of data sets that allowed him to determine normal anatomy, and the technique for recreating a perfect virtual image. In collaboration with one of the oncologists, he began to screen elderly men in search of prostate cancer, and found that he could be as accurate as a biopsy, and even find tumors where the prostatic specific antigen blood test was negative.

Subtle bone fractures that had been missed after numerous examinations were obvious to him. With each refinement of the software, he could extract more detail, until his radiological dissections were cleaner and more direct than the bladed explorations of the pathologists. It seemed that his skills and discoveries would be limited only by the amount of time he had to spend working in the laboratory.

After his conversation with the Dean, Spencer had been skeptical, but decided it was best to wait and watch before pushing his request. Waterhouse had always come through for him in the past, and so he was content to return to his research — at least for the time being. He needed to get the project to the point where he could turn it over to other researchers if he was going to have time to be Dean.

Only a few other people besides Waterhouse knew the details of his work, because the data were preliminary and could only be used under strict investigational protocols. For one such study, Frank Klawitter had been asked to identify patients with uterine fibroid tumors, so that Fred could work on pelvic anatomy. The men had long ago become close friends, as much in recognition of their mutual concerns for the medical center as for their respective clinical acumen. Fred always made time to interpret Klawitter's toughest radiology studies, and went out of his way to refer to his gynecologist friend as one of the shining stars in the medical center. Frank had complete confidence in Fred, which was more than could be said for his opinion of certain other doctors at Branscomb. Frank knew that Fred Spencer would never have any of his cases presented for discussion at the Quality of Care Committee.

At first, becoming Dean faded as a priority for Spencer. The work was going exceedingly well. As his discoveries progressed, he thought about calling Waterhouse and telling him to sit tight on their discussion for awhile, but then thought better of it. There was no harm in keeping his request active.

The timing of the phone call from Boston couldn't have been better — or worse. He would have never thought he could leave Branscomb. If being offered the opportunity to apply for the position of Associate Dean for Graduate Medical Research at Harvard wasn't the ultimate compliment, it was close. Spencer had rebuffed innumerable feelers from lesser institutions over the years, but you had to respond to a call from Harvard. It was quite a package. He could become the Associate Dean, which of course put him in direct line for succession to the top job, and continue to direct his own research, with as many lab assistants as he needed. All of his grants would be transferred, and he could come any time in the next six months. There was a search committee, but the background checks and letters of support would be perfunctory. There was one other candidate, but it was inconceivable that the Board of Trustees would not find Spencer to be the clear choice. Branscomb or no Branscomb, he needed to check this one out.

Spencer went to Waterhouse's office.

"Come in, Fred. What's on your mind?"

Spencer was nervous. He wouldn't make eye contact, but glanced quickly around the room. The portrait of Louis Pasteur, the marble mortar and pestle, the citations in their heavy frames, the diplomas, the candy jar full of multicolored jellybeans. It was so familiar, like home really. And now he badly wanted to leave. "Wiley, I need your help. I have to make a decision. Along the lines of what we talked about before."

"Now Fred, you've got to give me a chance. I've called some of the trustees and they're just starting to get back to me."

"No, you don't understand." Fred laughed. "It's not Branscomb. I've been invited to apply for a position as Associate Dean at Harvard, and they need a letter from you. I'm sure it's only a formality, but it's probably best not to take any chances. Can you knock it off over the weekend?"

Waterhouse was dumbstruck. That couldn't be allowed to happen. If Harvard could get their hands on someone like Fred, they'd do it in a heartbeat. Stealing prized faculty was academic sport, and a Fred Spencer came along once in a deanship.

"But...but...your research! How will you finish your research? You're sitting on a Nobel Prize!" As soon as the words came out of his mouth, Waterhouse knew it sounded all wrong. Selfish. He had to control his voice, erase the panic. Fortunately, Spencer's mind was elsewhere, at Harvard. He answered calmly.

"Oh, that won't be a problem. They've assured me that I can take my work with me. The way the grants are written, so long as I give notice and proper justification, there won't be a problem transferring funds. Look Wiley, I know that this can't make you happy, but I appreciate your dilemma at Branscomb. It's above and beyond the call of duty for you to promote me here. I see that now. Look at it this way: if I go to Harvard, you don't have to stick your neck out for me. I can do a great job there, and maybe come back. You never know." He took Waterhouse by the arm. "Hey, c'mon now. You look like you just lost your best friend. You'll still be a co-author on some of the papers. It'll still say Branscomb on a lot of the stuff. Faculty always move around. Everybody knows that."

"It's just that you mean a lot to me, Fred. As a person. And as a friend." And as a fundraiser. And as a direct pipeline to the NIH. And as a ticket to more media attention than Waterhouse could have arranged if he were appointed the next Surgeon General.

"And you to me. I'll always be grateful for what you've done. So, will you do it?"

"I'll do better. I'll match their offer. You can stay here as *my* Associate. We'll create a special position for you by tomorrow morning. It's never been done before, but I don't see why we couldn't."

"That's tremendous! I really didn't come here to push for the position at Branscomb. Wow. I need to think about that." Fred suddenly felt empowered. It was a nice feeling.

"What's there to think about? That's what you asked me for, isn't it?"

"Yes it is." Spencer grew reflective. "But now that they've come to me, I feel that I have to respond. Wiley, it's Harvard. And I didn't have to twist their arm. Why didn't you get back to me?"

"I was going to." Waterhouse sounded pretty unconvincing.

"Fine. I appreciate it. You know how much I love Branscomb. If we had worked this out before, I would have told them no right away. But now I have to play this one out. I'm going to find out more. It's the sensible thing to do. So will you write me the letter?"

The Dean knew it would be senseless to protest. Spencer was right. "Of course I will. Do you want to see it?"

"No. I'm not supposed to. I trust you. Besides, nobody reads those things, anyway. Not at this level."

Waterhouse needed to regroup. He offered his hand to Spencer.

"Congratulations. I'm proud of you. Things won't be the same without you around here."

"Hey, don't look so glum. I haven't decided anything. I might hate the place. Let's wait and see."

Richard L. Moffitt, M.D., Ph.D.
Dean, Harvard Medical School
Boston, Massachusetts

August 31, 1995

Dear Rick:

I am writing at the request of Frederick P. Spencer, M.D., who has informed me that he is being considered as a candidate for the position of Associate Dean at the Harvard Medical School.

As you know, Dr. Spencer was well regarded as a medical student and house officer, and thus a highly sought-after addition to our faculty. His clinical skills in radiology have resulted in numerous awards, and his research is poised to attain national recognition. He is a valued member of our faculty and I am understandably regretful of his interest in your institution. It would be a great loss to Branscomb to have Fred Spencer leave our radiology department.

At a personal level, I find Fred to be quick-witted and in enormous possession of the details. He is a tireless worker who brings great creativity to his work. The impact of his work upon our medical center is difficult to predict, but I suspect that it may bring us great attention. There will be great scrutiny by the press. I am working with him to prepare for that eventuality.

In summary, you are wise to consider Dr. Spencer as a candidate for Dean. Please feel free to contact me if I can offer further support for his application.

Sincerely yours,

Wiley R. Waterhouse, M.D.
Professor and Dean
Branscomb University School of Medicine

It was a good ol' boys network at the deanship level. There would be no mistaking the cue. The communication was clean but provocative. The unwritten protocol would have Moffitt call the Dean at Branscomb, which he did as soon as he received the letter. The tip-off phrases could not be ignored. "The impact of his work..." was brilliantly crafted. In its imprecision, a red flag was raised. Any reference to the press had to be explored.

The phone call was placed an hour after the letter was read.

"Hello, Rick. How are you? The Patriots going to be worth a damn this year? Or is it Superbowl and bust like usual?"

"Probably the usual. I shouldn't waste my money on tickets, but you know what they say about New England football. Hands like their heads." Moffitt paused before moving to the main topic. "By the way, was it my imagination or did I catch a glimmer of something in your letter about Fred Spencer? He's blown everybody away up here. The superstar medical student returning to his days of glory. The second coming. Your comments were awfully brief, sort of cryptic. He's been successful at Branscomb, hasn't he?"

Waterhouse had to be perfect. Any hint of jealousy or sour grapes would be seen for what it was and blow the whole deal. Moffitt would expect Waterhouse to try to keep Spencer at Branscomb, but he wouldn't anticipate what the desperate Dean had in mind. If this worked, it would be a crime without a trace; if it didn't, Waterhouse would forever be branded as an untrustworthy SOB.

"He's a great one." Waterhouse waited.

"And?"

"And what?"

"And what else? Just a great one?"

"Rick, I'm not sure quite how to say this."

"Say what?"

"First, you have to promise me that you will never under any circumstances discuss what I'm about to tell you with anyone. Ever."

"Wiley, you know me better than that. What should be kept confidential will be kept confidential. Before you say anything, however, remember that we have a search committee and they need to be kept informed. But that's an entirely closed operation. There's no requirement for minutes to be kept. I handpicked them. There won't be any leaks, I promise you."

It was decision time. Waterhouse would have preferred to do business solely with his Harvard counterpart, but he knew that Moffitt would have to tell the others. He would have said the same thing. "OK, but remember, if this gets out, we'll all pay for it."

"Enough angst, already. Do we have a problem with our boy Spencer?"

"You don't. I do."

Waterhouse recorded a lengthy sigh from the other end. Moffitt was sliding into his trap. It wasn't the kind of news that a recruiting Dean liked to hear. "I'm listening."

"All of his data may not be clean."

"Oh my God."

He was buying it. "I know."

"Which study? You're a co-investigator on at least one, aren't you?"

"Don't you think I know that? Fortunately, *our* work together is clean. It's the earlier stuff, the CT spine enhancement project he did when he first got here. Maybe one other. I'm not sure yet."

"Are you absolutely certain? What's wrong?"

This was critical. If Moffitt were hooked, he'd take the rest on faith. "I can't tell you yet. We're still investigating. It might never come out. Then again, it might. We're trying to keep this thing under wraps. I can promise you this much — the patients will never know. The conclusions are correct, just a little bold. He wanted to get ahead. You know, the numbers." The implication was that Spencer had used fictitious patients. Fraud was the most reprehensible type of research abuse, worse than plagiarism, worse than kickbacks. "You can't imagine how difficult this is for me. I think the world of Fred. But if somebody found out after I recommended him to them — well, what would *you* do?" Waterhouse's revelation showed Moffitt that his colleague greatly trusted him.

"Does anyone else know?"

"I don't think so."

"Good. Then let's leave it there. Hopefully, no one will ever find out. You don't need to say anything else. I can take it from here. Wiley, I owe you. You didn't need to stick your neck out like that."

"Of course I did. We can never forget that there's still some honor left in this business. That's why we're all here, isn't it?"

CHAPTER 6

After nearly three years of self-imposed celibacy that followed disso-
lution of a crummy marriage and a devastating divorce, Frank Klawitter's
cousin Eleanor finally decided she was entitled to a little stimulation over
and above *Horton Hears a Who*. But with two young daughters, dating
was difficult. That didn't leave many options. With so little free time, she
was forced to transform from a model legal secretary and PTA mother
into a cocktail party woman. She had never been promiscuous, so the
mindless small talk and blatant come-ons were frightening at first. In
time, she learned to loosen up at office gatherings where she could hide
in the wine and frivolous chatter.

It was bound to happen sooner or later. A great party at the firm, a
surge of loneliness, too many margaritas and one episode of furtive not-
so-great sex with a co-worker landed her a trip to the hospital. In April
when Eleanor missed her period, she wasn't overly concerned, because
she'd been irregular ever since the birth of her second daughter. A few
months after the baby was born, she had tried to resume taking birth
control pills, but there were problems with splitting headaches and high
blood pressure. Frank advised her to stop using the oral contraceptives
and to begin using a diaphragm and foam. When she'd been married that
was a nuisance, but she complied with the recommendation. However, at
the age of 39 and recently divorced, she didn't think she had any need to
carry a birth control device. She also never thought she'd get drunk and
hop in bed with a friend. It was Murphy's Law. The second missed
menses and the abdominal cramping were ominous. When she began to
bleed, it was time to visit the doctor.

Eleanor scheduled an appointment with Frank at the gynecology
clinic, but she sat for hours and was cancelled two days in a row because
each time, he was called out to do a delivery. She didn't tell the nurse
that it was urgent. The receptionist asked if she wanted another doctor,
but Eleanor refused.

By the third morning, Eleanor's abdominal pain wouldn't let up. The
waves came more often and grew more intense, so she was enormously
relieved when Frank could finally see her, especially while the children

were at school.

When he was with her, Frank was always upbeat, so Eleanor immediately sensed his somber mood as he faced her in the examination room. When he took her hand to talk, Eleanor's heart sank. He had never done that before as her doctor. It was a gesture he hadn't made since her father died. A person remembered things like that.

"Eleanor, even though the rest of your exam was pretty normal, that tenderness I felt in the left lower part of your abdomen was concerning. I sent a urine pregnancy test. I'm afraid I've got some bad news. Eleanor, you're pregnant, probably eight or nine weeks. No question about it. The test is strongly positive." It was difficult for Frank to hide his disappointment.

Oh shit, thought Eleanor, *this isn't what I need right now. How can I have another baby?* The gnawing ache deep within her pelvis continued to worsen.

"But it appears that the pregnancy may be tucked up in the corner of your womb or in one of your fallopian tubes, which are outside your uterus — what we call an ectopic pregnancy. In either case, you might need an operation to remove the fetus and try to repair the uterus and tube. There's really not much choice. I'm sorry."

Half-relieved by the prospect that there was a justifiable medical indication for terminating the pregnancy, Eleanor asked, "What would happen if we decided to wait and see what happens? Couldn't I just have a miscarriage like everybody else?"

"That's possible, but pretty unlikely. Although there's a small chance that the baby is situated properly inside your womb, I'd be surprised if it is. From the way you're behaving, it's more likely to be planted in your left tube. That's why you're having so much pain. Unfortunately, most ectopic pregnancies as far along as yours rupture the tube and there can be a lot of bleeding. Sometimes we can't control it. If you really have an ectopic, then we need to operate as soon as possible to keep you from having a bad hemorrhage or even from dying. I'm not trying to be overly dramatic, just telling you that this is a serious situation where we can't sit around and daydream for very long. I'm going to send you over for an ultrasound, so we can see exactly what's going on. You've had that before

— it won't hurt."

In the midst of the long explanation, Eleanor suddenly became woozy. The room spun around her. Eleanor nodded to her cousin in feigned understanding. The reason she was lightheaded was because she had just painlessly dumped nearly a liter of blood into her abdomen in less than five minutes.

"I feel dizzy," she said, clinging to the siderail of the examination table.

Frank ordered his nurse, "Start an IV and draw some bloods. Send a blood count and serum pregnancy test, get some 'lytes and clotting studies, and type and screen her for four units of packed cells. Call ultrasound and tell them we'll need the study as soon as possible. While you're at it, call the O.R. and see if they can add a case after lunch. Actually, better make that to follow. Also, find out who's on call for anesthesia add-ons." The nurse hurried off.

Frank patted Eleanor on the cheek and forehead and bent down close to her ear. "Don't worry Kiddo, you'll be OK. We do this kind of thing all the time. I'll take care of you." He turned and left the room.

An ultrasound technician wheeled Eleanor into one of the small examination areas demarcated by a hanging curtain, with no explanation or introduction other than that her name was Heather. The young woman slathered Eleanor's abdomen with translucent blue, water-soluble gel. She began to pass the cold steel transducer probe over her abdomen, gliding in a figure eight pattern through the slimy lubricant. The procedure wasn't uncomfortable, but evoked a visceral fear in Eleanor of baring her insides to this seemingly aloof examiner. The young woman couldn't have been much older than twenty, and she was smacking her chewing gum loud enough to be heard all the way down the hall.

For the first few minutes, the technician's expression remained blank, almost bored. Thus it was doubly terrifying to observe her quizzical brow furrow as she progressed farther into the procedure. She kept pressing down precisely over the area that hurt, staring at the monitor with squinted eyes as if she couldn't make out what was on the screen. To control her fear, Eleanor tried to imagine that the young woman was an artist, painting a landscape upon the canvas of her lower abdomen.

When the ultrasonographer began popping her gum as fast as she could and shaking her head from side to side, Eleanor couldn't stand it any more.

"What do you see? Am I pregnant?"

"I can't say for certain, ma'am, but if you are, the baby's not in your uterus. There's a house there, but nobody's home. I'm gonna look around over here a bit where you're hurting. I need to see whether I can find a mass in your left lower quadrant."

Her tone was too casual. It was dreadful. A *mass*?

"What's a mass? Could you explain that to me in English?"

"I'm sorry. A mass is a lump, you know, something that's not supposed to be there. Something that shows up on the ultrasound like a big shadow; you know, say, like a tennis ball or a tumor or something. It doesn't have to be cancer. Your left lower quadrant is down here." She pressed with the transducer and a sharp pain shot through Eleanor's flank. "Right *here* where the doctor told me you're having all of your pain. It's where we might find an ectopic. Hold still now."

Tumor? Cancer? Ectopic? Oh my God, I have cancer. Frank didn't say anything about cancer. Eleanor tried to read the tech's face as the youngster slid the metal transducer over her skin. She mustered her courage.

"You see something, don't you. Go ahead and tell me, I really want to know."

"I think I can see something, but I'm not sure. We'd better do a trans-vaginal. Did anybody tell you what that is?"

"No, but from the sound of it, I can imagine."

Heather remained seated on her stool on wheels and reached down to a tray on the shelf below the ultrasound power unit. She picked up an object that had been covered with a surgical towel. It was a metal probe with a pigtail wire connector. She unplugged the small cigar-shaped transducer she'd been using and plugged in the larger probe. She covered it with gel and held it up for Eleanor to see. The phallic eye dripped blue goo.

"This is the vaginal probe. I'm going to insert it inside you and get a better picture of your female organs. It'll be cold, but it won't hurt. Try to lay back and relax. Spread your legs a bit, just like you do for Dr.

Klawitter. Sorry, that didn't come out right. You know what I mean."

Eleanor put her head back on the pillow, much too scared to be embarrassed. "Ugh! That looks horrible." She allowed her knees to fall apart. She could feel blood trickling down the insides of her thighs.

"Hmm. You're bleeding a little bit. Let's go on and get this done, so you can go back to the clinic. Here goes. I'll go slowly. Don't move. That's it. Whoops! Sorry. All right, it's in now. Am I hurting you?"

Yes, but Eleanor shook her head "no."

"Good. This'll just take a few minutes." The technician switched on the machine and the probe began to vibrate. She rotated it back and forth in Eleanor's vagina. It was freezing cold. Eleanor began to shiver uncontrollably. She was growing increasingly uncomfortable, so she tried to think about other things. As hard as she concentrated, it was hard to ignore the human arm between her legs that recorded images of her insides with the humming pelvic sonar.

Heather finished. She pulled out the probe and wiped off the blood clots with paper towels. When it was apparent that she wasn't going to speak, Eleanor broke the silence.

"Well, any news? Did you see what you expected?"

"I'm not supposed to say anything to the patients. The radiologist will be by in a few minutes to read the ultrasound and then he'll tell your doctor, and your doctor will tell you."

"*Please.*" Eleanor was frightened and fighting back tears.

"I'm really not supposed to." Heather stared at Eleanor for a second. "Oh, OK. But remember, I didn't say anything. I think you have an ectopic pregnancy, but it doesn't look ruptured. My guess is that you'll have an operation today or tomorrow. I'm sorry." Heather stopped chewing her gum. "You kinda knew that, huh?"

Eleanor was silent for a moment, then whispered, "Thank you," and gave the technician a quick squeeze on the forearm. She breathed a sigh of relief. So, that was that, a baby in the wrong place. Well, it could have been worse. It could have been in the right place. Eleanor flushed with shame at her thoughts.

As an orderly wheeled her gurney back to the clinic, it all caught up with her. She began to sob and pulled the sheet up over her head to hide her reaction from passersby in the corridor. As soon as he reentered the examination room, Frank Klawitter read Eleanor's weepy face and realized that she had been informed of the ultrasound results. A flash of exasperation at the breach of protocol passed quickly. He understood that she needed to know at once. Most of the time, Eleanor was his spunky soulmate, but now she was frightened and dependent. Frank gnawed on his lower lip.

"Eleanor, I'm afraid our fears have been confirmed. You have an ectopic pregnancy. My recommendation is that I take you up to the operating room as soon as we can get on the schedule."

"Tomorrow?"

"No, Eleanor. Today. When was your last meal?"

"I nibbled at breakfast this morning and hardly touched dinner last night. I guess I ate about three bites of chicken and a little applesauce. I feel sick to my stomach, but not enough to throw up."

"Well, let's see, it's three o'clock now, and by the time we get everything arranged, it'll be five. Unless something changes we should be fine." Frank was talking more to himself than to his cousin. "Eleanor, this surgery will require you to undergo general anesthesia. It's very likely that you'll require a partial or total hysterectomy. Besides, you look like you could use a little rest."

"Yes, a little rest would be nice right now."

"I'll come back and explain everything to you in detail so that you can sign a consent form. It's all pretty straightforward."

The nurse interrupted him. "Doctor Klawitter, Doctor Spencer's on the phone. He says it's urgent."

Frank took Eleanor's hands in both of his and squeezed them tightly. He hesitated, then leaned down and hugged her around the shoulders.

"C'mon, Ellie. It'll be OK. I'd never let you down. I love you." He called back to his nurse, "I'll take it outside." He turned away and walked outside the room.

"Fred. What's up?"

"Sorry to bother you, Frank, but I was just passing through ultrasound and I caught a peek at your patient with the ectopic. Her study's pretty impressive. Look, this may or may not make a difference, but she's leaking right behind what looks like an adhesion on the left side. Maybe some old colitis or PID. I can't tell for sure."

"You can see all that on the ultrasound?" Frank shook his head in amazement. Fred was unbelievable. Nobody else could discern that degree of detail on a routine ultrasound.

"I'm pretty sure. So when you go in there, look for a thickened segment of bowel and you should be able to follow it right to the bleeding. I don't know if that's helpful, but I thought you ought to know. She sick?"

"Yeah. Real sick. Thanks a lot, buddy. You always seem to be in the right place at the right..." Frank's nurse interrupted his conversation with Fred by wagging her finger to summon him to another phone. He said goodbye to Fred. The nurse held her hand over the mouthpiece and whispered a few words to Frank. He looked at the floor and kneaded the back of his neck.

"Dammit," he grumbled. "Tell them I want a *real* doctor. Let me see the schedule. Damn! OK, call and tell them I won't do the case now and to make it an add-on in O.R. 9 after the hip. By then, someone'll have to be free to help me out. If that won't work, tell them to get me the Chief Resident on call, and if that doesn't work, tell them I'll take the goddamn intern. I refuse to work with Schmatz."

"Maybe *you* better talk to them."

Randolph Schmatz, Professor of Anesthesiology, was a sore point to every operating surgeon at the medical center, and particularly to Frank. Schmatz had become a lackluster anesthesiologist and besides, he was arrogant and often late for the start of cases. Frank Klawitter was one of many surgeons who avoided him in the operating room. Frank's cases were too complicated for a has-been like Schmatz. Klawitter knew all about the patients who woke up in the middle of their cholecystectomies or who got so much fluid that they floated off of the table.

Frank picked up the phone and after a brief conversation said, "Thanks, but I'll handle this," then hung up so that he could dial the private office number for the Chairman of the Anesthesia Department.

"Hello, this is Frank Klawitter. Sure, I'll hold."

While Frank cradled the phone between his cheek and shoulder so that he could write on Eleanor's medical record, his nurse signaled frantically for his attention. When he waved her away, she mouthed the words "We need you now" and flew out the door. Frank raised a finger to indicate that he would just be a minute, but she was already gone. The Chairman of Anesthesia came on the line.

"Frank. Sorry about that. What's up?"

"I've got an ectopic down here in the clinic that really needs to go to the O.R. this afternoon, but I'd prefer to do the case with someone other than Schmatz."

The usual excuses began. Everyone else was tied up. There was nothing special about this case. Schmatz was a perfectly competent anesthesiologist. If he did it for Frank, then he'd have to do it for everybody. If Frank put up with Schmatz just this one last time, he'd see what he could do about it in the future. Blah blah, blah blah.

"Yeah, I know this is a straightforward operation and that the man is a living legend and that you don't want to call someone else in because Schmatz will be insulted, but frankly I don't give a shit. Look, the last time I operated with Schmatz he damn near killed my patient. It was tattooed on her forehead that she was allergic to gentamicin and he gave it to her anyway. We came damn close to losing her. So I'm sorry, but you have to give me somebody else."

Sterner words of refusal followed. He wasn't going to budge. They traded unpleasantries, then Frank rumbled, "Thanks for nothing, as usual," and both men hung up hard.

Frank's moment of self-indulgent anger was interrupted by a loud call for help from the clinic nurse.

"Dr. Klawitter, *please* come in here. We're having a problem."

Eleanor was clutching her abdomen and had her knees drawn to her chest. A broad splash of bright red blood interspersed with dark maroon clots soaked the sheets between her legs, and the young woman's color was ashen. Eleanor was shaking violently and her breaths came between huge racking sobs. She was trying not to panic, but the bleeding and pain broke her defenses and she was frightened beyond control. The nurse was having a difficult time handling Eleanor, who began to roll from side to side on the gurney. She gushed again and flooded the mattress.

Frank had been through bad situations like this with critically ill women many times before. Eleanor ceased to be his cousin. He swiftly marched into an inquiry and examination of the patient. With one big hand he controlled her hip and pelvis, while he kneaded and poked around her navel with the other.

"Is this where it hurts the most? All right, take a deep breath and hold it. That's good. Now breathe. Spread your legs a bit, so I can see what we've got here on the sheet. OK, I know that this is uncomfortable, but it will just take a second. Good girl. Slow your breathing down, you're making yourself feel worse. C'mon now, slow it down. That's better. Let me have your arm for a second. Let's see what we have here for veins. That 'a girl, Ellie, you're going to feel a little stick here in a second."

As he spoke, Frank smoothly inserted a second intravenous catheter into a small vein on the back of Eleanor's left wrist.

"Her pressure's eighty over palp."

"Let's run in a liter of Ringer's wide open." The salt-containing crystalloid infusion would be life sustaining until the internal bleeding could be stopped and Eleanor's lost blood replaced.

"Eleanor, I would've liked to do all this in a more leisurely fashion, but I'm afraid that you're bleeding a bit faster than we can tolerate. We need to take you to the operating room as soon as possible and get everything fixed. Don't worry, we were gonna do all this anyway. We just have to get started a little sooner."

"Oh, Frank. I really don't feel very good right now." Eleanor leaned over the bedrail and vomited the little bit of food and bile that was left in her stomach. "I'm sorry. I can't help it. Can I have something for the pain? My belly's killing me." Eleanor felt extremely lightheaded. She retched again and needed to make a great effort to stay conscious.

"Sure. If we can get your blood pressure up a little bit, we'll let you have some morphine. Because you're going to be under anesthesia pretty soon, it's dangerous to give you too many narcotics. We'll put you to sleep as soon as we can."

Eleanor winced.

"You know what I mean."

The color drained completely from Eleanor's face. She began to swoon. Her skin was cool, clammy and moistened with sweat. Frank reached out and clutched the underside of her wrist. Her pulse was rapid and could barely be felt. Eleanor was slipping quickly into shock, most likely because of massive bleeding into her abdomen, which was now protuberant and firm. Frank rested his hand below her navel. Her skin felt like a wad of dough. He was certain that the pregnancy in her tube had ruptured. There could be no delay to surgery. Eleanor's eyes rolled back in her head and she began to breathe slowly and heavily, almost like she was snoring.

"Please, please. I can't make it stop. I can't breathe. Please help me."

"Call the O.R. and tell them we're on our way up. We'll take any room that's available or share a room if we have to. I don't care. Have Schmatz meet us in pre-op. Call the blood bank. Have them cross the first four units right away and stay ahead of us with another four. Tell them to fire the bags upstairs as soon as they're ready. Throw some oxygen on her and let's go!"

Frank spun the heavy gurney around as easily as if it had been a shopping cart. He grabbed the stretcher and rocketed into the hallway and across the clinic toward the main elevators. All of the bystanders backed away when they saw the urgency on his face and witnessed the distress of the young woman who moaned and writhed underneath the sheets. Large drops of blood on the gray granite floor marked a trail from the clinic into the elevator.

"Push 3. Pull the No Stops button."

Even though it lasted less than twenty seconds, the ascent seemed interminable. Klawitter timed his push with the opening of the elevator doors. He thrust the gurney through the wide electric doors that led to the pre-operative holding area.

The scene was hospital green, all wires and tubes, with two parallel rows of gowned patients in various stages of preparation for their operations. Each patient was attended by an orderly, many of them moonlighting medical students assigned to shave away hair, administer final enemas, resecure intravenous lines, tape nasogastric tubes or just keep the anxious patients company.

"Do we have an O.R.? Which room are we going to? I need a scrub nurse. Where's Schmatz? Is there any blood ready for this patient? Didn't anybody call and tell you I was coming? What the hell is going on here? Get off your ass and make something happen!"

Frank barked at the nearest orderly, who was up to his elbows in shaving cream scraping away the final vestiges of pubic hair from the perineum of a markedly obese woman about to undergo a "tummy tuck." His shouting caught the young man off guard. He jerked his arm and nicked the poor woman's vulva, which aroused her from a peaceful, sedative-induced sleep.

"Ouch!"

"Sir, I'm just an orderly. A medical student. I really can't help you."

"What's your name?"

Well, Jesus, thought the student. *He's pissed at me and I've got nothing to do with this.* Right or wrong didn't matter when a surgeon got mad at you. Medical students were nobodies. The doctor-to-be made a quick decision.

"Appington, sir, Bart Appington." The youth looked away, covered his mouth with his hand and mumbled his answer. His real name was Philip Slocum, but he gambled that in the heat of the moment, this irate doctor wouldn't remember his answer. Even if he did, the fictitious name wouldn't get him or anyone else in trouble.

"OK, son, drop what you're doing and help me wheel this patient into the trauma room."

Slocum rearranged his surgical mask and shower cap scrub hat to cover as much of his face as possible, and grabbed the foot of the gurney. The two men moved swiftly with Eleanor through the main corridor, which snaked through the center of the operating room complex.

Frank's shouting had attracted the attention of the Chief O.R. nurse. Pat Malley was a formidable presence in the medical center. She was very Irish, very tough and very much in charge. Malley grabbed Slocum's arm with the grip of a stevedore and put her nose right in his face.

"Hold your horses, Dr. Kildare. Where do you think you're going with this sweet little lady?"

Given the opportunity, Slocum would gladly have traded places with the patient. He was nearly felled by Malley's nicotine breath. It was true, Malley ate cigarette butts and medical students for breakfast. He quickly scanned the hallway for an escape route, and seeing none, began to kneel in supplication. Pat turned to the larger doctor.

"Frank Klawitter, what have we here? You know better than this. This is the trauma room, and if you'll beg my pardon, I don't believe that this woman has been injured. Aren't you still a gynecologist?"

Malley had worked with Frank since he'd been a resident, and she had enormous respect for him. He was a great technician. She had registered the concern in Frank's face and assessed the patient's critical condition. In eighteen years up in the O.R., she'd seen it all and then some. She never panicked. Malley grabbed the stretcher and pulled it in the opposite direction.

"I'll forgive you this time, Frank. Let's just turn this stretcher around and mosey over to O.R. 20. I'll have a crew for you before you can clean your fingernails. Who's passing the gas?" She twisted her head around to glare at Slocum. "And who's this little shit-for-brains medical student trying to help you break the rules?"

"Applegate, ma'am. Bill Applegate." He was so flustered that he couldn't remember the other name he had just made up. Another name, another lie. Who cared? He just wanted to get it over with. Slocum figured that if he got out of this alive, he'd turn in his scrubs and quit his job. The hell with his paycheck. Hopefully, Klawitter and Malley would forget who he was.

"Mr. Applegate," Malley said, "I never forget a name and I never forget a face. There's no Applegate on my payroll. When you come back up here on your surgery rotation, better hope I'm retired." Slocum decided that he would grow a moustache and beard like a fugitive on the lam. Maybe he'd also shave his head.

While she was putting the fear of God into Slocum, the nurse kept her fingers on Eleanor's wrist in order to assess the rate and quality of her pulse. It was rapid and thready, and Eleanor was starting to drop a few beats. Blood was dripping off the stainless steel side rails. Eleanor was ashen. Malley understood better what had gotten into Frank, who was ordinarily a cool customer.

"OK boys, let's keep moving. This little lady needs an operation. Did you order any blood?"

"Four units. Should be ready by now."

As Klawitter and Slocum headed for O.R. 20, Malley trotted to the central communication desk situated near the entrance to the operating rooms. She punched in a three-digit code on the intercom. A loud horn blast sounded throughout the area and in the lounges. Malley barked her instructions into the perforated metal box.

"On-call scrub team to O.R. 20, STAT. On-call scrub team to O.R. 20, STAT."

She deactivated the intercom and picked up the telephone to dial the hospital page operator. She instructed the operator to locate and deliver Randolph Schmatz to the operating room. Then she called the blood bank to double check that the blood had been ordered. When she heard the response, she couldn't believe her ears.

"No way. You've got to be kidding. No blood? Wasn't any ordered?"

Malley listened to the answer and then raged in anger.

"Oh, you were gonna call when you got a chance. Why do you think we order blood for patients? Did it ever cross your mind that some people bleed to death? Did you think that bad tubes mean that we don't need the blood anymore? What's your name?"

The standard alibi followed. The blood specimens were hemolyzed. The technicians in the blood bank always said that the red blood cells had inexplicably disintegrated whenever they dropped a tube or got behind in their work. It was a convenient lie and furthermore, it was impossible to tell whether or not it was the truth. Malley replied in a terse whisper.

"Yes, I see. Do yourself a favor. After you do exactly what I tell you, fill out an incident report with your version of the story. Now listen carefully. If you screw this one up now, I'm gonna make you an organ donor. Send up four units of O-negative whole blood right now. When you get the tubes from the O.R. that I'm gonna send you, do the cross-match as fast as you can. If *these* tubes hemolyze, you're the one that's gonna need the operation. Certainly. Malley. M-A-L-L-E-Y. Be careful. I'm losing my sense of humor."

Randy Schmatz had a difficult uphill lie on the fringe off the green. He decided to use his putter rather than try to chip it close. Just as he completed the backswing for his attempt at a birdie, his pager vibrated on his belt.

"Double or nothing."

"Double or nothing what? This is the 17th hole and we're all even. It doesn't matter what I do here. Either I'm one up or you're one up with two holes left. That means either one of us could still win." His pager vibrated again. "Doggone this ding-blasted thing! It always goes off when I'm in the middle of something important." Schmatz pushed a small button on the top and the liquid crystal display flashed the main number for Branscomb Hospital.

"What is it, Randy?"

"It's probably nothing. If it's really important, they'll page me again." The preoccupied anesthesiologist knelt down on the edge of the green and dangled his putter to read the line. A money putt always came first. "So, d'ya understand now? You can't double or nothing, because nobody's ahead. You do the books in the ER?"

"Quadruple then. I wanna quadruple our bet."

Schmatz stepped back from his ball and threw an incredulous look at his golfing partner. "Clyde, are you nuts? I'm not betting two thousand dollars on a round of golf. That's heinous. You ER docs make too much money."

Clyde Resnick pulled the pockets out of his shorts. "Not true. I just wanted to keep it interesting. Besides, you putt like my grandmother."

"OK, OK. Enough already. Quadruple the bet. But don't say that I made you do it."

Schmatz stepped up over his ball and took a practice swing, then changed his mind. He walked over to the electric cart, put his putter back in the bag and pulled out his eight iron. Resnick shook his head. Schmatz returned to his golf ball, took three abbreviated practice strokes, then chopped at the ball. It bounced twice on the green, then hit the pin and dropped straight down into the hole. The anesthesiologist fell to his knees, lifted his arms over his head and let loose a war whoop.

"Yes! What'd I tell you! Happens every time. You should know better than to mess with me." The pager vibrated one more time. Schmatz turned it off. "Won't they ever learn? Let's finish up. I'm sure whatever it is can wait."

"Maybe you'd better answer your page. That's the second one."

"The third. But no way, Clyde. You're not getting out of this one. Besides, what're they gonna do about it? Fire me? It'll never happen." Schmatz gave Resnick a wink. "Nope. Let's keep playing. Just one hole to go. Let's see, two thousand dollars. That's a new set of Pings and an alligator bag, with change left over. Thanks, buddy." Schmatz pulled a cellular phone from his bag and answered his page. "This is Dr. Schmatz. Can you tell me what the page was... Oh. I see. Yes, I know the number. Sure, you can connect me." The operator transferred Schmatz to the O.R. main desk.

"Dr. Schmatz, they need you in Room 20 for an emergency lap. Frank Klawitter's case. The place is hoppin', so there's nobody in the right seat. Everyone else is tied up, so they're holding the case for you. Uh, you know what I mean. All the other rooms are going and no one's free, so we really need you to get in here quick. The patient's pretty sick. I don't think they can wait much longer."

"OK, I'll be there as soon as I can. Give her some atropine and Bicitra. I can put her to sleep as soon as I get there. Got it? Good. See you in ten minutes." He turned back to Resnick. "Remember where we were. Gotta go earn a living."

Out of the corner of her eye, Malley watched Randy Schmatz trot into the dressing room, hugging the drug box like a freshman tailback on his first carry. Malley used the local intercom into O.R. 20 to tell Frank about the blood. He was furious, but now was not the time to do anything about it. Besides, the blood bank was the least of his worries right now. Frank had wasted precious time waiting for Schmatz. Eleanor had plummeted into a shock state. Unless her bleeding was controlled in the next few minutes, the minuscule amount of oxygen and nutrients being pumped to her blood-starved body would be inadequate to sustain her. She was hemorrhaging to death internally from her ruptured fallopian tube and the operation to remove it had to begin immediately if her life was to be saved. There was an axiom in medicine that there were few genuine emergencies. This was one.

Schmatz made his entrance into the O.R. with a flurry. Before anyone asked, he tried to make an excuse for his tardiness by announcing that the batteries in his beeper had gone dead. That damn thing was always breaking down.

In their rush to try to get the operation started, no one paid any attention to him. Klawitter didn't look up when he began to address the anesthesiologist.

"Randy, cut the crap. Listen, we need to get this patient to sleep right now. She has a ruptured ectopic and has been hypotensive off and on for nearly 45 minutes. After you tube her, start another big line and get some more blood for type and cross. I don't trust those dummies downstairs. The blood bank screwed up and we're gonna have to fly with O-negative for awhile. Remember, we need a *big* line."

"Not a problem."

"Randy, I think we ought to go with a rapid sequence induction and stay light on the pentothal. She's pretty much out of it, anyway. You agree?"

Eleanor was in and out of consciousness, and comprehended none of the commotion around her. When she opened her eyes, no image registered in her brain that she would ever remember. Frank continued to bark orders.

"I'm going to paint while you set things up at your end. Applesauce, you can assist me. Go scrub."

Phil Slocum walked out and hesitated for a minute outside in the anteroom next to O.R. 20, where the surgeons scrubbed for their cases. Although he knew he was totally unqualified to assist with any surgery, he also knew that opportunities like this didn't come along every day. It wasn't very often that medical students were actually invited into the operating room. Most students were lucky to stand three rows back on a circumcision once or twice before they graduated. What the hell. He'd do exactly as he was told. All he was probably going to get to see were their backs anyway. He'd watched other surgeons scrub for cases, so he figured he could at least get past that part.

Using his foot and knee to work the stainless steel apparatus below the porcelain sink, Phil turned on the water. He grabbed a bristle brush and scrubbed his hands for all he was worth. Lather rose up to his armpits, and he completely soaked the front of his scrub shirt.

Back inside the operating room, the lead scrub nurse handed the masked and gloved Klawitter a stainless steel bowl full of dark mahogany brown povidone-iodine solution and a stack of surgical sponges. He drenched the pads and used them to hastily swab the solution over Eleanor's lower chest, abdomen, perineum and upper legs. He poured what was left into her navel and slopped it around. There was no time to shave or prep any further. Meanwhile, Schmatz held a clear padded face-mask over Eleanor's mouth and nose and instructed her to take deep breaths. She was incapable of following commands. Eleanor's respiratory efforts were shallow, as muscular fatigue dominated the desperate demand of her body tissues for oxygen.

Eleanor's chest was barely moving. It was obvious to everyone that she was running out of gas. Without an endotracheal tube through which to force air into her lungs, the oxygen content in her blood was dropping precipitously. At any moment, she would simply stop breathing. Eleanor lost control of her bowels. The alarm on the cardiac monitor sounded a loud warning after a series of irregular and ineffective heartbeats.

"I think she needs a bedpan," said Schmatz.

"Jesus Christ, Randy, she can't breathe! Stick a tube down her throat before she arrests!"

The elderly anesthesiologist spent most of his clinical time in Day Surgery, where none of the patients were very sick and people just didn't die. He continued to assemble the endotracheal tube. He began to test the balloon at the business end of the tube to be certain that it inflated and deflated properly. Frank watched in disbelief.

"Randy, tube her, or give me the goddamn laryngoscope!" Frank tossed the empty bowl of antiseptic into the corner with a loud clang and made a move for the head of the bed. Schmatz saw him approach, so he ceased the preliminaries and inserted the laryngoscope blade neatly into Eleanor's mouth.

Slocum entered the room and held his hands up in the universal surgeon's gesture to ask for gloves, as he had frequently seen doctors do on television.

Frank looked up at Phil's drenched scrub suit and realized instantly that this was probably not the right person to assist him. "Applebaum, hustle down to the blood bank and see if the blood's ready. Sorry for the scrub."

Although he was disappointed that he might miss part of the operation, Slocum was more than happy to lower his personal risk. He ran off to the blood bank.

"A little cricoid pressure, please." Schmatz wanted a clear view of Eleanor's vocal cords. Frank used two fingers to press on the front of Eleanor's neck, which pushed the circular, inflexible bony cricoid cartilage against her esophagus. This gave Schmatz a clean look and prevented Eleanor from inhaling her vomit during the procedure. The tube passed easily. "We're in." Schmatz connected it to a blue, football-shaped rubber "ambu bag" and began to force oxygen into Eleanor's lungs. Although her color didn't improve substantially, the aberrant activity on the cardiac monitor subsided for the moment. Her oxygen saturation was nearly normal, but she lacked precious red blood cells. The anesthesiologist connected the endotracheal tube to a mechanical ventilator, which assisted Eleanor's breathing. He injected her with a sedative and a long-acting paralytic agent. She became totally limp on the operating room table.

Frank stripped off the nonsterile rubber gloves he had worn to prep the patient and began to gown formally for the operation. Schmatz was feeling good after the intubation and tried to be useful.

"Where the hell is that kid with the O-negative blood? He should've been back by now. I'm going downstairs to find the blood myself. Watch the machine."

Schmatz bolted out of the room before anyone had a chance to object. As he stepped immediately outside the door to the operating room, he collided with a transportation clerk who was carrying four units of blood bound together with a heavy red rubber band. The blood was tagged for O.R. 10, where a splenectomy was in progress. The scrawl on the piece of paper with the room designation was partially obscured by the rubber band. Glancing at the crumpled label, Schmatz read the "10" as a "20". He assumed that it was the blood requested for Eleanor.

"I'll take that," barked Schmatz. Not one to argue with a doctor, the clerk obediently handed over the blood. Schmatz didn't bother to further inspect the documentation. He darted back into O.R. 20, held up the blood and announced flamboyantly, "Nothing to it! Just have to know who to talk to." No one was paying attention.

As the anesthesiologist unbound the package, the marker paper floated to the floor. Schmatz grabbed the top unit of blood and spiked the bag with an elaborate blood administration filter set so that he could rapidly infuse it into Eleanor. He was as concerned as the others about her deterioration. Unfortunately, he didn't compare the patient identification number on the blood bag label with that on Eleanor's wrist band. The blood administered by Schmatz was type AB positive, not type O negative. Eleanor had type B negative blood. The viscous maroon fluid dripping into her vein was totally incompatible.

"She's got blood going. You can tee off now."

Frank pinched Eleanor's abdominal wall with a towel clamp to see if she would respond to pain. She was breathing an anesthetic gas mixture and didn't react to his stimulus, so the surgeon began the operation. He deftly carved a vertical skin incision that began a few inches below her breastbone, curved around her umbilicus, and stopped at the top of her pubis. Because time was of the essence, he didn't bother to meticulously cauterize small residual "bleeders", the tiny arteries and veins that coursed through the fat and muscle layers overlying Eleanor's intra-abdominal contents. It didn't make much difference, because her blood pressure was so low that there wasn't much bleeding, anyway. Frank used his instruments and fingers to advance rapidly through the muscle layers of her abdomen to reach the peritoneum, the fibrous tissue sac which lined her intra-abdominal cavity. He noticed that it was dark and bulging, which confirmed his worst fear. Her belly was full of blood. Frank knew that as soon as he incised the peritoneum, the bleeding would be torrential.

"How much blood have you got hanging? She's gonna bleed like crazy. Before I open her up, you'd better hang another two units. Better get up some fresh frozen too."

"Roger," replied Schmatz in an irritated tone of voice. He was being talked down to and he knew it. Frank stared a dagger through the older man's heart. No matter what, he would never operate with Schmatz again.

Schmatz plugged a Y-shaped connector tubing into two more units of the blood intended for another patient. He slipped each unit into a circumferential pressure bag designed to hasten the infusion, which allowed the precious fluid to pour precipitously into Eleanor's bloodstream.

"That should do 'er. She's got three units hanging. Go ahead with your incision."

"Here goes. Hold on." Frank made a small slice in Eleanor's peritoneum with his scalpel. He was instantaneously greeted with a swirling torrent of bright red blood laced with dark maroon clots the consistency of jellyfish. The scrub nurse, who was serving as Frank's first assistant until Slocum returned, used a stiff-tipped plastic suction unit to clear away the river of blood and allow Frank to see his surgical field. At first, they were successful. Then all hell broke loose.

"Clamp. Tie. Clamp. Suck. C'mon, c'mon, put the tip over here. Jesus, she's bleeding like stink. Hang in there, Ellie. Where's it coming from?" Frank felt her slipping away, then remembered what Fred Spencer had told him, to look for an adhesion on the left side. He began to run his hands quickly over her bowel, until he came to a thickened and immobile segment. He slid his fingers behind the lump of matted tissue and barely felt the blood spurting through a pea-sized hole in a knot of scar tissue. His brilliant radiologist friend was right. "OK, here's the tube, blown to smithereens. Poor kid, I'm amazed she held out this long. Looks like it blew an hour ago. Small clamp. Tie. No, goddamn it, big tie! OK, this should slow things down a bit."

Frank had isolated the ruptured tube and cut off its blood supply by wrapping large sutures around the feeder vessels and pulling them taut. In the nick of time and with supreme agility, he sewed purse string patterns around all of the bleeding sites. In just a few moments he had converted a flood to a trickle.

"Suck here, so I can see if that's all of it."

Frank continued to work rapidly to isolate the segment of Eleanor's left fallopian tube which had been thinned and eroded by the improperly situated pregnancy. He stripped off the adherent bowel and then began to meticulously tie off all of the smaller blood vessels traveling to and from the area. Finally, he pruned away the nonviable damaged tissue. In less than fifteen minutes he completed the critical portion of the operation and brought Eleanor's hemorrhaging under control. He began to relax a little.

"We're going to be all right down here. How are you doing up there?"

"Fine.

The response wasn't entirely accurate. Even though Eleanor had been transfused with three units of blood and was now receiving her fourth, her blood pressure wouldn't come up over 75 millimeters of mercury. That would have been acceptable if she was heavily anesthetized or was a small child, but it wasn't right for her. Schmatz decided not to tell anyone. Instead, he opened up the flow regulators on the blood bag and added two bags of normal saline to the infusion. He assumed he was merely behind on her fluids.

Meanwhile, Slocum had been fighting the usual blood bank bureaucracy. His quest for the blood was impeded by the usual backlog of requests. Furthermore, one of the technicians talked him into waiting for fully cross-matched blood, which she promised would only take a "couple extra minutes." Unfortunately, she misread the requisition as asking for two units instead of four. Phil decided it was probably better to wait for the additional two units than to return shorthanded. After thirty minutes of pondering new careers, he dashed from the blood bank with four units of packed red blood cells, type B negative, matched precisely to the sample originally extracted from Eleanor's vein.

He reentered O.R. 20 to witness a scene of utter pandemonium. After the most difficult part of the operation was completed and while her abdominal wall musculature was being sutured back into alignment, Eleanor once again began to bleed. Only this time, she not only bled into her abdomen, but from every single site where her skin had been punctured or a mucous membrane irritated. Blood oozed briskly from around each of four intravenous catheter sites, began to well up in small rivulets within her abdominal incision, trickled into her nasogastric tube, and discolored the urine that flowed through the catheter which had been placed through her urethra into her bladder.

The first sign of coagulopathy had been a little bleeding from her major incision. At first, Frank denied that anything was out of the ordinary. He released a few sutures, assuming that he had missed a bleeder and needed to buzz the cautery a bit more just under the skin. But it was far worse than that. Eleanor was bleeding from every minute blood vessel that had been severed, even the ones that had already been torched. Frank touched the red-hot bovie tip to a few of them, creating wisps of smoke that filled the air with the odor of burning flesh. The bleeding continued. At the same time, blood began to well up out of the wound. There had to be a tie undone or a torn artery he had missed. Frank quickly snipped all of the suture lines he had just placed. He quickly worked his way back down to the peritoneum. To his horror, it once again bulged under the pressure of an abdomen full of blood. Something horrible was happening. The locking sutures in the fibrous sac would hold, but Frank knew that he had to go back in.

Frank was beside himself with frustration and fear. He couldn't imagine what the hell had happened.

"Randy, how much blood has she gotten?"

"Almost four units."

"Did you hang any fresh frozen?"

"Nope, not yet. She's only had the four units. We usually start the plasma with the sixth unit."

As much as Frank needed a simple explanation, he knew that Schmatz was right. Frank racked his brain and ran through a flurry of differential diagnoses. Eleanor appeared to have disseminated intravascular coagulopathy, a condition of uncontrollable bleeding that occurs when a human's blood won't clot. Had he allowed amniotic fluid to enter the blood stream inadvertently? No, that was impossible. The embryonic sac had ruptured freely into the abdomen and an ectopic just didn't cause this type of problem. If it did, this would have to be the first reported case. Besides, the bleeding was too severe. She wasn't on any anticoagulants, and no heparin had been administered. Maybe he was overreacting. Maybe this had a simple surgical cause. Frank bit the bullet and reopened the peritoneum.

Blood poured out of her abdomen and Frank knew in an instant that he'd made a very bad decision. He grabbed a fistful of laparotomy pads off the tray behind him and began to stuff them into the surgical abyss. If he couldn't control the bleeding with this crude method, he knew he wouldn't have a prayer of finding the source before his cousin bled to death.

"Open up her fluids, Randy. Jesus, she won't stop bleeding. You didn't give her any heparin, did you? She's not a hemophiliac. Stat page one of the hematologists. Give her all the fresh frozen you have. Try some calcium."

"Don't have any fresh frozen. Her pressure's 60 and I'm having a little trouble squeezing the bag." Schmatz referred to the fact that Eleanor's lungs were beginning to stiffen. He disconnected her from the machine and took over assisting her manually. Pink frothy fluid began to appear in the translucent endotracheal tube. Now she was spewing blood that had leaked into her lungs.

Frank resumed his mental checklist of pathology. Had Eleanor's previous period of hypotension triggered a cascade of altered coagulation? He'd never seen it happen. Was she allergic to the anesthetic? Had her core body temperature slipped below 90 degrees and allowed the onset of hypothermia? What could possibly be going on?

Eleanor lost ground rapidly and began to bleed profusely from everywhere. Bright red blood ran from her nose. The skin around her puncture wounds and incision were puddled with crimson fluid, which appeared more watery by the second. Her heart rate soared to 170 beats per minute while her blood pressure plummeted. Bloody foam filled the tube that ran from her throat, and all of the alarms on Eleanor's electronic physiological monitors harmonized in a macabre symphony.

"I've got the blood," announced Slocum, who hoisted the precious cargo high above his head for all to see. No one heard him at first, so he shouted at the top of his lungs. "I've got the blood!"

There was absolute silence as everyone turned to the medical student. The realization of what had happened hit them all at the same time. It was a transfusion reaction.

"Oh my God," whispered Frank. "Check the labels on the blood we gave her. Randy, I swear I'm gonna have you hung for this one. We need to get some fresh frozen plasma and platelets. Give her a hundred of Solumedrol. Call the blood bank and tell them we need ten units of crossmatched whole blood. This is a mess. Call the unit and tell them to set up for dialysis. If she's got any kidneys left, that's her only shot."

Frank lowered his voice so that he could barely be heard.

"I don't want a word of this to anyone," he intoned. "This mustn't be discussed outside of this operating room with anybody. I'll make a full report to the legal office." Without looking at Schmatz, he said, "Randy, I'm going to hang you."

"Hindeminth, Susan." The dead silence was broken by the circulating nurse.

"What?"

"Hindeminth, Susan. The blood was labeled Susan Hindeminth. Plain as could be." She held up three empty plastic transfusion packs that Schmatz had thrown on the operating room floor.

After a few more minutes of futile pharmacological manipulation, Frank realized that nothing he could do was going to help. He had no other choice but to pack each bleeding site with layers of gauze and a tight wrap. The surgical team raced the critically ill young woman to the intensive care unit. Eleanor lost her blood pressure entirely three times in the corridor, and Frank nearly lost his composure watching his cousin deteriorate. She was greeted by a swarm of intensivists, but to no avail. Frank never left her bedside. During the next eight hours Eleanor received an additional 45 units of blood, 10 units of fresh frozen plasma and 18 platelet packs. Without regaining consciousness, she hemorrhaged massively into her liver, lungs, kidneys and the right side of her brain. When her heart finally stopped beating, she endured a prolonged and extremely brutal resuscitation attempt. The inevitable fatal cardiopulmonary arrest occurred less than 10 hours after she had received the wrong blood. From the moment she left the operating room until she died, Randy Schmatz never again laid eyes on her.

Frank was stricken with relentless, gut-wrenching grief. Like every other surgeon, he had lost patients before, but Eleanor was his own flesh and blood. This was a personal nightmare he would carry with him the rest of his life.

Fred Spencer came up to Frank at the wake. "I'm terribly sorry. Frank, I haven't been able to sleep. You've got to tell me. Was I wrong? Dear God, Frank, did I misinterpret her study?" The radiologist was trembling.

"Oh Fred, no. You were right on the money." Frank's voice cracked as he struggled to keep his composure. "It was stupid, senseless that she died..."

Randy Schmatz went into seclusion. He was devastated by what he had done, but was too fearful of Frank to approach him. God, he wanted to quit, but there were a few more loans to repay, and an admission of guilt might lead people places he didn't want them to go. If he got through this one, he'd be more careful. He swore an oath to himself, and to others.

Sam sat in the rear of the church during Eleanor's funeral. He wished there was something he could do for his mentor. Frank was taking all the blame, but there was something about the way he did it that made Sam suspect that there was more to the story. It was as if he were protecting someone. He'd seen him do it before.

The funeral and burial were hard on Frank. His nieces would live with their grandparents. The younger girl was confused, but her older sister fully understood that something terrible had happened. As Frank clutched her to him, she kissed his cheek and whispered in his ear. "I love you, Uncle Frank. Grandma said it wasn't your fault." He felt her tears run down his cheek.

The nights that followed were worse. There was no way to drive his thoughts from his cousin. Every time he revisited the vision of Schmatz in the operating room, he was seized by fury — a blood-red fury that pulsed through his veins and filled his brain with manic energy.

Schmatz had to be removed, better yet, thrown in prison. Frank detailed everything to the Chairman of Anesthesiology, who instructed Frank to go through the Quality Assurance Review Committee. Frank prepared to take his case to the committee. He transcribed the incident in every gory detail. He gathered written descriptions of what had happened from all of the nurses present, as well as from Slocum. If any of this had gotten into the hands of a malpractice attorney, it would have been a dream case. He packed everything into a thick manila envelope and turned it in to the Risk Management Office. He was going to nail the bastard.

Frank was excluded from the review because of "conflict of interest." After an investigation coordinated by the Chairman of the Quality Assurance Review Committee, the cause of death was recorded as "intravascular coagulopathy secondary to mislabeled blood." Nothing about a stupid, improper blood transfusion. No physician reprimanded for improper practice. Despite Frank's vehement protest to the Dean and implied threat of a lawsuit, Schmatz was held harmless. Citing personal reasons, Philip Slocum dropped out of Branscomb Medical School, and quietly enrolled as a transfer student at the University of Nebraska.

CHAPTER 7

"Unit 35 with a surgical stat. Unit 35 with a surgical stat."

The announcement from the ambulance telecommunication unit blared loudly over the public address system in the ER. The clerk at the main desk punched into the intercom.

"Dr. Resnick, please pick up the radio for Unit 35 with a surgical stat. Dr. Resnick, pick up the radio for Unit 35."

Clyde Resnick was the faculty physician assigned to the ER for the night shift. He'd been retired from his surgery practice by the Chairman of the Department of Surgery because of erratic work habits and a series of stupendous screw-ups. The final incident had been when he took out the pericolic fat, but left in the gangrenous appendix, of the contractor who built the new wing of the hospital. Resnick kept the peace by becoming a member of the Branscomb Society, signifying an annual donation of $100,000 or greater. Most people assumed that these donations allowed him to stay at the medical center.

"Dr. Resnick, *please* pick up the radio for Unit 35."

The ex-surgeon was in the library reading the magazine *Diversion: for Physicians at Leisure*. During an assigned shift, the Attending Physician was never supposed to be out of the clinical area. Clyde Resnick was used to bending the rules.

"Unit 35 needs a doctor for a surgical stat. Do you copy my transmission? Ambulance Unit 35 to base hospital. Do you copy?" The paramedic in the field was agitated.

Gloria Koslofsky was the evening charge nurse in the ER. She grabbed the microphone and began to stall for the delinquent doctor.

"Unit 35, this is Branscomb. We copy your transmission. Please stand by for the doctor."

As soon as she released the transmit button, she shouted down the back corridor.

"Hey you, get up here and take this radio call."

Koslofsky had spotted a surgery intern. It was late August. With only two months of internship under his belt, this young man probably didn't know his ass from a hot rock, but she needed a doctor.

The intern ran through the maze of stretchers, linen hampers, infant warmers and crash carts that lined the hallway and scooted onto the stool in front of the radio unit. Koslofsky handed the intern the microphone. He didn't have Clue One about paramedic field protocols, what it was like to ride in the back of an ambulance, or the proper medical management of anything in particular.

"Branscomb, this is Medic 42 on Unit 35. We have Code 1 traffic. Gunshot wounds to the neck, chest and abdomen. Request permission to initiate the trauma protocol. We'd like to start 2 lines, insert an ET tube and run Code Three. When we get loaded, we're 15 minutes to your facility. Do you copy?" The voice on the radio was breathless and unnerved.

The intern turned white and opened his mouth, but no sound came out. While he sat dumbfounded, the paramedics were struggling to keep their patient alive. After thirty seconds without a response from the base station, they called in again. Koslofsky and the intern could hear sirens and angry shouting in the background.

"Branscomb, this is Medic 42. Did you copy our transmission? We're lookin' at alligators here, and there ain't no way to drain the swamp. The situation is critical. I repeat, *the situation is critical.* The victim's been shot three times, and we have a hostile crowd. We need orders *now* to start lines and stick in a tube. Also, we'd like to throw on the MAST trousers and blow them up. Branscomb, do you read me?" The paramedic was a former navy medic, the cream of the crop. It was a hot night and he and his partner wanted to get *out* of there.

Koslofsky read the intern's glazed expression. She mouthed the words, "get the vital signs."

"Vital signs?" he squeaked into the radio. Koslofsky pinched his arm, hard, to get him to speak up. "What are the patient's vital signs?"

"Branscomb, this is Unit 35. We're in the projects. The victim is a black male, shot all over. He has wounds in the neck, chest and abdomen. He's unconscious, pulse 140 and weak, blood pressure 60 palp, respiration's 25 and labored. There's blood coming from his mouth and nose and we're having a difficult time managing the airway. Request permission to do our stuff. Over and out."

"Go for it. We'll be ready."

The intern slumped on his stool while Koslofsky instructed the hospital operator to page Clyde Resnick and the senior surgery resident on the Trauma Service. Then she called the operating room to alert them that a major trauma was on the way.

The senior surgery resident answered his page quickly. He had a medical student relay the message that he was in the midst of an abdominal aortic aneurysm resection. There was no one to cover and he couldn't break scrub for at least 30 minutes. Gloria protested, but he said no way, and that was that. He told Gloria to let the Emergency Attending and the intern run the resuscitation. It was a weekend and there wasn't anybody else in-house.

Resnick was sound asleep in a study carrel when he was aroused by the shrill series of beeps from his pager. It was the ER. He got up slowly and meandered down the hall. At a stairwell, he collided with Frank Klawitter, who had just been called into the hospital to do an emergency C-section.

"Hey there, Frank. How's it hangin? Fought in any wars lately?"

Klawitter didn't have time to chat, especially with someone as worthless as Resnick. Frank knew all the horror stories and had a few of his own. The last time Clyde had called him in to see a patient was to repair a hideous vaginal tear created by forcing a delivery in the ER that could easily have gone to Labor and Delivery. The time before that, Frank examined a young woman with obvious gallstones that Clyde had labeled as pelvic inflammatory disease. He'd never forget when Resnick had paged him out of a wedding reception to come to the ER to diagnose a teenager with her first menstrual cramps.

"Sorry I can't stop and talk, but I've got to get upstairs." Frank picked up speed and rounded the corner.

Resnick resumed his stroll. He stopped in the cafeteria to grab a cup of coffee, then made his way to the ER.

"What's goin' on? Did somebody page me?"

The ex-surgeon arrived fifteen seconds before the paramedics burst noisily through the entrance with the wounded man sprawled on a gurney. Blood flew everywhere. The paramedic had to yell to give his report over the advancing din.

"This is a 30-year-old black male from the neighborhood who got in an argument with his brother and some dude during a card game. They were all drunk. The stranger pulled a gun. When we arrived on the scene, the patient was face down in a pool of blood. We estimate at least two liters on the floor. Initial blood pressure was 70 palp. Our man was having difficulty breathing and wouldn't follow commands. When we called in, he was going downhill fast. We haven't been able to get an IV started. My partner stuck him twice in the arm and once in the neck, but they all blew. It looks like he's a user and his good veins are gone. The shit he's got left is collapsed. We didn't have time to tube him."

The report was interrupted by violent convulsive jerking by the victim, who began to gag and spew vomit and blood from his mouth. Large fragments of hot dog floated in the putrid eruption.

"Aw, Jesus Christ, he just ate. Damn, he's gonna aspirate. Turn him on his side!" screamed the paramedic. "Turn him, now! Goddamn it."

"No, don't move him," commanded Resnick. "He might have a cervical spine fracture. Use the suction to clean out his mouth." It didn't mean anything to him that the man was choking to death. Resnick held the victim flat on his back. The injured man's stomach continued to contract, forcing waves of gastric contents to well up out of his mouth and nose. The rancid mix of blood, partially digested food and alcohol smelled even worse than it looked.

The intern looked behind him for a suction catheter while the paramedics ignored Resnick and turned the choking man, still strapped to the wooden backboard, on his side so that they could sweep his mouth with their fingers. The paramedics scooped out handfuls of vile muck and threw them onto the floor at the feet of the intern. He started to gag.

Gloria Koslofsky turned to Clyde Resnick and snarled, "Why don't you roll up your sleeves and make yourself useful? For starters, this man doesn't have any lines. He's bleeding to death. If we don't get some fluid into him pretty soon, this party's over. And you, stick a tube down this man's throat." Koslofsky wanted the intern to perform an endotracheal intubation.

Resnick grabbed a fistful of intravenous catheters from a large plastic cup on one of the counters. He walked up to the victim and started poking around on his forearm looking for a vein. He didn't find anything, so he looked at the other arm. Nothing. Since the patient's legs were covered by the inflated plastic pressure suit, he couldn't get to the saphenous vein in the ankle. He ripped open the Velcro seams that held the MAST garment on the lower torso and legs of the victim. In doing so, he caused the patient's already low blood pressure to free fall.

"Oh no, you idiot," mumbled the EMT. "What are you doing? You can't just pull the pants off like that." The men watched Resnick in horror and disbelief. All of their efforts in the field had been undone in a few seconds by this dinosaur.

Resnick glanced up and noticed that the intern was holding a laryngoscope in one hand and an endotracheal tube in the other. The intern wants to do this by himself, thought Resnick. That's OK with me. This guy's probably not going to make it anyway. Probably deserved to get shot. Damn addict.

"You boys step back now. Nice job you did. We'll take 'er from here. Resnick blindly pierced the victim's skin with the IV needle four times while he was talking, all dry taps. He looked up again at the intern. "Go ahead son, put the tube in."

His helper began to whine softly. Although the intern had watched a few intubations during an anesthesia elective, he had never before inserted an endotracheal tube into a live human being. In slow motion, he inserted the laryngoscope blade into the victim's mouth and jammed his tongue down his throat. The patient retched the remainder of his bellyful of blood.

Wrongly assuming that the man was bleeding from his lungs, rather than merely regurgitating his stomach contents, the intern freaked out.

"We can't intubate this man. He's bleeding from his chest. He needs a tracheostomy now! Somebody get me a trach tray. Turn him over! Suction! Oh my God, what's his pressure? Can somebody tell me his pulse? What have we got for lines? Page anesthesia! Call the O.R.! Open the trach tray! I need a knife! Dr. Resnick, help!"

The young intern hoisted a scalpel. His trembling hand initiated a vertical incision directly over the Adam's apple, and sliced on down for four inches, finishing well below where he should have.

Resnick stood by and watched silently, because it had been a long time since he had performed an emergency cricothyroidotomy. The victim was barely breathing, but nobody noticed. After completing the skin incision, the intern became completely confused by the anatomy. He carved deeper and encountered a pink fleshy mass laden with small deep purple veins. Having never operated in the neck, he didn't recognize a living thyroid gland.

Blood ran into the wound in half-hearted spurts. "Oh man, I can't see a thing. Dr. Resnick, can you tell where the blood is coming from?"

"Just hold pressure and it'll stop bleeding." Clyde pushed the boy's hand away and replaced it with a stack of gauze dressings under his gloved hand. "We'll look in a minute and see if we can continue."

"Pressure's 50 over palp now. We've got a lot of ectopics on the monitor. You're choking him to death," rumbled Koslofsky. "He's not breathing. I suggest you do something quick."

"Another goddamn coroner's case. Another fuck-up," muttered one of the paramedics. "Why do we have to bring patients to these bozos? Why can't we do something besides stand here like a couple of statues?"

"Back off, buddy," answered his partner, who was already seething with anger. "This isn't our territory. The last time I tried to say something to one of these assholes, I got docked two shifts pay. I'm leaving. I can't stand to watch this anymore. It's obscene."

The senior paramedic turned to leave the room. As he took his first step, the bradycardia alarm on the cardiac monitor signified that the heart rate had dropped below 30 beats per minute. The patient began an agonal slide into catastrophic cardiopulmonary failure.

"Atropine," stated Resnick without an ounce of emotion. "One milligram, IV."

"We don't have an IV doctor, remember?" popped Koslofsky, who had positioned herself on a stepstool next to the victim. She looked up at the cardiac monitor and watched the lime green waveform flatten into a straight line. She placed her hands on the young man's chest, locked her fingers, straightened her elbows and began to lower the weight of her upper body down in the compression phase of cardiopulmonary resuscitation.

"He's gone flat line, doctors. We've got a code."

In a few seconds, the loudspeakers throughout the hospital blasted "Code Blue, Emergency Room" six times in rapid succession. Twenty bodies descended on the ER. Out-of-breath doctors, respiratory therapists, blood bank technicians, medical students and assorted bystanders poured in. The hospital chaplain elbowed his way through the crowd to administer last rites.

An anesthesiology resident quickly performed the endotracheal intubation without difficulty. A second-year surgery house officer started an intravenous line in the victim's groin by ripping down through the fat with his fingers to locate the prominent femoral vein. CPR was all for naught, as the resuscitation team couldn't generate a single blip of spontaneous cardiac activity. In a desperation maneuver, the surgery resident sliced open the victim's chest to directly expose his heart. It was empty and flaccid. Everyone hated to give up, but after a 20-minute flog, they threw in the towel.

The ambulance crew gathered up their blood- and vomit-covered equipment and rinsed it in the utility shower. Koslofsky poked her head in.

"Sorry, fellas. You did everything right." There was no answer from the paramedics. "I guess that wasn't the prettiest job we've ever done. I hope you understand. The kid's brand new. He did the best he could."

The paramedic was crestfallen and bitter. "Gloria, we've got no beef with the intern. They're always stupid. It just gets a little old watching Resnick stand around and get paid for dishing off our saves to the coroner. He's a public menace. Why can't you guys unload that bastard? He wouldn't last two minutes in any other hospital."

The charge nurse clutched his arm. "I don't know why he's still here. If there was something I could do to get rid of Resnick, believe me, I wouldn't hesitate for a second. Remember, I'm just a nurse." She shrugged her shoulders and emphasized the last sentence.

"Yeah, yeah, Gloria. And I'm just a paramedic. Don't give me that bull. Walk me back to my rig. No offense, but right now this place makes me wanna throw up."

As Koslofsky and her paramedic friend exited the doors to the parking lot, they walked past Clyde Resnick, who was standing with the dead man's sister. She wobbled and sobbed uncontrollably. Her wails expressed a wild combination of grief and skepticism.

"I'm very sorry, ma'am," explained Resnick to the young woman over and over. "We did everything we possibly could for him. He just had injuries he couldn't survive. I can promise you he didn't feel any pain. He didn't suffer."

"But *she* will when she gets his bill," whispered the paramedic to Koslofsky, who answered the paramedic with a quick glance. The look in her eyes made his blood run cold.

"It should've been you, Clyde," she heard herself say, "It should've been you."

CHAPTER 8

Gloria walked into her tiny cluttered office at the back of the ER and threw herself into the chair in front of her desk. Clyde Resnick had always been a lousy doctor, but now he was out of control. The paramedics would have this tale out on the street before the ambulance left the parking lot. She could imagine their response. They already told everyone that Clyde Resnick used trauma care as a form of population control. Clyde's incompetence was all the more frustrating because he was so nonchalant about it all. He really didn't seem to care if the patients lived or died.

Resting her head on her hands, Gloria reached up and punched in the numbers to the operating room. The phone rang three times before someone picked up.

"O.R."

"Hey. This is Gloria down in the ER. Where's Pat? Is she around?"

"Yeah, I think so. I'm gonna put you on hold while I page her. OK?"

"Fine."

"Are you all right? You sound beat."

"I'm real tired. Let me talk to Pat."

"Sure. Here goes. Let me see if I can find her. Hang on."

The receiver went dead as the red hold button began to flash. Gloria used the moment to gather her thoughts. She had dialed with the intent to let the O.R. know that they wouldn't be coming up with the patient, because he hadn't made it out of the ER. Now that communication didn't seem like enough. She needed to talk to someone.

"Hello, this is Pat Malley. Can I help you?"

"Hi Pat. This is Gloria. Got a sec?"

"Gloria! The princess of emergencies. What's up?"

"First, you can cancel the trauma. It won't be coming up. Clyde just notched another one. Clean kill. The poor son of a bitch never had a chance. He would've been better off if the paramedics gave him a trach set and let him do it himself. What a flail."

"Oh, mother of mercy. That old boy's caused you a lot of heartbreak. Haven't you talked to anybody about him?"

Gloria sighed loudly. "Sure I have. But the Director's so old he's got Alzheimer's and the Big Doctors wouldn't know how to find this place if their lives depended on it. The last time I saw the Chief of Surgery was when they interviewed him for the job. That was in 1975, and the only reason he came through was because he wanted a shortcut to the credit union. Nobody cares about the ER. If they did, how could they possibly let a disaster like Clyde keep on torturing patients? He's brain dead."

"I know the feeling. We had the worst one *I've* ever seen about six weeks ago. Let's see if you can guess who."

Gloria thought for a second, then answered with confidence. "That's easy. Ingelhart did a bypass."

"No, don't be silly. This is for real. Guess again."

"Give me the specialty."

"Anesthesia."

"Schmatz! What'd he do this time?"

Pat lowered her voice. "I wasn't there for all of it, but I got the details from Frank Klawitter. This is the worst. Schmatz basically killed a young girl with an ectopic by transfusing her with the wrong blood. She DIC'd and died."

"No!"

"Yes. And it's worse than that. She was Frank's cousin!"

"Who's cousin?"

"Frank's. Can you imagine?"

"Oh my God!"

"Frank went ballistic. He turned Schmatz in to QA. I haven't heard what happened."

"Good luck. I've been writing up Clyde for years. Not only does nothing happen, I don't even hear back from those guys. You'd think that they'd at least ask me some questions. Nope. Not a word. Zip. Zero. I've stopped writing, because it's just a waste of time."

"No kidding. That's funny, because Frank seemed to think that that was the way to go. Come to think of it, though, Schmatz is still here. Maybe you should talk to Frank about what to do about Clyde."

Gloria shared Pat's high opinion of the gynecologist. "Well, it couldn't hurt. I've talked to everybody else. Anyway, I didn't call to cry about my problems. I just wanted you to know that you could release the trauma room. We won't be needing it, at least for now."

"OK, Sweetie. I appreciate the call. Don't let the sons of bitches get you down. Remember, what goes around comes around."

"I hope so."

Gloria hung up, leaned back in her chair and massaged her temples. *What the hell.* She grabbed the hospital directory and flipped through the M.D. pager listing, then picked up the phone and punched in the numbers for Frank Klawitter.

CHAPTER 9

"Dottie, this is Frank Klawitter. I wonder whether you could do me a small favor."

"Sure, Dr. Klawitter, anything you say."

"Great. This shouldn't be too hard. I need some information about billings, salaries and bonuses for a couple members of the Faculty Practice Plan. I was hoping you could pull some records for the last two or three years."

Frank kept his tone of voice low and casual. Hopefully, Dottie wouldn't consider this to be too unusual a request. Like many other women who worked in hospital administration, she'd been his patient for a long time and considered him as much a friend as a personal physician. Most of Frank's patients were fond of him; he was always courteous and took the extra time that made a person feel special. If a patient worked at Branscomb or was poor and struggling, he never sent a bill beyond what the insurance would cover.

"Could you be a little more specific? I'll do what I can, but it depends on what you're looking for, exactly."

Frank wanted to keep this vague. "I'm doing a little survey to see if we've been getting the right reimbursement for our services. I want to be certain the new coders are doing their jobs right. You know what I mean."

She didn't yet, but that wasn't important. What harm could there be in pulling a few records? "Oh, I see. Go ahead. What would you like me to do?"

"If it's not too much trouble, could you pull the financial sheets for myself, Clyde Resnick and Randy Schmatz? That would give me a good start. I know that we each receive a report by procedure code, but if you could sort the list a few different other ways, like by patient name, procedure code and date of service, that would be great. If not, don't worry, I can do that myself."

"No problem, sorting shouldn't be a big deal. I've never seen it done the other ways, but it sounds pretty straightforward. But doctor, why do you need data for Dr. Schmatz? He's an anesthesiologist and you're ob-gyn. Wouldn't you rather have someone else from your own department?"

Frank was ready for that one. "No, Dottie. I want Schmatz's stuff because we sometimes use the same coders and I want to see if it's me or them. You know Schmatz. He would never forget to document anything that would lead to a charge. Same with Clyde."

Dottie agreed. "You're right about that. Let me see what I can do. I'll ask someone down in Patient Accounting to give me a hand."

"No. Don't do that!" Frank's tone changed abruptly. He followed quickly with an explanation. "I mean, I really don't want you to go to any extra trouble. I didn't intend for you to have to get extra help. If the sorting'll be too much work, I'll just take the master list and get my secretary to do the rest. You're being too nice."

Dottie was put off at first, but she warmed back up. "OK, Dr. Klawitter. It's really not a big deal. I'll do it myself. Let me help you with the sorting too. I can run through it with the computer in a flash. If it's done by hand, your people will be at it for a week."

"Are you sure you have the time? I want to keep this kind of confidential. You know how doctors are about having people review their incomes."

"The other doctors don't know?"

"No, and I'd prefer not to tell them."

"OK. For you — anything. I'll have it in the morning. I've got some free time this afternoon, so it really isn't a problem. It'll give me something to do."

"Thanks. You're terrific. What time do you come in?"

"Nine."

"See you then."

It didn't take very long for Frank to pick up the pattern. There were blanks where the salaries and bonuses for Schmatz and Resnick were supposed to be listed. Frank didn't have any choice, because he needed to know the precise numbers. He telephoned Dottie and explained to her what was missing. She told him she'd see what she could do. The next morning, there was a soft knock on his office door.

"Come in."

"Dr. Klawitter, I wanted to bring these to you myself. I don't trust the hospital mail." Dottie wore a concerned expression when she handed him the revised reports.

"Is something the matter?"

"I don't think so, but perhaps you'd better decide that yourself. Anesthesia and Emergency Medicine certainly seem to be lucrative professions." She was blushing. "I haven't been able to get the bonuses yet, but look at the salary figures."

Frank opened the envelope and scanned the documents. "Dottie, please don't tell anybody about this. It may all just be a mistake. That's why I'm reviewing it."

"Of course I won't. I'll get you the bonus info as soon as I can. Will there be anything else?"

"I wouldn't think so. You've been an enormous help. Thanks. And remember…"

"Don't worry."

Their compensation was up in the stratosphere. It was possible that an anesthesiologist could bill a tremendous amount, but Schmatz wasn't that busy anymore, because none of the doctors familiar with his clinical performance wanted him anywhere near their patients. And if Resnick had actually earned that much, then Frank was the man in the moon. These kinds of payments required authorization from someone high up in the medical center. The Dean was usually the man with the checkbook. It didn't make sense.

Schmatz and Resnick had been made into multi-millionaires. And that didn't even include any bonuses. Was there more? No one in his right mind would lay it all out for the accountants to review. There had to be something else, information or income that wouldn't be picked up in an audit. He sensed a connection. But without the presence of raw data, a more definitive link to someone or something that kept these lethal incompetents on the payroll, he was powerless. For Ellie and everybody else to come, Frank swore he'd find out what was going on and put an end to it.

CHAPTER 10

Harvard didn't even have the decency to call before they announced to the press. Harry Baraff was the new Associate Dean at Harvard. Fred Spencer was stunned. Only two weeks ago, he had been told that he was a shoo-in for the position. They had discussed moving expenses and furnishings for his new office, and had a realtor from Boston take him on tour. This didn't make sense. What could have possibly happened to make them change their minds? And why the cold shoulder?

Fred telephoned the Dean's office. Richard Moffitt was on vacation for ten days in France? Impossible. He would touch base on something this big before he left. It wasn't just business — it was fundamental respect. Why? Why!

The Department of Radiology secretary handed Fred Spencer a letter which had arrived yesterday, the same day as the newspaper story in Boston. He opened it with trepidation. This had to be a bad dream.

Dear Fred:

I'm sorry to inform you that the person chosen to be the next Associate Dean of the Medical School at Harvard is Harry Baraff from the University of Chicago. This was a very difficult decision for us. You are one of the most illustrious graduates of our medical school and represent a remarkable combination of clinical and research abilities, but in the end, the committee felt that it had to go with more administrative experience. As you know, Dr. Baraff is an extremely well regarded scientist and program director, and has been largely responsible for the new curriculum in the school at Chicago. Despite your favored son status, we had to address our immediate organizational needs.

I want to personally thank you for participating in our search process and being forthright in our discussions. While I imagine this will be somewhat of a disappointment to you, I have every confidence that your career will continue to cast a beacon which will soon attract other offers, more than you will know what to do with.

Unfortunately, I will be gone until the middle of the month. Alumni affairs and a much-needed rest call me away. Please forgive the nature of this communication, but I am certain that you understand.

Sincerely,
Richard Moffitt, M.D., Ph.D
Dean, Harvard University School of Medicine

Fred read and reread the letter. It was absurd. He and Moffitt had discussed all of the issues mentioned, and had agreed that Fred's lack of administrative experience wasn't important. In fact, Moffitt had told him that he welcomed a fresh, unbiased outlook, and preferred a younger person for the job. No mention had been made of his competitor, other than to dismiss him as an unrealistic choice. Fred knew Baraff. He was nothing special.

Moffitt's switchback was totally unexpected. Fred was completely demoralized. He needed to speak with someone from Harvard, and it couldn't wait until Moffitt returned from Europe.

Fred called an old medical school classmate who had stayed on the faculty at Harvard. When Fred asked him to snoop, he became circumspect. It was an outside chance, given the nature of the inquiry, but he'd see what he could find out. One of the trustees lived in the neighborhood.

The next day Fred learned the explanation. He dropped to his knees, insane with rage. Because of what Waterhouse had told Moffitt and the speed with which that kind of defamation spread in an academic medical center like Harvard, there would never be a chance for him to go back there as an Associate Dean, or anything else. Unless he confronted both Waterhouse and Moffitt in public, he was a marked man.

Fred held his head in his hands as he sank into despair. The more he thought about it, the more he realized that there was no effective way to do damage control. Deans talked to deans and trustees to trustees. You were guilty until proven innocent, but even then, the doubts would always remain. Like a charge of sexual harassment. Even when you were innocent, people believed what they wanted to believe. It was an act of inexplicable cruelty.

When Fred burst through the Dean's door, Waterhouse knew immediately that his treachery had been discovered. He jumped up from his seat and ran to close the door.

"I want to know why the Dean of a medical school, who could have anything he wants, and who is usually surrounded by contemptible idiots, would screw the one person who has never asked for anything. Why, after years of helping a friend hold it together, my thanks is a big blade in the back. I thought I knew you, but I didn't know anything at all. Why didn't you have the guts to tell me what was really on your mind — what you intended all along? You stooped to this just to keep me here? We could have worked something out."

"Fred, this isn't the time to talk. You've got to take a step back."

"A step back! You take a step back! Take a step back to when you told me that I was the one person you could count on, that I was the only reason you had for staying at Branscomb, that I was the only one who made sense. How could you do this to me?"

Fred had given him his out. Try sympathy first. "You know. Because I couldn't stand to see you go. It was too painful to think about. I need you here."

"Need me? Need me for what?"

"To maintain some equilibrium when things get crazy. To make the others understand that the rewards are for greatness, not for manipulation. To make this the greatest medical center on the planet. You do see that, don't you?"

"I'm having a hard time seeing anything. Why didn't you come to me? I didn't have to leave right away. For Christ's sake, you offered to make me a Dean. Why did you feel like you had to ruin my career? What have I ever done to you?"

"Nothing. I just didn't think you were ready, that's all."

"Goddamn it! Ready for what? For this crap? For making up stories and smearing reputations? For character assassination?" Spencer made a move for the door. "You're crazy. You're greedy and you're stupid and you're crazy. You didn't do this for me. You did it for you. You don't want me to go because without people like me, you're nothing. Well, fuck you,

Mr. Bigshot. You won't get away with this. I'm better than you at *everything*. I'm gonna track down Moffitt and blow the whistle on both your bullshit."

"You can't."

"What do you mean, I can't?"

"He won't believe you. You should know that. He can't take a chance."

"You don't have any proof. I have all the original data in my files."

"No you don't."

Spencer was dumbstruck. The studies which Waterhouse had maligned were done years ago, and all of the records had been kept on paper. Wiley knew where the original materials were kept. By Wiley's expression, Fred realized that the documents were now in the Dean's possession, altered maliciously.

"You bastard."

"I'm really sorry. There'll be other jobs. Other chances. You can still be an Associate Dean here if you want. I can do that for you right away."

"I want to go *now!*"

Waterhouse shook his head and looked away. "No, you can't. Not until I say so. Look, you can have anything you want. More space. More money. I meant what I said. You can work in the Dean's office. We're a team, aren't we?" The Dean started to offer his hand to Spencer, then let it rest at his side.

"You're sick. No, worse than sick. You're a demon." Fred's face turned white as he stepped forward. Waterhouse was afraid that Spencer was going to strike him and backed away. The radiologist turned around abruptly and raced out the door, slamming it behind him. Waterhouse sat down, breathing hard. He had never before witnessed such hate.

The stunned radiologist ran back to his laboratory, barely able to hold back the tears. He was a prisoner at Branscomb for as long as the Dean wanted. Even if Waterhouse changed his mind, he would still have a difficult time undoing the nightmare he had created. Nothing that Spencer had achieved could counter the repulsive evil of this jealous man.

Spencer turned on his computer and pulled up a set of MRI data on

Waterhouse, whom he had imaged long ago when their project was first getting started. The beams of light intertwined behind him and created the perfect image of a short, fat naked man standing on the platform behind him. He rotated it slowly while he reflected back on the decades of work it had taken him to get to this point in his career, and how quickly Waterhouse had devastated him. In a surge of anger, the radiological genius pushed a series of buttons and spun his dials. The image behind him became decapitated, and then lost its limbs, so that a holographic torso hung behind him. Fred Spencer surveyed his creation, then made it disappear completely. He brought the image back, and cut off its balls.

CHAPTER 11

The Quality Assurance Review Committee met once a month to discuss cases. The members of the committee included its physician Chairman, six other physicians, a medical center attorney, the Director of Risk Management, the Nursing Director from the Pediatric Intensive Care Unit, and an administrative assistant from the Chancellor's office. The meeting was held in a plush conference room. The issues were sensitive and the discussions often became contentious.

The Chairman was Bob Stoner, an orthopedic surgeon who specialized in total joint replacements. Stoner had been a medical student, house officer, and faculty member at Branscomb, so he knew the hospital politics cold. He was considered to be an extremely competent surgeon, and very effective at gathering consensus. The Dean had no difficulty convincing the Chief of Staff to appoint Stoner as Chairman of the QA Committee. His levelheaded demeanor was effective at steering the committee through complex ethical and legal considerations.

The six other physician members served for three-year rotating terms. The holdovers from the previous Chairman were Frank Klawitter and Joe Masterson, the latter a classically assertive trauma surgeon. Stoner's appointees were a dermatologist, a general internist who specialized in adolescent disorders, a psychiatrist, and a soft-spoken immunologist who specialized in rheumatoid arthritis. He had clearly chosen a group of individuals who would bring diverse experience to the deliberations.

The Director of Risk Management, Ferdie Gooch, was a good ol' boy who hailed from Amarillo, Texas. Even though he himself wasn't a lawyer, Ferdie loved to mix it up with plaintiffs' attorneys on behalf of the medical center. Every year, the risk manager took a vacation out West in his mobile home, so that he could drive around the Dakota plains and shoot prairie dogs. When he got time off in the winter, he headed to Yellowstone and roared through the park on a snowmobile, frightening the daylights out of the elk and bison.

The medical center attorney generically hated doctors, mostly because she hadn't been able to get into medical school. The Chancellor was represented by a dyed-in-the-wool preppie tattletale who spent most of her spare time arranging Junior League benefits. All she knew about medicine was how to drop the names of celebrity patients and when to call the doctor if she got sick. She was regularly grossed out by the committee's graphic descriptions of human excrement, gangrenous scrotums and dislodged catheters.

The members varied in their approach as they reviewed episodes of unlucky coincidence and twists of fate. Klawitter and the ICU nurse took a fairly hard-nosed position on the matters of record, insisting on full reviews and appearances before the committee by alleged perpetrators of malpractice. They were skeptical of quick explanations, and became exceptional analysts. The immunologist, psychiatrist, dermatologist, and internist were more contemplative, less willing to be harsh in judgement, and occasionally reticent to find fault with marginal transgressions.

The Chairman of the Committee was often circumspect. At times, it appeared that Dr. Stoner wanted to serve his time with a minimum of controversy. He more often than not spoke in defense of physicians under investigation, reminding the group that after all, they never knew when *they* might stumble.

Before any case was presented to the committee, Stoner reviewed it in private and rendered a preliminary opinion. By the time everyone else got a shot, it was nearly a done deal. There were a lot of predictable mishaps, such as take-backs to the O.R. for missing sponges or postoperative bleeding, wound infections, medication errors, slips in the shower and the like. Every once in awhile, there would be a worrisome indicator, like operating on the right knee when the left one was the target. Then there were the spectacularly scary examples of stupidity, like transplanting the wrong organ into a patient — crazy mistakes that one wouldn't imagine a cerebrating creature capable of committing. Finally, there were the errors of omission, which followed fatigue or were acts of outright laziness. Unnecessary procedures were rarely discussed, because that was business, not medicine.

The last case of the day involved the operating room. Stoner read from his text. Case number 854-A. Reported to the committee by Pat Malley. The patient was taken to the operating room at 7:48 A.M. for an unscheduled liver transplant. The on-call anesthesiologist was paged at

7:55 to inform him that his patient was in the pre-op area, but he didn't respond. A second page was entered at 8:10, but was also not answered. All of the other faculty anesthesiologists were doing cases or unavailable, so the Chief Resident was paged. He was in the middle of a mastectomy, so the first year resident on the ICU service was called. He had to finish floating a pacemaker before he could come to the O.R. The procedure was complicated, so he got held up in the ICU. He left the ICU and reported to the OR at 10:00. Pre-operative medications were given and the case was started at 10:45. At noon, the missing faculty anesthesiologist called in from outside the hospital to check his messages and was told that the case had started. The case continued with two complications before the anesthesiologist arrived midway through the operation.

"What were the problems during the case?" asked the nuclear radiologist.

Stoner replied, "Apparently, the perfusion pump to the donor liver bath was intermittently turned off or set on the wrong temperature. It's not entirely clear what happened. Anyway, this wasn't noted until just prior to the transplant by the circulating nurse."

"Unbelievable," muttered the trauma surgeon Masterson. "How do you like your liver cooked? Who was responsible for the pump?"

"The pump is usually handled by the anesthesiologist."

"That's a rookie error," said Klawitter, who had steamed up quickly during the narrative. "Who was the on-call faculty anesthesiologist?"

"I'll get to that in a minute, Frank," answered Stoner, who waved Klawitter away. "There was one other problem with the case. The resident spiked and hung a bottle of citrate that was supposed to be used for anti-coagulant instead of the dopamine pre-mix. It was piggybacked into the central line. A few times during the case, the patient dropped his pressure, which as you know is fairly common during a liver transplant. It was felt that he needed a trickle of dopamine, so he got infused with the wrong drug."

"I'll say it was the wrong drug," broke in Masterson. "You need an ocean of fluid and blood during a liver transplant. That's basic. The only time you need dopamine is if the patient has heart failure. That almost never happens. This isn't one mistake, it's four. First, I'll guess not enough blood. Second, not enough salt. Third, major medication error. Fourth, where was the frapping faculty anesthesiologist? This one *really* torks me off."

Stoner held up his hand and continued dispassionately, as if he'd never been interrupted. "Late in the case there was an episode of prolonged bradycardia and hypotension, so the faculty anesthesiologist infused more citrate, because he thought it was dopamine. Things went from bad to worse. Apparently, the anesthesiologist never told the surgeons that he was having trouble until it was too late. The patient arrested on the table, so the team went up into the chest to get control of the aorta. It's hard to tell from the notes, but approximately ten minutes into the resuscitation someone figured out what had happened. The patient was given a mega-dose of IV calcium and came back pretty quick."

"Did he live?" whispered the Chancellor's mole. "What happened next?"

"The transplant was completed. He's doing just fine now," answered Stoner. "There was a relatively rocky ICU course, but no residual neurological deficit. He wasn't informed of the reason for his thoracotomy, other than it was a complication of the transplant surgery necessary to save his life. At this point, he appears to be accepting a minimal explanation."

"So what's the problem now?" asked the dermatologist.

"As far as I'm concerned, perhaps not much. We have to review the case because it was submitted and Ferdie won't let me dismiss it preliminarily. Ferdie?"

The wily risk manager folded his hands in front of him and peeked over his bifocals around the room. No one in the room loved Branscomb more than Ferdie or had a better understanding of how destructive a failed malpractice defense could be. "Boys...and ladies... this one smells bad to me. Whooey! If a jury gets a look at this one, that'll pretty well chew up our self-insurance funds for this century. But I'm cheatin' a little bit, because I know more about this one than y'all do. Bob, you need to tell 'em the rest. Go ahead.

"Unfortunately, the patient has rejected his transplant. It's hard to say whether or not what happened to him in the O.R. has anything to do with it. A lot of these cases don't work out, and nobody particularly knows why."

"Wait a minute, Bob," interrupted Frank. "Are you telling me that you want us to believe that an improperly perfused liver and a cardiac arrest during the operation aren't the cause of organ rejection? Are you telling me that you can take a donor liver, beat the hell out of it with a tire iron, put it into a patient and expect it to live? Man, I'm getting tired of the hit squad. Who was the anesthesiologist that didn't show up for the case?"

"I don't think that's the major issue, Frank."

"Of course it's the issue."

"No it isn't. The issue is whether or not the person who was actually there and did the case was in error. All of us have been late for cases. That's not a crime."

"Bullshit! Not four hours late. And we all have real backup, not puppy dog backup. I'm sick of the horses around here doing whatever they goddamn feel like and us rolling over for their horseshit. Who was it? What was the excuse?"

"I must say that this is a bit disturbing," said the psychiatrist. Everyone except Stoner nodded in agreement. "I agree that the young man who made the error needs to be counseled. He's probably beside himself with guilt. But perhaps it would be useful for us to know who the tardy anesthesiologist was. Maybe this is a pattern."

Frank and Masterson looked at each other and rolled their eyes. Everyone turned to Stoner. He hesitated.

"Got to tell, Bob," said Ferdie Gooch.

"OK, it was Randy Schmatz."

"Well, surprise surprise," laughed Masterson as he leaned back from the table and threw his hands up over his head.

"That malignant son of a bitch," growled Frank.

"For the love of God," said the internist. "Where was he?"

"Who cares?" chuckled Masterson. "The first-year resident probably knew more anesthesia than Randy boy. It's just as well that he didn't show up. The only transplant Schmatz understands is when he takes money from your wallet and transplants it into his big fat bank account."

Frank had to let it pour out. The death of his cousin had erased his restraint as far as Randy Schmatz was concerned. He nearly broke down. "What will it take to put this moron away? If we let him go on this one, somebody ought to take *us* to court."

Ferdie Gooch stood up. His heart went out to the gynecologist, but Frank's response was dangerous. He wanted to defuse his grief without embarrassing him. "Now fellas, I mean fellas and ladies, we have to stop this kinda talkin'. We keep minutes from this meeting. Even though they ain't supposed to be discoverable in a court of law, the lawyers know how to get their hands on anything and everything. For you surgeons, let me put it this way. Those suckers smell it when you're bleeding inside, and they'll make the diagnosis by slittin' you open on the witness stand. So we'd best be real careful how we talk in here and stick to the important issues. Don't be so hateful. This ain't a courtroom. Schmatz ain't on trial here. We're talking about a specific case, and I don't want anyone to say something now that they might regret later on. Now calm down. Thank you for lettin' me speak my piece."

"Ferdie, you know that I think the world of what you folks do in Risk Management, but I just don't agree," said the Intensive Care Unit nurse. "I'd like *someone* to answer my original question. Where was he?"

"Where was who?"

"Schmatz."

Frank turned to Stoner. "Bob?"

"He wouldn't tell me. He said he was sorry."

Verbal pandemonium erupted. Everyone in the room tried to talk at once, spouting expressions of incredulity. Frank turned to Stoner and snarled, "We've got to nail him this time." The nurse shook her head from side to side. Gooch scribbled furiously on his yellow legal pad and admonished the psychiatrist not to put anything in the minutes. Even the usually silent immunologist said to no one in particular, "We really should bump this one up to the Medical Board."

Stoner zeroed in on her comment instantly. "Before we go any further, let me tell you how I've assessed this situation. I know it seems pretty bad, but we have guidelines for how we're supposed to grade these cases. First of all, we have to confine ourselves to the persons present at the time of the incident and the activities that occurred at the time. It's not our role to pass judgment on people who weren't even present. Therefore..."

"Now wait a minute," argued Frank. "You can't be serious. That son of a bitch was on call. He was told that he had a transplant starting. There was no excuse in the world for him not to drop everything and race in to the hospital. Do you mean to tell us that it's OK for an anesthesiologist to miss, no, I mean to *ignore* a case and let it be done by someone who is totally unprepared for the operation? How can you possibly condone what he did? For Christ's sake, Bob, you're the best orthopedic surgeon at this hospital. I know that you won't let him do any of *your* cases any more. Why is that?"

"Frank, you've got to let me finish! I know you're upset about this, but there are some principles of the committee involved here. You've got to understand that..."

"Understand? I understand, all right. Tell me what you consider to be malpractice. I mean, where do we draw the line? Does Randy have to stick somebody in the heart with an ice pick before you'll admit he fucked up? C'mon, Bob, don't be a company man. They should have retired Schmatz twenty five years ago, and if nobody else has the balls to do it, then we have to."

Frank's tirade was interrupted by the entrance of Dr. Wiley Waterhouse. The portly Dean of Branscomb Medical School stood in the entryway and glanced quickly around the room. He acknowledged everyone by nodding his head a few times, then occupied a vacant chair in the back of the room. He folded his arms in front of him and crossed his legs.

"Please go on, I don't want to interrupt anything. What were we talking about? Got a good case this month? Somebody have an adverse reaction to his bill?"

Stoner spoke. "I think the Dean is already familiar with this case. Dean Waterhouse, we were discussing the episode of the liver transplant where Dr. Schmatz couldn't get to the operating room on time. Our discussion this afternoon has centered around the issue of whether it is our role to comment on the case as it transpired or whether we should also deal with Dr. Schmatz's inability to arrive in time to commence the case."

Waterhouse responded, "It's always been my understanding that the committee is supposed to confine itself to issues of care rendered."

"Spoken like a true bureaucrat," hissed Frank. "Dr. Waterhouse, the real issue now is how many times we're going to let Randy Schmatz off the hook."

To Frank, it seemed more than a coincidence that the Dean had once again appeared during a discussion about Schmatz. He had also been at the last two meetings when Schmatz was discussed. In each instance, Schmatz's shortcoming had been sufficient to merit consideration of throwing him off the clinical staff, or at least putting him on probation. Both times, a far-fetched procedural interpretation had been invoked to clear Schmatz of any culpability.

In the case of Frank's cousin Eleanor, Waterhouse fenced Frank and Stoner for over two hours. While the Dean finally yielded on the issue of erroneous transfusion, he let Schmatz slide because he felt the blood had been "inadequately tagged." The tags were supposed to have been glued to the plastic blood bags, but for some reason, they weren't. Frank argued the absurdity of the excuse, since no one would *ever* transfuse blood without checking off the unit against the patient's ID bracelet. When the session became untenable, Waterhouse pulled rank and closed the case. In a private session with Frank and Stoner, he swore to limit Schmatz's privileges. This had obviously not been carried through as promised.

"It has always been my view that one mustn't judge one's colleagues too harshly, particularly since all of us have transgressed in one way or another during the course of our illustrious medical careers," intoned the Dean. "I don't believe that a man who misses an appointment because of a scheduling error or a flat tire is responsible for the performance of another man who takes his place. This may be worthy of a reprimand, but hardly devilish enough to merit a public hearing."

My God, thought Frank. *He's gonna do it again. A whitewash. Some poor slob just lost his new liver and probably his only chance to live, and now the man responsible gets off scott-free. I can't take it any more.*

"Illustrious career?" Frank raged, "Dean Waterhouse, I think you're missing the point. Do you really consider screwing up a liver transplant to be the same as getting a flat tire? This is the third time in the past year Schmatz has blown one bad enough to come before this committee, and we're about to let him off the hook again. He's a monster. I can't sit here and accept responsibility for the next person he kills. If this one doesn't score a four, I resign from this committee right here, right now."

Waterhouse got hot in a hurry, which wasn't very typical for him. He stood up red-faced and walked to the head of the conference table so that he could address the entire group. He pointed his index finger at Frank.

"Dr. Klawitter, you're way out of line. Dr. Stoner sets policy for this committee and decides who goes and who stays. You can't resign. You have an obligation to me and to this medical school to stay on the committee and to support its decisions. And you have my word, the behavior of Dr. Schmatz is about to undergo a radical improvement. There will be no more transgressions."

Everyone turned to Frank, who had never before shown any of them this side of his personality, in private or in public. Frank glanced quickly at Stoner, who averted his eyes and shuffled the pile of papers in front of him.

Frank turned to the Dean. "Sorry, but I'm out. Maybe I don't understand the process, but I know shitty medicine when I see it. The only option here is to be a good ol' boy. I can't play it your way. You want it, come get it." Frank stood up, put on his long white coat and left the room. As soon as he walked out, Masterson raised his hand.

"Joe." Stoner beckoned to the trauma surgeon.

"Bob, I've got to say in Frank's defense that he knows what he's talking about. Schmatz is a disaster. Hell, if I needed anesthesia and Randy was the only one around, I'd go get a mirror and put myself to sleep. I can't believe that he won't be held responsible for this one."

Waterhouse didn't give Stoner a chance to respond to Masterson. "Listen everybody, he will be. I'm sure there's liability in this case. But I also have great concern about the performance of the house officer. His ineptitude is not in the Branscomb tradition, and I plan to suspend him from the training program. That should serve as an example to the other residents that they must be properly prepared before they presume themselves to be capable of administering anesthesia."

"No! That's bullshit! He did the best he could. At least he was there."
Masterson was livid.

"Dean Waterhouse, I don't think we should do that," argued Ferdie.
"We'd face a legal action for sure. Maybe you should reconsider."

Stoner agreed. "The house officer should be held harmless."

The others were ready to chime in, but decided to keep their mouths
shut for the moment. They sensed that Waterhouse had another agenda,
and now wasn't the time to argue.

The Dean sought a legal opinion.

"Dr. Waterhouse, from a lawyer's perspective, it's debatable whether
we can hold Dr. Schmatz accountable for what occurred in the operating
room. The fact is that Dr. Schmatz wasn't present. Therefore, he cannot
be held strictly accountable for what happened. The surgeon should not
have allowed the case to begin. Therefore, I recommend to the committee
that we consider these events to have been unpredictable, but within the
standard of care. I don't think any lawyer would disagree with my interpretation."

Joe Masterson wore a look of total disgust as he rose from his seat.
"What do you do when a lawyer has a seizure in a bathtub?" No one
answered. "You throw in the laundry." Masterson made his way to the
door. "Sorry folks, but I can't stomach this either. It's a sad day when
we've got the lawyers telling us that a bad doctor is a good doctor and
the Dean figures to run some young buck up the flagpole 'cause we don't
want to get the Branscomb flag all wet. Your shit stinks too, Waterhouse,
maybe worse than the rest of us. Hell, you know what anesthesia is
around here? A way to keep the pathologists in business. Count me out
too."

Masterson and Frank collided at the water fountain.

"Hey Frank." Masterson held out his hand. "Put 'er there, big boy.
What you did took real courage. Waterhouse can be a vindictive SOB.
You better watch your back."

"What are you doing out here? You're the only hope left for the committee."

"Not any more. So, what do you think we ought to do about this?
Schmatz is gonna get away with this again."

Frank hesitated for a second, then pulled Joe close to him. "Maybe there *is* something we can do. If the system isn't designed to fix the bad problems, maybe we should try something a little different. Ever since Eleanor died, I've been checking things out, and I'm sure I'm on to something. I'd like a few of us to get together to talk this over. I need to be sure that I'm not the only one who's had a problem lately. But not a word to anyone. You know how this place is."

Frank and Joe were interrupted by Waterhouse, who had wrapped up his comments quickly so he could follow Joe out of the room. "I want to talk to you two. Right now! What do you think you're accomplishing by storming out of a committee meeting?"

The doctors looked at each other, then back at the Dean. Neither man answered.

"Answer me! What are you trying to prove? You have a responsibility to the others."

Frank didn't raise his voice. "What about our patients? What about the oath we swore as physicians? You're damn right we have a responsibility. That's why we got out of there."

"You have a responsibility to *me*."

"Please. There's no audience here. He killed my cousin! Why don't you go work on a budget or something? You wouldn't recognize a suffering human being if one collapsed in your office."

"Frank, don't you think I understand how you feel? I told you in there, Schmatz will toe the line. But there'll be no public hanging. So, I'm asking you, Frank. Don't push me. I'm cutting you a lot of slack. Your cousin's death was tragic but it's not an excuse for you to abandon your duty."

"Wiley, I told you I'm out, and I'm out."

The Dean was losing ground. He tried an old standby. Sexual harassment. "There are people who come to me very upset about your behavior. They confide in me. Women who don't appreciate the things you say to them."

"What are you talking about? Are you out of your mind? Who are these women? Give me one name."

"That would be breaking a confidence. I can't do that." The Dean's bluff immediately lost ground. He wanted to intimidate Frank, but the gynecologist wasn't having any of it.

Joe chimed in. "Excuse me Dr. Waterhouse, but you aren't by any chance *threatening* Frank, are you? I mean, are you trying to say that there's a problem with Frank?"

"I'm not talking to you, Joe."

"Well, I'm talking to you, Wiley. We're off your committee. You go tell anybody anything you want. Why don't you start by telling Schmatz that he's not an anesthesiologist. Tell him he's a serial killer."

Waterhouse felt his collar tighten as the blood rushed to his head. He would give no ground. "This is my final advice to you two. Be careful. If I get one more complaint about either one of you, I'll need to reconsider your appointments. Loyalty to the Dean's office is extremely important at Branscomb. Some would say that loyalty is everything."

"And here's my advice to you." Joe squared off directly in front of the Dean. "I don't give a rat's ass about titles, promotions or any of the other goodies you dangle in front of all those sniveling slimebuckets who suck up to you for a handout. You know, I'm beginning to think you're trying to protect someone. And don't you *ever* threaten me again. Unless you want a tour of the ER flat on your back looking up at the lights. Now get out of my sight!" Waterhouse was frightened. He turned and walked away quickly.

Frank grabbed Joe's arm. "That pompous prick! He protects a sleaze-ball like Schmatz and threatens to take *us* out. That's it!"

Masterson dropped his voice to a whisper. "You don't know the half of it, Frank. We've got one worse than Schmatz in the Department of Surgery that hasn't even made it to the QA Committee. Why do we stay here? I'm sick of this. Maybe it would be better for everybody if we just resigned and went someplace else to work."

"No, that's not the answer. I owe it to Ellie to see this through. Something's very wrong, and I think that we've already let it go on for too long. I'll call the meeting."

"Mind if I review the guest list?"

"Not at all. How about my place on Saturday night? Ten o'clock. I'll handle the invitations."

CHAPTER 12

The QA meeting was dismissed soon after Klawitter and Masterson walked out. Waterhouse strode quickly back to his office. He was shaken badly by what had happened. This was the closest call yet. In a fury, he snatched the phone off the hook and dialed the Department of Anesthesia.

"This is Dr. Waterhouse. I need to speak with Dr. Schmatz. Yes, this is very important. I'll wait until he's off his call, thank you. Slip a piece of paper under his nose and let him know that I'm on the line. No, I don't want him to call back. I want to talk to him *now!*"

Calm down. Calm down. The idiot's not worth a heart attack. Waterhouse tried to lower his blood pressure and slow his heart rate by taking a few deep breaths and working the muscles in his feet and lower legs. Stress reduction exercises. The best stress reduction would be to ship Schmatz and the others to the moon. He loosened his tie.

The voice at the other end was loud and cheery. "Professor Waterhouse, the distinguished Dean. What can I do for you today? Perhaps you'd care to join me at the country club for a late nine holes and a prime rib dinner. Whaddya say? Your putter still working that old black magic?"

Waterhouse roared, "Shut up! The only nine holes I want to talk about are the ones I'm going to drill in your head. I just left the QA Committee. They wanted to crucify you. What's the matter with you? Enough is enough!"

"I know. I'm trying. I promised you that I'd retire soon, and I will. I just need a little more time. I don't want to go in disgrace."

"We're beyond that. Your reputation is long gone. Randy, I can't hold them off much longer. What in the hell have you been thinking about? I've given you all the rope I can, but missing a liver transplant case? You've gone too far. I may've gotten you out of this one, but I'm not sure. They were really hot for you this time, Randy. They want you out. I want you out. We agreed that you'd do your job right. Be on time. Stick to simple cases. You're not keeping up your end of the bargain."

Schmatz was frightened and angry. "Don't give me that bargain shit!

We don't have any bargains anymore. You're in this as much as me, buddy boy. You pull anything now and the cat's out of the bag."

"Jesus Christ. What do you think you're doing? You're going to ruin all of us. You killed Klawitter's cousin. He's hot. You know how close we came on that one. It still isn't over. Now Joe Masterson's on my case. I can handle them one at a time, but it's becoming an assault. And you're providing them enough ammo to blow us all out of the water. You can't come up again. Please, Randy. Retire. You know I could just kick you out of here."

"And what would that prove? That you're a big man? Don't get delusions of grandeur. You may be the Dean, but any one of us can break you in a heartbeat."

"It's not just me anymore, Randy. You know it's more complicated than that. Remember, the QA Committee leads directly to the Chancellor, so when they talk about you, it all goes upstairs. I can't prevent it. He's already hinted to me that he wants to start sitting in on the meetings. What do you think'll happen then? I'm telling you, find another way to make your money." He hesitated. "We can fix that."

Schmatz chuckled nervously. "OK, OK. I'm sorry. How was I supposed to know that the case was gonna be that tough? I'll try to do better next time."

"No. I can't find any more experts to defend you against the lawsuits. The last one settled for a million and a half. We can't afford another next time. The best thing is to quit while you're ahead. Use your head. You're the one person in all this I can really trust." Waterhouse tried to sound sincere.

"Now wait a minute. Let's go over this one more time. What is it precisely that you're asking?"

"Randy, think about it. I need your help with the others. It'll never work if *we're* the ones on the witness stand."

"Wiley, you're right. You can't touch me and I can't touch you, or any of the others for that matter. That's pretty obvious, because if we could, we'd all be long gone by now."

True enough, thought Wiley to himself. Until he had a better idea, he had to continue to appeal to reason. "Randy, all I want you to do is consider how your behavior affects our ability to continue with our current lifestyle. If the QA Committee had taken you down, there actually would have been nothing I could do to prevent it."

"Don't give me that bull. You can do anything you want."

"*Almost* anything. But I can tell you this much. If you botch a case again, you're on your own. If you miss a dose by as much as a milligram and somebody says something, I'll have to feed you to the lawyers myself. And no matter what, you hand in your resignation by the end of the year."

Schmatz had heard it all before. He knew when it was time to end the conversation. "I hear you. Don't sound so depressed. Guess you probably don't want to play golf today."

"No, I don't. Goodbye."

Something had to be done about Schmatz. Waterhouse knew him well enough to tell that he had been frightened, but not enough. Wiley realized that time was growing short. The others had their moments, but Randy had become intolerable. Wouldn't it be nice if he could be convinced to retire or just keeled over one day?

Either would do.

"Dot, this is Frank Klawitter. I just wanted to tell you that you did a fantastic job with those reports for me. They were just what I needed. Thanks a lot."

"That's good. I'm glad I could help. It was a little confusing in the beginning, but once I figured out the system, it didn't take very long to crank them out."

"I wonder if I could ask you for another small favor. I need one more report. I don't think I'll need any more after that. Would it be too much trouble? If it is, forget I asked."

"No, not at all. When do you need it?"

"Would tomorrow be too soon? You tell me. I'm totally at your mercy. I was hoping to put together a report over the weekend, so it would be nice to have all the data as soon as possible."

"Dr. Klawitter, if it were anyone else, I'd say no. Give me the names and I'll have the spread sheets for you by late this afternoon."

"There's only one more name. Bob Stoner. Run the reports the same way you did for Schmatz and Resnick."

"Are you sure that's all? It isn't any more trouble to run extra people. I might as well get it all done at one pass."

Frank thought about the recent activity of the QA Committee. "Actually then, if you have the time, it wouldn't hurt to take a look at Myron Ingelhart. That way, I'll have people from surgery, medicine and outpatient services. Plus myself, of course. Is that too much?"

"Tell you what, Dr. Klawitter. I'll run everybody from those departments."

"The entire faculty?" "

"It's not a big deal. You can go through the stack and use whatever you need. But remember, please don't tell anybody. I don't want everybody up here asking for special reports."

"Of course not. I really appreciate it."

"My pleasure. Is that all?"

"Yes, except to tell you that I owe you a favor."

"No you don't, Dr. Klawitter. Too bad there aren't more doctors like you at Branscomb."

"Thanks, Dot."

That evening in his office, Frank pored over a mountain of spreadsheets. What he observed was no less than incredible. Ingelhart was just like Schmatz. Stoner was clean. The newest addition was a surprise. Joe had explained that she was becoming a bad doctor, but taking money was totally unexpected. Dottie had been able to dig down into another layer. The dollar amounts were staggering. Still, it had to be more than the money, at least for the Dean. His name wasn't on the list, so Frank couldn't tell for sure. He could understand how the recipients would benefit, but what was in it for Waterhouse? This was criminal. Perhaps the men he had invited into his home could help him understand what drove this cabal of doctors, and help him devise a scheme to put them out of business. Rewarding horrible medicine didn't make sense, unless it wasn't about medicine.

CHAPTER 13

Frank Klawitter's study was his pride and joy. It was finished to precise specifications, with all the accoutrements of a man who liked to relax in solitude. The floor was burnished polished oak, laid down tongue and groove with cherry strip inlay and plugs. The entry had a sliding oak door that latched with sterling silver marine fittings. Along the side walls were cherrywood bookshelves with large openings for framed photographs of hunting dogs and geese in flight. A collection of antique pistols hung on the wall above the flagstone fireplace. The mantle held a picture of Frank's parents and another of his beloved cousin Eleanor.

Frank's desk rested on an enormous rug woven in Katmandu. In its corners were four golden dragons devouring rainbow-colored serpents, with a setting sun over a blood red river in the center. His desk was piled high with journals and stacks of correspondence. There were four tall antique wood filing cabinets, secured by dead bolts.

Since Frank's home was a bit off the beaten track, it was a good place to meet without drawing attention. The visitors arrived after dark precisely on time. They were all used to being punctual and getting their business done quickly. Frank greeted them at the front door and then ushered them quickly into his study. This was a gathering of strong wills, so he took charge right from the opening bell.

"Gentlemen, we all know each other, but we've never gotten together on something like this before. As I explained to everyone on the phone, we might have an opportunity together to fix a problem that's been tormenting the medical center for a long time."

"For everyone's sake, I hope you're right."

"Remember, we have to trust each other. Please agree that what we're about to discuss won't leave this room. Does anyone object? If so, I'd like you to speak up now or leave before we bring up any sensitive issues."

That was a daring comment coming from Frank to the elite men who had been invited into his study. Each man turned and inspected the person seated next to him. Frank studied Raymond Montague, the Chief of Surgery, who stared directly across at Joe Masterson. Masterson nodded his approval to Jonathan Herbert, the Chairman of the Department of

Medicine, who nodded in concurrence to the brilliant radiologist Fred Spencer. Frank surveyed his guests to look for the slightest hint of weakness or collusion — a wink, a frown, a shrug of the shoulders. He detected nothing.

"Good, then I think we should get right into it. We all know why we're here. There's a terrible problem at Branscomb. Everyone talks around it, but so far, not a single person has come forward and put himself on the line to tackle it." Frank's visitors glared at him. They knew he was addressing them, but they weren't about to be intimidated. There would be no averted eyes in this group. Frank stared back. "Simply stated, there are doctors — you know who they are — who won't practice up to a decent standard. What they do isn't even medicine. The institution can't take it anymore. We need to find a way to convince them to leave."

"Frank, I think you're being too nice," chimed in Masterson. "It's not that they can't meet a decent standard, whatever that is. It's that *they're* indecent. Those quote unquote doctors don't seem to care what happens to their patients. Let's call it like it is. They've become killers."

"Here here," said Montague. "Can someone tell me what the hell is going on with this place? In the old days, we would never tolerate incompetence. If we had slackers like this, we'd either work their butts to the bone or kick 'em out! Frank, what's all this talk about convincing people? Why can't somebody just fire them?"

"Maybe you should tell us, Ray. From what I hear, if Elaine Mahnke leaves one more clamp, they're going to have to pass the patients through a metal detector on the way out of the O.R. If she took a drug test, her urine wouldn't just turn colors, it'd probably dissolve the test tube. She's a walking advertisement for AA, the DEA and Betty Ford all rolled into one." John Herbert spoke without any inflection in his voice. He wasn't goading the Chief of Surgery, just stating the facts. Montague was taken by surprise and embarrassed.

"It isn't that simple, Jon."

"No, it's not," agreed Spencer.

"If it were simple, I suppose we wouldn't be here."

"What about Schmatz?" added Masterson. "Holy Christ, he's maybe the dumbest doctor — no, maybe the dumbest human being — that ever lived. Ray, you're the Chairman of the Department of Surgery. You know how bad he is. Everybody does. How in God's name does a guy like that get to keep his O.R. privileges? I mean, why the hell does he keep sliding through the QA committee without even a slap on the hand? He's bumpin' 'em off right and left and we all stand around with our hands in our pants. Something's wrong, all right."

Montague jumped up livid with anger and faced Masterson. "Now, hold on a minute, young man. Who do you think you're talking to? I've tried to get rid of Schmatz and Mahnke. The Dean won't let me touch them. This problem isn't all mine. And you Jon, what have you done about that maniac Ingelhart? For Christ's sake, he isn't just a terrible doctor, he's a certifiable wingnut. As long as you still have wackos sticking catheters in people's hearts, don't talk to me about a lousy anesthesiologist." He turned back to Masterson. "And don't you forget that you work for me, young man. I won't stand for this sort of insubordinate innuendo."

The provocateur cowered momentarily. Frank started to step between Montague and Masterson, but didn't get there before Herbert addressed Montague in a cold and steely voice. Jon Herbert was one of the few men in the medical center powerful enough to withstand a frontal assault from Montague.

"Ray, forget that you're the Chief of Surgery. For the purposes of this meeting, we're all equals. No power moves. No intimidation and no threats. If you think that the standard behavior of the surgical hierarchy applies in this room, get up and go home. Starting here and now, we need to stop coming after each other, because the fact of the matter is that the blame is shared and a lot of it's in this room. I agree with Frank. For some reason, these very bad doctors haven't been called on the carpet. That makes us as bad as them. If the dregs of this hospital continue to define an extraordinarily low level of competence for which we're all ultimately responsible, then it'll be the end of the medical center as we know it. I for one am willing to hear what Frank and Joe have to say about our current situation and how we can bring an end to it."

Montague looked at the other faces and saw he was outnumbered.

He sat down in stony silence, and Frank grabbed the opportunity to steal back the conversation.

"Fine, now that we've got that over with, let's get down to business. Branscomb is a great medical center, a world-class institution. But like every other hospital in the world, we've got our rotten apples. It's just that ours are taking down the tree. Elaine Mahnke. Randy Schmatz. Myron Ingelhart. Clyde Resnick. They've gotten away with murder. We've watched them pull stuff so bad at Branscomb that not only should they have been kicked off staff, they should have been drawn and quartered. But nothing's happened. We've been forced to turn a blind eye, and lately it seems that things are getting worse. Each time the QA Committee tries to crack down, Waterhouse floats in like the blue fairy and waves everybody off. The Chancellor either doesn't know or won't do anything. Well, Joe, you're right. It never made sense to me before."

"Didn't make sense to me either."

"They're protected by someone for some reason. They have to be. Their screw-ups have been so phenomenal and so blatant that they truly have to believe that nothing can bring them down."

"In a place like this, can you blame them? It's all a game. A great big fucking power game." Spencer spoke with a bitterness that surprised the others.

Joe followed Fred. "I'll bet somebody else's ass that Waterhouse hasn't been keeping these guys out of trouble out of the goodness of his heart."

"Right," said Frank. "I've been doing a little research, and there's definitely something fishy going on. But before I tell you all any more, I think it'd be a good idea if we let each other in on some personal history and what we know. That's the main reason why I brought us together. There's a link, and perhaps it'll become clear if we can find a common thread. We already know that this isn't just one man's problem. Jon, why don't you start? Tell us what you can about Ingelhart."

Herbert cleared his throat and sipped from his glass of water. "Myron's nuts —everybody knows that. But it wasn't always this bad. He used to be a semi-decent cardiologist, but something went wrong."

"Went wrong? What do you mean, went wrong?"

"It's not entirely clear, but apparently, this all goes back farther than even I know. I've been told that he started losing it when he was a new Assistant Professor. Maybe even before that, when he was a Fellow. It wasn't his medicine per se, it was how he behaved. Weird things, like practical jokes on rounds and asking out female patients. In those days, there weren't any faculty mental health programs. So my predecessor pulled him off the service and tried to rein him in. From what they tell me, it was a running battle. Myron would go off the deep end and the Chief would put him in time out. Myron was unpredictable. One day he'd seem normal, the next he was weird. One time he got so excited examining a patient that he hyperventilated, went into carpopedal spasm and dropped his stethoscope. He became a wrecking machine on the wards."

"And yet he was allowed to stay. How'd he get to be Chief? That seems more than absurd, given what you just told us."

"From what I understand, it was an inside deal. When the old Chief of Cardiology, Max Weinstock, left Branscomb, there was a search, except not really. Waterhouse brought through a few stale bodies from the outside and offered them nothing. Naturally, they all walked away. Myron applied and Waterhouse handed him the job. It was a joke."

"Did Ingelhart ever do his job as Chief?"

"Hell no! He's never worked. But Myron was a crafty son of a bitch, and most of the time his antics didn't interfere with the service. Whenever it did, he'd go off on a sabbatical. The med students loved to invite him to their parties, because he'd get shitfaced and jump out a window or puke all over somebody's date. From what I understand, he still shows up every now and then."

"Why didn't the med school unload him a long time ago?"

"That's the part that's never made sense. It all has to be on the Dean's shoulders. I know that everyone else was pretty fed up. Before my predecessor retired, we argued about Myron. He told me that I shouldn't ever try to lay off Myron if things got bad, because Waterhouse had insisted that he had everything under control, and that Myron was in no uncertain terms a matter for the Dean."

Joe Masterson was amazed. "Incredible! You mean to tell me that you just let Myron keep on stumbling around and playing with people's hearts because someone told you that the Dean said he would take care of everything? That's astounding! Did you talk to Waterhouse?"

Herbert felt the hairs rise on the nape of his neck, but he restrained himself. "Of course. But Waterhouse said back off. So I did."

Masterson shook his head and let out a derisive sigh.

"Look Joe, when you're a new Department Chairman and the Dean tells you to lay off, you lay off. He controls your salaries, your space, your bonus income, your faculty promotions, your secretaries, your housestaff positions, and whether or not you get to go to the bathroom. If you mess with the Dean, you might just as well shoot yourself in the nuts. So don't climb up on your high horse and preach to me about how I should've been tough with the Dean. You don't have the *faintest* idea how bad that could be."

"Jon, nobody's accusing you of anything. Calm down." Frank tried to smooth things over. "Listen guys, we're in this together. We've all made mistakes, myself included. We're not gonna get anywhere if we take it out on each other. Joe, stop acting so much like a surgeon and use your brain a little. Jon and Ray have been around the block a million times and we haven't even gotten off the porch. It's a dogfight out there. Just listen up for awhile."

"I'm sorry. I guess I'm just tired of hearing excuses."

"Be patient. Jon, keep talking. We're with you."

Herbert relaxed a little and settled back into his chair, then tensed up and shifted forward. "Things went from bad to worse. Myron's patients started having horrible outcomes. Then he added harassment to his repertoire of sociopathic behavior. He had periods where he became a skirt-chasing devil, interspersed with public displays of garden variety mania. When he was manic, he decided to become a body builder. What he really became was an exhibitionist. After he asked the fourth CCU nurse to feel his biceps, I went back to Waterhouse and begged him to intervene. He kept trying to stall, but I had to do something because everybody in the hospital knew how Myron was behaving. That was about three years ago. Since Waterhouse wouldn't make a move, I had to do it for him. I yanked Ingelhart's clinical privileges and made him swear he'd keep his hands to himself. I told him that if he showed up at one more party, touched one more nurse or even got near a patient, I'd turn him in to the State Board of Medical Quality Assurance."

"How'd he take it?" asked Masterson.

"He threatened me, but I didn't back down."

"What was his threat?"

"The usual. He'd run to the Dean. I told him I didn't care. He could run to the President of the United States."

"And?"

"At the time, I thought I had it knocked. Waterhouse seemed relieved. Myron all of a sudden became penitent and said that he understood why I did what I did. He agreed to cease and desist. He offered to step down as Division Chief. I accepted his resignation. It seemed to be over."

"But it wasn't."

"That's right, it wasn't. Myron disappeared for a few weeks, then I got a call from Waterhouse. He pulled me in and told me that Ingelhart would be staying on as Chief of Cardiology. He explained that in the absence of a formal charge or investigation that I was violating university human resource regulations and that he would have to deal with Myron in a different manner. I asked him to be more specific, but he wouldn't. What I think now is that he couldn't. When I told him I wasn't satisfied, he suggested in fairly simple terms that he hadn't yet made his decision about the new cancer research building. I'm sorry now, but I backed off again. It seemed like it wasn't worth trashing the whole Department of Medicine for a jerk like Myron."

"Get used to it," growled Spencer. "We're dealing with the master."

"You were blackmailed," Masterson said.

"Wake up, Joe. It happens all the time. It seemed like we were making progress, because Waterhouse said that Myron had agreed to stay away from the patients. He was just going to be Chief, that's all. Administrative stuff. We could cover for that."

"But he's still at it. The patients, I mean."

"Yes. Fred can tell you about that."

"Fred?"

"In a minute. Jon, keep talking," Frank instructed.

"What have you done since to try to actually get rid of him?" asked Montague.

"First, I suggested to Waterhouse that we terminate him for cause. You can pretty well figure out that the Dean wouldn't even listen to that one. He said that Ingelhart's outstanding record — can you believe that — wouldn't allow him to consider termination. Besides, he said, Ingelhart had tenure and it would take an act of God to get him thrown out. No, he just wanted me to help keep him away from patients, but to let him stay on as a figurehead. I argued until I was blue in the face, but he stonewalled me. He also said in so many words that it would be better for Myron to stay than to have the funding for my new Division of Molecular Biology go to build another locked ward for the Department of Psychiatry."

"Incredible. You were blackmailed twice!"

"Not in any way that I can prove, but yes. Welcome to academics. You give a lot and you get a little. Unfortunately, the story still doesn't end there. What happened next didn't make any sense then, but maybe it will now. After Waterhouse pitched me the line about money, I had a brainstorm. I asked why couldn't we make Myron an offer he wouldn't refuse? I suggested that we offer him a half a million dollars to step down. You know, buy out his contract just like the university does for lousy football coaches. The President of Branscomb does it all the time, and I know that it's been done before at the medical center. We could weave Myron a golden parachute. Remember that worthless knucklehead in Pathology? He got a bundle to say that he had to run his family business in Boca Raton and volunteer for early retirement. It can be done. But when I proposed the same thing for Myron, Waterhouse said that it was reprehensible for me to suggest that we stoop to such an ignominious level, if I recall his exact words. He said that if I wanted to pay Ingelhart, I would have to take it directly out of one of my grants. It was impossible for me. But it would have been so easy for Waterhouse."

"Yes, it would have," agreed Frank. "He could do it for one, but not for the other. It all fits."

"I don't think anything fits." Montague stood up and walked over in front of the fireplace. He raised his head and shook a clenched fist. "This makes sense, does it? Protect your worst doctors and threaten the ones who make everything work right? Save the sinners and burn the saints? Well, it's my turn to talk. But I think I need a drink first."

"And my bladder's about to burst." Fred Spencer winced.

"Sure," said Frank. "Let's take a little break and get some refills."

The men dispersed for awhile, trying to let loose some of the tension by admiring the handsome fittings of Frank's study. The moment was broken when Montague tapped on his glass and called the group to order. "Fred, you were going to say something?"

"Just that Ingelhart is still on the loose. It's horrible. I'm sure you'll hear about it soon. Two days ago I got a call from one of the cardiology Fellows about a young woman with fainting spells. Myron ordered every test under the sun, then decided to recommend against a pacemaker. The Fellow was nervous and asked me to review her chest CT. I worked it through my computer and found a big fat scar in her heart. Her conduction system was blocked. Without a pacer, it was only a matter of time. I called Myron myself."

"I don't like where this is headed."

"Myron totally ignored my advice, and now the patient is dead. Cardiac arrest while visiting with her family out by the fountains. Can you imagine? Her family's devastated. The preliminary autopsy confirms what I saw. Damn it! She was a teenager! Why are we doctors? I could save lives, but what good does it do when these monsters don't have to listen to me? With our knowledge, we should be able to change the world — for the better. Something has to happen. I want them out." Spencer was livid. "*However* it has to be done."

Montague took his turn. "After Jon's story, I don't think that what I'm about to say will come as a great surprise to anyone. I've been trying to straighten out the mess with Mahnke and Schmatz for the last two years, and getting nowhere because of you know who. I'm not sure you want to hear the details."

"Yes, we do," replied Herbert. "Maybe there's a clue in the story."

Frank agreed. "Always the diagnostician, Jon. You're right. We need all the information we can get. The connection's in there someplace."

"OK. First, Schmatz. Everybody knows what a hit man he is. There isn't a surgeon in this hospital who hasn't had a case delayed, cancelled or botched because of that idiot. As head of the O.R. Council, I've submitted report after report to the QA Committee. The ones I don't submit are turned in by the nurses from the O.R. or Labor and Delivery. He's probably the single biggest fuck-up artist in the hospital. But one of two things always happens. Either the report gets previewed by the Chairman and dismissed without coming to the committee or when it does, nobody finds anything wrong and Schmatz gets off. Lately, Waterhouse has been jumping in to save him. Last week after the QA meeting I was desperate. I went to the Dean and suggested that we give Schmatz a big trophy and a pile of money, name a chair after him and then send him off to Timbuktu. I even volunteered to take it out of my departmental reserves. Waterhouse said no way. Said he had never heard of such a thing, that it was against every decent principle of academic medicine. But listen to this. He also said that no one had ever before come to him with such a contemptible request. Now, Jon's just told us, that isn't true. Colossal bullshit."

"Same thing with Mahnke?"

"No, not really. Elaine's more pathetic. I hinted to Waterhouse about six months ago that even if she made it through rehab, we should try to sell her to another program. He got real angry real fast and chewed me out for being an insensitive chauvinistic boor. I've never seen him so mad. He said that if I tried to do anything to get rid of her that he would have no choice but to report me for gender discrimination. That's absolutely ridiculous, but can you imagine what would happen in my department if there were an investigation of how women are treated? I run a Department of Surgery. We discriminate against human rights in general. The press would hang us before they finished the first interview. It would be quicker and a whole lot less painful if I just exploded a grenade at a faculty meeting."

"Is that it, Ray?"

"Just one more thing. I'll tell you what really burns my butt. After Waterhouse finished telling me how he'd turn me in if I tried to even so much as counsel Elaine Mahnke, he leaned back in his big leather chair, lit up a cigar and blew smoke in my face. He said, 'You know Ray, you really need to learn to do things the Branscomb way.' That's exactly what he said. Are you kidding me? Do things the Branscomb way? That pompous bastard is *killing* Branscomb!" Montague threw his glass into the fireplace and shattered it into a thousand pieces. His face was contorted with rage. "Maybe we ought to kill him."

Jon Herbert rose to his feet. "That's OK, Ray. Frank, I'll clean it up. Somebody pour him another drink." The Chairman of Medicine walked over to the fireplace, knelt down and began to retrieve shards from the floor. Montague watched for a moment, then joined him.

Montague's distress caused Fred Spencer to flash back to his recent encounter with Waterhouse. "No, we can't kill him, as good as that's beginning to sound. Deans are too well protected. But then again, maybe we can, in a matter of speaking." His audience looked confused. "You know, eliminate his support."

"Right, Fred." Frank addressed the group. "I think we're all beginning to recognize a pattern. Waterhouse is systematically protecting these people. The only one we don't know about is Resnick, but I'm sure there's a link. I don't know exactly why it exists, but I'm certain I can prove that it *does* exist."

"Nobody would protect Resnick."

"Don't be so sure," whispered Fred. "Did you know he's tenured?"

"No! You've gotta be kidding. In what department? Surely not in Surgery! I'd know about it if he were. I have to approve all promotions." Montague was dumbstruck. "You can't get rid of anyone who's got tenure unless he commits an outright atrocity. Who in the name of God gave Resnick tenure?"

"Guess." Frank posed the question.

"Waterhouse!"

"He did it when you shifted Clyde down to the ER. You probably thought he'd be on a short rope. Nope. The Dean wangled him a tenured appointment in Family Practice."

Montague was dumbstruck. "I never knew."

"No way you would have. Somehow Waterhouse finessed it without any hoopla, probably because he didn't want you to find out. I can only imagine how he twisted somebody for that one. Now Branscomb's stuck with Resnick for life."

"Frank, I've got something to say," interjected Masterson.

"Sure Joe. Go ahead."

"I never had to go nose to nose with Waterhouse until last week, but that was enough intimidation to last a lifetime. We've got to stop behaving like we're helpless. Damn it, look around you — all of you. You're the *good* guys. Waterhouse has figured all of your weaknesses, and he's played them to the hilt. And furthermore, he's been able to keep the finger from pointing at him. Does *he* ever come up in committee? No way. Can't you see what he's doing? It seems to me that he's a big part of the problem. Frank, aren't you going to tell them about your cousin?"

"No. I don't want to talk about that. There are reasons enough to do what we're doing without that."

"What's this about your cousin?" asked Montague.

"Schmatz killed her," answered Joe.

"You didn't tell me." Fred was disconsolate. He stared at his friend, who had turned crimson. Frank's pain was theirs.

"Why didn't you sue the bastard?"

"I started to, but then I stopped. Everyone would have thought I was trying to protect myself, even though that isn't true. Besides, that wouldn't finish it. It runs deeper than one bad doctor. And this may sound stupid, but I love Branscomb. I want to do something to save it. Picking off one of them in court makes the whole place look lousy, and still doesn't finish the job. I want them all."

Masterson continued. "He gave away your cousin, and Waterhouse let him walk. Frank, I can't listen to this stuff anymore. What are we gonna do?"

Frank unlocked one of his filing cabinets, pulled out the top drawer, and extracted a thick stack of computer printouts. He held them up for the group to see. "Here's what I've found. These are reports from the practice plan of all the bonuses paid out to the faculty for the last five years. Pull up your chairs." Frank leafed through the documents slowly as he explained what he was showing them. "First, look at this report. This is what you'd see if you somehow figured out how to crack into the practice plan database. Remember, normally only the Dean can authorize a report, so I don't believe that anyone would ever get to look at these unless he managed to get into the computer himself."

"How did you get your hands on these?" whispered Montague in awe. "I've been asking for years. Waterhouse always says that I can only see the sheets for my department, and he makes me beg to get those."

"Trust me — they're unfiltered and accurate. Now, focus on the top stack of reports. Here's the incentive column. Everyone in the practice plan has a bonus listed, except for our friends Ingelhart, Schmatz, Mahnke and Resnick. Curious, isn't it?"

Klawitter leafed through the pages and pointed out where he had highlighted the lines that followed the names of Myron Ingelhart, Randolph Schmatz, Elaine Mahnke and Clyde Resnick. Under the column for "Incentive", there was a "**" where a number should have been listed.

"Now, here's the great part. After I reviewed these reports, I asked whether there was any way I could get the incentive numbers. It seemed impossible at first. But there *was* a way. One time the whole system crashed and they called in some wizard from IBM to fix the mainframe. A friend of mine was assigned to help him. In the process of getting the computer fixed, they discovered a program buried in the operating system that bypassed everyone's password on the network. The computer guy knew how to get into the system using a special access code. No one knows what we know. Here's the modified report."

Frank moved the bottom stack of paper to the top. "This is the same thing you just read, except look at the places where the numbers were missing. Let's start with this past year." He led them to the numbers next to each name. Myron Ingelhart: $500,000. Randolph Schmatz: $500,000. Elaine Mahnke: $500,000. Clyde Resnick: $500,000.

"Now, the year before." He flipped to another page. $500,000 four times again. "And the year before that." Same names, same numbers. For every one of the last five years, the four doctors had each received a $500,000 bonus.

"This is incredible," said Montague. "The Dean's been paying them at least ten times more than anyone else and using the practice plan profits to do it. But for God's sake, how does Resnick fit in? How do any of them fit in? Why is he doing it? They're the *worst* doctors at Branscomb. Could anybody else possibly know about this? Why would Wiley be so stupid to keep a record of everything?"

"Because he's arrogant. Because he apparently doesn't know much about computers. As to whether anyone knows, I doubt it, Ray. Even Waterhouse couldn't get away with this if anyone knew. He's been doing this for at least five years and probably longer. I tried to dig deeper, but we're locked out for the years before 1988. But hang on, I'm not finished. There's more. Look at this."

Frank moved his finger to another highlighted section. "This is medical school administration. Nice bonus for Waterhouse, eh?"

"That thieving scoundrel!"

'We're not finished yet."

"What else could he possibly be doing?" asked Herbert. "He's already robbing the other members of the practice plan and giving the money to the biggest bums in the medical center. He's skimming twice as much for himself. Let me guess — he's embezzled the money from Children's House."

"That's a good thought, Jon, but unfortunately, I can't tell. Nothing like that shows up in the computer. There could be other kickbacks. We'd have to look under his mattress, which is probably where he keeps the loot."

"So, what else did you find?"

"Something very interesting. After all this, I got curious to find out the details about their individual clinical practices, and I uncovered the damnedest thing. Look at this."

Klawitter leafed through another pile of paper. He ran his finger down a few columns until he found what he was looking for.

"This is the spreadsheet on Resnick, broken out by patient name in alphabetical order, with procedures listed horizontally across the page. Notice something unusual? Here's Myron Ingelhart on his patient list. Not once, but seventeen times, more than any other patient. Look at the procedures. Chest pain - emergency/complicated exam. Acute abdominal pain — emergency/complicated exam. Oleander intoxication — emergency/complicated exam with overnight observation. Keep on reading down the list. There's not a single visit for a sore throat or cut finger or anything less than what would generate a major physician fee. Now, look at this list, which does the same thing with Ingelhart's patients. Surprise, surprise. It seems that Dr. Resnick has had some very serious heart problems that none of us ever knew about, because he's been in to see Myron Ingelhart 43 times over the last five years, including a visit for an echo, a treadmill, a thallium scan, two catheterizations and an angioplasty. The funny thing is, their medical records are signed out."

The men spoke in unison. "Waterhouse."

"That's right. The medical records of Clyde Resnick and Myron Ingelhart are signed out to the Dean. And have been for as far back as I can tell. This is a criminal case."

"Frank, how can this be going on and nobody pick it up?" Spencer asked.

"Easy, Fred. First of all, the reports aren't usually generated this way. Second, the clerks have no way of verifying that any patient encounter actually occurred. They never see the records, just the codes. You or I could do exactly the same thing if we were willing to take the risk of getting caught if we were audited. I can tell you that if the Dean decided that we were *not* to be audited, it would be one of the great scams of all time. So, what I'm driving at is that not only are these greedy bastards getting it straight off the top, at least two of them are also committing insurance fraud on an everyday basis. They're probably making money other ways too, but I haven't had time to figure that out yet."

"This is worse than I ever imagined," said Montague. "No wonder the Dean won't pitch these guys. He's in it up to his eyeballs."

"There's got to be something else," Frank insisted.

"You're kidding. This isn't enough?"

"Nope."

"What do you mean?"

"I don't know yet, but think about it. Waterhouse is too smart to choose these lunkheads for business partners. There has to be another reason."

"Like what? The money seems enough reason to me."

"No, I don't think so. Look at it this way. Waterhouse is playing way out of bounds. He likes to joust, but my read on him is that he's fundamentally a coward. Even if he's making a ton of money on kickbacks, that doesn't change the fact that he's also a control freak. The other four are flawed individuals. He can't possibly trust them. He would never have chosen them. There's some other link, and we have to find out what it is."

"Why? Why not just go to the Chancellor and let him do it? Let's pull the plug now!" Herbert wanted a solution.

"Because for all we know, he's in it too. Look, you don't stay the Dean at a place like Branscomb for nearly three decades and not have your roots tangled in everyone's business. There may be others. If we want to nail Waterhouse, we need to do some more tests to find out how far the disease has spread. Otherwise, *we* could end up being the growth that gets cut out."

Frank let it all sink in, then got to the main point of the meeting. "Gentlemen, what do you want to do?"

No one spoke. Montague pulled a small pocketknife from his pocket, flipped open the blade, and scraped under his fingernails. Herbert stared at the fireplace. Frank bounced the spreadsheets on his knee, and Joe went over to the bar and poured himself a Jack Daniels straight up. Fred was deep in thought. Finally, Frank spoke in a hushed voice.

"Look, we're all ethical men. That's why we're here. Our medical center is being destroyed by four very bad doctors, maybe more for all we know. The Dean should be the one to clean house. Instead, he's in bed with the scoundrels. Something is very wrong."

"I agree."

"Me, too."

"So do I. But what can we do? Do you have an idea?"

"Yes, I do," Frank answered. "Schmatz and company aren't gonna disappear out of the goodness in their hearts. They've been pulling this off for years. I think we need to consider something a little more drastic."

"Like what?" asked Joe.

"We need more information. Learn what keeps them together and use it to drive them apart. I promise you, it's more than money. Somebody has to get close. But we can't all personally risk getting caught."

"Then who'll do it? Are you going to hire a spy?"

"In a manner of speaking," Frank said. "I have some ideas. I'll take responsibility for checking them out for now. If I need help, I'll ask for it."

"Too risky for one person. Let me help." Masterson was the first to volunteer. Spencer followed.

"No. I'll be careful. If something happens to me, we need a fall back position."

"What makes you so sure you can pull it off?" asked Montague.

"That's right," added Herbert. "Besides, I need to know more of the details."

"I think you may be onto something, Frank. Let's go for it," said Spencer. "They have it coming." He brushed his hair back. "I may be able to help in my own way."

Herbert began to pace. "I need time to think about it."

"No! The reason we're in this mess is because all we've done is to think about it." Frank spoke without a quiver of indecision. "Me first. I promise to ask for help if I need it."

"I'm in," said Masterson.

"It's about time," declared Montague.

"We must be careful," warned Herbert. "If we're wrong and something happens, our careers will be finished."

Frank respected Herbert. "This isn't for us — it's for our patients. They're being held hostage at Branscomb Hospital by men who honor willful incompetence. We're watching what amounts to murder. If we don't stop them, we're as bad as they are. This goes way beyond malpractice. And they're getting rich doing it. If something goes wrong, I'll take the heat. This is a risk we have to take for the sake of everyone else."

Herbert nodded. "Yes then, I'm with you. Heaven help us."

CHAPTER 14

After Sam Anderson moved into his apartment, Frank gave him an open invitation to dinner. The food was great and Sam felt so welcome that it was hard to stay away. And having company was good for Frank. They quickly settled into an every-other-night pattern, which they both knew would stop once school started. Sam peppered Frank with questions about science, medicine, and morality. Since Frank had accepted the responsibility to be Sam's advisor, he encouraged him to ask difficult questions. Their free-ranging discussions were never dull.

Tonight was different. Medical school orientation started in the morning. Sam was excited and wanted to talk, but Frank was subdued and seemed preoccupied. After dinner, he sat with Sam in the study.

"Sam, I'm sorry. It's been a long day. A long month, actually."

"You don't need to apologize."

"Yes I do. Today they delivered the memorial stone for Eleanor's grave. I went to inspect it, and the instant replay started all over again. I wish I could tell her how sorry I am."

"I understand."

"Not completely. There's no way you could." Frank hesitated, then was overwhelmed by the urge to explain. "There's a situation here at Branscomb."

"Sir?" Frank's choice of words triggered Sam's military response.

"You can stand down, young man. I want to tell you what really happened to Eleanor. Just in case."

"In case? In case what?"

"Forget I said that. Do you have a few more minutes to spend?"

"Of course I do. I'll stay here as long as you need. And whatever you tell me..." Sam sensed Frank's reserve. "...Is between you and me."

"Good. It needs to be that way. OK, here goes." Frank explained what had happened to Eleanor in the operating room, and portrayed Randy Schmatz as totally incompetent. He didn't mention anything about the Dean or any of the others. Sam sat spellbound.

"So now what? I know how you feel about lawyers, but it seems like the logical thing to do would be to take him to court. How else can you get any justice?"

Frank clenched his teeth and worked his jaw. This was just what he would have expected from Sam. It was why he trusted him.

"It was my first thought too. Sam, it would get me some money, but that doesn't bring back Eleanor. It also doesn't solve the problem. It's bigger."

So that was it. A "situation at Branscomb." From Frank's tone of voice, Sam knew that this was serious. "How big? What do you mean? Has this happened before?"

"Yes. Remember overseas, when you asked me about how we deal with mistakes in medicine? I told you that we had a process, a way to evaluate our peers. Something at Branscomb has gone wrong lately, and the mistakes are getting through without any discipline. I'm afraid that's what happened with Eleanor."

"Who would let that happen? She was defenseless. Are you saying that you're taking the rap for Schmatz? Why?"

Now Frank had to decide where to go. He wanted some help with what he was about to do, but the wave of insecurity was passing. "Because if I push it, I might lose the others."

"Others?"

"Perhaps. I have my suspicions, but it's too soon to tell."

Sam was intrigued. "Tell me what you'd like me to do." He sensed where Frank was headed.

"Nothing. I just wanted you to know that there's a lot going on, and that I'll snap out of it. You know how it is when everything hits all at once."

Sam took Frank's hand with a firm grip. "Yes, I do. And I'll never forget what you did for me. You're not telling me everything, and that's OK. But remember, if you decide that there's something I can do, I'm right here. Are you sure there's nothing?"

"I'm sure. At least for now. I'll let you know."

"OK."

"And not a word, right?"

"Not a word."

After Sam left, Frank was unsettled. He read for awhile, but he couldn't get his mind off his mission. He drank a glass of red wine, but it didn't help him relax. He had two more, and the warm buzz prompted him to pick up the phone.

"Hi."

"Hello? Oh, *hello*."

"Just thought I'd call and see what you're doing."

"At this time of night, what did you think I'd be doing?"

"I don't know. But I know what I'd like to be doing."

"And what might that be?" Her voice became soft and seductive.

"You know."

"No I don't. Tell me. Tell me exactly."

Frank sipped at his glass. She was in the mood; that was great. "Here's a clue. I only want to do it with you."

"Oh, Frank...me too."

"What are you wearing?"

"Your favorite nightgown."

"The red one?"

"Yes. That one."

Frank heard a faint rustling through the receiver. "Tell me how it feels."

"Sure. Give me a second. There. Now I can move it."

"This would be more fun in person."

"So who's stopping you?"

"Oh, it's getting late. What do you think?"

"It's soft and silky. I'm sliding it over my legs."

"I have a better idea."

"I can't imagine."

"Let's play doctor."

"Come on over. We've got all night."

CHAPTER 15

Clyde Resnick was late for his shift in the ER for the third afternoon in a row. The faculty member who preceded him couldn't leave until Resnick showed up, because he needed to wait for Clyde to be able to properly sign out his patients.

"Where've you been, Clyde? It's 4:30 already. I need to get out of here to make it to the Disaster Committee meeting. I told you about that yesterday. Damn, I hate to be late!"

"Sorry, buddy. The Ferrari again. I need to unload that son of a bitch."

"You can unload it on me, Clyde. It's worth more than my house." The car today, a long-distance telephone call yesterday. Three days ago, Resnick's dog had supposedly coughed up a tapeworm. What would it be tomorrow, an invitation to the White House? "Clyde, you're full of crap. I don't have time to listen to this. Try to get here on time tomorrow, will you? Otherwise, you can write me a check for the hours. I've got everything pretty well cleared up for you. C'mon, let's make this quick."

The doctor going off duty flipped through the charts on the rack. He fired off a sentence or two about each patient. When he was finished, he gathered up his stethoscope and briefcase and dashed out the door. Clyde was in charge now.

It didn't take long for business to pick up. "Dr. Resnick, please walk to Room 7." The overhead page interrupted Resnick's evaluation of a construction worker who had poked a deep hole in the bottom of his foot. A rusty nail had penetrated the man's boot and carried a wad of bacteria-laden debris. The infection was heralded by an angry red streak all the way up to mid calf, a sure sign of blood poisoning.

Clyde spit a few orders at the nurse. "Find out if he's allergic to any antibiotics. Date of last tetanus shot. Clean up his foot and start an IV. Get an x-ray. I'll be right back."

The patient in Room 7 was lying on his back with his foot propped up on three pillows. His pants had been ripped up the seam to his hip. One of the interns was pressing a thick wad of gauze pads against his shin, which caused the patient a great deal of pain. The blue diaper sheet under the man's calf was soaked with blood.

"Well, what have we here? Let's take a peek." Without explaining to the patient what he was going to do, Resnick pushed the intern's hand away and yanked off the bandages. The patient inhaled sharply through clenched teeth as a searing sensation shot through his leg.

"Take it easy, will you? It hurts like hell!"

Clyde didn't look up. "Sorry. Got to look. That's ugly. Looks like you got chopped by a chainsaw, unless it's a shark bite. What was it?"

"You've got it, Doc. Chainsaw. Sucker kicked back on me."

The damage was extensive. The blades had carved a canal below the knee, leaving a shallow groove in the bone. The steel chain twisted and tore the skin badly, so that it was macerated, bruised, and impregnated with wood chips and grease. Shards of denim dotted the traumatic landscape.

"Wiggle your toes. Good. Now move your ankle. Close your eyes. Can you feel this?" Resnick touched the man's toes.

"Yup."

"Feel normal?"

"Yup."

"Good. Feel this? This? What about this?" As Resnick completed the neurovascular exam, he sized up the wound. It would be a bitch to clean. He didn't want personally to take the time, but he had an intern. "I think we're in business here. You missed everything important. All we need to do is numb you up, get the dirt out, trim the edges, and stitch you up. You'll be good as new."

"Excuse me Dr. Resnick. Are you sure you want to do this down here? We had a case like this a few weeks ago and I was told that it had to be done up in the O.R. Infection, you know."

"Young man, come with me. I want to show you something." Resnick hooked the intern's arm as he turned his back to the patient. "Excuse us. I just need to talk to this young doctor for a second. We'll be right back." The chainsaw victim fell back on the gurney.

Outside the room, Resnick lashed into the intern. "Don't you ever do that again. *Never* contradict me in front of a patient!"

"I...I...I..."

"I what? I don't have a brain? I don't have any respect for my fellow physicians? I don't want to get kicked out of the program?" The color drained from the intern's face. "Now, you go back in there, explain to the patient how you were confused about this case, and start irrigating the daylights out of that laceration. If it starts to hurt, inject a little Xylocaine. When I come back, I want it clean enough to eat off of. Do you understand me?"

"Yes sir. But...don't get mad...I wasn't trying to give you a hard time. I'm sorry." The mollified intern hung his head.

"That's better. Do a nice job and I'll let you close it." Clyde knew that interns loved procedures more than anything. "Actually, wait. I've got a better idea. We'll let *you*..." He pointed at a nurse in the hallway. "...Clean the cut and I'll take you..." Clyde collared the intern. "...With me. How else are you gonna learn? Let's go."

The men walked back to the patient who had punctured his foot on a nail. His foot had been scrubbed and awaited inspection. Resnick picked up the x-ray and snapped it onto the bedside lightbox. "Hmm, let's see. Looks pretty good to me." Resnick turned to the chart and studied the preliminary x-ray report. "No foreign body seen. Early degenerative changes at the plantar attachment of the Achilles' tendon. Hairline fracture of a 5 mm bone spur with small amount of air from puncture wound. How can anybody see that? Oh. Fred Spencer's reading tonight. Now I understand. He's unbelievable. Son, if he sees it, it's there."

Resnick pulled down his bifocals and put his face close to the wound. "Put on a dressing, give him a tetanus shot if he needs it, and hang some antibiotics. Write him a scrip for the cephalosporin de jour. We'll see you back in two days. Stay off that thing if you want to get better."

Behind a curtain in the next bed lay a heavyset young woman who was holding her head and moaning. Tears ran down her cheeks as she explained her ailment to the doctors. "I was putting a box of groceries in the back of my Suburban when I felt something pop in the back of my head. My vision went blurry and I threw up all over the sidewalk. It was awful. I got real dizzy and passed out. Some lady helped me. She wanted to call an ambulance, but I wouldn't let her. This is so embarrassing. I've never been this sick before."

"Do you have problems with headaches? Does your head still hurt?"

"I had a migraine once. This is sort of like that, except there's no flashing lights. I feel like my head's gonna explode."

"Hold still and follow my finger with your eyes. Touch your nose. Now touch my finger. Put your chin to your chest." Resnick led the woman through a brief neurologic exam, looked in her eyes with an ophthalmoscope, and asked a few more questions. When he was finished, he ordered a CT scan of her brain. "Just to play it safe. I can't find anything wrong, but she might have a brain tumor or something. My x-ray vision's only fifty percent accurate." The clerk told him that the CT scanner was down, but that they could sneak his patient in for an MRI. That was even better. Resnick sent her off for the test.

Murphy Hawkins was an 85-year-old ex-roofer who had spent most of his life crawling around under apartment rafters installing asbestos and wads of fiberglass padding. Now he had terminal lung cancer that had metastasized everywhere. He also suffered from Alzheimer's dementia, so most of what went on around him was a blur. He wasn't really suffering, just dwindling away. He'd been registered in the ER because his family couldn't handle his incontinence and wandering. They also reported that he might have vomited up some blood. Resnick asked the intern to drop a nasogastric tube.

"Hey, Mr. Hawkins, you probably don't understand any of this, but you need a tube stuck up your nose and then down into your stomach. It'll make you feel better. Is that all right with you?"

Hawkins was nearly deaf. He watched the intern's lips move, but all he heard was muffled garble.

"Can't hear ya. Whadja say?" Murphy responded. "I need a lube job?"

"No. I said we need to stick a tube in your nose," the young man shouted. "That OK with you?"

"What? There's a tub in my room?"

The intern grabbed a nasogastric tube wrapped in a sterile cellophane wrapper and a big squeeze tube of clear KY lubricating jelly. He extracted the tube from its wrapper and stretched it out, working the silicone sucker between his hands like a snake handler loosening up a python. He held it against Murphy to measure the correct length from the tip of his nose to his stomach. Then he squeezed a big gob of clear jelly from the tube onto the perforated tip with the holes destined to enter Mr. Hawkin's nose.

"Hold still now." The doctor placed his left hand against the victim's forehead and with his other hand jammed the hard tip of the tube with the dangling daub of medicinal grease up into Murphy's left nostril. He immediately met resistance, so he pushed as hard as she could. There was a sickening crunch. Hawkins pulled his head back and the intern jumped away.

"Aaaargh! Dad blame it, that hurts!" The old man sputtered and cursed as bright red blood ran freely from his nose and streamed in rivulets over his mouth and chin. The startled intern hadn't evaluated the patency of his nostril, and Murphy had a slightly deviated septum. By forcing the hard plastic tube into the wrong side of Hawkins' nose, he had gouged a divot into the soft mucosal lining, rupturing a cluster of delicate veins. Hawkins shook his head wildly from side to side.

Resnick couldn't pass up the teaching opportunity. "Son, the most important thing is to get the patient to cooperate. If you know what you're doing, the whole thing's a piece of cake. Actually, I've never had any trouble with one of these. You've just got to explain carefully to the patient what you're going to do."

Clyde turned to Murphy and began to talk to him in a normal tone of voice. Hawkins didn't comprehend one word.

"Now, Mr. Hawkins, I'm going to slide this tube into your nose and when it gets to the back of your throat, I want you to swallow it down. It may be a bit uncomfortable, but once it's in you won't notice it too much. Don't fight me. And remember, the most important thing is to swallow. Do you understand?"

The patient stared blankly out into space and didn't utter a sound. His assailant turned away from him and nodded affirmatively to no one in particular.

"Great! We're ready. We'll try the other nostril."

With a quick thrust, Resnick forced the tube through Murphy's narrow nasal passage and into the back of his throat. He slid it too far, so the tip lodged just above the opening between his vocal cords, blocking his air passage. Murphy sequentially coughed violently, choked, gagged and turned blue. He spit blood and phlegm all over Resnick, who twisted and turned to avoid the spray while he pulled the tube back to allow the patient to breathe. Hawkins stopped bucking.

"Heh, heh, heh. Guess I pushed it down the wrong pipe. No problem, that happens sometimes. It all depends on the anatomy. At least we know he has a good laryngeal reflex. OK, time to put this puppy where she belongs."

Resnick put his face directly in front of Murphy and exaggerated his lip movements. "Now, when I say swallow, I want you to swallow over and over for all you're worth. Just keep swallowing. Don't stop for a second. If you do that for me, this'll all be over in a minute. Remember, you've got to *swallow*." Murphy had that blank look again. Resnick talked over his shoulder to the intern.

"The most important thing is to get the patients to swallow. If they do that for you, there's nothing to this." Clyde yelled into the old fellow's ear as loudly as he could while he pushed the remainder of the tube through his nostril.

"Swallow! Swallow! Swallow! Swallow!"

Murphy Hawkins swallowed for all he was worth. His Adam's apple bobbed crazily up and down his scrawny neck with each gulp. Resnick fired the hose up his nose hand over hand and imagined that he felt a give in resistance with each of the old man's swallows. In just a few seconds of screaming and pushing, the nasogastric tube was buried to the hilt, with only a few inches left dangling from Murphy's nostril.

"There. Piece of cake. Right up the old schnozole. Damn, that's nice!"

He kept on talking while Murphy sat stone-faced in front of him, continuing to swallow with his lips slammed shut.

"You can stop swallowing now," he shouted. "It's all over." Murphy nodded like an Indian chief affirming a peace treaty. His eyes watered profusely. The man had been tubed. He contorted expressions of something bad-tasting with the facial elasticity that comes from having no teeth. "The last thing left to do is to make sure that it's in his stomach."

Resnick grabbed a huge empty syringe and attached it to the opening in the tube that hung free from Murphy's nose. He pulled back on the plunger, expecting to aspirate gastric contents, but only got back air and spit.

"Sometimes you don't get anything back. Maybe his stomach's empty. We can check it another way. Here, listen through my stethoscope." The intern lifted up Murphy's gown and placed the diaphragm over the left upper quadrant of his abdomen.

"When I squirt air into his stomach, you'll hear a big rush of gurgling like the bubbles in a hot tub. That way, we know we're in the right place. Ready?"

The intern nodded.

"OK, listen up. Here goes." With a forceful plunge, Resnick injected.

Murphy's cheeks and lips fluttered as the air blasted out of his mouth. The tube, which Resnick had neatly coiled like a garden hose in the back of Murphy's mouth and throat, flopped out in a revolting shower of blood, phlegm and lunch across the hair and neck of the intern leaning over the patient. When the intern felt the slimy cold plastic on his neck, he jumped back, collided with Resnick, tripped and fell to the ground. The tube was hooked in the intern's name tag, so he dragged Murphy over the side of the bed by his head and nose, since the other end of the tube was anchored to his face by the large syringe which had been yanked up and jammed into his nostril.

Resnick disentangled the tube and whipped it out of the man's nose. When the intern asked him if he was going to try again, he replied, "Nah, he probably doesn't need it anyway."

"Dr. Resnick, the headache's back from MRI. Here's the preliminary report."

"Great. Let me see." Clyde read quickly. "Just as I thought. Nothing there." The patient was relieved to learn that her test was negative, but she still had a splitting headache and her neck was a little sore. Resnick recommended that she undergo a spinal tap, just to play it safe, but she refused the procedure. He prescribed a potent analgesic. "Come back if you're not feeling better by tomorrow morning."

"We're ready for you back in Room 7." Clyde reentered and assisted the intern. It took over an hour to cut away the shredded skin, scrub out the grime, and figure out how to approximate the skin without leaving a huge defect. The repair was only moderately successful, because so much tissue was missing and the stitches were under enormous tension. As they finished, Resnick peeled off his surgical gloves and snapped them like rubber bands into the garbage can.

"That's that. This fine young surgeon did an excellent job. We're going to hope for the best. It was worth a try to keep you out of the operating room. If you get an infection, the worst that'll happen is we might have to take out the stitches and let it heal open."

Resnick felt good about how the shift was going. He articulated his sense of accomplishment to the trainee at his side. "That's what I really like about medicine — the chance to do something *good* for people. Step in, figure out what's wrong, and call the shots. It doesn't matter how long you've been in this business, son. When you have a great day like this, there's nothing to compare. I hope you're learning something."

"I think I am."

Exactly 24 hours after Clyde sealed the chainsaw laceration and entrapped a horrendous inoculum of microscopic grease and germs, the patient suffered a shaking chill. By the time his family got him to the hospital, he had a fever of 104 degrees. It ultimately required three operations and a skin graft to reconstruct the contour of his leg.

The woman with the headache went home and tried to sleep, but her headache was relentless. In the middle of the night, her leaking cerebral blood vessel burst.

The Chairman of Surgery wanted to reassure himself that drastic measures were necessary. Resnick's most recent medical blunder was incontrovertible, and the Dean would know that. Montague wanted to give it one more try before he was willing to admit that it had to be done Frank's way. Medical records in hand, he kept his appointment with Waterhouse. The titans greeted each other coolly.

"Here are the cases we've gone over before. An intravenous drug user with a fever gets admitted to rule out endocarditis no matter what. You don't transfer a kid with a head bonk because he doesn't have insurance, and you never — but never — sew up a snakebite with silk! I think it's time for Clyde to retire, don't you?"

Waterhouse flipped through the paperwork he had been handed and shook his head in dismay. He agreed with Montague, but there wasn't an easy solution. "I've seen these before. They've all been resolved. You have something else?"

"Yes I do. A woman with a subarachnoid hemorrhage."

"I've already heard about it. It'll go to the committee," Waterhouse said coldly. "And I'll talk to him."

Montague shook his head. "You'll talk to him to fire him, right?"

"Maybe. I have to discuss it with Clyde."

"What's there to discuss? Am I missing something? Is there a way to defend missing a potentially lethal bleed? Really, Wiley. Young woman plus sudden headache on exertion plus stiff neck equals a burst aneurysm. He should have held her for observation. Thank God she's doing well. Is there any question about what's right here?"

"Ray, don't start this again. The MRI was normal. You know the procedures. I'm happy to talk to Clyde, but this all has to go through QA."

"Like everything else, right? Well, if the past is any indication, I imagine this horrendioma won't see the light of day. Damn it! Whatever happened to clinical judgement? Wiley, why are you so afraid to let Resnick go? Has he got something on you? Did he save your life or something? If he did, that's pretty amazing, seeing as he's never been able to save anybody else."

The Dean blanched. He spoke slowly and emphasized every word. "I told you I'd talk to him." He couldn't control his fear. "And if you ever again insinuate that what I do in the Dean's Office is improper, I'll shut you down so tight that you'll need a goddamn blow torch to cut your way back into the operating room. Don't you *ever* think that you can show me this kind of disrespect. I'm the Dean!"

"You certainly are. Forget I asked. I won't bother you again." Montague was convinced. Frank was right.

CHAPTER 16

The first year class gathered in the auditorium for their introduction to medical school. They possessed some of the finest undergraduate records in America, and they were eager to get started.

Wiley Waterhouse sized up his audience. This was his twentieth year at the podium as Dean and unquestionably his favorite moment of the year. The students would hang on his words as if they were the Sermon on the Mount. He cleared his throat loudly.

"Welcome to Branscomb University Medical School. You are already way behind and will spend the rest of your lives trying to catch up. In the great tradition of Sir William Osler, Alfred Blalock and Albert Schweitzer, you are beginning a sacred journey. The knowledge and skills you will acquire during the next four years of medical school will form the foundation upon which you will build careers that shall carry you around the globe. Do not despair at the difficult tasks which lay before you. Thousands of young scholars have entered and successfully completed the rigorous academic program at Branscomb. We will attempt to strengthen you for postgraduate training in a way that will make you better prepared than your peers from other institutions. Branscomb medical students typically score in the top five percent on the National Board examinations."

Waterhouse paused to sip from a glass of water that rested on the podium. His audience kept him fixed in their collective gaze.

"In the first year, you will focus upon the basic science of medicine. You will dissect the human body in Anatomy, study cells and microbes in Physiology and Pathophysiology, wrestle with the tangles of DNA in Biochemistry and Genetics, learn about bacteria, viruses and fungi in Microbiology, and become familiar with drug kinetics in Pharmacology. In the spring of your first year, you will master Histology, Human Behavior, Neuroanatomy, and Fundamental Laboratory Techniques. One year from now, after you have been rigorously instructed and supervised in the art of Physical Diagnosis, you will begin the clinical rotations of Internal Medicine, Surgery, Pediatrics, Obstetrics and Gynecology, and Psychiatry. In the third and fourth years, you will have the opportunity to pursue the subspecialties of medicine, complete at least one research project, and seek other ways to distinguish yourself sufficiently so that you may become competitive for a prestigious internship. The time will fly by faster than you can imagine. It takes a lifetime to become a great physician. Heed these words of advice: there is no question that those who approach their responsibilities lightly in the preclinical years become failures and flawed physicians in later life."

Waterhouse paused again. They were squirming a bit now. This was not exactly the warm welcome most had hoped for.

"You are the new blood, the future of medicine. You must learn to work hard to be successful. Look forward to eight hours of classes a day, six days a week. Prepare to study five to seven hours a night. Do not plan to pursue sports or romance. For those of you with families, a half-day with the children on Sundays will probably be possible. You will need your summers to get ready for the following year.

Observe the men and women that occupy the seats around you. Of this entering class of one hundred and three, five of you will flunk out, two will decide that medicine is not what you really want to do, and a few will transfer. Someone will get caught cheating and another will succumb to an illness."

Sam Anderson scrutinized the proceedings from his vantage point at the far end of the tenth row. He had chosen his seat out in an area of near total darkness, where he could observe but not be observed.

The orator at the podium droned on and on until he became background noise for Sam's daydreaming. He was about to slump out of his seat when he was awakened by a nudge in the ribs by Lauren Doopleheimer, a young woman who was sitting in front of him.

"Ssshh! You were snoring."

Sam sputtered and sat up in time to catch one last rhetorical outburst from Waterhouse.

"Duty and honor are the cornerstones upon which the house of medicine is erected. This Dean will expect no less than completely exemplary behavior from all of you. From this moment forward, your one and only duty is to your studies."

CHAPTER 17

"Thanks. I was about to go down for the count. After listening to that bullshit, maybe I would've been better off asleep."

"Not if he saw you." She slid her hand between the seats to shake hands. "My name's Lauren Doopleheimer. Nice to meet you. My friends call me Doopie."

Her handshake was firm, though her hand was soft. She smiled warmly and looked him straight in the eye. He was intrigued. "Sam Anderson. I'm from Rutgers. What are you doing sitting over here in the dark?"

"Same as you — hiding. I was warned. Thought I might drift off. From what I understand, it's all downhill from here."

"Heads up, Lauren. They're starting again."

"It gives me enormous pleasure to introduce to you some of the distinguished men and women who teach in the medical school." Wiley Waterhouse gestured with a sweeping motion to the row of white coats that occupied the front row of the auditorium.

"You will recognize many of these persons as pioneers in their fields, as figures of unmatched international stature. Pay close attention to their words of wisdom, for you will find clues to the methods and diligence which will be required of each of you to acquire the precious degree of Doctor of Medicine."

Waterhouse delivered the last three words in a contrived basso voice that was more sinister than confidential. A Williams graduate couldn't restrain himself. He crooned, "Woooooooooooooo." Unfortunately, he chose a moment of absolute silence in which to express himself. All eyes turned to him in unison, including the eyes of the Dean and the faculty seated in the front row. Waterhouse wouldn't forget his face. He became a marked man.

"Criminey, what an asshole," whispered the petite young woman sitting in front of Sam. That idiot's gonna get us all in trouble. Somebody better set him straight."

Lauren Doopleheimer was barely four-feet-eleven in her stockinged feet and weighed all of 98 pounds. She was a Teutonic anomaly, a woman of German ancestry who was blond, blue-eyed, and small. And beautiful, Sam thought, although he had never heard such an adorable-looking woman talk so tough. Lauren pushed herself hard to compete with her tall siblings, especially her two older brothers, so she acquired a major talent for drinking beer and brash behavior. She graduated number three in a class of thousands, but one would never guess by the irrepressible way she acted. Her bold approach was a front for the loneliness that came from measuring all men against an unattainable standard. Lauren never held onto a boyfriend for very long, because they couldn't keep her stimulated. She enjoyed physical contact, but sex usually signaled the beginning of the end of a relationship, a default move from her mind to her body. Sam didn't know any of this — not yet — but he was instantly intrigued by this Lauren, who seemed to be offering him instant friendship.

Sam cleared his throat softly. "Let it go. He'll learn."

"Yeah, you're probably right. I'd hate to see a big mouth spoil it for everybody." Doopleheimer slid down in her seat and reclined as far as she could to talk to Sam. "You look like you could handle a tough place like Branscomb."

"What makes you say that?"

"Woman's intuition. Check it out."

"Check what out?"

"Pay attention to what's going on up front, before they mark your fanny like Mr. Wisenheimer over there."

Sam faced forward and suppressed a laugh; he was going to get to know this compact fireball.

"Let us begin. I have the great privilege to introduce Dr. Clayton Thomas Geehr, who serves as Chancellor, President, and Chief Executive Officer of Branscomb University Medical Center."

The audience applauded vigorously for this pillar of medicine, as they would for each subsequent speaker. Clayton Geehr deliberately placed his hands on the sides of the lectern, gripped it firmly and gazed out across the auditorium to survey his audience.

"Well, here you are. The class of 1999. There are 103 of you. Seventy-three men and 30 women. You come to Branscomb University from 86 universities in 37 states and eight foreign countries.

Thirty of you majored in biology, 15 in biochemistry, and 44 in pre-medical studies. Two of you are Rhodes Scholars, ten have already achieved advanced degrees, and one of you is a dentist.

Twenty-nine men and seven women have collegiate athletic letters and one of you was a medallist in the 1992 Winter Olympics. Nine of you love animals, 64 of you have owned a dog at one time or another, and two of you profess to hate cats.

Sitting among you is one pinochle champion, two eagle scouts, an ordained Methodist minister, an ex-bartender, and a former finalist for the astronaut program.

One of you worked as a broker on Wall Street, another as a dam builder in the Peace Corps, another was a professional bouncer, another a Congressional aide, and another a booking agent for a rock band. Two of you are classical pianists, four play the guitar, one the trombone, three the trumpet, two the violin, and one the drums.

In your class are an ex-paramedic, a police officer, and the youngest candidate for political office in the history of the State of South Carolina. You represent the finest class that could be assembled by our Admissions Committee.

It is my expectation that you will perform remarkably well at Branscomb University Medical School. I hope that you're up to it."

The students remained silent, more intimidated than inspired. Waterhouse was uncomfortable with the silence, so he scurried back up to the podium.

"Thank you, Dr. Geehr, for that eloquent introduction. Next, I would like to call up our distinguished Professor of Radiology, Dr. Frederick Spencer. Professor Spencer."

Fred Spencer had a reputation as a "good shit." He was known for his vision of the future of medical education and had developed an exciting curriculum in radiology. Computer simulations of multi-layered anatomy were substitutes for human dissections that would soon be the death knell of laboratory sessions, boring stand-up lectures and slide shows.

"Never underestimate the importance and extent of the foundation of knowledge upon which you must base the practice of medicine. You cannot communicate without a complete understanding of the normal landmarks where a disease has made a turn or detour. It is not enough to know that it is a leg or an arm or an elbow. You must know each specific tendon, each nerve, each minute blood vessel. The pathologist's microscope may show you the interior of cells, but man is more than a collection of cells. He exceeds a tangle of DNA or a cauldron of enzymes. Man is flesh. In learning to identify each tiny bit of that flesh, you become a doctor rather than merely an observer. Without the study of radiology, medicine is nothing more than empiricism."

Translation: Radiology is a fourth-year elective course that no one ever flunks because it's taught so well. Spencer is a maestro who brings to life shadows within the mazes of the systems that make up the human body. He pushes his students to see the world through his penetrating eyes. The massive trivia crunch all comes together with his masterful teaching.

Waterhouse regained the podium. "Thank you, Dr. Spencer. Our next speaker hardly needs an introduction. Raymond Fletcher Montague is the most important man in American surgery, perhaps in the world of surgery. Dr. Montague is the current President of the American College of Surgeons, International Society of Surgeons, Western Surgical Association, and Academic Council of University Surgeons. Graduates of his residency program are virtually guaranteed positions as academic leaders in major medical centers."

Well, thought Sam, this is a real power hitter. Definitely someone to avoid, and certainly nobody to fuck with. It was nationally known that Montague was ruthless when he wasn't obeyed. The reputation of the program was that it was the hardest and most dehumanizing. His residents took call in the hospital every other night for as long as they were trainees. It was a standing joke that the divorce rate was 150%, since you could be around long enough to ruin two marriages. Montague expected surgery to be your life, and if you couldn't cut it, there were plenty of aspiring young men and women with impenetrable sphincters to replace you.

"The life of a surgeon epitomizes the glory of a career in modern medicine. From the days of Ambroise Paré, we have revered the contributions of the men of steel. You will appreciate the discipline. Expect to live like surgeons. You'll be on the wards at 5 A.M., in the operating room before breakfast, in the recovery room and ICU in the afternoon, and on teaching rounds in the evening. Dissections will be completed on weekends. The average amount of sleep during your surgery rotation is four hours per night. You will read extensively about your patients, and present them at conferences hosted by visiting professors. This rotation will be the highlight of your experience in medical school. Please arrive for your surgery rotation well rested and appropriately attired."

Translation: We will own you. You will shave off all of your facial hair and keep the ones on the top of your head trimmed well above your ears. Every waking minute during these eight weeks will be devoted to the surgery clerkship.

Doopleheimer leaned back and whispered in Sam's ear. "I wonder what it takes to get so famous?" Lauren was wearing flowery perfume and her unruly blonde hair flicked Sam's nose. He leaned forward so that they were nearly cheek to cheek.

"Don't think much about it, Doop," replied Sam out of the side of his mouth. "You'd be amazed if you really knew what some of these Big Doctors were like. The medicine's easy. It's staying human that's hard."

"That's a pretty profound thing to say on opening day. You a philosopher?"

Sam smiled. She was gorgeous. "I'm just like you — here to be a doctor. Look, it's hard to talk in here. Let's get together for a glass of wine after this is over."

"That's cool."

"Next we'll hear from the Chief of the Division of Cardiology. Everyone who knows him agrees that there's no other physician quite like him at Branscomb." Waterhouse ducked for cover.

That was an understatement. When he walked to the podium, a muffled gasp rose from the students. Myron Ingelhart was the Arnold Schwartzenegger of doctors, an iron pumper who loved to show off his muscles. As he preened in the front of the auditorium, he behaved more like a body builder in a pose-off than a world famous Professor of Cardiology.

"What is cardiology? What is a cardiologist? What does it take to have a heart? These are not easy questions to answer. Look within yourself and ask, Why am I here? Who are these people around me? Is the heart the most important organ in the body? What is a heart, anyway?"

Myron posed briefly to let the audience drink in his physique. He stretched and flexed his arms over his head. "This is real power. If you want to understand the heart, you have to reach within. Pull it out. Let it pulsate in your hands. Cardiology is extremely complex, but it doesn't hold a candle to what goes on in the brain. If you can't hack cardiology, you sure won't make it as a neurosurgeon. Have a nice time in medical school." He bowed and waved to the crowd. They clapped loudly and cheered, and more than one student rotated an index finger against the side of his head in the universal gesture of insanity. They had been tipped off.

Translation: Who could possibly know? Ingelhart amazed most of the newcomers. It was hard to imagine an academic peer accepting Myron as legitimate, let alone as Chief of Cardiology. When did he have the time to develop those biceps?

"That one's fried," Doopleheimer laughed. "And a faculty member, no less. I'll tell you, Sam, I'll bet he turns a few heads in the nursing home."

Waterhouse bounded back up the steps to the podium and spoke quickly to squelch the laughter and loud chatter that followed Ingelhart's verbal hallucinations.

"Thank you very much. Our last speaker is the Associate Dean for Student Affairs."

Valerie Snell was the only faculty member who chose not to wear a white coat. She flashed her theatrical violet contact lenses at the men in the front rows, and captured the heart of every male in range. Sam caught her eye for a second and cast her a wicked grin, which she threw back full on. She pulled the microphone from its stand and worked it like a torch singer in a piano bar. She brushed her auburn curls back from her forehead, which accentuated the curves against the green silk of her blouse. Wiley Waterhouse was not alone in his lustful thoughts.

"I'm delighted to welcome you to this class. This has been a long afternoon, so let me just say that I look forward to getting to know each and every one of you personally. Welcome to Branscomb."

As Valerie replaced the microphone and walked from the stage, she glanced back at the students. Nice selection this year.

Waterhouse regained the podium for the last word. "So begins your odyssey. Go now to your tasks. We will gather again like this only once in the next four years, when I will bestow upon you the degree of Doctor of Medicine."

CHAPTER 18

The reception for the faculty and first-year class was always held at the palatial home of the Chancellor on the Sunday before classes started. Sam introduced Lauren to Frank.

"I hope you like it here." Frank shook her hand. "Sam mentioned how lucky you were to find good living arrangements."

Lauren smiled broadly before she swallowed the remainder of her second beer. The sundress and sandals gave her a country girl look that made it difficult for Sam to take his eyes off her. "Yes, a pleasant room-mate, too, on short notice. There she is." Lauren pointed to a slender brunette conversing in the middle of a group. "She seems quiet, but nice enough."

"Great. Well, welcome to Branscomb. I'd like to stay and chat longer, but I have extra rounds to make in the hospital this afternoon."

"But it's Sunday afternoon."

Frank chuckled. "Lauren, we don't get to choose when the patients get sick. It's a 24-hour-a-day, seven-day-a-week business. You'll see. Sam, you should bring Miss Doopleheimer over to dinner soon." Frank turned and walked away.

"What a nice man," mused Lauren, watching him go.

"He's pretty dedicated." Sam looked after him in admiration. "Well Lauren, what do you say? I've had enough meeting the professors. Ready for that glass of wine?"

"On top of the beer? Forget that. Tell you what. I've got a couple of six packs in the fridge at home. Let's just go to my place. But wait! There's my advisor. We've got to say hello." Lauren led Sam over to a tall, gray-haired man who had just walked out from the house. Lauren reached up and tapped him on the shoulder. "Dr. Spencer. Hi. You made it."

"Hello, Lauren. Yes I did. How are you?"

"Fine. I'd like you to meet a fellow medical student and a new friend. Sam Anderson, this is Dr. Frederick Spencer. He's already trying to talk me into becoming a radiologist."

Spencer barely acknowledged Sam's presence. He scrutinized Lauren while he spoke, "A pleasure." He shook hands softly with Sam.

"My advisor, Dr. Klawitter, mentioned you to me."

"Klawitter, eh? You're a lucky fellow. He's one of the best."

"That's what he said about you."

The radiologist laughed. "Mutual admiration society. It helps." He turned to Lauren. "You look lovely. I've set aside some time tomorrow to go over your courses with you."

"Thanks, Dr. Spencer. I'll be there at seven, sharp. Isn't that what we said?"

"Excellent. Nice meeting you, young man. Goodbye, Lauren."

"Gonna go over your courses, huh?" said Sam when Spencer walked away. "I'll bet that's not all he'd like to go over."

"Sam! He's my advisor. And he's old enough to be my father."

Sam felt foolish. "I'm sorry. Just a reflex. You *are* the prettiest woman here. I guess I shouldn't be surprised that people notice."

"Stop it. You hardly know me. Let's go."

Back at the dormitory, the two drank and swapped stories. With each beer, Lauren slid closer on the couch, until they were side by side and Sam had his arm around her. He had a healthy buzz going, but Lauren was way ahead of him. They were flirting like teenagers.

"You know what I like about this medicine stuff?"

"No. Why don't you tell me?"

"I like the idea that we'll be able to rub up against..." Lauren ran her hand through his hair. "...Some of the great minds in medicine. Truly brilliant people. But I hope it doesn't take too long to get out of the class-room. I want to get my hands on some patients. Somebody told me that if we push the Dean, we might be able to get on the wards sooner. If that's true, do you want to come with me to talk to him?"

"Lauren, Lauren! We haven't started classes yet. I think it would be a good idea to see how much work we have to do first. From what Frank...Dr. Klawitter...tells me, we'll get plenty of clinical experience. Until we see how much work we have to do, I don't think we should look for more. I'd give it at least a couple of weeks."

"Aw, c'mon. Where's your spirit? Come with me to talk to Waterhouse."

"The Dean? No, Doopie. Not a good idea. I'm not in a big hurry to spend a lot of time with the Dean. Besides, we should probably be careful."

"Be careful?"

"Yeah. Be careful."

Doopleheimer polished off another bottle of Miller Draft. "Whatever in the world would make you say something like that? Be careful of what?"

"Nothing. Too much work. Too much attention. You know." Sam was feeling good, but his confidentiality alarm had been triggered the moment he entered her dormitory room. Lauren wore a quizzical expression. "Oh, forget it. I just think it's a good idea to be careful, that's all. I've seen places like this before. The army, for instance. Where there's power, there's egos. I'll bet at least some of these guys didn't get to where they are by being nice. I'd rather hang with Frank for awhile. You stick with Spencer." Sam stood up quickly. "Anyway, you haven't shown me around yet. Let's have a tour of the mansion."

Sam pulled her off the couch. Lauren led him through the four-room apartment. "This is Malinda's bedroom. Over there's the bathroom. I guess you already know that. This is *my* bedroom." Sam held back at the door. "You can come in. I won't bite." Lauren sat down on the bed and motioned for Sam to join her. He sat down next to her.

The liquor had loosened Lauren's inhibitions. "I'm hungry. Feel like eatin' something?" Lauren put her head on Sam's shoulder and ran her fingernails up and down his leg. On an impulse, she grabbed his quads and squeezed for all she was worth. When Sam started to squirm away, she latched on with the other hand and began to wrestle. He held her off easily, laughing, which made her want to tackle him in earnest. Lauren slid her hands up under his shirt and tried to tickle his armpits. He locked her arms with his elbows and pushed her back on the bed.

"That's not fair. You're wearing a dress. There's nothing I can do."

"Oh yeah? Use your imagination." Lauren lifted her head up and kissed him quickly. She wrapped her left leg behind him so that he couldn't pull away.

"Now hold on..." Sam let go with one arm and reached behind him to pry her leg loose. Her skirt had pulled up around her hips, so he grabbed a smooth muscular thigh that moved instantly with his touch. She ran her heel up and down his calf. Sam slid his hand up. Lauren was wearing bikini panties that barely covered anything. The couple rolled over so that she was on top.

Lauren opened her mouth to his. Grinding together, they kissed in earnest. It wasn't romantic, but it felt good. After a few minutes of dry pelvic grindings, Lauren stood up and began to pull off her dress. She lectured Sam at the same time.

"If we make love now, I might never talk to you again. I just wanted you to know that," she said as she straddled him.

"What?"

She took his hand and put it between her legs. "You know, something changes. *You know.*" She opened his zipper. "Oh, forget about it. It doesn't matter. Let's see what you've got here."

"Wait a minute!" Sam pushed her hands away and slid himself out forcefully from underneath her so that they were facing each other from opposite ends of the bed. "What are you talking about? You bring me up here and get drunk, take your clothes off, and then tell me that if we have sex you'll never talk to me again? Are you nuts or something?" He'd heard about the women in med school having their quirks, but this was too much. Still, it took all of his will power not to throw off his clothes.

"No. I just think I might really start to like you, that's all. So I had to tell you. If we make love right now, then I probably won't ever see you again. I mean, of course I'll see you in class. But we can't go out or anything. But don't worry about me. I'll get over it." With twisted alcohol logic, Lauren crawled forward and put her face in Sam's lap. She bit him through his pants. For a split second, he drew her head against him, then reluctantly pushed her away.

"Stop! You're plastered. C'mon, get up. I've gotta leave. You're not ready for this yet." He let his eyes drink her in. "Doopie, you're beautiful, but you're loaded. Let's just be friends for awhile."

"Mmmmmmm." Lauren was too drunk to protest and Sam knew it. She'd do whatever he decided.

"Sorry. I don't like your one-time-only conditions." Sam crawled away from her and rearranged his clothes. Lauren sat back and made no attempt to cover up. She looked like a two-year-old who'd been scolded and was about to cry.

"Now you'll never talk to me again."

"Au contraire. In case you don't remember tomorrow what just happened here, I'll write it down for you. We didn't make love."

"Why not?"

Sam was halfway out the door. "Because it was the right thing to do. I had a great time. I really want to see you again. And not just in class. Get some rest. We start at eight."

"Malinda. You're back early."

"Early? No, I don't think so. It's nearly eleven o'clock."

"Oh. I guess I fell asleep. Well, did you have a good time?"

"It was all right. You've been doing some entertaining."

"Don't worry, nothing happened."

"Hey, that's your business. So, who was he?"

"One of the guys in our class. Sam Anderson. What a jerk!"

"Don't tell me he threw a move already! I take it you showed him the door."

"Actually, he found it himself. I had too much to drink, so he turned me down. Can you imagine that? I'm humiliated."

Lauren blushed and looked away. Malinda exploded. "What kind of a fool are you? You never shit where you eat! Take it from me. Jesus, Lauren!"

"Hold on! You don't even know me. What gives you the right to be so damn self righteous? We didn't *do* anything."

"Because I've been there, and take it from me, you don't want to be there. The minute you trust him, he'll have you for lunch. Maybe it's a good thing this happened. Now you'll be more careful."

"Funny. That's sort of what he said." Malinda was outraged, and Lauren was flustered. They argued about whether or not it was acceptable to have sex with another member of one's class, about men in medicine, and finally about whether or not they should remain roommates. In the end, Lauren conceded Malinda's experience and wisdom.

"Look Lauren, this Sam Anderson may turn out to be good or he may turn out to be bad, but after tonight, he's ahead of the game."

"Thanks, Malinda. I'm guess I'm lucky to have found a roommate like you."

"Yes, you are."

Lauren got dressed and put on a jacket.

"Where are you going? It's nearly midnight."

"I'm hungry all of a sudden. I'm going to Burger King and grab a Whopper. Want anything?"

"No thanks."

"I'll be back in twenty minutes."

As soon as Lauren was down the hall, Malinda went into Lauren's room and began to go through her chest of drawers. There wasn't anything specific she was searching for. It was just a precautionary measure. She never took any chances. There was nothing of interest in Lauren's closet or bureau, so she rifled quickly through her desk. Nothing there except a diary. Malinda flipped through the pages and didn't see anything of interest.

Sam Anderson *was* good-looking. But Lauren should have shown better judgement. Malinda knew what could happen if she didn't.

CHAPTER 19

The door to Professor Spencer's lab was half open, so Lauren didn't bother to knock. When she stepped into the vestibule, she let out a gasp. She was staring straight into the eyes of a naked male ghost. It took a half step toward her. She'd seen that face before. The Dean.

"Don't be frightened. It isn't real. What do you think?"

"My God, what is it?"

"An image. What you are looking at is a laser hologram of millions of bytes of data, reconverted by a computer program into a three-dimensional reconstruction of a human being. Do you like it?"

"Well, it's certainly...it's certainly, er, different." Lauren's gaze drifted down. "Pretty complete." She blushed.

Spencer flipped a switch and the apparition disappeared. "Sorry about that. I didn't expect you so early. You can add or subtract the clothes. It's always easier for me to get the motion right without any distractions. After you've been through gross anatomy, nothing'll bother you."

"So I hear. What else have you got?"

"Plenty. I'll show you later. I've got a lot to do this morning and so have you, so let's get down to business. Now, weren't we going to go over your courses for the first year?"

"Uh-huh. I brought the catalog with me. It looks like everything is required. I don't have any curriculum choices until the Spring quarter. My only real decision is whether to take Death and Dying or Introduction to Human Sexuality."

Spencer wanted to smile, but he kept a poker face. "Take Death. You have plenty of time for the other later."

Lauren moved over in front of the control console. "Can you show me another one?"

"Sure." Spencer punched a few buttons and twisted some dials that brought up a menu screen on the computer monitor in front of him. He clicked on a column of categories, then tracked the cursor down. "Hearts OK?" Lauren nodded. "Great. Let me find my favorite." Spencer browsed across his list until he spotted a certain name, then selected it. The futuristic light generator in the ceiling slowly changed orientation as it shot intersecting beams of light onto the platform below. The image of an extremely muscular male appeared. He was clothed from the waist down. "What you have before you is the image of a twenty-year-old male athlete in the prime of his wrestling career. Intercollegiate runner-up in the 142-pound weight class. All-American. World Games alternate. A sure bet to win the NCAA this year. Except for one problem."

"What's that?"

"Come over here. I'll let you do this yourself. Sit down next to me. Turn this knob slowly until his skin begins to melt. Good." The image shed its skin, revealing a layer of well-proportioned muscles.

"This is science fiction."

"No it isn't. It's the future. Now, let me expand the chest." Spencer worked the keyboard and eliminated every part of the man above the neck and below the waist. Then he enlarged him. A huge torso hung suspended in front of them. "Turn the dial again. Slowly. No, slower. That's it."

As Lauren moved her fingers, the muscles peeled away. First there were ribs, then lungs, then a round central ball of muscle. She recognized a human heart.

"Good. Stop there and let me explain. You're looking at the outside surface of his heart. See the little worm-like lines? They're his coronary arteries. The big U-shaped tube that takes off down the side is his aorta. This isn't the best view for the lungs. What do you notice?" Lauren was speechless. "Turn the knob just a trifle more. Good, good, good. Stop! There it is."

"What am I seeing?"

"The inside of his heart. What you'll learn over the next few months is that there's something terribly wrong with this picture. The septum — the muscle that divides the heart into chambers — is thickened. In fact, the entire heart is too big, too fat, too muscular."

"But he's so strong. What happened?"

"This young man used steroids to make himself strong. You're look-ing at an early cardiomyopathy. If he kept taking the drugs, in a year his heart would be a floppy useless bag. Then, without a heart transplant, the kid would be a goner." Spencer turned off the machine again. "What's incredible about all this is that nobody knew. I was the first to find out. He just answered a campus ad to make a few bucks, and when I imaged him for the collection of normals, I found out. He admitted it right away."

Lauren looked stricken. "Will he really die?'

"No, probably not. I was just being a little dramatic. What's incredible is that if he hadn't come in here, he would still be popping the steroids. He isn't an idiot. When I showed him the picture, he gave it up. On the spot."

"So, you saved his life, really. Wow. That's pretty amazing. And you developed this? That's what Dr. Klawitter told me. That the whole world wants you."

Spencer turned off the machine. "The whole world?" He became distant. "The whole world? No. A few do. But I'll stay here. I started this work at Branscomb and I'll finish it at Branscomb. You can count on that." He snapped out of it. "Now, where were we? I remember, your courses. So, take Death and Dying, and if you get a chance, try to get into Policy and Politics. Believe it or not, that might be the most useful course you have the whole time you're here."

"Dr. Spencer, can I work with you?"

"Excuse me?"

"I'd like to work with you. I took the advanced placement tests and got excused from Physiology, so that gives me an extra ten hours a week easy. I was going to pick up another course, but I don't have to. It would be great to earn a little extra money, but that's not really important."

"Lauren, you just got here. You haven't even started school yet. Give yourself a chance to adjust. Besides, my assistants do the other work. I do this project on my own." He didn't have the time now to teach her what she would need to know.

"We're supposed to get together every two weeks anyway. There must be something you could have me work on that would bring me up to speed."

"Most of my work is done in confidence. It's still research. I don't use trainees."

"I've worked in a lab before. I'm a quick study."

Her look caught him off guard. "It can be very dull work."

"Not for me."

Spencer chuckled. He could stand a smiling face these days. It was easy to give in. "Pull up a chair."

CHAPTER 20

The telephone awakened Sam on the tenth ring. He had dozed off and sat up slowly to drag the receiver off the hook.

Sam was exhausted. Biochemistry, anatomy and physiology had become brutal, and he took his studies seriously. It was October. He'd been hitting the books hard and keeping long hours.

"Hello. Anderson."

"Hi Sam. It's Frank. I hope I haven't interrupted anything important. How's the studying for the biochemistry midterm coming? I hear that the test is a bitch."

"Hey. You don't happen to know what time it is, do you?"

"Sure I do. Eleven o' clock. I thought you might be studying late. I guess not, huh?"

"Hardly. I was just catching a nap. What's up?"

"I know how that goes. Wait until you're an intern. So, how are your classes?"

"Fine. Everything's a breeze except biochem. For the life of me I can't figure out why I'm having so much trouble. I took almost the same course last year and managed a decent grade. This stuff seems harder."

"Are you in trouble?"

"I don't think so. I bombed the first pop quiz, but the second one put me back into the course. Besides, they wouldn't actually flunk some-body, would they?"

"Unfortunately, they would. If you really tanked a quiz, you need to get a decent score on the midterm. I wish I had known sooner."

"Why? What could you do? Frank, you can't help me with every-thing."

"No, I suppose not. Well, keep pounding the books."

"OK. So Frank, you didn't call to talk about biochemistry."

For weeks, Frank hadn't been able to learn anything that would bring him and his colleagues closer to the information they were seeking. He was growing impatient, and now he thought some fresh eyes and ears might help. Until he had a feel for how to get inside the circle, his approach had been extremely cautious. He had drawn a blank, and now the others wanted to participate. It was time to reconsider Sam's offer to help him. "Remember what we talked about? Eleanor's death. I told you about Dr. Schmatz."

"And maybe others. I remember."

"It doesn't look good, Sam. There *are* others. I need your help."

"My help? Go on."

"I know the timing's bad, with exams and all. I just thought that you could snoop around and no one would suspect."

"Anyone in particular?"

"Myron Ingelhart would be the easiest. He seems to be pretty much out in the open. Any clue that links him to the Dean is what I'm after. If you come by in the morning before class, I'll tell you everything I know."

"I can do that. And Frank, don't worry. I'll be careful."

"You have to. I don't want any heroics. See you tomorrow. Thanks."

It was late in the evening in the medical school office building. All of the doors were unlocked and the lights were on so that the custodians could clean up. Many professors prepared their lectures and stored exams in this bank of small office cubicles. Despite the modern multimedia education technology available to the faculty, most mid-term tests and flash exams were still old-fashioned multiple choice, true-false, or fill-in-the-blank.

Frank Klawitter walked softly in the shadows to approach the rear entrance to the building. He gently turned the old tarnished brass knob on the massive wooden door and quickly pushed it open. He slid through, then shut the door behind him. He knew exactly where he was going. With a deft surgeon's hand, he tried to rotate the handle on the door to the Biochemistry cubicle. It wouldn't budge. He slid Jon Herbert's key into the lock, then tripped it open. The door made a little squeak as it moved, so Frank stood motionless to listen for a human response. There was none.

After what Sam had told him, he couldn't take a chance that the Dean would focus his attention on the lad. Still, it was difficult for Frank to contemplate an academic crime. It wasn't unusual for faculty members to come in late to get caught up on their work, so he had to anticipate another professor paying an unexpected visit. He had formulated a good story explaining why he would be in the building after hours.

Frank walked in pitch blackness to the locked filing cabinets. Using a tiny pocket flashlight to quickly glance at the keys, he ran his fingers to the one that corresponded to the steel cabinet in front of him. He opened the cabinet and began to rifle through the rows of hanging folders laden with papers and envelopes. He flipped through the files until he came to a stack separated from the others by a tab marked "Biochemistry 100 Midterm: A through L." He read the names on the top two exams. Aiello. Anderson. The tests were ungraded. Paydirt.

Frank pulled an answer sheet from his pocket, unfolded it and compared it to Sam's exam. He smiled and shook his head in amazement. Most of the questions were answered correctly. Still, no point taking any chances, in case the test was graded on a curve. Frank changed a few of Sam's answers, then returned the exam to the folder and slid the drawer closed. *Who knows,* mused Frank as he left the building, *he might even get honors.*

CHAPTER 21

Despite Frank's admonition to exercise extreme caution, Sam shadowed Myron Ingelhart like a hunter trailing a deer. He learned what time Ingelhart left his house in the morning, the route he drove to the hospital, what he ate for lunch, and what time he went home. The student pulled all of the journal articles the cardiologist had ever written and struggled to understand them. His task was to find out whether Myron had any information he cared to share about the Dean.

Ingelhart's agenda was erratic, since he no longer had much of a clinical practice and because he wasn't teaching any courses. Fortunately, most afternoons, Myron stayed late to work out on the exercise machines in the "gym," an old janitor's storage area on the sixth floor assigned to the housestaff.

Every expense was spared. There was no window to the outside save for an eight-inch square of reinforced safety glass in the heavy cafeteria-style door. The floor was wall-to-wall blue Astroturf. The exercise equipment was purchased used and in some cases, battered. There was a multi-station Universal machine with bench press, pull-down bar, leg press and sitting press stations. A wrought iron rack held pairs of forged steel dumbbells. A number of the ex-athlete housestaff complained that there wasn't enough equipment, so the administrator added a bench, Olympic bar and iron free weights. A small water cooler with paper cups sat in the corner.

Myron Ingelhart lifted weights for an hour or two at a time, and performed exercises designed to give him bulk and definition rather than strength. While the younger men grunted and groaned under iron loads twice their bodyweight, Myron pumped the light stuff repetitively. He didn't do much leg work, because he knew that his gams were hopeless. Myron would never be as strong as the others, but he looked a hell of a lot better than men half his age. Like everything else he did, it was all for show.

Most of the time, Ingelhart had the room to himself. The interns and residents were too dog-tired to work out, and when they did, they usually only lasted for ten or fifteen minutes until they pooped out or got beeped. He would have preferred to have some company, because then he could babble his rhetorical nonsense and flex his muscles. When Sam Anderson strolled in, Myron was glad to see him.

"Hey there, son, come to build your body? That's good, building your body. You build your mind too much, it gets to the point that you push something in your left ear and something falls out the right. You need muscles to get by in this world, not brains. I'm living proof of that! Excuse me, I need to do another set." Ingelhart slipped underneath the pronghorned tubular shiny steel lever which operated the bench press on the Universal, and lay supine on the vinyl-covered bench. He assumed an attitude of profound intensity and gripped the rubber handles, then began to breathe rapidly in short bursts of feigned hyperventilation, as if preparing for an enormous effort. The stack of iron weights was set at 115 pounds.

Sam turned away so that Myron wouldn't have a chance to catch his involuntary grin. What an imposter! A big guy like Myron Ingelhart ought to be using that for a warm-up, not an exhibition of strength. The performer waited until he thought that Sam was paying attention, then pushed the weights up and down slowly, forcing a loud explosive exhalation with each repetition. After ten reps, he finished with a mighty grunt, and let the weights crash back onto the stack. He looked at Sam for his reaction.

Sam nodded his approval and began to swing his arms back and forth across his chest to warm up. He was dressed in a baggy old sweatshirt and sweatpants. The sweatshirt hood was pulled up over his head. He didn't want Myron to notice the taut muscles concealed underneath.

That's pretty impressive. I'm just coming back after a layoff and I need to warm up a little. Would you mind giving me a spot on the bench over here? I've never used a machine, so I think I'll just stick to what I know." Sam walked over to the bench with the Olympic bar and free-weights.

"Certainly, young man. Here, let me help you."

"Thanks." Sam placed the bar in the metal saddles welded to the uprights at the sides of the weight bench. He picked up a 45-pound plate and slid it onto one end of the bar, then walked around and slid its mate onto the other end. Since the bar also weighed 45 pounds, that was a total of 135 pounds.

"Hey there, little fella, that's a lot of weight to warm up with. You sure you don't want the bar by itself?"

"Oh, I'll give this a try. Take it if I look like I'm having trouble. I don't do this very often, so we'll see how this turns out. My shoulder's been bothering me, so I'm gonna kind of take it easy."

Sam lay down on the bench and positioned himself directly under the bar. He took his time positioning his hands, then pushed the bar up and over his chest. With a measured effort, he glided through eight repetitions, then pretended to struggle a little with the final two. He eased the bar noiselessly back into the rack and folded his arms across his chest.

"Man, that was hard!" he exclaimed. "Am I out of shape! You want to give this a try? I don't know, it might be too much for you. It's amazing how much you lose when you get older. You probably know what I mean." Sam massaged his triceps and winced. He wanted Ingelhart's undivided attention while he figured out what might make the man confide in him.

"Young man, don't be fooled by external appearances. Over this interior of rotten innards and foul political motivations lies a shell of steel. I was lifting weights this heavy when you were learning how to twang your pistol. Move over."

Sam slid off the bench, then grabbed his towel and wiped the vinyl shiny. He made a sweeping gesture for Ingelhart to sit down in his place. Myron straddled the bench and quickly took his position. He measured a precise distance from the center of the bar with each hand, then gripped as tightly as he could. Huffing and puffing loudly, Myron pushed upward and hoisted the iron over his chest. Despite the fact that the weight wasn't much more than he had maneuvered on the Universal, he was forced to balance it, which made it seem a great deal heavier. His arms quivered, not from weakness, but from the effort to keep his upper extremities from swaying too far forward or backward.

"Sewing machine arms," announced Sam matter-of-factly. "I could show you how to fix that."

"Hmmmph!"

Once he felt that he wouldn't drop the weight, Myron eased it down to his chest. He rested the bar on his pectorals for a split second, then pushed it straight back up, wandering a bit too far back. Sam reached out and gently pushed the bar forward with his index finger. Myron was annoyed.

"I've got it. Don't help unless I ask! It screws me up." Ingelhart adjusted his grip and lowered the bar again. It went back up much easier this time. With growing confidence, he began to pump the iron up and down faster. That young weasel had done ten, so Myron did fifteen. The last three repetitions weren't easy, and Ingelhart trembled with the effort. When he finished, his shoulders burned and his wrists were sore. No matter, he had shown Sam what he was made of!

Before this moment, Sam had only sketched in his head how he might deal with the useless cardiologist. It was information he was after. Now he was beginning to form an idea. It was time to try a man's work-out.

Ingelhart stood up and walked over to the water cooler. He poured himself a cup and tossed it down like a gunslinger doing shots of whiskey. Sam waited until he was sure that Myron was paying attention, then began to load up the iron bar. Judging by the ease with which Ingelhart had worked with 135 pounds, Sam estimated that he could handle 155 without too much difficulty. That would be a good weight to tire him out.

"If you're not gonna do anything for a minute, I'd appreciate it if you could give me another spot. I'd like to see how many times I can get this up." Sam sounded tentative.

"Sure, kid. At my age, I'm happy if I can get anything up." He gave Sam an over-exaggerated wink.

Sam chuckled and said, "Yep. I sure know what you mean. Look, when I'm finished with this, can I ask you a couple of questions? You've been around awhile. Maybe you can help me."

"Suit yourself." Myron stood over Sam and watched him heft the bar. Pretending to strain, Sam slowly lifted the barbell and weights up and down six times. On his seventh attempt, he stopped short of full exten-sion and wavered, then whispered, "Med school's kind of rough. Give me a hand."

Ingelhart reached over and gripped the bar between Sam's hands, so that he could help him complete the exercise. As Ingelhart pulled, Sam relaxed so that Myron would think that he was doing something. They struggled together to return the bar to its original position. Sam exhaled explosively.

"Whoof! That was a bitch. Man, I tried to get the last one, but I just wasn't psyched." Sam stood up and started to remove one of the iron plates. "Want me to take it back down to 135 for you?"

"Hell no. I'll stay with you. Give me a spot."

"Whatever you say." Sam tried to sound incredulous and displeased. Ingelhart was loving it. "What's the story with the Dean?"

"What?"

"He's driving me crazy. As if first year isn't hard enough, that son of a bitch has to mess with my schedule. Like he owns us."

"Welcome to Branscomb. You'll learn. Quit whining and pay attention here."

Myron took even longer to set up this time. Just as he was about to attempt to lift the bar, he let go of his grip, sat up and rubbed his hands together. Then he climbed off the bench, walked over to a cardboard box full of powdered chalk and dusted his palms with the white talc.

"Hands are a bit slippery."

"Yeah, you don't want any excuse for not being able to do ten reps." Myron hadn't said anything about how many repetitions he was going to do, but Sam wanted him to crank out as many as he could. Tire him out. Ten would probably be all the cardiologist could manage.

Myron lay back down on the bench, reached up and started pumping. He coasted through the first three presses, struggled a bit with numbers four through six, then really had to strain on the seventh, eighth and ninth. He held the bar straight over his head and breathed heavily.

"Want me to take it?"

"No fucking way."

Ingelhart breathed in and out in three staccato bursts. He dropped the bar onto his chest and threw it back up by arching his back and hips. The same maneuver got him two more repetitions, but he could barely get the bar up at the end of the final thrust.

"There. Son of bitch! Twelve reps. Told you I could do it."

"Awesome. You're stronger than you look." Sam clapped his hands softly and shook his head. "You must have been something else when you were younger."

Myron smiled as he mopped the sweat off his forehead. "Not much to it. It's all leverage. I guess I *am* pretty strong for a man my size."

"Yeah, you sure are." Sam paced for a moment and ran his fingertips over the bar. "Well shit, if you can do that, I've gotta try one more time. I can't let you show me up."

Ingelhart laughed hard and slapped his thigh. "Some people never give up. Son, let it rest. Tonight's not your night."

"No, really. I want to see what I can do. So, Dr. Ingelhart — you *are* Dr. Ingelhart, right? - I need to know how to deal with Dr. Waterhouse. What a pain in the ass. Always trying to intimidate people. He's making my life miserable. You've been here a long time. What do you say to a guy like that?"

When Sam saw that Ingelhart wasn't going to be quick to answer, he removed the ten-pound plate from each end of the bar. He replaced them with 45-pound plates. That was 225 pounds. He lay down under the bar, grabbed it, then changed his mind. He sat up. After he rested on the bench for a moment, Sam added another ten pound plate to each side. The bar and plates now weighed 245 pounds. Sam reclined under the iron configuration.

"Now young man, don't be ridiculous. I don't want to be responsible if you hurt yourself."

"That's OK, this is my idea. You don't have to help if you don't want to. I can probably get by without a spot."

Ingelhart shrugged his shoulders and took his position at the head of the bench. He poised over Sam with arms outstretched like an eagle set to swoop.

"Want a lift-off?"

"Nope. If I can't get it off, I can't get it up." Sam waited a second, then added, "Maybe I've got that backwards. Here goes. One. Two. Three."

Sam gave a firm grunt and pushed the weight up out of its resting-place and over his chest. With military precision, he lowered the bar to his chest and smoothly returned it up over his head. To be certain that he provoked Ingelhart, he lifted it twice more, then let it settle back in the rack with a loud clang. He sat up and breathed deeply.

"Damn! That was the best lift of my life!" he exclaimed. "I'm sure glad you were here to share that with me. Now, I don't suppose you'll want to try that, too."

"Maybe I would," muttered Ingelhart.

Sam mimicked Myron's previous taunt. "I don't want to be responsible if you hurt yourself."

"Move over! It's my turn."

Myron powdered his hands again and put his back to the vinyl-covered foam. He walked his fingers into position to grip the bar and once again began his stertorous breathing routine. As soon as he finished, he pushed up on the bar. It didn't budge.

"I'll need a lift-off."

Sam placed his hands together at the center of the bar and squared his hips to Myron's head. He moved in to the bench as close as he could and placed his feet slightly underneath the overhang under the cardiologist's head. He knew that he'd have to do most of the work, and he didn't want to hurt his back.

"On the count of three," barked Myron.

"Whenever you're ready."

"Here goes. One. Two. Three!"

When Ingelhart shouted, "Three!" Sam rowed up hard. Together, the men hoisted the bar off its resting-place and positioned it over Myron's chest. Sam let go, and Myron kept the bar aloft only because his elbows were locked. As soon as he began to bend his arms to lower the weight, it plunged down and careened into his chest, forcing him to cough loudly in a forced exhalation. He tried to push it off, but it only sank deeper into his chest. He was way out of his league. With a frightened whisper, he gasped, "Take it."

"You sure you need help? I thought you said that this was gonna be easy."

"Don't fool around. This thing hurts. C'mon, get it off me." Ingelhart was running out of breath. The bar sank and formed a groove across his chest and sternum. Sam offered Myron a crooked smile and reached down to take the bar. He put his hands just inside of Ingelhart's.

"OK, let me give you a hand. But don't stop pushing. You've got to help me get this up now. C'mon! Keep pushing."

Sam leaned way out over Myron's head and pulled up on the bar. Their combined effort raised the steel off of Myron's chest. Sam let him struggle. Ingelhart's face was beet red from the effort. Anderson helped him just enough to keep the bar in motion. Three quarters of the way up, Sam shifted into neutral, so that the bar went nowhere. There were only a few inches to go, but Myron couldn't do it without Sam's help. He pushed for all he was worth.

"Jesus H. Christ, take the thing, will you? I can't push any more. You've got to help me. What the hell are you thinking about?"

The door to the workout room swung open. In walked Lauren Doopleheimer, of all people, with Malinda Dwyer at her side. Lauren was dressed in surgical scrubs over a fluorescent green body leotard with black tiger stripes, pink high-top Reeboks and a bright red headband. She saw Sam and yelled out a big hello as she started to strip out of her scrubs.

"Look what we've got here! It's Sam the man! I knew I'd find some he-man up here. Hot damn! Will you look at those weights. Who *is* that Hercules under there? Is that Chuck Norris? Oh my God, it's Dr. Ingelhart. Holy shit, I can't believe how strong you are! What is that, a million pounds?"

What horrible timing! The second that Sam saw the door begin to move, he secured the weight in his hands and took all of the pressure off Ingelhart. As Lauren ran through her greeting, he helped the exhausted cardiologist hoist the bar up and set it back into its resting-place. Myron took his time sitting up. He wanted to say something to Sam, but not with the women present. He directed his breathless comments to Lauren.

"Nope, not a million, but close. It's about 315." He couldn't tell the truth even when it didn't matter. He squinted his eyes and stared at Malinda, as if he were trying to figure something out.

Sam walked away from Ingelhart and over to his classmates. "Good to see you guys. Doop, I didn't know you pumped iron. I thought you just tortured your friends." Since their aborted tryst after the Chancellor's reception, Sam and Lauren had become extremely close and saw each other whenever they could. He adored her. "You better stay away from this stuff, so you don't mess up that beautiful body."

"Yeah, nice to see you too, Conan. You know my roommate." Malinda nodded at Sam, then held her hand out to Ingelhart.

"And it's so nice to make *your* acquaintance. Professor, I'm amazed at what great shape you're in. By the way, I really enjoyed your talk at the orientation. It was nice to hear someone talk about the real problems in medicine." Myron examined Malinda with a quizzical look, than lost his thought.

"We have this room reserved," Ingelhart said.

"What? You can't..."

Lauren looked at Sam, who shook his head and motioned with his eyebrows for them to leave. Even though she knew that Ingelhart had no right to order them out, she prepared to acquiesce.

"Sorry, Doop, but Dr. Ingelhart's got the room reserved. We're having a little contest."

"No prob, you guys. We just stopped in to catch a few sit-ups. We can come back later." She tugged on Malinda's arm.

After they left, Myron walked directly in front of Sam so that they stood toe to toe. His flash of anger was gone, but he wasn't about to let the incident slide by. He interpreted Sam's behavior as a taunt, rather than a threat. The women's appearance made it all worse.

"You pushed me pretty hard a few minutes ago, son. I like that. Pushing people makes them do better. You're a heck of a weightlifter. But you just caught me on an off day. A few years ago, I could take a weight like this and twirl it over my head like a baton."

"Sure, sure. I'm sure you could. Just today you had a little problem. Really, I understand. We all have off days. Anybody could tell how strong you are."

"I'll tell you what. I'll see you back here in three months. Just you and me. Give me three months and I'll press this as many times as you did. You have to go up fifty pounds and do the same. That's the deal."

"Deal? What deal? Is this a bet?" Sam wanted information, not a competition.

"It is. You told your friends that this was a contest, so let's make it one. You lift 295 and I don't lift 245 and you win. Or I lift 245 and you don't lift 295 and I win. We both do it or we both don't do it and it's a tie."

"What's the bet?" Sam saw it now. He'd use it.

Ingelhart had been so eager to issue the challenge that he hadn't thought about the specifics of the wager. He scratched his head, then decided to do a little pushing of his own. For a change, it wasn't money he was after.

"You getting hassled by the Dean? OK. I win, you walk up to the Dean, turn around and drop your pants to the floor. Then you tell him that you heard from Dr. Resnick that he really knows how to party."

"What's he gonna do?"

"Oh, probably kick you out of school. But no matter what, you can't tell him who put you up to it. That's the deal."

"Great. I moon Waterhouse and he ends my career. So what happens if I win? Do you climb up on the Dean and piss in his lap?"

"That's not a bad idea, but no, that's not what I had in mind. You win and I give you five hundred bucks. Cash. Now be honest, you could use a little money, couldn't you?" Ingelhart's eyes were blazing. The money was nothing. He wanted to see the expression on Wiley's face.

Soon. Sam whistled. "Man, that's a lot of money. Five hundred dollars. You *really* mean five hundred?"

Ingelhart nodded. "Five hundred dollars. If you want, I'll bring it with me."

Not yet. "Two hundred ninety-five pounds is a lot of weight. I'm not sure I can do that. I need to think about this one."

"No thinking. Answer me now! Take it or leave it. You lift the weight and I don't and you get the money. It's that simple. Otherwise, get out of my face."

Now. "Tell you what, Professor. I don't want your money. You're a big man at Branscomb. I need something *really* good to embarrass

Waterhouse. He's a pig."

"Like I said before, welcome to Branscomb. You should study harder."

"I don't think so. Look, he's picking on me. You must know how he is. All I did was ask him whether he became a Dean after he passed his prime as a doctor. I didn't mean anything by it. I don't understand. Now he won't get off my case." Sam was watching Ingelhart intently. He had his full attention. "I need something to say to back him off."

"What good would that..."

"C'mon. You guys know everything about us, but we never learn a thing about you. Look, I actually came up to the weight room to meet you. You're one of the reasons I wanted to be at Branscomb. You're famous — everyone's heard of Myron Ingelhart. I've read all your papers. I figure if anyone can help me, it'll be you. Hell, look at how tough you are. Please. All I'm asking for is a few tidbits I can use. There has to be *something* he doesn't want to hear."

The flattery worked. Ingelhart had no doubt that he could win his bet, so where was the harm? If Sam didn't want money, that was his choice. The kid was perceptive — information *was* power at Branscomb. He congratulated Sam on his choice of award.

"That's sensible, son. You'd never believe the things I could tell you."

Sam's confidence was building. "Nobody'll ever know who told me. Tell you what. If you win, I'll moon the Chancellor, too. But will you still talk to me?"

"You drive a hard bargain, son."

"What's your answer?"

"Sure."

"One more thing. Three months is too long. Can we make it one? Look at you — you can do it." Sam reached out and offered his hand. "Don't break it."

Ingelhart flexed a biceps and grinned. "Better get to work, 'cause I'm comin' after you. See you in November."

CHAPTER 22

Frank decided it would be best for Joe Masterson to know that he had asked Sam to help out.

"I don't like it. He's just a boy."

"He was a soldier, Joe. I know what he's been through. I was with him. He'll do fine. And look, we're making progress. Sam thinks he has a way to get to Ingelhart. It could be the big break we need."

"I hope so, Frank. I know you don't want to hear this, but we might even want to consider switching him over. You probably haven't heard the latest."

"Don't tell me."

"I've got to. It's your best buddy again. He's notched another one."

"Schmatz?"

"None other. I would've never found out if Resnick hadn't tried to blame it on the Chief Resident on the Trauma Service."

"Resnick, too? They did this together? What happened?"

"Hold onto your hat. You've never heard one this bad..."

The police had called ahead to the ER to warn them that the ambulance was coming in soon from a freak accident only a mile from the hospital. A bus had pulled out from the curb without signaling and had been struck from behind by a car, which careened to the side and skidded into a pedestrian. By the time the official paramedic call came into Branscomb, the ambulance and victim were already at the door. He was packaged in the usual manner, strapped to a backboard with a rigid cervical collar supporting the neutral alignment of his head and neck.

Clyde Resnick performed a rapid assessment and was right on the money. "This man's in a coma." He lifted his eyelids and swung a penlight across his pupils. They were dilated and didn't react. He put his pen between the man's fingers and squeezed his digits to elicit a response to pain. Nothing. There was a long laceration on the left side of his face and a deep gash across the bridge of his nose, but the bleeding was minimal. "What happened to him?"

The paramedics gave a quick report. "He's still a John Doe.

Bystanders said he was trying to get out of the way of the bus, but he wasn't quick enough and it hit him. Apparently he fell backwards against a street sign, spun and struck his head on the curb. His sunglasses were shattered. That's all we know."

"Any seizure activity?"

"None noted."

"Vital signs?"

"He's been stable since we got to him. Blood pressure 210 over 150. Heart rate 75, but it dips into the forties. He's been breathing OK, but we have to keep suctioning him to keep the blood out of his mouth. We didn't have time to work on his airway. We figured we were so close that it was best to get him in here. "

"You're right," replied Resnick. He peeled back the old man's lips and removed a fractured upper denture plate, which had sliced a clean gash across the upper gum line. "Keep his mouth clear. C'mere." He motioned to one of the paramedics. "Hold this gauze tight against the cut. Right. Let me think for a second."

An old man had fallen and stuck his face hard enough to crack his false teeth and split open his face. Now he was deeply unconscious and showed signs of raised intracranial pressure. He needed a CAT scan.

"Call radiology. We're coming over for a head scan right now. Page Dr. Schmatz and tell him we have an emergency intubation from the ER. Tell him we'll meet him in scan land. I'm pretty sure he's in house." Whenever he could, Clyde referred the paying customers to his friend Randy. The victim was dressed in a three-piece suit, so it was a safe bet that he had good insurance. While he was waiting for the anesthesiologist, he performed a rapid neurological exam. Clyde tapped on the patient's knees and his heels with a reflex hammer. Although the injured man still didn't respond to pain, he appeared to have faint reflexes.

"What have we got here?" bellowed Schmatz as he charged into the CT room. "I got paged to do an emergency intubation. Is this the fellow? What's the problem? I need to make this quick, because I'm supposed to be somewhere in fifteen minutes."

"Randy, this fellow got hit by a bus and smacked his head on the pavement. He's been in a coma ever since. We needed to scan his head right away, but now that that's finished, we've got to protect his airway. I was hoping you'd do a rapid sequence intubation."

"Is he moving at all?" Schmatz lifted one arm off the scanner table and let it fall with a thump back to the man's side. "Any response to pain?" As he waited for the answer, he moved quickly to the head of the bed and looked into the victim's mouth. "Bad cut. We'll try to stay away from that."

"Not since he's been here. I don't know what's going on inside his head."

"Let me borrow your light. Thanks." Schmatz peeled back his eyelids and inspected the pupils for any reaction. "Not looking too good up here."

"Yeah, I know. I've done that already." Resnick called out to the technician in the viewing room, "Got a wet read on our scan yet?"

"Sure do. Small subdural. C-spine's normal down to C5, but all the cuts aren't out yet."

"Who's reading?"

"Fred Spencer."

"Great."

"Well, it looks like he got dinged pretty bad." Schmatz touched a finger to his head. "Hold his squash. I need to have a feel of his neck. These damn collars are a nuisance." With a nurse's assistance, the anesthesiologist removed the Philadelphia collar and began to run his fingers up and down the front and back of the old man's neck. He wiggled his Adam's apple and worked the man's jaw up and down. There was absolutely no resistance. "Hey Clyde, are you sure about this scan? I'm happy to put him to sleep, but I think he's brain dead. Let's see if he has doll's eyes."

Schmatz cut in front of the nurse and clutched the man's head between his hands. With a sudden forceful snap, he jerked his head from side to side.

"His *neck*!" shouted the trauma resident. "We haven't x-rayed his neck yet!"

"Don't be such a worry wart. The scan's OK. Well, I guess I was wrong. His eyes move all right. Let me paralyze him and we'll pop in a tube so he can go to the scanner. We'll bag him up first." Schmatz pulled a syringe of pentothal from his coat pocket and injected it into the IV tubing. He followed it with a dose of succinylcholine. The paralytic agent took effect in less than a minute. Immediately after the anesthesiologist observed the patient's facial muscles flutter, he performed an effortless endotracheal intubation. "Ahhh. I love it when things go the way they're supposed to." He turned to Resnick. "Thanks for this fascinating consult. He's all yours now."

The CAT scan showed a small insignificant subdural hematoma and some brain swelling that didn't require surgery. The patient went from the scanner to the intensive care unit, where the trauma resident assumed complete responsibility for his care. On follow-up neurological exam, the patient had no deep tendon reflexes and remained completely flaccid, long after the curare derivative should have worn off. Recalling what had transpired in the ER, the astute young clinician raced his patient back to the scanner. Special cuts through the base of the skull revealed complete atlanto-axial dissociation, the most insidious and devastating form of broken neck. There was every reason to believe that Randy Schmatz had irreparably damaged the man's spinal cord.

"Wait. You haven't heard the best part," Joe said to Frank. "You'd never guess this one in a million years. The guy's wife finds out he's been hit by a bus, so she's not very happy. While the resident is interviewing her, she tells him that her husband just came home from an appointment with the eye doctor, who put drops in his eyes to dilate his pupils! That's why he was fixed and dilated. That nincompoop Schmatz assumes he's brain dead and piths him! Let me tell you, his wife is pissed."

"She knows everything?"

"I don't know how, but she does. Great PR for Branscomb, huh? I heard she's got a lawyer already. Waterhouse is ready to shit a brick."

"It's about time. Are you going to review the case in Morbidity and Mortality?" Frank wore an expression of defeat before Masterson even began to answer the question.

"Why bother? We'll go over what happened, but what can I possibly accomplish? Randy and Clyde don't belong to me, so I can't do anything to them directly. You know where it goes from there. This case is too weird and they've already got all kinds of excuses for what happened. Hoping for anything out of the QA committee is just wishful thinking. Besides, if we're in a lawsuit, the Dean'll shut this one down tight. Nope. I'm afraid they've got us again."

"Not us. They don't have *us*! They've slaughtered another poor unsuspecting slob who got brought to the mecca for a cure. God damn! We've got to stop them."

"Frank, why don't you let me help? You shouldn't take them all on yourself."

"Not yet. Waterhouse has radar, and he already knows how we feel. Let me chew on this tonight. Sam's coming over for dinner. I'll give him a pep talk. I have a feeling about Ingelhart. He's such a lunatic that I don't think it would take much to get him to tell us everything he knows."

"All right. We'll sit tight. I hope this works."

CHAPTER 23

Frank was a fabulous cook. Even though he usually cooked for one, he devised culinary creations that would have been the envy of many a skilled chef. It wasn't the results that he necessarily sought. It was the process. Slicing, sampling, tasting, making all the proper adjustments — it was creative, and Frank was very good at it. Preparing a meal was a welcome respite from the mental stress of the medical center. Entertaining friends gave him that much more pleasure.

Like his study, Frank's kitchen had been remodeled to precise specifications. It was the hub of the house, figuratively and literally. Offset from the main entryway, it was a rotunda with bay windows that looked out across an expansive deck onto a broad grassy area dotted with dense clusters of birch and Japanese maple. The kitchen countertops were solid black granite flecked with sparkles of silver and pink. The individual sections had been cut from a slab Frank personally chose from a quarry he visited in West Virginia. Oak cabinets held an epicure's collection of kitchen implements, spices and well-worn cookbooks. A large skylight above the central workstation was sufficiently ample to transmit moon-glow when the sky was clear.

Tonight he served one of his favorite meals. Buckwheat cakes with smoked duck and grilled mushrooms, avocado and yellow tomato salad with a citrus-mango salsa dressing, followed by lightly charred silver salmon in gingered soyu accompanied by triple rice pilaf. For desert, he decided to keep it simple and offer bittersweet chocolate mousse and fresh strawberries.

Lauren and Sam relaxed at the table as Frank served them cappuccino.

"That was a great dinner, Dr. Klawitter."

"Thanks, Lauren. Now tell me. Why did you change from political science to a pre-med major?

"It wasn't convenient after all that work, but being a political scientist became an oxymoron. I wanted to get away from politics. Do something useful. I started to think about medicine. It seemed logical."

"There are politics in medicine too."

"I suppose, but you don't have to get elected to be a doctor. You earn it. You know what I mean."

Frank understood. "I do. But times have changed. People like you and Sam will make it better for all of us." Frank stood up.

"Are you sure I can't help?"

"I'm fine." Frank gathered up the plates. He didn't allow anyone else in his kitchen during the preparation or serving of a meal. Frank called back through the passageway. "Don't misunderstand me, Lauren. I didn't mean that in a derogatory fashion."

"Mean what?"

"Mean that politics in a medical center have to overwhelm you. But it's a fact of life."

"Why?"

"Because there are egos." He returned to the table with more coffee. "You need to walk softly and read the signs."

Lauren sensed that Frank was disturbed. She felt awkward, and tried to lighten things up.

"You just don't like any competition," she kidded.

"Hardly. Look, I'm sorry. We were talking about you. Please go on."

"The rest's not very interesting. I took my courses and here I am. So far, so good."

Frank had a faraway look again. Lauren read him correctly and paused in her conversation. Her host broke the silence.

"Being a doctor isn't everything it's cracked up to be. Things can go wrong. People can make mistakes."

"Certainly, but what about the work I'm doing with Dr. Spencer? It's brilliant. You have to believe that it's people like you and him that make medicine worthwhile."

Sam interrupted. "Frank, thanks for setting that up. Lauren showed me the lab the other day. When do you suppose we'll be able to use that stuff on our patients?"

"Not for awhile, I'm afraid. It all has to go through the usual peer review process. Papers, presentations, and validation. Everything has to be justified."

"Dr. Klawitter, Sam told me something about your time together in

Kuwait... "

"I was explaining to Lauren about the time you gave me your philosophy about relationships. Remember? About how important it was to be supportive of each other. About the difference between an honest mistake and malpractice."

That triggered it. Frank fell back to his preoccupation. "Lauren and Sam, I want you to look me in the eye and pay close attention. There is no upper boundary on greed. The easiest way to break through any glass ceiling is with a hammer, but the more common instrument is usually a compromise. Before you trust anybody, put them in a position of power over you and give them a little test. Put your fate in their hands, but not really. Then watch. See in whose interest the decisions are made. Watch where the money flows. Remember, when you get to this level, everybody's smart. The question is, who's honest? Who'll stick by you when it hits the fan? You've got to be careful. There are a lot of dirtballs out there."

"Really, Frank, I don't think you should..." But there was no stopping him now, Sam realized.

"Lauren, I don't want you to take my word for it, or anybody else's. Just be alert, that's all."

Sam and Lauren had the same instinct simultaneously. They stood up. "It's getting late and I think we probably should get going. We've got an early class tomorrow."

Frank was slightly embarrassed. He hadn't meant to give a speech like that.

"It's been a wonderful evening," said Lauren.

"I'll give you a call tomorrow," added Sam.

"You can call tonight. I'll be up late."

In the car, Lauren nestled close to Sam. "What got into him? All of a sudden he just withdrew. And sounded bitter."

"There's a whole lot about this place that most people don't know."

"And you do? Tell me!"

"I'd rather not."

"Don't start that again. Look, I showed you how everything worked in the lab. I don't think that Dr. Spencer would be too happy with me if he found out. You can't just tell me that you know something and then say it's a big secret. Who am I gonna tell? C'mon!"

"I don't know."

"Sam."

"OK. The reason why Frank went off is because he hasn't just seen some bad medicine. He's been victimized by it. Dr. Schmatz gave his cousin the wrong blood. It was horrible." Sam told Lauren the story of what had happened to Eleanor.

Lauren shook her head and wore a worried expression. "No wonder he's bitter. But I don't understand. If Schmatz is so bad, how come he's still here?"

"Because it isn't that simple. He's just part of it, I think."

"Part of what?"

Sam was suddenly alarmed at how much he had told Lauren and so he said that he suspected there were more, but that he didn't know who they were. Lauren knew that he was holding back, but she also knew when to quit.

"Thanks for tonight. You were right. Frank is special." She leaned over and gave him a kiss on the cheek.

"See you tomorrow."

Malinda had been reading in preparation for a gross anatomy lecture. She was half-asleep in her favorite tattered Princeton sweatsuit when Lauren woke her up by opening the door.

"I'm sorry. I didn't know you were resting."

"Did you have a nice dinner?" Malinda was groggy.

"Sure did. I'm sorry you weren't there. Next time you should come along. Dr. Klawitter was really provocative."

"What do you mean? He came on to you?"

"No! Man, have you got a one-track mind. He talked about good medicine and bad medicine and good doctors and bad doctors. I couldn't figure out where he was coming from, but Sam explained it to me." Lauren hung up her jacket and began to undress. During their first few months as roommates, she and Malinda had warmed up to each other, but Lauren was far and away the more communicative.

"So?"

"So, you'd think that if there was a rotten doctor running around, someone would've done something by now."

Malinda was suddenly wide awake. "A bad doctor. Anybody we know?"

"No. I mean, not yet. Some guy named Schmatz." Lauren stretched and yawned. "I'm bushed. Gotta do the diary. See you in the morning."

Frank lifted the receiver on the first ring. "Hello?"

"Hey, Frank. It's Sam. So are we ready to go after any of the evil professors?"

Frank didn't like Sam's tone. It was too lighthearted. "One at a time. This isn't a game. It could get nasty. You need to be very careful." He hesitated. "Maybe you should forget everything."

"Don't worry. Nothing will go wrong. Ingelhart's just the way you described. I'm pretty sure he'll talk."

"All right, go get him. But Sam, I mean it. Be careful."

"I'm always careful."

CHAPTER 24

It was a crisp autumn afternoon, and the leaves had finally turned, painting a perfect background for the ivy-clad gothic towers on campus. Lauren could have jogged on forever, but she had to be back in Dr. Spencer's lab before dinner.

The shower felt great as Lauren lathered up her calves and ankles. Her legs were hard — she was pleased. Sam told her she had great legs. Lauren smiled as she remembered how he had mentioned it. Since their first fumbling encounter, Lauren and Sam had become comfortable in their physical relationship, although she was the more aggressive of the two. For some reason, Sam was hesitant to make love, even though she reassured him time and again that her initial warning was no longer valid. Now she had to be content to wait, although having him so close yet so far away was torture. They kissed and touched, and Lauren longed for the day when Sam would acquiesce. His chaste approach made him all the more desirable.

Lauren scrubbed her abdomen, then ran her hands over her shoulders and breasts. As she was about to finish washing her left side, her soapy fingertips slid over something firm that she had never noticed before. Without consciously thinking about it, she began to massage the underside of her breast. She felt it again. Concerned, she added her other hand and initiated a self-examination. No question about it — something was there.

In front of the bathroom mirror, she held her arms straight out in front and then over her head. Nothing abnormal was visible from the surface. She explored each armpit with the fingers of the opposite hand and to her horror discovered there might be an enlarged lymph node down deep on the left. She hadn't noticed any soreness before, but then she hadn't been looking for it. Four years ago her mother had been diagnosed with breast cancer, but it had been a controllable case managed with a simple mastectomy. This might be different. Lauren imagined the worst.

There was no one to turn to at the moment and Lauren needed to get to the lab. She dressed quickly and walked to the research center. She tried to immerse herself in her work, but her concentration was shot. Spencer had asked her to pull up all the bone images and sort them by anatomic region, then work on removing the artifacts — all of the extraneous false markings outside the body that had been manufactured by the machine. She was only allowed to work with the two-dimensional flat views, and it was a laborious process that required her complete concentration. Ordinarily, she could crank through five or more images an hour, but this evening she couldn't get past the first one. What if the cancer had already spread to her bones? To her brain? She had to know.

"Hey, Lauren. How's it going? You just about finished with those? I've got some other stuff I need you to start on as soon as you get a chance. Big presentation coming up."

"Dr. Spencer, I'm having a little problem."

"Really? Let me see." He leaned over her shoulder to observe the screen. Her newly washed hair smelled wonderful. He inhaled deeply, but Lauren didn't notice. "Oh, that's very good. What's the problem? You still have a few more marks to take out." He looked closer. "Actually, you have a lot more marks to take out. How many more shots do you have left?"

"All of them."

"All of them? What time did you get here?"

"An hour ago."

Spencer stepped back. It wasn't like Lauren to be flat or slow.

"Are you OK? Feel all right?"

"Sure. Well, no. I don't. I'm scared." Lauren was ready to cry.

The radiologist had grown extremely fond of Lauren and was immediately moved by her vulnerability. He spun her chair and took one of her hands.

"What's the matter? Did something happen in class? At home? With Sam? Are you in trouble?"

He thought she might be pregnant. "Oh no, nothing like that. Impossible. Everything's OK."

"What then?"

"Oh, Dr. Spencer. I'm embarrassed. I don't want to bother you."

"Look Lauren, don't be ridiculous. You can't sit here in front of me, sound like you just lost your best friend, tell me you're scared, and then not let me know what's wrong. If it's something personal, that's fine, but you can trust me. You should know that by now."

He squeezed her hand, then reached out and brushed her hair away from her face.

"I think I might have breast cancer." Lauren fought back the tears. "There's something there."

"Where? When did you find out?"

"In my left breast. I felt it tonight, just before I came to work. In my armpit, too. My mother had breast cancer. It runs in my family."

"Ever noticed it before?"

"No. This is the first time."

Spencer was gentle, but methodical, with his questions. "Is it painful? Have you noticed any discharge from your nipple? Have you been losing weight? Any night sweats? Have you ever had any cysts? Are you using birth control pills? Anyone else besides your mother with cancer in the family?" The answers were all no.

"Lauren, you should have a good breast exam, but I imagine how you must feel. Maybe we can do a little something to ease your mind. Do you want me to do a scan right now?"

She hadn't thought of that. "I don't want to put you to all that..."

"Nonsense. Of course you do. Come with me. We'll just run a few quick cuts and take a look at this thing. You know, even if someone can't feel the lump, you're going to want to know, right?"

Lauren agreed. "Are you sure you don't mind?"

"Let's go. You know the routine. Put on a gown while I warm up the machine."

Spencer began to turn on switches while Lauren walked into a small dressing room with shelves of hospital gowns. She stripped down to her panties and slipped on the cotton garment that tied in the back. "Where do you want me?"

"On the table. I'm ready." Lauren positioned herself supine on the cold white MRI table. It was weird. She had now helped scores of people do exactly the same thing, but this was the first time she had actually done it herself. "All set?"

"Yes."

"OK, I'm going to slide you back now. Breathe slowly and wear the earphones. You'll hear me talk to you. When I tell you to be still, try to stay as motionless as possible, especially your arms. If you need to come out, talk in a normal tone of voice and I'll hear you. The microphone picks up everything." The table moved with Lauren up inside the immense circular magnet. Lauren had a brief flash of claustrophobia. Now she understood why some people freaked and couldn't go through with it. "You'll hear some clicking first, then some clangs, and then a loud hum. When the clicking stops, you can't move."

The procedure took forty minutes, which seemed like an eternity. A limited scan usually only lasted for ten or fifteen minutes. Lauren was worried. Her back was stiff when Spencer helped her sit up. He was quick to explain.

"Sorry about that. I wanted to be sure we got everything we needed, so I repeated the scan a few times. You can get dressed now while I take a look at the data."

When Lauren came out of the dressing room, Spencer wore a huge smile. He pointed to the screen behind him. "No problem. It's a lump of fat. A lipoma. As benign as the nose on my face, but smaller. You don't have cancer. And there's nothing in your axilla."

Lauren's eyes watered, almost crying in relief and gratitude. She hugged her supervisor. "Thank you."

"Feel better?" Spencer held her at arm's length. "Now we can get back to work. There's much to be done."

CHAPTER 25

The emergency department was always unpredictable. Ten minutes of doing nothing, then the sudden craziness that accompanied motorcycle wrecks, schizophrenic tantrums and babies born in the parking lot. A lull never lasted for long.

Dave Ring was rushed to the ER in the middle of Monday Night Football. His chest pain started right after the second half kickoff. San Francisco ran it all the way back, and as the points went up on the scoreboard, Dave felt something press on his breastbone. It was no stronger than the feeling he got when his grandson kneeled on him, just a tweak, nothing really painful. He had felt an identical pressure a few times over the past month, but hadn't paid much attention. He'd been playing golf on the weekends and attributed the tweaks and twinges to a pulled muscle. Dave rubbed his chest and shifted around in his chair. The discomfort gradually subsided. He grabbed a handful of peanuts and a bottle of Michelob Dry. He relit his half-smoked cigar and took a couple of puffs.

There was nothing Dave loved more than sitting down in front of the tube and watching a good football game. He was a municipal engineer who put in a 60-hour week, between the time he spent at the office and all the work he brought home. He used to take it easier when the kids were living in the house, because his wife scolded him if he didn't spend enough time with the family. But now that the last one was gone, his wife had backed off and resigned herself to the fact that she'd married a workaholic. Whenever Dave was comfortable, he always rubbed his feet together. She watched him work his stockinged toes and warmed with a surge of affection.

Ten minutes before the end of the second period, Dave got kicked in the chest by a mule. Without warning, he became nauseated and started to sweat. A split second later, he felt a steel band tighten around his upper body. Something was ripping inside him. It took away his breath and made him fall out of the armchair onto his knees. He started to cough and gasp for air. The pain intensified and traveled through to his back between the shoulder blades. Not knowing what else to do, he reached for his wrist to feel for a pulse. Nothing. The engineer breathed rapidly until his fingers and lips tingled. Sudden weakness overwhelmed him and he dropped face down on the floor. He vomited up a tidal wave of meat and mashed potatoes, beer and peanuts.

His wife heard him fall. When she saw her husband lying on the carpet in a pool of vomit, her first thought was, *Oh my God, he's dead.* She knelt down beside him and called his name over and over, but he was too weak to respond. Dave could hear her, but his heart wasn't generating enough blood pressure to enable him to roll over, let alone get up. His chest still hurt, though not quite as bad. He had never felt so miserable in his life. He didn't remember falling down, and wondered whether he had just lived through an earthquake. His wife dialed 911.

The paramedics arrived quickly and carried Dave out to the ambulance on a stretcher. Inside the ambulance, they gave him intravenous atropine, which bounced his heart rate back up to 80. His blood pressure came back and he rejoined the land of the living. When he reported the pressure sensation in his chest, the ambulance attendants sprayed nitroglycerin under his tongue. The unit pulled away from the Ring residence as the 49ers' coach began his interview on the postgame show.

By the time he arrived at the ER, the pain had subsided to a 2 out of 10. Maybe he would live after all. When Dave got wheeled into the cardiac bay, he was one of two patients in the department. Within five minutes, there were 20 more patients and 22 on the way.

The registration clerks got bombarded. A hysterical babysitter ran into the waiting room with a toddler wailing at the top of her lungs and scald blisters across her face. At the same time, a paramedic rig rolled up with three victims from a collision. One had a broken femur and a scalp laceration. The other two complained of abdominal pain. A nurse from the neurosurgery intensive care unit needed to be seen because she'd been stuck with a needle from an AIDS patient.

The other fifteen patients who came back into the treatment area were mostly the post-Monday Night Football rush. True to form, there were four mothers with children who had fevers and an assortment of runny noses, diarrhea and rashes. One college coed had twisted her ankle that afternoon playing softball. A young hemophiliac with hepatitis had a cluster headache. Another person suffered from mild asthma. Two bar rats got into a fistfight over the televised game's outcome. One needed his eyebrow stitched and the other had a broken hand. There was a frequent flier who had slashed his wrists for the three millionth time in order to spend some time in the isolation room and get a free meal. A woman lost her contraceptive sponge and thought that it still might be in her vagina. A ninety-seven-year-old nursing home resident had tripped over her walker and was driven in by her grandson. She had a broken nose and wrist. A husband and wife who had eaten fried chicken at a convenience store came in puking their guts out six hours after they had eaten the offensive fowl. The last patient was a 45-year-old cocaine addict who wanted a mole removed. To top it all off, Charge Nurse Gloria Koslofsky had just received a call over the radio that they would soon receive 22 Chinese acrobats from a traveling circus. They had been stacked in a human pyramid when one of the performers lost his balance, and caused the entire formation to collapse in a tangled heap of arms, legs and black Lycra. None of them spoke English and they all were pointing to their necks, so the paramedics were bringing them in for x-rays.

The name of the game was to keep 'em moving. Ordinarily, Dave Ring would have had a one-to-one nurse assigned to him, but that just wasn't possible at the moment. The physicians were expected to pitch in and pick up some of the nursing tasks, like arranging for transfers upstairs. In Dave's case, that was just fine with Clyde Resnick, the doctor on duty.

When Dave came in, nurse Koslofsky greeted the ambulance and wheeled the gurney into one of the special bays reserved for chest pain patients. She placed the sticky electrode patches on his chest and wired him up to the cardiac monitor. She recorded his vital signs and hooked him up to the transcutaneous oximeter. The oxygen mask which he had been given by the paramedics was swapped out for nasal prongs. While all of this was going on, Gloria asked Dave a few questions.

"How are you feeling? What happened? Are you having any pain now? Just relax. We need to do a few things here, and then the doctor will be in to see you." The charge nurse ran off a quick electrocardiogram and drew three tubes of blood from a vein on the inside of Ring's arm.

"I feel a little something here." The patient pointed to his breastbone.

"It's not nearly as bad as it was, but I still notice it."

"Is it sharp or dull? Does the pain go into your jaw or arms?"

"Sort of. It's sharper now. It went into my left arm before, but now it's just here." He reached around to his back.

"Put one of these under your tongue." Koslofsky placed a nitroglyc-erin tablet under Dave's tongue. "Don't swallow it. Just let it dissolve. If you feel a little lightheaded, we know that it's getting into your blood-stream. It's the same medicine the paramedics gave you on the way in, just a different strength. Tell me if it helps the pain." Gloria shouted out to the entryway, "Would someone please find Resnick and ask him to come in here? Right away." She turned back to Ring. "How's that? Notice any difference?" She didn't like what she saw on the monitor.

"Absolutely," he answered in amazement. "That took all of the pain away. My head hurt for a second, but I feel OK now."

"Good. Things are a little busy here now, so I'm going to step out of the room to help out. If your chest starts to bother you again, call some-one for help. I'll be right back. Are you sure you aren't having any pain right now?"

"Yes ma'am. I'll be fine. Thank you. I'm just a little tired, that's all."

Gloria tidied up quickly and placed the tubes of blood she had drawn in her pocket. She took the electrocardiogram and put it on the top of the clipboard which would hold the doctor's notes. She hung the clipboard on the baseboard of the bed. She left the room and went look-ing for Clyde Resnick.

He was out front in the registration area arguing with a young father who was carrying a small boy in his arms. The child's mouth was bleed-ing and he was wide-eyed in fright. His father held a washcloth wrapped around an ice cube against the little fellow's face to try to keep the blood from his lacerated lip from dripping all over his clothes. It wasn't work-ing.

"I'm sorry, but your Medicaid card is expired. Unless it's a life-or-limb-threatening emergency, you'll have to go to the county hospital. It's not my decision. I just do what the hospital tells me."

That wasn't true. The ER doctor knew that this "cash account" wasn't likely to pay his bill. But he could still treat him if he wanted to. The extra work wasn't the point. Resnick wanted to give this man a lesson in medical economics.

"Aw, c'mon Doc. I've got money." The father juggled his son while he fumbled to pull out his wallet. "Can't you just throw a couple a stitches in his lip so we don't have to wait six hours over at the General? I hate that place!"

"I know you do. But unless you're willing to pay two hundred and fifty dollars up front, which is about what it'll cost by the time we're finished, I'm afraid I can't help you. We don't work for free around here."

Koslofsky interrupted. "Dr. Resnick, I've got the patient in 1A set up for you. He came in with a history of chest pain and bradycardia in the field, which responded quickly to atropine. He had a small amount of chest pain when he arrived, which was relieved by one nitroglycerin. I've drawn his admission bloodwork and done an EKG. Sounds like a keeper to me, probably a small MI."

"Great. I'm on my way in to see him." He watched the man carrying his son storm out of the waiting room. "'I've got money.' *Sure* you do." *These people are all alike. They all want something for nothing.*

"Clyde, do me a favor will you? The rest of the place is filling up. If he's having a heart attack, he's going to be admitted. Let's get him a cardiologist and ship him upstairs. I don't think it'll do him a lot of good to watch the sideshow. Ed Ashley's in the hospital. I saw him come through about a half an hour ago." Gloria was hinting that Resnick use a specific cardiologist, one skilled at catheterization and the most modern interventions. Ashley was aggressive and clinically superb. "Want me to give him a call?"

"Thanks, but no thanks. I need to see the patient first. I'll keep that in mind, though."

Resnick strolled up to Ring's bed and picked up the chart. There was nothing on it except the paramedic report, EKG and vital signs. It wasn't like Gloria to leave the nursing notes uncompleted. She must really be busy, thought Resnick.

"I'm Dr. Resnick. You're Mr. Ring. I'm sorry to hear you're not feeling well. Tell me what brings you in to see us."

Ring related his story as best he could while Clyde looked at the electrocardiogram. He explained how he had been watching the football game and suddenly felt weak and dizzy, then sort of went blank for a moment. When he came to, he was in the ambulance. He wasn't clear on the details. It was a combination of actual loss of memory for what had happened and trying to minimize his symptoms. Dave Ring wasn't a complainer, and he wanted to go home. He didn't like the idea of being in the hospital.

For his part, Clyde didn't like the look of Dave's EKG. The ST segments in leads 2, 3 and AVF were elevated and there were a lot of extra ventricular beats, known as "PVCs." With nothing else to go on but the heart tracing, this would be an inferior myocardial infarction. With the history, the diagnosis was a slam dunk.

"You're not having any pain now?"

"Not in my chest, doctor. Maybe a little in my back."

"Good. Let me just take a little listen to your heart. Resnick pulled his stethoscope out of his pocket and put it into his ears. He listened to Dave's heart, then reached behind him and sat him forward so that he could auscultate the back of his chest. He didn't like what he heard in either location. Ring had a cardiac gallop, which indicated that his heart muscle wasn't functioning properly, and had a few crackles in the bases of his lungs, which suggested mild heart failure. If Dave hadn't already suffered the big one, it was right around the corner.

"Mr. Ring, you did the right thing coming in."

"Well, Doc, I didn't have much choice in the matter. What do you think? Am I going to make it? I feel a whole lot better now."

"You know, much as I'd like to tell you that you can go home, I think that there are a few things here that are pretty worrisome. You may have suffered a heart attack. I'd like to bring you into the hospital and see that you get some tests done right away. You sure don't want to walk out of here and get brought back in a box."

Ring was taken aback. "Well, uh, sure Doc. When you put it that way, it's kind of hard to argue. Whatever you say."

"Do you have a regular doctor or a cardiologist?"

"Yes and no. I've never needed a cardiologist. My regular doctor's a family practitioner. We've been going to him ever since I can remember."

Resnick frowned and wrinkled his forehead. "Hmmm. A family practice guy. You need a specialist. I know a good cardiologist here at the medical center. I'm sure that your doctor would approve. If I give him a call and tell him about you, he'll be right in. I really don't think we should wait too long."

"Whatever you think is best."

"Fine. We'll snag a chest x-ray and then I'll send you upstairs to the coronary care unit and give the cardiologist a call. His name is Myron Ingelhart."

The cardiac care unit was the most high-tech unit in the hospital. Every patient was attached to a heart monitoring system that displayed waveforms at the central nursing station, where the alarms could ring and be instantly noticed. Each private room had a curtained glass panel to the main hallway. It was a remarkable unit, with a fine nursing staff that had a reputation for really knowing their patients. The Charge Nurses in the CCU worked closely with their counterparts in Emergency, because they were always taking reports on patients coming up from downstairs.

Trish Hurley was working Charge when the call came from Dr. Resnick. He told her that he had a patient named Ring coming up with a probable inferior MI, and that the Attending would be Myron Ingelhart. She was concerned on two counts. First, it was highly unusual for the ER doctor to call up a report, unless there was going to be something tricky about managing the patient. Second, Ingelhart hadn't had a patient in the CCU in over 18 months. It was common knowledge that he was there just for show. On a hunch, Trish called down to talk to Gloria Koslofsky to get the scoop, but Gloria couldn't come to the phone. The receptionist told Trish that Gloria was busy with 22 Chinese acrobats. What a strange night!

Ring showed up at the double doors to the unit as white as a ghost and clutching his chest with both fists. He was moaning and belching, with an occasional hiccough. Trish and another nurse whipped him around the corner into his room and looked at the tracing on the portable monitor connected to his EKG leads. The ST segments were sky high and every third beat was a premature ventricular contraction. The experienced CCU nurses knew what to do. Working on standing orders that applied to any patient in the unit who didn't have a doctor in attendance, Trish sprayed nitroglycerin under Dave's tongue, squeezed an inch of white nitroglycerin paste out of a tube onto a piece of paper and slapped it on his chest, and injected 100 milligrams of lidocaine into his intravenous line. Over the next 60 seconds, the PVCs disappeared. However, the ST segments stayed up.

"Mr. Ring, are you still in pain?"

"Yes ma'am, it still hurts pretty bad. Isn't there anything else you could give me?"

"There sure is. Are you allergic to any medicines?"

"No."

"Ever had any narcotics?"

"No."

"All right then. I'm going to give you a little morphine just to tide you over until Dr. Ingelhart gets here. We were expecting him before this, so he should be here soon."

Trish went to the narcotics drawer and unlocked it with a key she had pinned to her yellow uniform. She grabbed a Tubex of morphine and brought it to the bedside. Dave was looking pretty miserable, so she injected five milligrams into his IV tubing. He experienced a small amount of relief, but it wasn't complete, so she gave him another five. Ring reported that his pain was gone for the moment. Then he had an episode of projectile vomiting and roared in agony. Trish looked up at the monitor and saw that his heart rate was up to 180. If anything, it should have been slowing down. Something terrible was happening, more than a simple heart attack.

Ring needed to get to the cath lab. Without a critical remediation, whatever was causing his demise would advance to the point where not even a cardiac bypass operation would help him.

"Page Ingelhart and tell him that if he still wants to have a patient when he gets here, to move his buns. Just page Ingelhart once. If he doesn't answer in 30 seconds, beep Ashley."

The desk clerk looked up Ingelhart's pager number and dialed it in. She looked at her wristwatch to time 30 seconds. Just as she picked up the phone to page Dr. Ashley, the rhythmic "beep beep beep" of a pager grew louder as it approached them. Myron Ingelhart entered the unit.

"Just a minute, somebody's paging me. Oh, it's for here! What's up?"

"Dr. Ingelhart, your patient's in 403 and he doesn't look very good right now. He's still having chest pain and the monitor shows marked ST segment elevations both anteriorly and inferiorly. I think he's infarcting right now. Would you like me to notify the technicians on call for the cath lab?"

"Whoa, slow down! Not so fast, Miss..." Ingelhart leaned closer to Trish so that he could read her nametag. "Miss Hurley. I haven't even had a chance to talk to the patient yet. Let me have a few minutes and then we'll see what we need to do."

"Certainly, doctor. It's just that I know that you'll probably want to study this man's coronaries and I know that Ed Ashley's in the hospital somewhere. It might be a good idea if I call and tell him to at least stick around. You wouldn't be doing this man's cath, would you?"

Trish had stuck both feet in her mouth. Ingelhart turned dark red and his jaw tightened. Even though it was widely rumored that the Chief of Cardiology was forbidden to use the cath lab, he had never been confronted with it by a staff member. The nurse immediately realized her mistake, but it was too late. She braced herself for the tongue-lashing.

"Well, you pretty young busybody! What business is that of yours? Perhaps this patient won't need a catheterization, but I wouldn't know that, would I? Unless of course you gave me your permission to examine him. Let's see, you've been to nursing school and probably can read and write, so I imagine that qualifies you as an expert on how to take care of a heart attack patient. Let's see how well you do with a few simple questions."

Trish started to back up, but Ingelhart matched her step for step. He put his nose in her face and glared at her with the wild malevolence of Captain Hook.

"Are you game, Miss Hurley?"

Trish swallowed and pleaded, " Please, Doctor."

"What is the enzyme defect in homocystinuria?"

"I don't know."

"Ha! Cystathionine synthetase. Who discovered leishmaniasis?"

"I don't recall."

"I thought you wouldn't. Sir William Leishman. Who is Chairman of the Department of Cardiology?"

"You are, sir."

"Good. You're one for three. Now, if you'll quit bothering me with your opinions, I'll go examine my patient."

Ingelhart left Trish and walked into the room with Dave Ring. Nurse Hurley ran into the staff bathroom and burst into tears.

The Chief of Cardiology held out his hand to the patient, who took it and shook weakly. He was losing his strength, and the pain had taken root deep in his chest. The morphine helped a little, but he had surges of pain that elicited beads of sweat on his brow and imbued him with a sense of impending doom.

"I'm Dr. Ingelhart, but you can call me Myron. That's what my friends call me. They tell me that you have a little pain in your chest and that your heart's slowed down a bit. Let me see here." Ingelhart took his own pulse, then the patient's. He pulled an old stethoscope from his pocket and offered it to the patient.

"Want to listen to my heart? It seems only fair, if I'm going to listen to yours. There's no magic to this, you know, just a hunk of muscle that keeps whapping away day in and day out. Then the oil gets old and the filter gets clogged and it's time to put in a new transmission. Want to guess what's wrong before I tell you? Might as well be like everybody else around here."

Ring thought that this doctor seemed a bit peculiar, but maybe he was just trying to put him at ease. The pain was so constant and severe now that all he could think about was how to make it go away.

"Doc, this hurts pretty bad. Is there something you can give me?"

"Oh, sure there is. How about a little morphine? When you have a pain in your chest, I've found that there's nothing like a good old shot of morphine." Ingelhart walked over to the door and yelled at Trish, who had straightened up her makeup and returned to the nurses station. "Hey, Hurley, bring us a little morphine in here. Mr...." He stuck his head back in the room. "What's your name?"

"Ring. Dave Ring."

"Mr. Ring is having a lot of pain. He needs some morphine. Please give him ten milligrams, and if that doesn't help, give him another ten. As far as I'm concerned, he can have as much as he wants, as long as he doesn't take any home."

"Yes, Dr. Ingelhart. I'll bring it right away." Trish unlocked the narcotic drawer once again and pulled out two preloaded syringes.

"Good girl. Now we're cookin'."

The cardiologist returned to the bedside. He pulled the most recent cardiogram, which had begun to normalize. The preliminary x-ray report was "unremarkable — questionable enlarged heart. Fred Spencer." It was time to watch and wait and hope for the best. In the old days, there wasn't much you would or could do about any of this. Before the advent of drugs to dissolve blood clots and balloon-tipped catheters to press the atherosclerotic plaque out of the way, a trial of medical therapy was the usual first maneuver.

Times had changed, but Myron Ingelhart hadn't. Ever since his clinical activities had been restricted, he stopped trying to keep up with the literature, so he was limited to techniques and prejudices he had adopted fifteen years ago. To make matters worse, underneath his void of self-esteem was still a vestige of pride that he couldn't reconcile with his morbid psychological state. This glimmer of ego would not allow him to seek consultation with a younger faculty member. He might be worthless, but he was the Chairman of the Department. The nip from Trish sealed the fate of Dave Ring. He was at the mercy of Myron Ingelhart's judgement, which was as flawed as that of Custer at Little Bighorn.

"This doesn't look good, my friend," mused Myron. "I think that you're having a heart attack. This is nature's revenge. I wish that there was something I could do about it, but I can't. However, I can take away your pain. I can put you in Disneyland with morphine. We should know where this is headed by morning."

Trish listened with horror. Ingelhart was flying blind. She administered the morphine through Ring's IV. He became visibly more relaxed as the intensity of the pain began to diminish. All the while, precious minutes elapsed while the undiagnosed aortic dissection, a huge rip, lengthened and continued to weaken the essential vascular pipe that carried blood from Ring's heart to his body. Meanwhile, the related coronary artery blockage continued to rob his heart muscle of essential oxygen. The morphine dulled Dave's senses and made him feel better, but it didn't provide any significant physiological benefit. His respiratory rate increased as blood leaked into his thorax and fluid collected in his lungs. Had he been taken promptly to the cath lab, the study would have revealed the true nature of his problem, and an operation given him a better than fifty percent chance of survival.

"So, is that better? Good, good. You see, I know what we're dealing with here. From a literary point of view, I find diseases of the heart most fascinating. Goethe wrote 'My peace is gone. My heart is heavy.' Interesting, isn't it? Even Oscar Wilde knew that hearts could be damaged. Do you remember that he said, 'How else but through a broken heart may the Lord Christ enter?' Listen to this. 'Cleanse the stuffed bosom of that perilous stuff which weighs upon the heart. Therein the patient must minister to himself. Throw physic to the dogs. I'll none of it.' So you see, Macbeth knew how little we can do."

By this point, the poor man who lay before Myron Ingelhart was physically and emotionally exhausted. His cardiac output was declining precipitously, he was numb to the world from 30 milligrams of morphine, and he'd been left in the dust by the disconnected rambling of his doctor. The pain had been reduced to a dull ache, and he could tolerate it. In the midst of Ingelhart's soliloquy, Dave Ring fell asleep.

"Ah, the patient rests. Perfect. Our therapy's working. Nurse Hurley, let's leave him be for awhile. I want him kept on oxygen and all other drugs discontinued except for the morphine. I'll come see him again in the morning."

"Do you want me to stop the lidocaine? He was having quite a bit of ectopy."

"Ectopy schmectopy. I don't believe in the stuff. Just do what I asked. No drugs except morphine. If he gets into any problems, you can give me a call."

"Yes sir."

"Please hand me the chart." Ingelhart signed his initials in a broad dramatic gesture. He handed the chart back to Trish and left the unit. For the moment, he couldn't have been happier. He was a real doctor again!

Trish looked at the chart and shook her head. She couldn't read a word that Myron had written. She wanted to call Ed Ashley and tell him about this patient, but she'd been told specifically by Ingelhart not to, and she could easily lose her job if she crossed him. For now, the patient seemed to be resting comfortably. She hoped so.

Dave Ring was asleep, but it was a tortured rest. He tossed and turned constantly, unable to find a comfortable position. The nagging pressure in his chest never completely went away. Even with the morphine on board, his autonomic nervous system registered his distress, so he was prodded by brief episodes of nausea and sweats. But Dave wasn't a complainer. He awoke in fits and starts, then the potent narcotic settled him back into fitful slumber. For the next hour, Dave was poised on the brink of cardiovascular catastrophe.

The expanding blood clot that extruded from Dave's ruptured aorta finally broke loose. The pain became excruciating for a few seconds and caused Ring to sit bolt upright in bed, eyes wide in terror. It happened too fast and hurt too much to cry out. As Dave reached for the nurse call button, his heart emptied into his chest and began to quiver. With no blood circulating to his brain, Dave suffered a seizure, lost his bladder and bowels, and sustained a cardiac arrest.

The alarm at the central nursing station rang loudly and all of the nurses on the unit rushed into room 403. Trish screamed for the unit clerk to "page a code," which signaled the hospital cardiac arrest team to respond to the unit. The nurses began CPR and poured fluid and drugs through Dave's IV. By the time the medical masses arrived, the rhythm on the monitor had gone flat line, which meant that Ring's heart had quit and was no longer even quivering. Although they continued to flog him with devices and drugs, they couldn't generate so much as a blip on the screen.

Gloria Koslofsky had noticed the overhead page for a code in the CCU. She had a premonition that this might be the patient she had seen earlier in the ER.

"Trish, this is Gloria. Hey, you know, I was just calling to find out about that code I heard a little while ago. That wasn't by any chance the guy from the ER we sent up, was it? What was his name, uh, David Ring?"

"It sure was. I'm sick about it."

"Oh, that's awful! He seemed like such a nice guy. I guess he never made it to the cath lab. Did Ashley get to see him? He must have had a pretty big MI."

"Ashley? Did you say that Ed Ashley was supposed to be his doctor?"

"Well, no. I mean, not exactly. I told our ER doctor that Ed was in the hospital, so I assumed that he'd give him a call. Didn't he? Who came in?"

"You've got to be joking! If I tell you who showed up, you'll never believe me. It was Ingelhart."

Ingelhart, thought Gloria. *Myron Ingelhart. Why the hell would anybody call Myron Ingelhart? Everybody knew that he didn't take care of patients anymore.*

Trish kept on talking. "You can imagine. I tried to suggest that he call Ed, but he jumped down my throat. To make a long story short, everybody including the janitor knew that this guy had to go to the cath lab. Ingelhart just watched him. That's from the dark ages. Oh shit, this is all my fault. I should've pushed harder. I should have called Ed anyway."

Gloria consoled her as best she could. "Don't torture yourself. This isn't your fault. When the big cheese tells you that you have to do something, that's all you can do. To be honest, I tried down here. I should have made sure that we had the right doctor right off the bat. Damn!"

"Well, that's what happened. What do you think I ought to do?"

Gloria thought for a second. Nurses who complained too much weren't long for their jobs. Even though she was in the right, Trish would get burned badly if she got into it with a loose cannon like Ingelhart.

"Copy all of the records and mail them to the QA committee. Make it anonymous. Don't put your name on anything. That's what you should do."

"You're sure I won't get in trouble?"

"I doubt it. When you don't put your name on it, that's the signal to them that you don't want to be identified. They won't point you out, or nobody would ever tell them anything. I've sent stuff in before and nobody's ever come after me. I think it's the only thing you can do."

"Thanks, Gloria. I'm sorry, I guess I dropped the ball."

"We both did. Don't apologize. Just make sure you send everything you've got to QA. Mark it 'Attention Bob Stoner.' That way it'll go right to the top."

Two days later, a package arrived in the Office of Risk Management marked 'Bob Stoner - Confidential.' It was forwarded to the orthopedist's office, where he opened it and read through the contents. He recognized it immediately for what it was. Another anonymous complaint. Except this one made him livid. It wasn't the obvious stupidity with which the case was handled that made him so furious. It was the identity of the perpetrator. Dave Ring hadn't seen his doctor in over six months, so his physician wasn't willing to sign the death certificate. A post mortem examination was performed. Stoner called for the autopsy report, then called Ingelhart.

"Myron, this is Bob Stoner. Somebody sent me all the records of a patient you just took care of, a patient by the name of David Ring. Are you familiar with his case?"

"Sure. Poor guy had a big heart attack. Never had a chance."

"Cut the bullshit. The man died from a ruptured aorta. You had two goddamn hours to get him to the lab, and instead you sat on him."

"How was I supposed to know? His x-ray was normal."

"Listen, you dimwit, you're ruining the medical center. There was an autopsy. The family knows. There'll be publicity. The heat goes straight upstairs. Waterhouse is crazy enough already. I see here on the chart that Resnick pitched you this patient. What is it with you two? Can you possibly be that greedy? Aren't you making enough money? You aren't even allowed to take rectal temps on dogs in the lab! This is it! I've had it. If I get one more complaint through the committee about you or Clyde or Randy, you're on your own." Stoner slammed down the receiver.

He was on a roll. Ignited by anger, he dialed the ER. "This is Bob Stoner. Let me speak to Clyde Resnick. Oh, he is, is he? Well, why don't you interrupt his big meeting with the drug rep and tell him that Dr. Stoner is on the phone. Tell him that he's about to go naked. Yes, I said go naked. Please use those exact words. He'll understand." Stoner fumed while he waited for Resnick to come to the telephone. "Clyde, I just got off the phone with Myron. He says he really appreciates you sending him the referral the other night. That's the good news. The bad news is that he killed the patient."

"Hey, Bob, you sound pretty angry. Are you mad at somebody?"

"Mad at somebody? Mad at somebody?" Stoner put his lips as close to the speaker as he could and then lowered his voice. "I'm so fucking mad that I could walk over to the ER right now, drag your ass out into the parking lot and rip your head off. I'm so mad I could take your left nut and stitch it to your forehead with a jackhammer. But you know what? I'll tell you how mad I am. Right now, I'm so mad that I think it's time to cut you boys loose, and see if you can make your own way in the world. Let's see what QA does with this one if Wiley and I keep our hands off it."

Resnick had been chewed out by Stoner before, but this had a different ring to it. Stoner was really off the deep end, and that wouldn't do any of them any good.

"You know, it isn't the way it looks. I tried to call Ed Ashley first, but he wasn't available. I'm pretty sure that Myron tried, too."

"Don't fuck with me, Clyde. You're a liar! I know damn well what happened. As rich as you boys are, you still keep greasing each other. Well, this is the end. I've got the paperwork on this one, and I'm turning it over to the committee. I have to. I'm gonna abstain. We'll let them decide."

Resnick couldn't let that happen. He carried an old familiar card, and even though Stoner had seen it before, Resnick had no choice but to play it again.

"Bob, before you do anything stupid, remember that you're in this as deep as we are."

"Maybe I am, Clyde, but I'm not sure that I care any more. Maybe what happened isn't so bad. It was a long time ago. I just watched, remember? Besides, I'm not taking a big bonus like some people I know."

"That's your problem, if it's even true. The bonus isn't the point. It doesn't change what happened. If anybody goes down, we all go down together. Bob, you're just like the rest of us. Don't be so self-righteous."

Stoner faced the usual hurdle. He knew that Resnick was right, but at this particular moment he couldn't bring himself to back down. At least he wanted the satisfaction of making Clyde sweat.

"Well, I haven't made up my mind what I'll do. Just in case, you'd better look into plane tickets to South America. See ya, buddy."

After he hung up on Resnick, Stoner still hadn't vented all of his anger. He called Wiley Waterhouse.

The Dean listened and barely spoke, except to interject a few "whens" and "whys." When Stoner finished relating the contents of the QA report and his conversations with Ingelhart and Resnick, he asked Waterhouse what he ought to do.

"Nothing."

"Nothing? I'm sick of doing nothing. We've got to do *something*. These guys are wearing us out. We can't keep covering for them forever. It's time to start pushing them around."

"Bob, use your head. We have to be able to push them in the right direction. It's a no-win situation. If you throw Myron to the committee, of course they'll nail him. Then they'll want to review all of the cases where he got let off. Then they'll get full of themselves and start looking at Randy and Clyde again. No, I don't think we can have QA do this for us. This is private business. Let me think about it. I'll come up with something."

"You used to, Wiley, but not for a long time. Try to make it stick."

"I will, my friend. You keep doing your part, and I'll do mine."

Waterhouse was beside himself. Despite his best efforts to keep the adverse publicity under control, the bad press kept breaking though. The Chancellor was demanding explanations and damage control. The Branscomb Board of Trustees didn't tolerate bad outcomes. If there was another Dave Ring, the Dean's head would be on the block.

After the autopsy, the body was released to the diener, the man in charge of the dead. Down in his basement department in the Anatomy Building, Woody Gump read the toe tag and got that old sinking feeling in the pit of his stomach. When the bodies came from the hospital, they were tagged by service, doctor, and tentative diagnosis. Woody got to see everyone's medical mistakes, but it was unwritten policy that they weren't to be discussed outside of the embalming suite. It was more than obvious who contributed the most to the mortality statistics. The tags on the stiffs from the O.R. were signed by Randy Schmatz two to one over any other anesthesiologist, and the ER death sheets more often than not by Clyde Resnick. The diener talked to himself.

"Well, lookee here. I haven't seen one of these in awhile. Ingelhart's back in business! Aorta blown apart. The history form says they didn't take him to the cath lab or nothing. Wonder why not? I thought they ran Myron out of town. You don't think they're lettin' him fool with folks' hearts again, do you?" In the old days, there had been quite a few contributions from Myron Ingelhart, but lately his numbers had dropped off.

Woody furrowed his brow and rubbed his temples. How on Earth could they still let him near people? He wondered if it would ever end. There had to be something somebody could do.

CHAPTER 26

Frank had avoided direct contact with Wiley Waterhouse, because he knew that if the Dean grew suspicious, he would be the most likely person to run for cover. But it was taking too long working on the others. Frank was impatient to find a way to get inside the sanctuary without Waterhouse suspecting that something was up. He was even considering a scouting session at the Dean's home when he got a message that led to a brainstorm. The Assistant Dean for Student Affairs had called to ask him to visit her office. She wanted to discuss his advisee's performance in biochemistry class.

Lauren tried hard to establish a friendship with her classmate, even though it was hit or miss, depending on Malinda's mood. Sometimes Malinda was receptive and open. Other times she was the icewoman. Although Lauren didn't always confide in Malinda, she appreciated her more experienced perspective.

There was little reciprocity. Lauren had been told next to nothing about Malinda's past, and had begun to accept that her questions would be answered with simple positives and negatives, sans any conversational embellishments. Still, she kept trying.

"Why are you so down on Sam?" Malinda hadn't dated the entire semester, which Lauren attributed to her fastidious attitude. Malinda disapproved of Lauren's relationship with Sam, even though she hardly knew anything about him.

"There's no place for romance in medical school. If you can call the way he treats you romantic."

"Malinda, I think you have the wrong impression. He's a serious, thoughtful person. If you spent some time with him, you'd see it in a second. And you know how fabulous Dr. Klawitter is. Sam worships the ground he walks on. It's absolutely amazing how they've taken to each other. Sam's lucky to have him as an advisor, because he's one of the most highly respected doctors at the medical center."

"Enough. I get the point."

"And you have to admit that Sam's kind of cute."

"Lauren, I'm not just a creature of the library. You're not the only person in the class that lusts after those buns. I've watched the other women. You have some competition." Malinda *had* noticed.

"Hey, hey, hey! Hands off! I saw him first."

Malinda smiled, then allowed herself a small chuckle. Under other circumstances, she might have enjoyed some time alone with Sam, but he was Lauren's. "Be careful, Lauren. I don't want to see you get hurt."

"Neither do I." There was an awkward moment of silence. "Let me buy you a drink."

"OK."

Lauren poured two glasses of wine. They sipped in silence for a few minutes. When Malinda tried to make polite conversation, it came out as interrogatory.

"So tell me more about Dr. Klawitter. How is he going to deal with the anesthesiologist who killed his cousin?"

"How did you know about that?"

"You told me, I think." Malinda had forgotten where their conversation left off and Lauren's diary began.

"How would I know? We haven't talked about it. Frank still gets pretty moody and depressed. Sam says he blames himself."

"That's ridiculous. I mean, that's probably ridiculous. He shouldn't do that to himself. It's bad enough that it happened. Self recrimination won't bring her back." Malinda was subdued, obviously affected by the subject. Lauren felt closer to her.

"You're right, but Sam says Frank's having trouble with it, so he's working on something."

"Working on something?"

"I don't know what it is. When Frank starts to get bitter or sad about his cousin, Sam reminds him to be patient. Or something like that. It's probably nothing."

Perhaps nothing, perhaps something. It was hard to believe that this could be a coincidence. Like a wild animal downwind from a thunderstorm, Malinda suddenly sensed danger. This could ruin everything. Sam and Frank had just taken on a new meaning for her.

CHAPTER 27

Myron Ingelhart wasted no time getting started on his new conditioning regimen. He was going to beat that cocky medical student if it was the last thing he did.

His workouts lasted all day. He awoke at dawn and jogged a couple of miles, then sat in the sauna. After breakfast, he headed over to the local YMCA, where he trained in the weight room. Even though he would have preferred the housestaff gym, he didn't want to take a chance that he would run into Sam again before their competition. There was no point in showing the young man any progress and motivating him.

Two hours of pumping iron in the morning were followed by a half hour on the exercise bike. After a high protein lunch, he took a nap. Most afternoons and into the early evening, he was at the gym lifting weights again. If he exercised his arms in the morning, he worked his legs in the late session. He began to look unusually fit, even for him, so he started spending two evenings a week in the tanning salon. If he was going to be a big-time weightlifter, he needed to look like one.

Despite the fact that Myron was in his fifth decade, his muscles toned and grew. The changes were imperceptible in the beginning. Myron had to irritate his muscles and tear down their fibers before the subcellular machinery of anaerobic fitness began to remodel and build. He was visibly rewarded in the third week when he gained five pounds, but his waistline didn't expand. He loaded 200 pounds on the bar and heaved it off his chest. It wasn't pretty, but he benched it.

From that point forward, Myron made steady progress. By the middle of November, he was up to 225 pounds, and by the fourteenth he could lift 250 pounds twice. He had exceeded his target and was still going strong. Unless he broke his arm or suffered a stroke between today and tomorrow, he was going to win.

On the appointed day, Myron wore a sweatshirt over a new black Gold's Gym tanktop with an iridescent green cartoon weightlifter hefting an enormous drooping barbell. Since he was early, he decided to warm up. He was finishing a dozen sit-ups when Sam walked in.

"Howdy. I'm glad to see you showed up. How are you feeling?"

"I think you're in for a bit of a surprise." Ingelhart pulled off his sweatshirt and tensed the muscles in his chest. Sam eyed Myron and whistled his approval.

"What did you do, get a gallon of silicone? Absolutely phenomenal. This isn't fair."

Myron grinned. "The body's a curious thing. You can do just about anything you want if you put your mind to it." He stretched his arms behind his back, then walked over to the bench. "Might as well get started. You wanna go first? I assume you remember what happens if I do 245 and you can't do 295?"

"Doctor, you've been sandbagged. I could already do 295 the last time we were here."

Ingelhart saw the scam. He didn't know whether to be angry or amused. How stupid he had been! He should have made him try 295 the last time, just to be certain that he wasn't being set up.

"You scoundrel! I would've never taken you for a cheat, but I guess I ought to know better than to trust a medical student. Now, who lifts first? Since this was my idea, I should be the gracious host and let you go ahead of me. Do you want to warm up, or are you going to try for the big one right off the bat?"

Sam looked closely at Ingelhart, then at the bench. "Two ninety-five's a lot of weight. I think I better do a few warm-ups, just to be sure I don't pull anything. That wouldn't be too good, now, would it? Let's just put on 145. I'll work my way up. You can do the same if you want."

"No need. I'm already warm. When you're completely finished, I'll go."

"Suit yourself." Sam dropped to the floor and did ten push-ups, then rolled over onto his back and stretched his hamstrings. When he lay down on the bench, Myron stepped behind him.

"Need a spot?"

"Not yet, but thanks. I should be fine until I get to about 250. After that, I'll need to be spotted on everything."

Myron stepped back and sat down on the bench. If he lost the bet... He hadn't forgotten that he was supposed to tell Sam something about Waterhouse. Well, *that* would be easy.

Sam reached up and felt for the bar. He slid his hands back and forth until he was satisfied with their alignment, then pushed up and locked his elbows. This was just a warm-up, so it was easy. Sam let the weight descend to his chest, then pushed it up slowly and deliberately, exhaling softly. Breathe in on the downstroke, out on the upstroke. He performed five repetitions, then set the weight back in the metal saddle.

"Nicely done. You look strong."

"My sister would look strong with this weight." Sam was having fun with Ingelhart. "Put on a couple of twenty-fives."

"That'll take it to 195. Are you sure you want to go up so fast?"

"I can add. I don't want to burn myself out in the basement when I have to get to the attic. This isn't a workout. It's a competition, remember?"

Myron put a 25-pound plate on each end. Sam stayed on the bench. He extended his arms quickly and snatched the bar off its rack. This time he exercised faster, doing three repetitions in less than ten seconds. Anderson set the bar back in its cradle with a crash.

"That felt pretty good. I'm gonna take a minute breather. Go ahead and swap the twenty-five for a forty-five. I believe that makes 235."

"Yes it does. You have a long way to go, my boy. A long way to go. This is just about where we left off last time."

Sam massaged his triceps and shook his arms at his sides. He didn't answer Myron, because he was pretending to concentrate on the next lift. He took three deep breaths, then nodded. It was the unspoken signal that he was ready to go again.

"Why don't you let me spot you this time? I won't do anything to break your concentration."

"That's OK. I really don't want any help until the next level. Stand back." Myron walked over to the water cooler. Sam nestled back into the bench and positioned his hands more deliberately. He stared at the bar, then pushed it up off the rack. In one impeccably smooth motion, he pumped the bar up and down twice. It appeared effortless.

Myron was getting nervous. He knew that there was a world of difference between 235 pounds and 295 pounds, but Sam looked extremely confident. The next interval would be critical. He watched as Sam added back the 25-pound plates, to bring the total to 285 pounds.

"I'll take a spot now."

"Do you want a lift-off?"

"No thanks. And don't help me unless I ask, even if it looks like I'm having trouble. Sometimes I pause in the middle of a rep and then explode at the end. It's a style I learned for the Junior Olympics."

"Junior Olympics? You were in the Junior Olympics? You didn't say anything about being in the Junior Olympics!"

"You didn't ask. But don't worry. I only took fifth in the Olympic trials. Somebody else holds the world record for my weight class."

Myron was angry. "I don't believe this! The bet's off! This is a con job."

"Listen, I didn't force you into this. If you want to quit, that's OK with me. I'm sure that everyone will understand. We can just sit and chat about Waterhouse." Sam got off the bench. "A deal's a deal."

"Forget it! The bet's back on. Get on the bench. You can't do any better than a tie."

Sam smiled and repositioned himself under the bar. He grabbed the bar, pushed it up, then pressed it once. He struggled and ramped up the theatrics, which weren't wasted on Myron. "Hmm. That wasn't as easy as it should have been. Let's see, I've got 285 on there now. I need another ten pounds. Why don't you add a five to each side? That should do 'er." Myron slid a plate on each end. He'd never seen someone Sam's size attempt that much weight before. Sam had no intention of hurting himself. It was time for a great performance.

"Listen up, professor. I'm gonna count to three. When I say 'three' I want you to give me a lift. I'm gonna try and do this once. Whatever you do, don't help me unless I ask you to. OK?"

"Son, I was lifting weights before you were born."

Sam put his hands on the bar, then took them off. He wiped his palms on his pants, then wiped them on his chest. He hung his arms down at his side and shook them, then wiped them on his pants again. As he grabbed the bar for the second time, he wiggled around on the bench. After a few seconds, he began to count, taking a deep breath between each shout.

"One. Two. Three." Myron grabbed the bar between Sam's hands and together they hoisted it straight up. Sam hesitated for a split second, then lowered the barbell quickly to his chest. He threw his thorax up off the bench and thrust his hips as hard as he could. The bar came up halfway. Sam held his breath and strained, reddening his face and making the veins in his neck and forehead bulge out. He grunted and groaned and huffed and puffed, but the bar went no further. It wasn't going to happen. He really couldn't lift it.

"Take it."

"What did you say?"

"I said take it, goddammit! I can't do it."

"That's what I thought you said." Myron was grinning from ear to ear. He leaned over and grabbed the bar to help Sam push it up. Together they returned it to its resting-place.

"Well damn! That really pisses me off! I lifted more than this yesterday. I don't understand it."

"Nice try, hot shot. Take the twenty-fives off." He had an afterthought. "Then put on a couple of fives."

"Just like that? Take the twenty-fives off? Don't you want to warm up?" Sam wanted Ingelhart to do as many sets as possible, at least to tire himself out. He needed the information. "You really ought to do at least a couple of light reps just to stretch a bit. You're gonna rip the daylights out of your back."

"Don't give me that bull. I warmed up before you got here. I feel great. Besides, I'm not a big stud like you. But evidently I'm smarter. No, I don't think I need to warm up any more. I'll just take 255 right here, right now."

"The bet was for 245. You only need to lift 245."

"Well, Mr. Junior Olympics, I'm going to teach you a lesson. This is what you can do when you put your mind to it. Are you going to help me or not?"

"Sure." Sam pulled the large plate off his side while Myron did the same at the opposite end of the bar. Myron flexed his muscles a few times while Sam added back the smaller plates. The cardiologist kept preening, but Sam wasn't looking. Myron lay down on the bench. There would be plenty of time to rub it in after he lifted the weight.

"Need a lift-off?"

"Not necessary, young man. Step back and watch a real pro go to work."

"What about a spot?"

"If you insist. I don't think you'll have much to do. On second thought, no. You can just sit down and rest. I'll be fine. Why don't you have a drink?" Sam shrugged his shoulders. It was his turn to stand by the cooler.

Myron put his hands on the bar and closed his eyes. "Aaaaarghh!" With a mighty roar, he lifted the bar up over his head. After a few quick breaths, he lowered it to his chest. With the euphoria of the triumphant, he threw it back up. Myron held the weight over his head. He chided Sam while he balanced the bar.

"Ha! Told you I could do it. Now watch this." Myron did three more repetitions, each with increasing difficulty. He barely got the last one up, having to arch his back way off the bench to do it.

"OK. You've made your point. You can put the weight back now."

"No, young man. I'm not finished yet. I can do one more. That'll make five. And you couldn't even do one." Ingelhart leered as he strained under the weight. His eyeballs were bulging. "I can't wait to catch Waterhouse's expression when you wiggle your fanny in his face." Myron grimaced as he lowered the bar to his chest for one last attempt. He pushed. Even though he threw his entire body into the effort, the bar would only go halfway up. Ingelhart's arms were spent and he couldn't get the weight high enough to lock his elbows. "Help."

"What did you say?" Sam held a cupped hand to his ear. He was pouring himself a cup of water.

"I said help! I need help. I can't get it up." Myron was out of breath and the weight sank slowly toward his chest."

"Nobody made you try to lift it five times." Sam approached to help him, but slowly, because he wanted Myron to agonize a little first.

Sam underestimated the cardiologist's fatigue. Myron panicked. With a convulsive promethean effort, he tried one last time to hoist the bar. Because his arms were like rubber, he lost his balance and the bar drifted backwards. Myron's grip loosened and the bar slammed down full force onto his neck. Sam watched in slow-motion horror as Ingelhart's larynx was crushed. The spent weightlifter's arms and legs jerked a few times, then hung limp. The bar tipped and one end crashed to the floor. Before Sam had a chance to react, blood was running freely from Myron's mouth and nostrils. Sam wrested the bar off Myron.

Sam felt for a pulse. There was none. He knew how to recognize death, but his mind refused to register that Myron was really dead. Something must be done to reverse that split second when it happened. He was just getting a drink of water! Sam moved toward the cooler, as though moving back in time, when utter panic seized him.

What could he do? Sam concentrated on regaining control, getting his brain to work properly. He returned to the body and leaned the bar back onto the cardiologist's neck. If Sam reported this accident, he feared he would be asked to leave Branscomb, at the very least. Worse, he might be accused of manslaughter — involuntary or not. Sam decided. No one saw him enter this room; he had to make sure that no one saw him leave.

Sam walked to the door, cracked it, and peered down the hallway. Empty. He slid out and walked away, more frightened than he'd ever been in his life.

Sam sat in the study. For the first time since Sam had come to Branscomb, the men exchanged harsh words. Frank was furious in fear of what might have been discovered. Sam's remorse was for the man who had been mutilated by the metal cylinder. He felt like a murderer.

"You didn't waste much time, did you. What really happened?" After tortured nights in which he examined every aspect of their relationship, Frank remained skeptical of Sam's claim that Myron's sudden death had been an accident. He shared his doubts with Sam, who was quick to defend himself.

"Damn it, Frank, it wasn't what it seemed! I didn't do it."

"Sam. Remember what we've been through. It's OK if it happened. You don't have to tell me how you did it. Just come clean about whether it only happened or you made it happen."

"I guess I made it happen. But I didn't mean to. I'm not a killer. I never meant for him to die. I was just trying to get some information."

"And?"

"Like I told you, nothing. As usual, all Myron wanted to talk about was himself. Right up to the end. Christ, I'm sorry! Frank, I'll do better with the others."

"Others! You've got to be kidding. Listen Sam, this was a bad idea. I think you should get back to your studies and forget all this."

"It was a freak. It could never happen again."

"Sam, the man is dead."

"Jesus, Frank, don't you think I know that? Remember, I didn't volunteer for this. I was only trying to help you."

That was true. Even though Frank had thought he knew enough about Sam to trust him without reservation, he was shaken by what happened to Ingelhart. He needed a chance to get his confidence back. He was trying as hard as he could to believe Sam's story, but he couldn't help thinking back to Kuwait, and how Sam had fired on that junkie. Perhaps there was a side of Sam that he hadn't fully appreciated. He suddenly wished he knew him better.

"Look, I want you to be more careful. No more crazy stunts. Do you think you can manage that?"

"I ought to be able to. There are plenty of opportunities that I've avoided, because that is the way I've been playing it. Let me just go slow and keep an eye on things. If you don't hear anything from me, you can assume everything is fine."

"All right. Let me know what you come up with." After a long pause, Frank added, "At least there's some consolation. There's one less of them now. He can't kill any more patients."

At the request of Ingelhart's family, there was no autopsy. The coroner did a superficial examination of the body and confirmed that it was an accident. Ingelhart's remains were sent to Woody Gump to be prepared for the memorial service. Woody read the official coroner's report over and over again. It was incredible how someone could miss the obvious. Woody had no idea who had done it, but he was certainly pleased by Ingelhart's mode of exit. He decided not to mention his observation that the bar had been found leaning on the wrong side of Myron's neck.

CHAPTER 28

Elaine Mahnke grew up in a working-class suburb of Harrisburg, Pennsylvania. Her parents divorced when she was eight and her brother Steve was twelve. The children stayed with their mother, Gladys, who was extremely bitter. Her philandering husband moved away with his secretary, and it was a constant struggle for Mrs. Mahnke to extract alimony payments. To support the children, Gladys worked full-time as a realtor, which meant that the kids spent a lot of time together alone.

From the time of the divorce, her mother lectured Elaine about the unreliability of men and the vicissitudes of marriage. The little girl listened constantly to harangues about the absolute necessity for a woman to be self-reliant and to have a career. To be a success in her mother's eyes, Elaine would have to grow up to be a doctor or lawyer. The impressionable child took it to heart.

Steve took on added importance for Elaine. She adored him. The age spread and sex difference were perfect for them, because they never felt that they were competing for anything. Even though Steve was Mr. Popular, he always made time for his sister. He seemed to have a special intuition about her, to understand her needs in an uncanny way that was remarkable and touching.

Steve's achievements became all the more outstanding because of his struggle with diabetes. Before anyone realized he was sick, the boy would come home from basketball practice more fatigued than he should have been, and developed an insatiable thirst. He lost his appetite, even for his favorite foods. One deathly cold winter night after practice, he asked to go to bed without dinner, and told his mother that he was going to take a little nap. It seemed odd, but Gladys didn't think that much about it. An hour later, a sixth sense told her to check on her son. When she walked into the bedroom, she found him face down on the floor, struggling to breathe thirty times a minute in a deep and unnatural way. She knelt down and shook him, but he wouldn't awaken. She rolled him over and saw his lips split and covered with blood. His breath had a foul, fruity acetone smell, and he was choking on his own saliva. Steve was in a diabetic coma. Gladys screamed for Elaine, who raced to her side. When she discovered her brother unconscious, she burst into tears and could barely talk to the operator as she pleaded for an ambulance. She was certain that he was going to die and begged God to intervene.

Steve's first serious struggle with diabetes was nearly fatal. He was in the hospital for two weeks before the doctors could bring his blood sugar under control with insulin injections. He was classified as a brittle diabetic. By the time he was discharged, he had lost fifteen pounds and looked like he'd been starved for a year. The tests showed that he had probably been diabetic for a long time, because his vision was diminished and his renal function was about half of what it should have been. Early kidney failure was a bad prognostic sign. Steve had the most severe form of juvenile onset diabetes, the kind that would be debilitating and relentless despite anything the doctors could do. In those days, all they had to offer were diet and insulin. Transplanting a pancreas was undreamed of, and kidney dialysis was cumbersome and extremely expensive.

During the first recovery, Elaine clung desperately to her brother. No human being could have been more devoted than she. The absence of her father was still a constant torment, and now the thought of losing her brother drove Elaine to lock onto Steve as if it was going to be her last task on Earth. On the other hand, Gladys was more pragmatic. She stepped up her unsophisticated emancipation rhetoric. Doctors and deities were men. Like the husband and father who had abandoned his family, heaven and hospital were about to stick it to the Mahnkes one more time. She knew that her son was going to die. Gladys wanted Elaine to understand that part of the reason such things happened was because women weren't empowered, they weren't successful, they weren't wealthy. It wasn't logical, but it helped to carry her through this dreadful tragic period.

Steve's diabetes alternated between periods of muted remission and horrifying descents into physiological hell. When his disease flared, he grew weak and nauseated, acquired pneumonias and disseminated fungal infections, and lapsed into episodes of ketoacidosis. It was the worst kind of torment, because his mind and spirit never weakened. Even when his blood sugar was nearly 1000 and he was so dehydrated that his skin wrinkled like an old man, Steve mentated with monastic clarity. He never grew angry, only sad, knowing full well what he was about to lose. Less than three years after his first bout of diabetes, he barely resembled the young teenager with everything in the world to look forward to. Instead, he became a pasty-faced ghoulish caricature with wasted muscles and scarecrow features. His retinas scarred, optic nerves atrophied, and the clear vitreous within his eyeballs became opacified by the cellular debris that followed frequent spontaneous hemorrhages. Both of his kidneys shut down and in doing so triggered his immune system to quit. The simplest bacterial infections were magnified a hundredfold, and in his final winter, Steve endured pneumonia, a spinal abscess and meningitis. In the end, he suffered constantly, and Elaine shared every moment with him.

After her brother's death, Elaine succumbed to her mother's rhetoric. The attempts to find peace were no match for the cruel verbal venom generated by a woman who had lost her husband and son in rapid succession. Gladys quickly was able to convince her daughter that although Steve might not have ultimately survived, it all could have been handled differently. In her renditions, the doctors had been insensitive, the scientists inadequate and the insurance companies deceitful. Elaine became a diligent student of her mother and swore academic revenge upon the forces that conspired to keep her and other women in their places. In the midst of her adolescent confusion, it was a sign of the strength of her character that she came away from the hate and sadness wanting to find a cure for diabetes, and in the process, to excel in ways that could bring her to the forefront of medicine.

Elaine became a profoundly capable student. She graduated as valedictorian from her high school and received a full scholarship to Pennsylvania State University, where she graduated magna cum laude as a student of biology and genetics. Studies became her life. She had no significant extracurricular activities. The pre-meds were a cutthroat and highly competitive group, but she sliced through them like a hot knife through butter. At least once a month, she drove home and spent the weekend with her mother, who now lived her life completely through the achievements of her daughter. Gladys remained militant, so Elaine wasn't able to make the transition away from the intense disappointment with life that drove her to academic success. She continued to push herself and was reinforced by the reward system of her mother, who meted out her love in larger measure following each successful report from the Dean.

Mahnke could have gone to medical school anywhere in the country. Although she was accepted to Michigan, Harvard and Branscomb, she chose the University of Pennsylvania in order to stay close to her mother. In her second year of medical school, two things happened that changed Elaine's life. One afternoon, she was called to the Dean of Students' office. He sat Elaine down and broke it to her. For the rest of her career, the words "I'm afraid I have bad news for you" would be difficult for Elaine to speak. Her mother had died instantly of a pulverized liver in an automobile accident after her car had been struck by a truck driver who ran a stop sign. It was a closed casket affair. There was no chance for a final visit, no exchange of hugs, nothing more to discuss. Whatever thoughts they had wanted to share would be left unspoken forever. Elaine's entire family was gone.

It turned out that Gladys had always had a fatalistic attitude. She left her daughter an inheritance of nearly a million dollars from life insurance policies she had taken out on herself and the kids when her husband walked out. The money meant nothing to Elaine in her grief. On the advice of a family friend, she invested in Treasury bills and the stocks of computer corporations. In less than a year, interest rates dropped and Silicon Valley blossomed, so she tripled her money. Elaine didn't pay much attention, because the dollars contributed nothing to the internal engine fueled by her heartache. Her sole purpose in life was to achieve for her dead brother and mother.

A month after Gladys Mahnke's death, Elaine noticed that her fingers twitched when she rested her hands on her lap. It wasn't noticeable to others, but it was bothersome to Elaine. In the past when she was tired, she had suffered from imperceptible facial twitches, mostly around her eyes, but never really paid them any attention. These hand movements were different — definitely involuntary — and seemed to be controlled by a puppeteer other than her own central nervous system.

At first, she subconsciously tried to attribute the phenomenon to stress and fatigue. Although Elaine was a solid medical student, her class-mates included some of the brightest and most ambitious young college graduates in the country. The academic environment at Penn was cut-throat. The constant one-upmanship took its toll emotionally. In the peri-od immediately following her mother's death, Elaine's moods swung wild-ly. Distracted by the slightest interpersonal conflicts, she literally tried to work herself out of her funk. Long stretches of 18- to 20-hour days drained her physically and emotionally. In the intensive care unit during a grueling six-week, every-other-night on-call ICU rotation, Elaine finally cracked.

One morning at 5:30 A.M. before rounds, the intern on the service walked into the unit and found her slumped in front of the glass parti-tion that divided the doctors' charting cubicle from the patient care area. Mahnke sat on the floor holding a chart in her hand and staring out into the unit. She intermittently cried softly and talked to herself, mumbling that she "couldn't do it any more." She had scribbled primitive stick fig-ures of a man with a stethoscope and an enormous penis and a woman with an arrow through her midsection. With a black magic marker, she had changed the name on the patient's chart to her own and then written orders: 'Vital signs - none. Diet - work and discrimination. Medications: love and rest. Do not disturb. I don't feel anything. There's no hope.' The words were penned in elementary block letters, the way she had written in second grade.

The intern who took call with Elaine's team led her like a tranquil-ized laboratory animal to the Dean's office. After a two-hour session with the Assistant Dean, Elaine was granted a three-month leave of absence. She spent most of the time alone and in counseling with a private psy-chologist. When she returned to school, she found out that she had been awarded credit for the full ICU rotation.

The first few months back were shaky, but Elaine seemed to worry less than before about her grades. She picked up steam. However, her hands began to shake worse than ever, particularly when she handled medical instruments. After three weeks of trembling, Elaine made an appointment with an outside neurologist. The doctor asked her to per-form multiple manual tasks. In the beginning, he was concerned that she was showing signs of multiple sclerosis or another progressive demyelinating disease that could profoundly affect her ability to function. After yielding a gallon of blood samples, completing cognitive tests and being irradiated for bone films, CT scans and finally a myelogram image of her spinal cord, Elaine was labeled with the diagnosis of "benign Parkinsonian intention tremor." Elaine could expect her hands to shake whenever she attempted to perform a complex manipulation, and sometimes during simple digital motions as well. The doctor told her that this would happen with increasing intensity over the years. There was no cure.

Through the remainder of medical school, Elaine was able to use medications to subdue most of the shaking. At one point she became habituated to low doses of Valium, which calmed her nerves and partially controlled her tremor. Alcohol wasn't that helpful, and her tolerance for the sedative-muscle relaxant set her at a baseline of neurologic excitation which demanded constant sedation if she was not to become jittery. If Elaine missed a dose of Valium she shook more. Elaine became an addict. It was subtle, but it was real.

The dependent medical student was able to achieve above-average grades and received glowing evaluations from the faculty. The only people who had an inkling about Elaine's drug dependency were the Assistant Dean, to whom she reported regularly, and the rotation supervisor on the psychiatry service. He noticed that Elaine identified more strongly with substance abuse patients than one would have expected from her background. However, his inferential observation wasn't deemed appropriate for Elaine's formal record, and was deleted by the Dean's office from the composite student recommendation which would go out under signature as she applied for internships.

Elaine matched as a first-year resident into the general surgery training program at Johns Hopkins in Baltimore, which was a huge and unexpected honor, particularly for a woman. During the ensuing five years of basic surgery training, her emotional and physical problems were minimal, which seemed a deserved respite in the midst of her run of bad luck. Perhaps she could get past her unfortunate circumstances and bad genes. As she had vowed off and on for the past fifteen years, Elaine would devote her life to the study of kidney disease associated with diabetes. She turned down an offer to be a rare female Chief Surgery Resident in order to become a postgraduate fellow in a combined program in endocrinology and renal medicine.

Many of her friends were married and starting families, but Elaine never broke from the influence of her mother. Her attitude toward men was dispassionate and removed. It was a calculated decision never to have children, although she felt the pangs. Elaine never wavered from her desire to be a transplant surgeon. She threw herself at her work in a way that made her shine among equally talented and classically male counterparts.

During her fellowship, Elaine cared for all of the patients on dialysis, and watched the emergence of renal transplantation as a major factor in the survival of diabetics with kidney failure. After four years of medical school, five years of surgical training and four additional years of fellowship studies, Elaine was accepted as an NIH research assistant, to begin yet another educational process.

Although Elaine was nearly 35 years old when she finally finished all of her training, she was still relatively young by surgical standards. With her background, she was heralded by her mentors in Baltimore and Bethesda as a phenomenon, and got scooped up quickly by Raymond Montague at Branscomb. Wiley Waterhouse, who had originally recommended Elaine to Montague, encouraged him to offer her a spectacular compensation package. Her research on immunosuppressive agents in organ transplantation was on the cutting edge. As a young surgeon with a brilliant future, she was to be the dream player on Montague's team of surgeons, and a role model for women in surgery.

Unfortunately, her peripheral neurons had long since refused to cooperate. Elaine had been able to finesse her way through surgical training with a minimum of attention called to her tremor. Still, at times it was quite noticeable. One time when she had been a resident, her arm jerked when she was changing a patient's dressing after a breast implant, and she nearly sliced off the woman's areola. It soon became apparent to most of the senior surgeons that something wasn't right. She was assigned easier cases, so that she wouldn't have to do a lot of detail work like vascular or nerve reconstructions.

As a junior faculty member, Elaine saw her physical disability worsen rapidly. During flares of unsteadiness that sometimes lasted for months, her surgical technique and speed in the operating room suffered. After all she had been through, it didn't seem fair. It was as though she was being punished for some immutable sin committed in a former life.

Elaine had to do something to retain her position and career. She had long since negated the option of having a family to fall back on. As her hands became more shaky, she rekindled her enormous dependency upon sedatives. Elaine once again became addicted, but this time her tremors broke through the pharmacopoeia of suppressors.

Within months, she derived no benefit from the drugs. Rather, they caused her to lose the coordination, reflexes and split second judgement necessary for a competent surgeon. She made small mistakes in the O.R., which at first translated into minor mishaps and "take-backs." There were cases where patients needed to be returned to the operating room to retrieve a missing sponge or to re-approximate a bleeding staple line. Although Montague knew about her increasing problems, he was too busy at first to spend time with her in the O.R. to see for himself. He had a hard time believing that she was truly as bad as might be believed from the gossip. Montague was used to everybody picking on everybody else. Surgeons were notorious critics, so in the beginning he wrote the problem off to the usual ego bashing that ran rampant in an academic medical center. Moreover, if he was forced to give the rumors credence, it would be a tremendous black mark upon the Department of Surgery. My God, how could he admit that his boldest draft pick was an addict?

Montague should have stepped in early when he had the chance. Bad went to worse, as Elaine made surgical errors that she couldn't explain. Even if she had recognized the specific times when she blew a knot or trashed a graft, to admit those sorts of failures would have been professional suicide. When Montague confronted her, she was totally unwilling to even consider giving up her career in surgery. She would operate until they threw her out or she died. He became her proctor, which offended her greatly, and they argued repeatedly.

After Elaine's cases came up at morbidity and mortality conference more often than all the other surgeons combined, the Chairman of Surgery finally felt that he had to seek advice from Wiley Waterhouse. In a place like Branscomb, Montague knew that he could wind up with more misery from the solution than from the problem. Like it or not, the Dean needed to be involved.

Montague explained as much as he knew to Waterhouse, including a recitation of all of Mahnke's recent problems and why in his opinion she should be yanked from the O.R. He wanted to start with random drug testing, which required the Dean's approval. It was a pretty convincing account. Therefore, he was flabbergasted at Waterhouse's benevolence. Montague tried to debate, but Waterhouse read him a Gettysburg Address-like litany of reasons why someone like Elaine should be allowed to continue at the medical center for as long as possible. She was a woman, transplants were extremely important to the mission of the medical center, this was an issue for Human Resources, and so on and so forth. In Wiley's opinion, it would have to be a joint rehabilitation project by Waterhouse and Montague — there would be no swift firing or hint of a public reprimand. The Chairman of Surgery knew Waterhouse well enough to know when to back off, so for the time being he abandoned his attempt at expulsion. The Dean promised that he would meet with Dr. Mahnke to try to get at the root of her problem, and that he would take action if he couldn't make things improve. The next day, after a meeting with Waterhouse, Elaine requested an early sabbatical, which Montague granted immediately. One week after Sam and Lauren started medical school, Elaine flew to Phoenix and entered a drug rehabilitation program for professionals. She was to be gone for five months. All of her patients were reassigned.

CHAPTER 29

The bad news was unremitting. Every time Waterhouse turned around, one of them botched a case. He would have thought with Ingelhart gone, life would be easier, but it wasn't. Worse, he was having trouble with the cover-ups. There were notices of lawsuits. That would mean interrogatories. The families would find out more than they were seeking. The Chancellor called and told the Dean to "clean it up down there." He wondered aloud to Waterhouse whether there was a pattern, whether Wiley was "getting tired." Perhaps the Chancellor should form a committee to "look into things." Waterhouse trembled. If there was a real investigation, his omnipotence would vanish like an ice cube in the desert. If the truth came out — he couldn't bear to think about it.

For the most part, Fred Spencer now avoided the Dean. He was spending prodigious hours in the lab, and he rarely shared his results with Waterhouse. What had been a fabulous partnership was now a standoff. Waterhouse couldn't afford to lose their project. The Dean needed Fred to create some good news to counterbalance the adverse publicity the medical center was suffering at the hands of Schmatz and Resnick. Spencer was having none of it.

"You know, Wiley, it seems like you're losing control of this place, what with all the bad press lately. For awhile, you could keep the bad actors out of the spotlight, but now it's center stage for the boys. You're slipping a bit, aren't you?"

"Be careful, hotshot," Waterhouse hissed, "I don't see where you've done much lately." That was a mistake.

Spencer smiled. "I know exactly what you have to be doing right now. It seems like all the practice is "mal" and you can't stop it. Have you reconsidered stepping down?"

"It wouldn't matter. Like everything else, this too will pass. Nobody in my position would be able to do any better."

"Do you want me to try?"

Waterhouse glowered. "You need to stay focused in this lab, where you can do the most good. We need to create something marvelous, to get everybody's attention onto something else. So where are we on the reconstructions?"

"What's this *we* crap? *We* can talk about projects after I become Dean."

Waterhouse barked before he thought. He was tired of demands. "No, Fred. Not now. Just finish the work. As soon as we publish the results, you can have my spot. I promise. But until then, our project's the most important thing in your life."

"The most important thing in my life. The most important thing in my life." Fred strained the air through clenched teeth. "I'll tell you the most important thing in my life... putting my hands around your god-damn throat."

"Fred! You disappoint me. We're so close. Don't you see that?"

"No, Wiley. Please leave now."

Waterhouse looked back from the door. "Don't worry about Branscomb. I'll see to it that things don't get out of control. You can count on me."

"I always do." Spencer turned to his computer. The most important thing in his life.

CHAPTER 30

The Dean was out of town, so Valerie Snell could relax. He was always sniffing around her. A hand on the shoulder, a pat on the back, offering to rub her neck and shoulders, whispered innuendoes. Valerie found him revolting. She was disgusted by his sagging belly and bad breath, even more so by the fact that he was a braggart and a liar. She put up with him because she had no other choice.

There was a soft knock at her door.

"Come in," she called.

Frank Klawitter swung the door open and stood in the entryway. He was dressed in khaki pants and a cotton shirt opened at the neck. Valerie fixed her stare on a wisp of hair below his collarbone.

"Please come in. Did you have an appointment?"

"Yes, ma'am. You called my office. Said that you were concerned about something."

"Oh yes," answered Valerie, "Of course I did. Shut the door. You may or may not know I review the test scores of every medical student on a regular basis. Your advisee Sam Anderson scored extremely well on the biochemistry mid-term." Valerie paused and tilted her head, waiting for a response.

"Oh, really? That's great. What was his score?"

"Ninety-seven, the highest score in the class by ten points. His professor is amazed. Actually, he's more than amazed."

"That's terrific! I know he studied pretty hard. That's pretty wild, huh?"

"It's not wild. It might be unbelievable."

"Pardon me?"

"Frank, given that he barely passed the pop quiz in biochemistry last quarter and that he's not exactly burning up his other courses, it's hard for his professor to understand how he's suddenly able to achieve a 97 on an extremely difficult examination."

"Now wait a minute..."

"I'm trying to say this gently." Valerie reached across the table and took one of Frank's hands between her own. She squeezed it gently, and stroked the inside of his palm with her fingernails. It was a reflex. He sat down in front of her. "Frank, this is a real problem. You have to help me. We need to have a good explanation for his sudden outstanding performance in biochemistry."

"Do you have any suggestions?"

Valerie scratched her forehead. "I've got an idea. Let's work this through. You know, role play. You be Sam and I'll be me." Her smile was lascivious. Frank knew exactly where this was headed.

Valerie was Frank's big secret. More than a year ago they had discovered each other. After the first time there was no stopping them.

The gynecologist dropped to his knees. "Dr. Snell, all my life, I've wanted to be a doctor. I could give a damn about biochemical pathways and test scores. Honest, I don't have a clue how I pulled a 97 on that exam. If I had it to do all over again, I'd answer a whole bunch of questions wrong. I just want to take care of people, to be a *real* doctor."

Valerie laughed. "A little hokey, but very convincing. OK, it's my turn. Sam, have you ever examined anyone?"

"Ma'am?"

"Have you ever played doctor? Have you ever taken anyone's pulse, or listened to someone's heart?" Playing doctor was her favorite game.

"Well, sure."

Valerie climbed onto the top of her desk and knelt directly in front of Frank. Her skirt rode up to mid thigh as she leaned forward. "What should we do?"

"Please, Dr. Snell, teach me what I need to know."

Valerie swung her legs around and sat on the desk, knees apart. "Stand in front of me." Valerie took the fingertips of Frank's right hand and pressed them firmly against her neck underneath the angle of her jaw. "Feel my pulse."

Frank had both hands on her neck. Valerie closed her eyes and moaned softly. Her pulse was strong and rapid. Valerie was getting excited. It was always that way. Sex was high-voltage and irresistible — they stole their moments, often incautiously.

She took his left hand and moved it onto her left breast. "Feel my heart beating."

Frank put his right hand on her other breast and brushed her nipples in a circular motion.

"Slower. That's right. Look into my eyes."

Frank stared into that unmistakable look. *Beautiful and brainy,* he thought, *a woman in a million.* He adored her and her freedom. "Nice eyes." He leaned forward and with a quick sweeping motion, flicked his tongue around her earlobe. "Nice ears," he whispered.

Valerie hopped off her desk. She opened a drawer and rummaged to retrieve a shiny new stethoscope. Although Dr. Snell never saw any patients, she kept the instrument for ceremonial occasions. She placed the earpieces of the stethoscope into Frank's ears, then stood directly in front of him and pressed her chest against him. "I'm holding it against my heart. What do you hear?"

"Drums in a rainforest." Frank placed his hand over Valerie's and slid the bell of the stethoscope down to her abdomen. "Bubbles in a Jacuzzi, with a waterfall in the background."

"That's called a 'rush.' Kiss me." He pressed his lips against hers while she pulled his hand lower. Valerie was totally without sexual angst — no guilt, only pleasure and joy. If Frank wanted marriage at this time in his life, he'd choose Valerie. But neither was looking for that now. Meanwhile, they made each other very happy. "Examine me. Everywhere. Now. He won't come in." She was a temptress, a siren. She wanted him — even here. She squeezed the bulge in his pants.

With her mention of Waterhouse, Frank suddenly lost the moment. He pushed out both hands to ward her off. "No, darling, not now."

Valerie pouted in disappointment. "Whoa! What did I do?"

"Nothing. I'd just be more comfortable if I knew we couldn't be interrupted. Tonight. OK?"

Valerie traced a fingernail down Frank's nose. "Are you kidding? Of course it's OK." She helped him straighten his clothes. "Too bad, though. We were just getting to the good stuff."

"Val, is there really a problem with Sam's biochemistry score? I don't want to seem paranoid or anything, but if you know about it, maybe Waterhouse does too. I care a lot about that boy. Can I look at the Dean's files? I need to know if I have to set the record straight on anything."

Valerie shook her head. "You've gotta be kidding. Let you go through Waterhouse's stuff? No way! If he ever found out that I let someone into his office, I don't think I'd just get fired. I think he'd have me shot."

"It's important. I don't trust him. If it'll make you feel better, don't come in with me."

"I don't know, Frank, this is pretty unusual. What if someone walks in?"

"Just lock the doors. You can stand guard. If someone comes to the office, tell whoever it is that you'll be with them in a minute, slam your desk drawer real hard so that I can hear it, then wait to the count of fifty. I'll be out of the room and gone from the area by the time you let them in."

"I suppose so," Valerie responded with hesitation. "But the deal is, you find anything good and you have to tell me. You're in luck, because Waterhouse's office is open for the janitors, and they don't come by until after dinner. Shut the door behind you, so that I can't see what you're doing. I don't want them to torture it out of me. Better be careful about fingerprints, too." Valerie had an afterthought. "You know, come to think of it, there's a small safe in the wall behind that picture of Louis Pasteur over his desk. Waterhouse doesn't know that I know about it, but I've seen him close it up. Maybe there's something in there, but I don't know how you'd get in. It looks like the real thing."

"Where *is* Waterhouse?" asked Frank.

"At home. I just talked to him. He's been at the Midwestern Convention of Medical School Deans, or some other bullshit meeting like that. He won't be in the office for a few days. He's working on his memoirs, you know, something totally bogus, like how he won the war in the Middle East. He's so full of it."

Valerie caught a ferocious look from Frank. Why did he suddenly care so much about the Dean? For his part, Frank had long since grown sick of the intrigue. He wanted to tell Valerie everything. But he knew her as a lover, not a confidant, and it was safer for them both if she didn't know the real reason for searching the Dean's office.

"Did I say something wrong?"

"No, Val, not at all. Forget it. I was just thinking about something else for a second."

Valerie walked up to Frank and gently put her arms around him. "If you crack the safe, you owe me another office visit." She grabbed his buttocks and started to squeeze. Frank laughed, pulled away, and brushed her lips with a kiss.

The Dean's office was a junkyard of memorabilia. Waterhouse's collection of medical artifacts and antiques were all replicas. There were the usual pencil sketches and watercolor portraits of 18th and 19th century physicians commissioned by drug companies to subliminally promote their products. Every diploma and plaque ever awarded to Waterhouse was displayed prominently. For the sake of the parents of medical students, he had a gallery of class composite photographs aligned on one wall. The Dean was a man of unwavering pomp, so he kept his graduation cap, ceremonial robes and vestments hanging from a wooden stand in the corner opposite his desk. Directly behind his chair hung a small oil portrait of Louis Pasteur.

The rest of the room was a veritable clutter of professorial trappings. On the top of the Dean's desk was a marble mortar and pestle, a desk organizer full of Mont Blanc pens, and a small hinged frame with a photograph of Waterhouse at his medical school graduation. There were stacks of medical journals, all in pristine condition and unread. Next to the telephone was his trademark enormous jar of gourmet jellybeans. He loved to munch them when he chastised the medical students.

This was the inner sanctum of the medical school; the secretive, ritual inner office where the deals were made. Long ago, Waterhouse had the room soundproofed beneath the dark wood veneer. He would have built a secret passage to a dungeon if he could get away with it.

Frank stood in front of the portrait of the Pasteur painting and ran his fingertips around the edge of the picture frame to see if there were any trip wires attached. Satisfied that the frame wasn't rigged to alarm, he attempted to tilt it from side to side. It wouldn't budge. Upon closer inspection, there were two small set screws drilled through the corners which fixed the portrait to the wall. Frank used the Phillips head attachment on his army knife to extract the screws and free the picture from its position.

Just as Valerie had told him, there was a small door behind the picture. To Frank's amazement, it was an old safe controlled by a simple tumbler combination lock. Frank pulled the Dean's chair to the wall, stood on it and put his cheek to the metal door of the safe. He twisted the dial and listened for the definitive clicks which indicated that he had triggered the lock. Child's play.

The inside was packed with neatly arranged stacks of small manila envelopes. They appeared to be in chronological order, with older faded and wrinkled packages on the bottom and newer clean papers on top. Four or five envelopes comprised a package. Most of the envelopes were dated and each collection was bound by a heavy red rubber band. Frank leaned back and inspected the arrangement. He wanted to put everything back the way he had found it.

Frank pulled out one of the piles of large unmarked envelopes. They were held shut with a pliable metal butterfly. None of them were sealed. He examined their contents and found a disordered hodgepodge of documents, including letters of reprimand to medical students, contracts with Chiefs of Departments, and a self-nomination letter for the Office of Surgeon General. Frank emptied envelope after envelope, but didn't find anything interesting or important. He was nearly through the entire stack when he came to a fatter envelope. He squeezed it softly and found that it was padded.

This package wasn't sealed either, but it was stuffed tight. In his haste, Frank accidentally tore the envelope, which appeared from the outside to be like all the others. Inside was a sandwich of the soft clear bubble foam used to ship wineglasses. The protective wrap held two pieces of cardboard wrapped with a rubber band.

Between the cardboards was a stack of faded color photographs. The two on the top showed the Dean, when he had hair, standing next to four men. Three women were on their knees down in front. The image was faded a bit, but Frank recognized younger versions of Randolph Schmatz, Myron Ingelhart and Clyde Resnick. The other man had his head turned to the side. His face was partially obscured by a hat. They were all naked as jaybirds. The kneeling women were holding onto the penises of the men standing behind them, except for a woman on one end, who was covering her face with both hands. Her partner hung limp. Frank pulled the picture closer for a better look. The woman covering her face appeared to be very young. She had stringy long brown hair and a huge port wine birthmark on her hip that looked like an outline of Texas, with the panhandle resting against her left hip bone and the western portion of the Gulf coast across the crease between her leg and pelvis. The rest of the state disappeared into her pubic hair. The man behind her who Frank couldn't make out was fairly tall and also young in appearance.

The rest of the pictures were pornographic. They depicted the same people in smaller groups intertwined in creative sexual positions. It must've been quite a party. Waterhouse could have been the photographer, because he never appeared in any of the pictures except for the group portrait. Myron Ingelhart was dressed as Tarzan, when he was dressed at all, and Schmatz kept popping up with different partners. Except for Miss Texas, the women's faces could be clearly made out, although not as well as their nether regions. The shooter liked to zoom in close.

There was nothing left to inspect in the safe, so Frank took one of the duplicate group photos and carefully placed the rest back between the cardboards. He returned all the envelopes to their initial positions and shut the safe. He set the dial to its original number. Frank rehung the portrait of Pasteur and screwed it back into the wall. He exited the room silently, tiptoed to Valerie's office, knocked gently on the door, and waited for a response. There was no answer from inside. Valerie had her head down and appeared to be asleep at her desk, so he slipped back out and walked away from the office building.

The Dean needed to review some confidential documents, so he took down the painting and opened the safe. As was his custom, he made a cursory inspection of its contents. Nothing seemed to be out of order. Waterhouse took out the bound packets and slowly flipped through them like a big deck of cards. When he picked up the envelope which had been torn by Frank, he grew faint. Someone had been into his safe, he was sure of it.

His worst fear was confirmed when he saw that the Polaroids taken 22 years ago in Chicago were out of order. Waterhouse went down on one knee. Someone had seen the photos. But why were they still there? Why would someone just want to *see* the photos? Why wouldn't they take them? *Oh my God! One was missing!* The others at Branscomb knew that he had them. They had some too. It didn't make sense.

There was no place to turn, no way to deny the guilt. After all these years, the deepest sore was lashed open again. The only assumption he could make was that someone was trying to get him. But who, and why? Bob? Not likely. Randy or Clyde? They were in hot water, but no worse than before. Myron was dead. Elaine? Impossible! Then who? *Oh my God. Not her. If the story went public...* They had all sworn a pact, but he would be considered more to blame than they. He couldn't get it to fit, but he couldn't call the others. It was one of them, and if he tipped his hand, whatever was in the works might happen sooner, before he had a chance to plan a counter.

Waterhouse called Valerie. "When I was away last week, did you notice anything strange around the office?"

"What do you mean?"

"Did you see anyone in my office who wasn't supposed to be there? Did any faculty come by to leave me a note or anything?"

"No, not that I recall."

Now it was Valerie's turn to sweat. She didn't know what Frank had done in his office, but now she feared that whatever it was must have been more than just take a look around.

The Dean rattled off the most likely suspects. "This is very important. I was expecting Randy Schmatz to drop off a memo that I need to edit and distribute to the faculty tomorrow morning. Are you sure that you don't recall his being here? It wouldn't be like him to forget something this important."

"No. If he was in your office, I didn't see him."

"What about Clyde Resnick? I gave him some documents to review. Perhaps you remember him dropping by?"

"I'm sorry, Dr. Waterhouse. I've been out of the office a lot. I don't remember seeing them anywhere this week."

"Elaine Mahnke was supposed to leave me a book. Did you see her?"

"Nope."

"One of the students? Malinda Dwyer?"

"No. Not that I recall."

"If you remember anything, Valerie, you'll let me know, won't you?"

"Certainly, Dr. Waterhouse. Is something wrong?" Valerie couldn't look him in the eye.

"No, not really."

"If I run into Dr. Schmatz, do you want me to let him know that you were expecting to see him?"

"Oh, no, please don't! It won't be necessary. I'm sure he'll call and let me know what's happened to the memo."

Waterhouse was in no better position than before, and perhaps even worse. He'd been forced to make up a story about a memo that he would now have to write, and to lie through his teeth to another person who could benefit from his demise. Waterhouse turned to face Pasteur's visage. Valerie had been awfully quick to answer his questions. The more he thought about it, the more he knew what he had to do. The next time he talked to Valerie Snell, he would offer a bigger inducement for her to recollect who had been in his office.

CHAPTER 31

Elaine Mahnke's first week back after the drug rehabilitation program in Arizona was horrible. She was dry, but at the cost of unmasking her tremor, which was much more pronounced now that it was no longer suppressed by pharmaceuticals. Her secretary, who tried hard not to stare, simply told Elaine how well she was doing, "considering everything." Elaine nearly bit her head off.

The word got out quickly that there was something dreadfully wrong with Dr. Mahnke. Amplified in the circles of gossip, it seemed that not only was her body failing, but her mind as well. Medical centers love rumors. Mahnke's offended secretary dropped a hint and soon everyone guessed that Elaine had been an addict.

A less determined person would have withdrawn and quit, but Elaine still had something to prove. She had hoped to be eased back into the operating room, but in Montague's opinion, she'd been on vacation, because rehabilitation certainly couldn't be work. If she couldn't cut it, there was no reason to keep her. When she met with him after her return, she was careful to keep her hands clasped together firmly in her lap.

Her work was surgery, so now that Elaine was once again officially on the payroll, she needed to be on the O.R. schedule. On her second day, she was scheduled for an emergency kidney biopsy and a transplant. She was to be monitored during both procedures.

When she found out about the operations, Elaine broke into a cold sweat. Sometimes one might have to rush a transplant when a donor organ became available, but there was no such thing as an "emergency" kidney biopsy. She was being tested and she knew it.

Mahnke looked at her hands. Even though she was able to hold her forearms nearly motionless, her fingers moved up and down as if she were a concert pianist rehearsing an arpeggio. Unfortunately, she was trying to rehearse the absence of motion. Elaine began to cry softly, then tried to scratch the tip of her nose. The combination of her tremor and agitation caused her to poke herself in the eye. In an outburst of pain and indignation, she swept her arm across the top of her desk and threw everything off.

Just before lunch, she walked to the procedure room outside the pediatric intensive care unit. Although it was customary to have a surgical assistant on a case like this, Elaine declined the help. She didn't want anyone to see her if there was a problem.

Ricky was a four-year-old boy who had suffered a rare complication after having a strep throat. A month after he finished what seemed to be a simple sore throat, his precious blood filters began to fail, as antibodies in his blood stream attacked his kidneys. After Ricky wet his bed with pink urine, his parents rushed him to the pediatrician. Ricky had post-streptococcal glomerulonephritis, the shadowy sequel to a routine bacterial illness.

The pediatrician wanted a definitive diagnosis. Although the most likely diagnosis was acute reactive autoimmune inflammation of the kidneys, there were other possibilities, like undetected cysts, a rare parasitic infection or even a tumor. Although all of these were highly improbable, a kidney biopsy was felt to be in order. The child would be sedated, positioned on his stomach so that he couldn't move, and the biopsy needle inserted into his flank to harvest a small core of tissue. This would be preserved and sliced into extremely thin sections for examination under the microscope. Normally, a renal biopsy took less than thirty minutes. It was the kind of procedure usually relegated to trainees and rarely performed any more by the faculty.

By the time all 45 pounds of Ricky was wheeled into the room, he had already been through quite an afternoon. In case anything went wrong during the biopsy that might lead to the administration of a general anesthetic, the little boy had not been allowed to have anything by mouth for the last six hours. He became ravenous and infuriated. To make matters worse, he was forced to relinquish his new blue sneakers. That was the last straw. When the ward nurse came to start his IV and wrestled him to remove his shoes, Ricky bit her on the hand. The nurse went nuts. She turned him over and raised her hand to give him a spank when a student nurse intervened. The young woman asked to accompany the child to his procedure, even though she'd never seen anything surgical before. Her supervisor immediately approved. She figured that she could stick the student with the tedious post-procedure observation, when the children were usually miserable and there was little that could be done to console them. Besides, she didn't like this kid anymore.

With the student nurse soothing Ricky and allowing him to keep his sneakers on, they were able to get his IV started. They changed him into a hospital gown that tied in the back and wheeled him quickly past the swinging double doors of the pediatric intensive care unit into the procedure room. They were met by Dr. Mahnke, the circulating nurse and a nurse anesthetist.

The nurse anesthetist administered a mixture of fentanyl and midazolam, a potent sedative combination. Within a minute, Ricky dozed off and began to exhibit deep and sonorous respirations, sounding very much like an old drunk. As soon as he grew limp, the student nurse took off his blue sneakers and put them into the wire metal basket underneath the gurney. She rolled Ricky onto his stomach and helped the anesthetist place an oxygen mask over the boy's nose and mouth. They taped a small pulse oximetry sensor over his earlobe to read the oxygen content of his blood via infrared light beams. Then they tied him to the bed using sterile sheets as restraints.

"Is this going to hurt him?"

"Nah. He won't feel a thing. He's pretty gorked from the meds, and Dr. Mahnke will numb him up before the biopsy."

"Is that the doctor who'll do the procedure?" The student gestured at Elaine, who was scrubbing her hands at the sink. "Is she a kidney specialist?"

Her instructor answered softly. "Enough questions. Dr. Mahnke hasn't been up here in awhile. I heard she was sick. She used to be a pretty good surgeon. We'll see."

Elaine heard her name mentioned and turned around. She glared at the two women at the bedside. Elaine hadn't heard anything besides her name, but surmised that the women were gossiping. That was nothing out of the ordinary for nurses, but she assumed that there was more of an edge than usual. She resented it.

"Can the small talk, ladies, and get the patient ready. I have another case to follow, and I don't feel like sitting around here while you tell each other your life stories."

They turned back quickly to their patient. The older nurse took a bottle of mahogany brown povidone-iodine solution and poured it into a stainless steel bowl. She donned a pair of rubber gloves and grabbed a stack of 4-inch square gauze pads, which she dipped into the antiseptic solution. Using broad strokes, she painted Ricky's back, coloring him all the way from between his shoulder blades to the top of the crease between his buttocks. She repeated this until the liquid ran into small puddles at his sides and pooled on top of the black vinyl mattress cover.

"Why don't you just pick him up by the ankles and dip him in the bucket? You need to kill a few germs on his back, not disinfect the universe," remarked Elaine.

"I don't feel very well," said the student nurse, who had become queasy from the medicinal smell of iodine and the realization that she was about to watch something gory. "I need to sit down."

Elaine was instantly annoyed. "Oh great, a rookie. Who let this woman in here? Somebody get her a chair before she keels over. Sweetheart, if you don't have the stomach for this, I'd appreciate it if you'd leave the room. If everyone doesn't mind, I'd like to get started now."

The pre-syncopal lass sat in a chair near the sink. She was sickened and sweaty, and thought that she might faint. She answered Elaine in a weak voice. "I'll be OK. I'm not really supposed to be here to help with the biopsy. I just came along to keep an eye on Ricky. I'll stay out of the way. Honest, I'm all right." She was far from all right. The real reason she didn't get up and leave was because she was too nauseated to move. Her palms grew moist and she felt like she was going to have diarrhea.

"Let's get started. Please hand me the biopsy tray." The circulating nurse unwrapped the sterilized set of equipment necessary to perform the biopsy. Elaine rummaged around and picked up a syringe upon which she screwed a long needle. She uncapped the needle, popped the vacuum on the syringe, and held up the needle with her right hand in the universal gesture to request medication. Her hand was shaking noticeably and she grasped her right wrist with her left hand to steady herself.

Oh my God, thought the student, *she's nervous! She's never done this before. I don't think I can watch.* Little spots of light flashed in her peripheral vision as she grew more lightheaded. The trainee's face was totally devoid of color and she had the sour taste in her mouth that comes right before you vomit. The petrified nursing student held her head in her hands and prayed that she wouldn't puke.

The nurse anesthetist held a small bottle of lidocaine upside down and pressed the rubber stopper against the sharp tip of the needle. The needle tip slid through the rubber and for a moment, the women were connected by needle, syringe and bottle. Together they shook. Elaine injected air into the bottle to pressurize it and then drew out a syringeful of clear anesthetic. She pulled the needle out of the bottle, pointed it at the ceiling, and squirted out the air bubble at the top until a few drops of liquid dripped from the tip. After she capped the large needle and unscrewed it, she twisted on a smaller needle and uncapped it. Elaine turned to the patient, who lay face down on the gurney. Ricky was in the Never Never Land of light anesthesia, undisturbed by the commotion around him, but still sensitive to sharp pain. As everyone in the room watched her, Elaine poked Ricky in the side with the needle. He flinched and gave a small whine, which made the needle pop out of his skin, leaving a tiny drop of blood where it had broken the surface.

"Damn," muttered Elaine. "He moved. Will you guys please hold him? I can't hit a moving target."

Oh Lord, please let me get through this, thought the student nurse. *I'm supposed to be protecting this small child and the doctor's torturing him.*

"Are you sure that this doesn't hurt?" she squeaked in a barely audible whisper.

"Please, someone shut her up or get her out of the room. She's really beginning to bother me." At this point, Elaine was losing her confidence. If she couldn't even administer a little numbing medicine, how was she going to do the biopsy, let alone a big transplant case later on?

The circulating nurse walked away from the table and talked silently to herself. *Moving target my ass.* "Dr. Mahnke, are you feeling OK? Perhaps I should call Dr. Montague and let him know that you can't do the case today. There's nothing wrong with canceling if you aren't feeling well."

"There's nothing wrong, the patient just moved. Now, if you all will do your jobs like you're supposed to, we can get this biopsy done before this little man wakes up from his medication."

Mahnke leaned on Ricky's back with her left hand and quickly jabbed his flank again with the needle, more like a dart piercing a target than the skillful slide of an experienced surgeon. The boy squirmed, but Elaine held him firmly and injected forcefully. She buried the half-inch needle to the hub and continued to press lidocaine into the boy's skin where she intended to follow with the larger biopsy needle. As soon as the numbing medicine took effect, Ricky settled down. Elaine took a long slender stainless steel needle off the tray. It was a hollow probe with a removable obturator within its core. Although it was no thicker than a pencil lead, when compared to the tiny needle used to inject the anesthetic, it looked like a booster rocket.

Elaine nervously worked the obturator up and down like the slide on a trombone, then locked it into place. The idea was to push the biopsy needle through the skin until it was just next to the kidney, then remove the obturator and push the cutting needle through the kidney's capsule. This would core out a small plug of renal tissue within the hollow opening at the tip. The most common complication of a kidney biopsy was failure to obtain an adequate tissue sample. Bleeding was rare. Still, the procedure appeared barbaric to the casual onlooker.

"More paint," ordered Elaine. The lead nurse soaked a few more gauze pads and mopped directly over the weal where the boy's skin had been numbed. "Thanks. Hold him tight now."

Elaine was conducting a symphony with the biopsy baton in her hand. She grabbed the shaft of the needle with her other hand to stabilize it and stabbed it into the boy's back with a brutal thrust. Ricky first felt the pressure and the "pop." Then he let loose a blood-curdling moan, because Mahnke had missed her trail of local anesthetic and plunged directly through pain-sensitive tissue. Ricky arched his back as his peaceful slumber was interrupted by the lightning bolt in his flank. His agony startled everyone in the room.

The student nurse's worst fear of child abuse was confirmed. She took one look at the child and passed out cold. As she fell over backwards from her chair, it sounded like someone dropped a coconut off a table. She suffered a concussion. The nurse anesthetist jumped up and raced to her side, but there really wasn't much for her to do except to cushion the young woman's head and lift up her jaw so that she wouldn't choke. The initiate gave a few post-concussive jerks, so it looked like she was having a seizure. One nurse left the table to call for additional staff. That left Elaine alone with Ricky, who still had the needle protruding from his back. He was whimpering. Since she assumed that the tip of the needle was at the proper depth, Elaine removed the solid obturator and pushed the needle in further to take the biopsy. The boy groaned again, but his torment only made Elaine more determined to complete what she had started. With great difficulty because of her loss of dexterity, she rotated the needle in her fingers and obtained a tissue sample. She yanked the needle from the boy's body and held a laparotomy pad to his back.

"There, there. We're all finished now. Your mother will be with you in a few minutes. You were a real good boy, which is a lot more than I can say for everyone else in this room." Elaine pushed the plug of tissue into its receptacle, snapped the lid on the cover, then placed a pressure dressing on the bleeding hole. She left the room. She didn't bother to help with the student nurse or stop to fill out the normal paperwork. All she wanted to do was get out of there before *she* fell down. The biopsy had gone horribly. She had no doubt that it would be telegraphed all over the hospital.

After about three minutes, the student nurse woke up with a softball-sized lump on the back of her head, fuzzy vision and the mother of all headaches. It took her a second to focus.

"What happened? Did I get hit by a train? God, my head hurts!"

"Don't think about the pain, sweetheart. You slipped off the chair and hit your head. Anyway, you didn't miss anything."

"What about Ricky? Is he going to be OK? Did Dr. Mahnke finish the biopsy?"

"Yeah, she got it all right. I think you were still awake when she skewered the kid. Remember?"

The young woman couldn't control the tears that began to run down her cheeks. "What will it show? Did she put the needle in his kidney?"

Her confidant leaned in close, counting on the fact that the student nurse would repeat the exaggeration to all of her friends. "I'll tell you what the biopsy'll show. She stuck that goddamn needle right through the kid. When the pathology report comes back, it'll read 'normal mattress.'" The student nurse pictured Ricky speared to the gurney. Her eyeballs rolled back in her head as she passed out again.

What little confidence Elaine had regained was obliterated by her poor performance during the biopsy. Although she hadn't damaged the child or botched the procedure, she felt totally inadequate. Her hands were shaking so badly that she could barely comb her hair, let alone tie a surgical knot. She began to cry as she replayed the little boy's shout of pain. There was no way that she could get through a transplant in her condition.

Mahnke had no other choice but to fall back on bad habits. She walked to her office, locked the door behind her and reached far into the lowest drawer of her personal filing cabinet. Tucked underneath the green hanging folders was a large brown plastic pill container filled with an assortment of Vicodin, Valium and Halcion tablets. Elaine opened the large vial and shook some pills into her hand. She selected two five-milligram Valium tablets and swallowed them easily without drinking any water. Then she sat back in her chair and waited.

In about ten minutes she began to relax. Although she didn't experience a rush, she enjoyed the smooth drugged feeling that had been absent from her life for the last few months. Elaine held her hands out in front of her and saw that although they were still trembling, it was nowhere near the fury of the previous few hours. Like most addicts who fall off the wagon, she promised herself that this would be a one-time thing to get her through this operation. After the transplant, she wouldn't touch the stuff for as long as she lived. The operation was scheduled to begin in two hours. The fellows on the transplant team who would assist her on the case had gone out in the helicopter to pick up the kidney, which was being harvested from a brain dead unhelmeted motorcycle accident victim at a hospital 250 miles away. Elaine popped a few extra pills for good measure.

Just as the "harvest team" doctors were packing the kidney on ice in a cooler for the helicopter ride home, they received notification that they were to remain where they were and continue to work on the donor. A recipient had been located for his liver and pancreas at another medical center. Since time was of the essence with both the donor and the second failing patient, the Branscomb surgeons would have to procure the organs. After they were done, they would catch a commercial flight back to Branscomb. The kidney would fly home on the helicopter and Elaine would have to begin the operation without any help.

When Elaine found out that most of her surgical team wouldn't be present for the operation, she called Montague and asked to be replaced. He refused. According to him, all of the other surgeons were tied up with scheduled operations and there wasn't anyone senior to spare. Elaine could have an intern to assist and a first-year medical student to hold retractors, but that was the best that could be done until someone else could be freed up. In so many words, if she couldn't do this case, she could resign her position.

She had to take it or leave it. If she wanted to keep her job, she didn't have a choice. After the conversation with Montague, the events of the last six months began to rain down hard on her psyche. Montague would expect her to withdraw, and then he could be finished with her once and for all. Well, fuck him! She'd be damned if she'd give into him now. Elaine reached again for the pill bottle. For the next three hours, she kept herself under control with a mixture of benzodiazepines and opiates.

In the hall outside the operating room, Elaine was joined at the scrub sink by an intern and Lauren Doopleheimer, who'd been yanked out of a surgery basic science lecture to lend a hand. Taking secret insurance against disaster, Montague had enlisted his best first year house officer, who intended to become a transplant surgeon. The medical student Doopleheimer was inexperienced in the O.R. but was impressively intelligent and diligent. Montague was certain that they could manage on their own if Mahnke should begin to fail in mid-operation. He instructed the intern to notify him immediately if the least little thing went wrong, and certainly if she appeared incapable of continuing the case.

Washing hands was a ritual before each surgery case. The surgeons stood at the sink and scrubbed their hands with a stiff plastic brush impregnated with hexachlorophene. According to tradition, you scrubbed your hands, wrists and arms to the elbows, then held your hands up to drip dry before the circulating nurse handed you a sterile towel. You didn't fool with surgical customs.

Lauren had only scrubbed for a few cases. She told this to the intern. He patiently explained everything that he could before Elaine Mahnke arrived at the sink. He'd never operated with Mahnke, but he'd heard about her problems.

Mahnke, the intern and Lauren finished their scrub at the same time and stepped back from the sink, holding up their arms for towels. The nurse handed a towel to Elaine, then one to the male surgeon. She turned her back on the student. The rites of initiation required a medical student like Lauren to beg for a towel, but she didn't understand what she was supposed to do. The intern looked back and saw her standing patiently, dripping water from her elbows. He called over to the circulator, with whom he had already scrubbed on a few cases.

"Irene, throw her a towel, will ya? She's OK. There's no time to fool around on this one. I think we're all you've got. The boys are still in Raleigh shopping for liver."

Irene was one of the best O.R. nurses, after decades of mollycoddling the phenomenal egos of her surgeons. She had worked with the best and the worst, and long ago had learned to make them come to her instead of vice versa. As far as the students went, she was willing to help the good ones, but they all had to play by her rules. Irene's Rule Number One was to let everyone know who was in charge.

"Sure, Doctor, anything you say. Does she need anything else, like maybe a back rub or her bottom wiped?"

"Irene, you can be a real pain in the ass, but I love you. I think you're the best nurse in the history of surgery." He threw her a huge grin. This kind of flattery seemed stupid and an incredible waste of time, but it was necessary. "Try and cut her a little slack. I think this may turn out to be a difficult case, if you understand what I mean." He looked in Mahnke's direction.

The patient had already been wheeled into the room and was lying supine on the table attended by the anesthesiologist. On a cart near the bed was a clear plastic tub containing the transplant kidney. It resembled a huge kidney bean, lifeless and floating in a soup of iced saline through which bubbled a flow of oxygen, like air through a tropical fish tank. Instead of anemone tentacles, there were the floating arms of vital blood vessels, the severed remnants of the donor's renal artery and vein. This particular kidney had already been dissected free of most of its natural envelope of fat, so that it glistened a pale faded maroon in the salty liquid.

The recipient for the donor kidney was a diabetic, as Elaine's brother had been. At the age of 43, he'd waited for this kidney for over two years. It had been difficult to find an organ for him because of his unusual tissue type, and until this day, a reasonable matching donor couldn't be located. It was a good thing, because his hypertension had already broken through medications and dialysis. Without a new kidney, it was likely that he would suffer a stroke or heart attack in the next few years.

The team assembled at the patient's side as Elaine explained how the case was to be done. Her elocution was slow, as if she were speaking in a trance. She had started for the operating room after taking so much Valium that she could barely stand up. If she weren't doing this case, she would be sound asleep. Just before she rode the elevator, she stopped in the cafeteria and bolted down two cups of expresso, so now she had caffeine jitters on top of her polypharmacy-induced somnolence. Her central nervous system was tuned into two different stations, and it all came out as static.

"I'm going to talk you through this case. It's time that you interns were allowed to have more responsibility. Young woman, I want you to stand on the other side of the table and pay attention to everything that goes on. You'll hold retractors for us and if there's a chance, we'll show you how to tie some knots. Otherwise, keep out of the way."

Elaine knew that the less she got involved, the less the chance for an error. One way or another, she would get the operation completed.

"Knife to the surgeon. Make your incision here. No, like this." Elaine reflexly reached to take the scalpel from the intern, but her arm was shaking so badly that she drew it back and clasped her hands together in front of her. "Make the incision longer, all the way down to where his pubic hair starts. Good, good. OK, zap the bleeders." The intern reached for the electrocautery and touched the red-hot tip of the bovie to small veins that oozed blood into the wound and obscured the field. Small wisps of acrid smoke rose from the charbroiled black spots of flesh, and the volatile vapors wafted through the facemasks worn by everyone in the room. The odor wasn't objectionable, more like the smell of a hot dog on the grill.

Mahnke continued to rattle off instructions. She managed to hang on to a few clamps and to keep the surgery moving forward. Her skillful surrogate didn't cut any major vessels or get lost in the abdomen. Lauren stood back and watched as the bed for the new kidney was cleared within the pelvis. It was fascinating to see the inside of a human being, and Lauren began to daydream what it would be like to become a surgeon like Elaine Mahnke.

The medical student also began to perspire, a tiny bit at first, then in buckets. The operating room was kept fairly warm so that the patient wouldn't become hypothermic. Everyone in the room wore disposable paper gowns, which were more convenient, but not nearly as breathable as their old cloth counterparts. No one had told the student to wear light clothing underneath, so she was wearing a pair of jeans, a long-sleeved shirt and wool hiking socks under her scrubs. Combined with the vapor barrier of the cloth gown, surgical cap, mask, goggles and rubber gloves, it created a sauna. Lauren began to sweat profusely, and the drops that ran down her nose made it itch terribly. She wanted to wipe her face, but she knew enough to keep her hands sterile.

"Excuse me, but could you please scratch my nose? It itches something awful," she informed Irene.

"No. Just let it itch. We're busy."

"Really," Lauren pleaded, "I don't mean to be a bother, but this is driving me nuts. I really need someone to scratch my nose."

"Sorry, toots, you just have to toughen up. We'll be able to take a break in the case in about 45 minutes. Until then, think about something else."

That wasn't going to work. Once you get focused on an itch, it becomes a total preoccupation. Lauren grew desperate, then had a brainstorm.

"Could I have one of those instruments over there on the scrub table that you aren't going to use?" Lauren wanted to take a clamp and scratch her nose. "That way, you don't have to bother with me."

Irene lifted her head up from her position next to the scrub nurse and snarled, "We don't have time to bother with you. The instruments are for operating, not for picking your nose."

Now it was a test of wills. Damn if the Dooper was going to roll over for this bitch. "Listen, ma'am, I'm not trying to cause any trouble, but I don't believe it's your job to harass me. Now, if you'll please hand me one of those small pinching things from that huge pile over there that you've already finished with, I'll take care of myself and you can go on doing what you're doing."

The operation stopped. What had begun as a harmless request had become a cat fight. Everyone looked at Irene, who wasn't about to let Lauren step over her line in the dirt.

"Look lady, if you can't take the heat, guess you'll just have to leave the room. Maybe you'll get better at this stuff someday." Now everyone turned their heads to look at Lauren.

Lauren hesitated, then stepped back from the table. She reached up with her gloved fingers and scratched her nose, then wiped the sweat off her brow with a long, luxurious stroke of the back of her hand. Irene's expression turned to one of horror, then disgust. She was about to order Lauren to leave the room, when the quick-thinking young woman lifted her arms up in front of her and announced, "New gloves please."

Mahnke smiled under her mask, looked down and shook her head from side to side, while the intern, anesthesiologist and scrub nurse laughed out loud. Irene was furious, but she'd been beaten at her own game. She couldn't refuse the impertinent Doopleheimer a new pair of gloves, or *she* would be out of order. Lauren knew that she had probably slit her political throat in the O.R., but at the moment it didn't matter.

Lauren got her new gloves, and the case continued. It was time to take the donor kidney, place it into the recipient, and begin the arduous task of connecting everything up so that the essential filter could begin its next assignment in the body of the man who so critically needed it. Mahnke asked the intern to bring the kidney to the table. He turned and walked over to the cart that carried the precious organ, reached into the bath, and gently cradled the kidney in his gloved hands. It was a bit slippery, but fairly easy to hold. He brought it back to Elaine and she motioned for him to lay it down on two blue surgical towels she had draped across the patient's chest above the abdominal incision.

What happened next was not clearly visible to anyone but Elaine and Lauren. Everyone else was looking away or doing something that had diverted their attention from the main operation. The scrub nurse was focused on her table, counting sponges and rearranging instruments. Irene was behind the anesthesiologist's drapes, where they were checking gauges and IV lines. The intern had his nose down into the abdominal incision, where he was mopping up a few bleeders and checking to be certain that everything was ready for placement of the kidney. Lauren happened to be staring at Elaine, who reached over to handle the kidney. She wanted to inspect it for any nicks or deformities. She lifted it up with both hands, then allowed it to rest in the palm of her trembling right hand so that she could view its surface. She lost her grip. The kidney became as slippery as a greased watermelon and squirted away from her. As if in slow motion, it bounced off the patient's side, hit the edge of the table and then fell to the floor with a sickening squish. Elaine fumbled after it as it went down, but she never came close to preventing its fall. She looked up quickly and saw that Lauren had seen the whole thing happen.

"You'll never guess what happened," Elaine said softly.

"What?" answered the intern without looking up from the abdomen.

"You'll never guess."

"I give up. What happened?"

"I dropped the kidney."

It was totally silent in the room save for the rhythmic hiss of the ventilator. The intern looked up aghast as Irene moaned, "Uh-oh." Everyone looked down at the floor, where the kidney now appeared much smaller and almost pitiful. No one moved. Elaine reached over and grabbed the intern's arm.

"Well, why don't you pick it up?"

He scurried around the table and picked up the fallen kidney. On the side where it had struck the floor, it had a stellate crack and was flattened a bit. He cradled it in his hands and began to rock it gently, as if it were an infant that could be soothed.

"What do we do now, Dr. Mahnke? There appears to be some damage to the kidney. Should I call for help?"

"No. Let me think for a minute. For starters, put it back into the saline solution." The intern plopped the organ back into its container. "There's no reason why we shouldn't be able to use this kidney. We'll just treat this operation like it was for an injured kidney. We fix cracked kidneys all the time. Irene, pour some kanamycin into the kidney bath. We need to wash it off."

Everyone knew that they were far out on the fringe. The correct thing to do would be to discard the kidney, close the patient, report the incident and face the music. Yet no one spoke up, because it was sacrilegious to go against the word of an attending surgeon in the operating room. The intern and everyone else had to follow orders.

Elaine walked over to the kidney and rubbed its surface gently. Irene added the antibiotic solution to the bath, and Elaine continued to massage the kidney for a few minutes. She told the intern to lift it out of the bath while she held out a sterile towel to wrap it in, which gave her a better grip. As she carried it back to the patient, the intern spoke up. He wanted to call Montague.

"Are you sure this'll work? Maybe we should call to see if the other kidney is available. If I can just use the phone..."

Elaine spoke with absolutely no emotion in a hushed voice that sent a chill through everyone in the room. "Listen to me carefully. No one saw anything unusual happen here. This kidney was never dropped. Do you understand me? The kidney never fell. Did anyone see this kidney hit the floor?"

"I didn't see it happen," answered the anesthesiologist.

"What kidney?" said the scrub nurse.

"You're in charge," said Irene. The intern said nothing.

Lauren was speechless. She'd seen the whole thing, and it was all so terrible, all happening so fast. Elaine turned to her. "What happened in here is no one's business. Do you understand?"

"Yes, doctor, I understand."

"Good. Let's get the kidney connected so that this man can get to the recovery room."

The intern grimly continued his work and finished the operation. He repaired the lacerations in the kidney and then completed the vascular anastomoses. This was malpractice and he had been forced to become part of it. He vacillated between rage at Mahnke and pity for the patient. Lauren felt admiration for the young surgeon who was trying to make the best of Mahnke's botched job.

Back in the recovery room, things didn't go well for the poor man who had received the fumbled kidney. It had been bruised severely, so the urine it produced was grossly bloody. Despite immersion in a potent antibiotic, the kidney had been inoculated with microbes from the O.R. floor. Administration of the immunosuppressive drugs necessary to fight rejection allowed the bacteria to flourish. Three days later, the man developed an abscess. The combination of infection and internal bleeding fueled an episode of sepsis. A week after it had been implanted, the kidney had to be removed or the patient would die. The official diagnosis listed on the medical record and signed by Elaine Mahnke was "infection and acute rejection, proximate cause unknown."

CHAPTER 32

For days after the kidney transplant fiasco, Lauren was tormented by what she'd seen. Her initiate's understanding of medical ethics had been turned upside down as she became silent conspirator to a physician who had made a heinous mistake. To make matters worse, she was immersed in the part of the first-year curriculum that emphasized physician morality. She was reminded every other afternoon to tell patients the truth, to accurately document everything she did with patients, and to uphold the highest Hippocratic standards. After what she had seen Elaine Mahnke do, it all turned into a bunch of bullshit.

In separate episodes, she swore Sam and Malinda to secrecy, then told them everything that had happened. She was astonished that neither one seemed the least bit upset. When she asked Sam what she should do, he told her to keep her mouth shut, which made her angry. Lauren thought he had more spine than that. Malinda suggested that she write a letter to her Congressman, for all the good it would do her. What a cynic! Lauren would have thought that as pious as Malinda could be, she would have more constructive advice to offer. Maybe Lauren had been wrong about her. Well, if no one else was going to do the right thing, she'd have to do it herself. After talking it over again with Sam and against his explicit advice to discuss it first with Frank, Lauren made an appointment to talk to Dr. Montague. He had given her the assignment. Of all people, the Chairman of Surgery would understand what a difficult position she was in and work out the best solution for everybody. They were lucky to have such an insightful leader.

The meeting went pretty well, she thought. He was extremely attentive and seemed to hang on her every word. He asked a lot of penetrating questions, but seemed most interested about whether she had discussed the incident with anyone else. Lauren considered informing him that she had shared her tale with Sam and Malinda, but decided that it was irrelevant since they weren't going to tell anybody. Besides, neither one was there when it happened and they wouldn't be able to back up her story. When she finished spilling her guts to Montague, Lauren felt a hundred percent better. She didn't do it to get Dr. Mahnke in trouble, just to be able to tell the truth. The Professor of Surgery promised her that in fairness he would talk with everyone involved, and said how proud he was of her behavior. He told her she was a credit to her profession.

Lauren's story was accurate. This was just the break Montague had been waiting for. He called in the ailing transplant surgeon and explained to her that even though he liked her as a person, she was dead weight in his department. Because she had been through rehabilitation and failed, the next step was a permanent leave of absence or resignation. Montague would help her find another job, so long as it didn't involve surgery on people.

This time, the doctor made no attempt to hide her trembling hands. She was resigned to immediate defeat. There was no struggle. She accepted his assessment of her condition and what had happened without a single contradiction. Elaine understood his position, and would do the same thing if she were in his place. However, she asked Montague if he could hold off saying anything to anyone else for a few days until she could get her life in order. He saw no problem with that.

The next morning, Wiley Waterhouse paid a visit to Montague. He hoped that Montague would be willing to listen to reason. The variation on the theme didn't invoke the usual recriminations, because after all these years, Montague knew it was senseless to argue. Besides, the Dean was in an uncharacteristically accommodating bargaining mood. The old adversaries worked from both extremes back to the middle. The settlement was that Montague would retain the highly lucrative Divisions of Otolaryngology and Vascular Surgery in exchange for a non-clinical faculty role for Elaine. Under no circumstance would she be permitted to apply a scalpel to a hangnail, let alone a complex surgical problem. She was, however, to have an opportunity to lecture in the classroom.

A week later, the Dean summoned Lauren Doopleheimer to his office.

"Please come in, Miss Doopleheimer. Thank you for coming. I appreciate your skipping lunch, particularly since I know how hard you've been working. Please sit down." The Dean motioned to a chair positioned in front of his desk. "I need to ask you a few questions."

"No problem, Dr. Waterhouse," replied Lauren. "It's not every day that a student gets a one-on-one with the Dean. I appreciate it."

"Yes, Lauren. We need to chat a bit about something that happened in the operating room recently. First, I'd like to clarify a few points. What were you doing in the O.R. with Dr. Mahnke? Were you given *permission* to be there?"

"Yes, of course I was, Dr. Waterhouse. Why do you ask?" There was something unnerving about the way he asked the question. He was being brusque, very cold. What did *he* have to do with any of this? Where was Montague?

"Lauren, you must know that your story doesn't match up in some aspects with those of other persons who were present. Is it true that you insisted on breaking out of scrub to scratch your face and then made an obscene gesture at the scrub nurse?"

"Absolutely not, sir!" blasted back the medical student. "The fact is that I needed to scratch an itch and I did. But I didn't make any obscene gesture. Did someone say that I did that?"

"Lauren, I am not going to say who said what about whom. They've asked not to be identified. But according to everyone present, your behavior was felt to be way out of line. It does not represent the attitudes we wish to have displayed by our medical students. This medical school will not tolerate unprofessional conduct."

"That's a lie!"

"Please watch your language."

"Yes sir. I apologize."

"Based upon everything I've been told, I have no choice but to put you on probation."

Lauren was stunned. "What? What did I do? Don't I get a chance to tell *my* side of the story?"

"You already have. Besides, young woman, this is not a hearing. Based on my investigation of what happened, I have decided that a period of probation would be most appropriate. You have no recourse, so it will do you no good to complain. Be grateful that I have not decided to suspend you permanently."

"Probation. You're putting me on probation. What does that mean? Does that mean that I have to sleep in the hospital every night? What can you possibly do to a medical student that's worse than making her feel like she's a convicted criminal? This is unbelievable. Now, what am I supposed to do? What's that poor man with the mashed kidney supposed to do? Should I tell him that we're sorry, but maybe next time we won't play hot potato with his guts?"

The Dean flushed with anger at the impertinence. "That does it! Miss Doopleheimer, I suggest that you pack your bags and go on a trip for awhile. After next week, you will be de-listed from all of your classes until the fall quarter of next year, at which time I will review your record and make a decision about whether or not you will be allowed to reenter this medical school. I can tell you based upon my impression of what has happened and your response today that you would be well served to investigate admission to another institution. If you wish to transfer soon, we will support your efforts and make no mention of this incident or your suspension. If you choose to try to stay here, it is possible that you will be left, as they say, holding the bag. It's up to you."

"You can't do this. I demand an investigation."

This was the critical point. Waterhouse chose his words carefully. "As you wish. We can do precisely as you ask. But think for a second, Miss Doopleheimer. It will be your word against four other individuals, all of whom are extremely convinced about what they saw and that you should be thrown out of school. I'm offering you your only chance to remain at Branscomb. You may reject that if you wish."

Waterhouse was lying. The O.R. nurse was glad to sacrifice Lauren for Mahnke after the itchy nose episode. But when the Dean sought verification from the intern, the house officer eyed him coldly. " Miss Doopleheimer behaved correctly and capably. Dr. Mahnke's behavior was another matter." With that, he turned and walked away. Waterhouse didn't dare pressure him.

"Dean Waterhouse, this is totally unfair! I've done nothing to..."

"Miss Doopleheimer, we must all uphold the Oath of Hippocrates. Our conversation is finished." The Dean stood up and turned his back on Lauren.

Just like that, she thought. *Something stinks real bad up here. That junkie bitch got to him.* Lauren fled the room.

Through a torrent of tears, Lauren told Sam exactly what had happened. He told her that he guessed that the Dean was just trying to do his job. She couldn't believe how little emotion Sam showed. Maybe he didn't believe her.

"I'm going to the Chancellor."

Sam knew better than to tell Lauren everything that he and Frank were doing, that until they could be certain that the Chancellor wasn't part of the problem, she could mess everything up by going to him. She couldn't escalate this further, for both their sakes. He thought he knew why Waterhouse was sticking up for Mahnke, but he had to keep that to himself. Sam was seething, but he couldn't let it show. If in the process of completing his assignment, he could score one for the Dooper, all the better. The thought of her having to leave Branscomb personalized the mission in a way he would have never thought possible a few months ago. He wanted to help her get even.

"Doopie, drop out of sight, but stick around. Maybe the Dean'll change his mind. You never know. Sometimes people cool off."

"I don't know, Sam. He didn't act like he was gonna change his mind. Anyway, what's it to you?"

"It's a lot to me, Lauren. *You're* a lot to me."

"Well, sometimes you have a funny way of showing it. Look, I have a problem right now."

"Don't go to the Chancellor. Give me a few days. I'll think of something. I promise. Trust me on this one."

"Sam, I need to know more than that. What do you have in mind?"

"I can't tell you everything, but Frank and I are pulling together some information on a few of the doctors at Branscomb. That's all I can tell you."

"So?"

"Well, we're getting closer. Look, I can't tell you exactly what it is, but Doctors Waterhouse and Mahnke might not be long for Branscomb."

"What? What the hell are you talking about? I'm being ruined here! Stop talking in mysteries. What's any of this got to do with me going to the Chancellor?"

"Maybe nothing. Maybe everything. We don't know. But for now, *please* don't do it. I'm asking as a personal favor. You know that the Chancellor won't mess with the Dean anyway. If he would, why would that slimebucket still be here?"

Lauren fell into the couch confused and defeated.

Sam couldn't stand to see her in such pain. "Look, the Dean has a safe. Frank found a *very* interesting photograph from a party. There may be something to it. He just needs a little time."

"I don't understand."

"I know. I can't tell you any more — just that. You can't do this alone. Right now, the best thing is to do nothing."

Malinda's reaction wasn't that different from Sam's. She reminded Lauren that she had warned her about the Dean before.

Lauren felt betrayed. First Waterhouse suspends her unfairly and then she gets no sympathy from her friends. "You two make it sound like it was *my* fault," she muttered as she left the apartment.

Malinda raced to Lauren's top drawer and ripped open her diary. "I think that Sam and Frank are getting close to what they're looking for. They have a picture from a party, whatever that means."

That was the last thing she wanted to read. *It* could *be over soon,* thought Malinda, *if somebody got scared and decided to turn on the group to save their own hide.* She was at Branscomb for a reason, and she needed more time.

Things were changing. In her own way, Malinda had grown fond of Lauren, and she didn't want to see her roommate hurt by somebody like Waterhouse. She'd seen him do it before. If Malinda was going to have her day and be the one to put an end to it, she had to get to them before Sam and Frank.

CHAPTER 33

"Hello, Wiley."

"Hello. How are you?"

"Just fine. How're things up in the Dean's office?"

"Couldn't be better. Lots of work and very little time for play. You know how it is."

Waterhouse's gut was doing somersaults. She *never* called to exchange pleasantries. Might as well get it over with. "So tell me, what can I do for you? Having problems with your new car? Trouble with the rent payments? Running a little low on cash? That's easy."

"No, Wiley. Nothing like that. I have plenty of money. You've been very generous. I called because there's something you should know about. It looks like the cat's ready to jump out of the bag."

He shuddered. Letting her come to Branscomb was a mistake.

"I just got asked to help a guy that wants to know about three very bad doctors at Branscomb. It would've been four, but one's not here any more."

"What?"

"You heard me. There's a guy here who's trying to find out everything he can about three doctors at the medical center. I think he wants to publicly humiliate them. Isn't that a coincidence?"

With the picture from his safe missing, the Dean was petrified. How could something like this happen after all these years? If any of the others were caught — if the truth came out — everything would come crashing down around them. The crime, the cover-up, the payoffs, the malpractice — it would ruin his career and probably send him to jail. He'd do anything to keep that from happening.

"Christ, Theresa...Malinda! Quit talking in riddles. Tell me what's going on."

"I don't know. I was hoping you could tell me. Now, what I really want to know is, what do *you* have to do with this?"

Wiley was confused for a second. He had absolutely no knowledge of what she was talking about. Then it dawned on him she might assume that he was trying to get rid of the others himself. If she believed that he had a part in this, it might tone down her behavior.

Wiley decided to try a bluff. "Thanks for the info. I figured it would start soon. Don't worry, this is just a little housecleaning. You don't have anything to worry about. Just remember who's paying your tuition."

"Cut the crap! Tell me what's going on with specifics or admit that you're dropping a load in your drawers. You're lucky I want to be a doctor. If I didn't, I'd tell someone to start barking under your tree. When you decide to cut me in on some real info, I *might* do the same. Better keep away from your old friends for the time being."

Wiley's ruse had failed miserably. Now he was truly frightened. She was a demon! "Believe me, I really appreciate it. A deal's a deal."

"Good. I'll call you if I hear anything you need to know. Oh, and lay off my roommate, will you? She's nothing to you. Mahnke deserved to get her ass kicked. You don't need to do anything. It'll just happen."

"That's none of your business."

"I'm making it my business. Lauren didn't do anything wrong. Ease up. Do you hear me?"

"I hear you."

"Let her back in class."

"I can't do that. I would lose face."

"You'll lose more than your face if you don't listen up. Back in class."

"All right, but she stays on probation. And one last thing. Who am I watching out for? Is there anybody else involved?"

"Forget it, Wiley. It's probably better that you don't know, so that you don't do something stupid, like offer free tuition." She hung up.

Waterhouse looked out the window. He was perplexed. He needed to know if she was telling the truth. She wasn't asking for money, and she didn't say anything about the picture. But they were *all* at risk — didn't she understand that? All she seemed to want to do was frighten him. But why?

CHAPTER 34

Waterhouse waited until his secretary left for the day, then called Valerie into his office. His voice was a low hiss.

"You lied to me! When I got back from my trip, I asked if you had seen anyone in my office. You said no. I *know* that someone was in here. If you don't tell me the truth, there will be severe consequences." He couldn't be sure that Valerie knew who had been into his safe, but it was his best shot. The Dean struggled for control as he popped a few jelly-beans into his mouth and chewed furiously. Valerie fought a terrible urge to giggle. Calmer now, Waterhouse adopted a reasonable tone. "Valerie, the last time we spoke, I didn't tell you everything. There have been items stolen. I'm not at liberty to say what they were, but it's extremely important that they be located."

"My goodness."

"Think hard, Valerie. I'm sorry that I said you lied. Naturally, this is very upsetting to me."

"Of course it is, Dr. Waterhouse. I'd be upset too if someone broke into my office and took something."

"Or overheard a little sex talk?"

"Doctor?" She blanched, then blushed.

"Yes, Val. What would people think about a Dean who asks her gyne-cologist to undress her with his mouth? Over the phone, mind you. The exact words you used were, I believe, I'm so hot, Frank. Put your lips on my..."

"Stop! You have no right to talk to me this way. You have no right to pry into my personal life."

"Not so, Dr. Valerie Snell. You're my responsibility. If your behavior is immoral, that becomes grounds for dismissal. So many torrid conversa-tions. Should we take it to the Ethics Committee and let them decide? Now, back to when I was out of the office. Do you remember anyone coming in here? Anyone at all?"

Her head was spinning as she projected the wreckage of her career. She closed her eyes and pictured Frank as he let himself into Waterhouse's office. It couldn't be him.

"Now that you mention it, I do. One of the medical students was up here and asked if he could borrow one of your old historical books."

"What was the name of the book?"

"I really can't remember. But come to think of it, I'm certain that he left empty-handed, so if you're missing something, he wasn't the one who took it." Inadvertently, Valerie said the wrong thing. Someone who had entered and exited empty-handed fit the precise description of the photo thief.

"Who was it?"

"Sam Anderson. He's one of the first-years." All she could think of was that afternoon. Sam and Frank. Frank and Sam.

"Please pull his file and bring it to me."

Waterhouse thumbed through Sam's admissions folder. There wasn't any useful information. He stared at Sam's headshot for a few seconds, then picked up the phone and dialed a familiar number.

"Hello."

"It's Wiley."

"Dr. Waterhouse, I do believe that you're starting to miss me. I've talked to you more in the last two weeks than I have in the last ten years. To what do I owe this pleasure?"

"There's no pleasure in this phone call, Malinda. Things have gotten a little hot around here. I need some straight answers."

"OK. Shoot."

"First of all, if you don't tell me everything I need to know, you can kiss your trust fund, car and diploma goodbye. Who's the mystery man?"

"Wiley, you sound upset. Did you sit down on a lawn sprinkler or something?"

"You're finished! Goodbye."

"Wait, Wiley."

"Who's putting him up to it?"

"I don't know. I asked him the same question over and over, but he wouldn't budge."

"We'll find out about that later. So tell me, are you good friends with Mr. Anderson?" He caught her by surprise. When she didn't respond, he knew he was right.

Waterhouse tried not to sound upset, so that she would believe he knew more than he did. "It figures. I'll look up his record and see if I can figure a connection. He didn't say anything about anyone else, did he? He didn't say he had any proof of anything, did he?"

"No."

"Well, Malinda, that may have changed."

"Go on. What?"

"He had one of the pictures."

Malinda feigned a gasp. "No! What are you going to do?"

"I don't know yet. Be careful."

"You do the same, Wiley."

Lauren was preoccupied with her impending suspension from the class.

"Get me out of here. If I spend one more minute with my eyeballs glued to the microscope, I'm gonna lose my mind. I can't tell the islets of Langerhans from the Rock of Gibraltar. What's the big deal, anyway? I won't be here much longer."

"Who knows? Maybe Waterhouse will change his mind. Remember, you're on probation, not expelled. Just let him cool off." Sam frowned. "This sure isn't what I had in mind when I applied to medical school. I wonder if we ever actually get to take care of anybody."

"Tell me about it." Lauren reached over and pushed the hair out of his eyes. "Why do you want to become a doctor?"

Sam told her everything about Frank and their discussions, about what had happened to him in Kuwait and how helpless he'd been. It was the first time he'd admitted any weakness and it made Lauren melt. She was riveted to his story, which was fine with Sam. She hugged him with all her might and planted an enormous kiss on his lips.

"I could fall in love with a guy like you." She kissed him again and stood up. "C'mon, let's get out of here. Sam Anderson, you're a great one. Not much to look at, but a great one."

"You are too, Doop. And try not to worry so much about

Waterhouse. You can't let the bastards wear you down. I think that we're closing in on him, and I'm fairly certain that he doesn't have a clue."

"Not in your life. And I sure hope so. More than you think. But don't get your hopes up. Malinda says he's got a mean streak that won't quit. You know, maybe you should get to know her better."

"There'll be time for that later. I know you like her. But you get along with everybody. So, can we get together later?" Sam's eyes twinkled. They had begun sneaking into Fred Spencer's lab after hours for a late evening snuggle.

"Sure. He's out of town. I need to catch up on my work."

"And I need to catch up on you."

CHAPTER 35

Before students were allowed to examine and treat patients, they were required to participate in a two-week "Patient Encounter Experience." Each freshman was assigned to a ward patient who agreed to a series of interviews. The purpose of the interaction was to open a window on a patient's thoughts and feelings, but there were rigid guidelines. The first-years were allowed to ask questions about family history and past medical problems in order to try to understand the psychosocial factors that led to the patient's disease. However, they were strictly prohibited from discussing the actual medical treatment or the decisions that went into therapeutic choices. That could lead to second-guessing. The faculty didn't want naive students to become patient advocates.

Usually, the patient volunteers were people who faced a long stay in the hospital and had time to kill, not the in-and-outers who were having hernias fixed or tubes tied. The interviewees were more likely to be genuinely ill, but not so sick that they didn't have an inclination to talk to somebody. The students learned all about how obese women got their gallstones, what a veteran who smoked like a chimney was going to do after he had half his larynx removed, and whose grandma on her father's side had also suffered from an overactive thyroid. Whether or not you learned anything useful during this exercise depended on whether you saw it as a privilege or a chore, but even more on whether a patient opened up to you and you opened up to the patient.

Sam Anderson was assigned to a young construction worker from Cookeville, Tennessee. Tony had been diagnosed four months previously with acute myelogenous leukemia, a tragic disease of young people. The stem cells in his bone marrow had gone berserk and were producing physiologically ineffective precursor blood components. If the process continued unchecked, the immutable release of huge immature white blood cells into his circulation would clog blood vessels and neutralize the normal mechanisms with which his body could fight infections. He would grow profoundly weak over a mere matter of weeks. Unless he was cured, he would expire from a fatal pneumonia, heart attack or stroke. This was Tony's third hospitalization since he had been diagnosed with the disease.

Chemotherapy was one option for treatment. The new agents were powerful, but there was only a one-in-five chance for inducing a remission. The side effects of the treatment were awful, and included intense nausea and vomiting and profound weight loss. Tony was well aware of the discomforts, because he had already been through two rounds of chemo. Each time, his white blood cell count plunged to nearly zero as the drugs decimated his blood marrow. He was administered the poisons with the intent of wiping out the proliferating leukemia cells. Unfortunately, as is often the case, Tony's disease would remit for a few weeks, then rekindle.

It was horribly frustrating, all the more so because he had been offered no choice other than chemotherapy. Tony was unable to take advantage of additional advances in cancer therapy. Ideally, Tony would receive a bone marrow transplant from a donor whose genetic profile matched closely enough to allow a small amount of transplanted bone marrow to flourish within his body and replace the malfunctioning blood-producing organ. The process had been honed in numerous medical centers over the years, so it was fairly straightforward and clearly the best option in a case like Tony's.

A bone marrow transplant candidate with AML underwent total body irradiation to wipe out the most radiation-sensitive leukemia cells; the normal cell-manufacturing machinery was also obliterated. At the point of the lowest blood count, when white cells could no longer be detected, the recipient would undergo an injection of normal donor marrow cells, which would assume residence and multiply rapidly. When the technique worked it was miraculous, and the leukemia victim could be cured.

Tony's problem was that no donor could be found. He was an only child, and both of his parents were dead. He only had one cousin, whose genetic HLA type was radically different from his. A national survey of available bone marrow donors had not as yet revealed a suitable match. Although he had three children, none was an eligible donor. If the chemotherapy did not drive his cancer into remission, he would die.

It was lonely in the hospital. Tony was more than happy to have the opportunity to converse with Sam. The second round of chemotherapy had been even more horrible than the first. The side effects were gruesome and demoralizing to a man who had first come to the medical center at six feet three inches tall and 250 pounds in weight. Now he was bald, his muscles ached constantly, and he had withered to 165 pounds.

Tony was wasting away from his disease, and even though he was a strong-willed and spirited man, he knew he was fighting a losing battle. The worst part was having his family, particularly the little ones, watch him suffer. In a mere matter of months, their daddy had been reduced from the pillar that supported the family to a ghost of his former self, unable to play with a small child or climb a flight of stairs without getting profoundly short of breath.

"How did you know you were getting sick?" asked Sam, who knew nothing about leukemia and little about disabilities. Sam had hardly been sick a day in his life and didn't enter medical school with any experience with cancer patients. On the surface, his questions were simple, but he was deeply curious.

From his first conversation with Tony, he had been drawn to the man, who was more self-effacing than anyone he had ever met. Even though he was dying, Tony was willing to take the time to explain his feelings to Sam, who felt more and more empathy as their visits progressed. At first, Sam was uncomfortable and limited his inquiries to superficial matters. However, he soon found that what Tony really wanted to talk about was not death and dying, but about life and living — who he was, not what he was about to become.

"I just started getting tired doing ordinary things, like carrying lumber or fooling around with the kids. I thought it was because I'd been working long hours, you know, we were working on some custom homes and they were behind schedule. When that happens, you have to put the cut men up on the frame and bring in the subs early, so it really turns into a forced march. I was there sixteen hours a day for a couple of weeks, so when I started getting tired, I thought it was the job, that's all. I wouldn't have gone to see the doctor if I hadn't started coughing up blood. The doctor says he guesses it's a good thing that happened, or I wouldn't be here today. Not that there's very much of me left." Tony flashed a wan smile, which didn't mask his anguish.

Sam desperately wanted to cheer up Tony, even though that wasn't supposed to be why they were spending time together. During the past ten days, he had watched Tony go through his most recent round of chemo, which had nearly killed him. It was painful to watch the man be normal one minute, then begin retching uncontrollably the next. The poisons were attacking the very fiber of Tony, and doing little to control his leukemia.

Tony's faculty oncologist had a reputation for flogging patients with drugs. His was a personal crusade against cancer and death. Despite the repeated agonies he had observed over the years, part of him had become numb to the suffering. If there were a chance in a million for a remission, he would never suggest that someone throw in the towel. It wasn't that he lacked compassion. It was just that to him, death was a personal challenge. People should live as long as they could, because why else persist in the struggle? Since he himself had never been stricken with a serious cancer, he couldn't identify with the torment, only with outcomes. The interns assigned to his service rarely became oncologists, because they were so turned off to his heartless aggression in the face of inevitable defeat.

Sam understood that he was only to be an observer. He was not supposed to write orders, administer medications or even apply a Band-Aid to a patient. With permission, he could observe procedures and interview patients, but hands-on activities were limited to listening through a stethoscope, taking a pulse and holding someone's hand for moral support. It was poor form to introduce one's self as "Doctor" so-and-so when you were still a medical student. It was "Mister" or "Miss" until you had your diploma in hand.

Tony knew that Sam was a medical student, and liked him the better for it. He didn't feel as intimidated as he did by the doctors. Even though his oncologist was putting him through living hell, he felt uncomfortable protesting his treatment, because for Christ's sake, the doctor was supposed to know what he was doing. Surely, if he thought that there was a better way to attack the disease, he would recommend it. What the attending physician wasn't in an objective position to see was that if there was ever a candidate for therapeutic nihilism, it was Tony.

Sam's visits with Tony were the high point of his experience in medical school up to this point. Over the two weeks during which he was officially assigned to spend time with the young leukemic, Sam found himself becoming increasingly attached. Tony confided a lot of details about his family and confessed his fears for what was going to happen to them in the future. The carpenter deteriorated rapidly. As Tony got sicker, he began to lose hope. The gut-wrenching side effects from the chemotherapy wore down his physical reserve.

Tony was on a slippery slope, and in many ways clung to Sam as a companion, someone who would listen to him talk about the sorts of things in life that others thought were trivial in light of his catastrophic illness. The man didn't want to talk about life, death and existentialism. As far as he was concerned, an out-of-life experience meant you were plain out of life. He wanted to know baseball scores and to hear about the weather. Sam kept up the banter, but it became painful to observe Tony in his demise. He hoped that Tony wouldn't die before this patient encounter business came to an official end, because he didn't know how he would react.

On the last evening of his rotation, Sam came by to tell Tony that it would be his final visit. Before he could give him the news, he noticed from Tony's reddened eyes that he'd been crying.

"Hey, buddy, what's the matter? You look like you just lost your best friend. Doctor tell you how much you owe?"

"No, worse than that. He says my counts are sky high and came up so fast again that he wants me to go through another round of chemo starting tonight. I asked him what he wants to use. Daunorubicin again. That stuff tears me up. I don't think I can take it any more."

Daunorubicin hydrochloride was a cell-killing antibiotic derived from a strain of bacteria. A potent chemotherapeutic agent, it was nicknamed "the red death" because the powder was mixed up into a candy-apple red solution. The poison was used to treat the worst sorts of cancers. Furthermore, it induced extremely bad side effects. While the drug was killing leukemia cells, it made your hair fall out, your gums bleed, made you throw up, and dropped your normal white blood cell count so low that you were virtually guaranteed a major infection in your skin, throat, lungs or kidneys. If it leaked out of the IV into the skin, it eroded a vicious sore that could take weeks to heal. One round with the red death was bad enough, but to get whacked again so soon seemed inhumane.

"Oh, man, that's too bad. But I'm sure that your oncologist knows what he's doing. He wouldn't give you that stuff if he didn't think that it'd make you better. What did you tell him?"

"I tried to talk him out of it, but he wasn't listening. I don't think he ever listens. I know that this isn't gonna to work." Tony started to sob. "I mean, I love my family more than anything in the world and I want to live, but it just isn't gonna happen. I can't stand it when they come here and see me like this. I'm gonna die soon, and there's nothing anybody can do to stop that. My wife and kids need to get on with their life. I don't want the medicine. I don't. I can't. I don't." He put his head down between his hands and cried.

Sam reached out and put his hand on Tony's shoulder. He felt awkward, but he didn't know what else to do. He reached an arm across his shoulders.

"So?"

"What could I say? He's never taken no for an answer. I just don't think he understands. He thinks he's doing it in my best interest."

"Yeah, a lot of doctors are like that. You know, it's really your decision. It's *your* life."

"What do you mean?"

Sam didn't know what he meant. He was just trying to console Tony, and some philosophy squeezed through. Like most first-year students, Sam was subconsciously wrestling with the moral issues. If there was one thing he had come to despise, it was the egos of the Big Doctors.

"I mean, if you don't want to go through another round of chemotherapy, it seems like that ought to be up to you, that's all. Maybe you should talk to him again and let him know how you feel."

Tony hung his head. "Nope. That'll never work. He kills cancers, that's all there is to it." Tony tried to smile. "Hey, I want you to look at these." Tony pulled a plastic accordion sleeve of photographs out of his nightstand drawer. "These are my kids. My wife brought me these pictures yesterday." He handed the snapshots to Sam.

Sam unfolded the stack and stared at the pictures. It was a happy family — two little redheaded girls and a towhead baby boy, all smiling, in strollers, on swings, sitting on the porch. At the very bottom was a picture of Tony and his family before he got sick. Sam almost didn't recognize Tony. He had been tan and muscular posing with his brood. Sam couldn't bear to look up at Tony.

"I know," whispered the dying man. It's hard for me to look at the pictures myself. Funny what can happen to a man so fast."

Sam swallowed hard and his eyes began to water.

"Listen, Sam, I want you to do a favor for me, OK?"

"OK."

"After I die, I want you to take my kids fishing for me, all right? They really love fishing, and their mom doesn't know how to rig the line and put on the hooks and worms and all that stuff. Will you do that for me? Those kids just love to fish. Please say that you'll take them fishing, just once or twice. Tell them that their daddy loved them and loved them. OK?"

Sam couldn't get out the second "OK." Tears ran down his cheeks and he began to weep with Tony, who was once again sobbing. They held each other's hands and squeezed with all of their might. Even though he was wasted nearly to his skeleton, Tony's grip was so forceful that Sam wouldn't have been able to pull away even if he wanted to. They sat like that for a moment before Tony spoke again.

"I don't want the red death. It isn't gonna help, and I don't want my family to see me die like that. What can I do?"

The men stared at each other. "I'll take care of it," whispered Sam. "I'm not sure how, but I'll fix it. Don't worry."

"How?"

"I don't know, but I'll do it."

"Thanks, man. Thank you."

Sam walked slowly out of the room, wiped his eyes on his shirtsleeve and took a deep breath. He walked over to the chart rack at the central nursing station and picked up Tony's chart. He flipped through to the Orders section and ran his finger down the most recent entries. Midway down the page was written "daunorubicin 200 mg IV by house officer before 6 P.M." It was initialed by the faculty oncologist.

The order couldn't be changed without the professor's approval. Sam had made Tony a promise. He walked to the telephone and dialed the hospital page operator.

"Please page Dr. Ernie Mustalish to 37865. Thanks." He hung up the phone and waited, tapping the top of the work station nervously with his fingertips. He ripped the receiver off the cradle before the first ring was completed.

"Hello, Ernie? This is Sam Anderson, the med student assigned to Tony Albers. You know, I was just looking through his chart and I saw that he's supposed to get some more chemo. You didn't know that? Well yeah, the boss ordered another round of daunorubicin, and I was kind of wondering whether you'd mind if I gave him the medicine. You know, I'd have the nurse come in and help me and everything. Tony said it would be all right with him. I could use the experience. Would that be OK with you?"

Mustalish was an intern in medicine and getting slaughtered on the hematology-oncology rotation. He was on call every other night for six weeks, which meant that he was on for 38 hours straight, then off for ten, then on for 38 and so on and so forth. He had forty-one patients on his service, most of them sick as dogs, so he never got any sleep on his nights on call. On his nights off call, he never got out of the hospital before 9 P.M., so he was lucky to get six or seven hours of sleep. After five weeks, he needed all the help he could get. He didn't know anything about the rule restricting first-year medical students, and even if he had, he wouldn't have cared less.

"Shit, yeah. Thanks. Read me the order."

"It says daunorubicin 200 mg IV by house officer this evening. Nothing else."

"OK. Does the patient have an IV?"

"Nope."

"All right. Start a line and make sure it's a good one, cause if any of that stuff leaks out it'll eat a hole through his arm you can drive a truck through. Have the nurse mix up the chemo and then push it in slow, like over five minutes. Don't push it in any faster. When you're finished, flush the line with about fifty of saline. Got it?"

"Sure, I think so. Start an IV in his forearm and push the medicine through no faster than five minutes. Flush the line with saline when I'm finished."

"Good, that's it. Oh, and don't write anything in the chart. I'll scribble a note when I get down there. I don't want the Attending to think he's wearing me out."

"No problem. Thanks a lot." Sam hung up and looked around. No one was paying any attention to him. He glanced at the bed assignment board and scanned over into the nursing column. 210 B. Albers. Nurse: Mary Ann. She was new on the unit, just getting a feel for the rules and regulations. At this point, she hadn't learned that every word out of a doctor's mouth wasn't gospel, and she hadn't yet been burned by a medical student who overreached his bounds.

"Excuse me. Are you Mary Ann?" Sam flashed his biggest smile and spoke as authoritatively as he could.

"That's what it says on my nametag. Yes."

"Good. I'm Sam Anderson. You've got Tony Albers in 210. He's got an order for chemo this afternoon and Dr. Mustalish asked me to give it to him right now. If you've got a second, I'd appreciate it if you'd mix up the stuff for me. He'll also need an IV."

They were both trying to be proper and impress each other. "Yes sir, I'd be happy to help you. Let me see the chart."

Sam handed her Tony's record, already opened to the order page. She read it and closed the chart.

"I'll have everything ready in a few minutes. Meet you in the room."

So far, so good. Sam walked swiftly to Tony's room and knocked on the door.

"Come in."

"It's me. Listen, the nurse is going to be in here in a minute. Let her start an IV on you. I'll take care of the rest. Trust me."

"What are you gonna do?"

"You know. What we talked about."

Tony's eyes watered up and he started to thank Sam. "Oh man, I don't know what to say. What can I do to..."

"Not now. Cut that out and wipe your face. If you act weird, you'll blow the whole thing. Save it for later."

Tony took a big breath and exhaled hard. "OK."

Sam punched him gently. "That a way, buddy."

The nurse walked into the room carrying a liter bag of normal saline, assorted tubes and needles, and a big syringe filled with bright red liquid. She put everything down on the bed next to Tony.

"Mr. Albers, you know that your doctor has ordered more medicine for you. I need to start a little IV in your arm so that Dr. Anderson can inject the medicine into your vein. You've had this done before, so you know that it won't hurt."

Tony looked away and nodded. He couldn't control his trembling.

"Now, don't be so nervous. I'll have this done in a jiffy and you'll get the medicine and then you can get some rest." The nurse applied an elastic tourniquet to Tony's upper arm and quickly located a linear blue bulge in his dwindled forearm. She wiped it with alcohol, neatly threaded an intravenous catheter into the vein, released the tourniquet, and connected the hub of the catheter to the bag of saline.

"There, all finished! Here's the medicine, doctor. Would you like me to stay?"

"Thank you very much, but that won't be necessary. This is gonna take awhile, and you probably have a lot of other things to do. I'll take it from here. I'll come and get you when I'm finished, so that you can take out the IV."

"Fine. Thank you, doctor." Mary Ann turned and left the room.

Sam walked over to the bedside and looked down at Tony. "Well, partner, if you want to change your mind, now's the time. Just say so. I'll understand."

Tony shook his head. "No. I don't want this stuff. Let's just get it over with."

Anderson walked into Tony's small bathroom and looked into the mirror over the sink. His forehead and nose were beaded with sweat, because he was scared shitless. How the hell had he gotten himself into this one? Oh well, what the fuck. If you can't kill your friends, who can you kill? This was what the man wanted, and he was going to die anyway. Sam squirted the medicine into the sink and flushed it down the drain with a blast from the tap. He walked back out to Tony and started to say something, but his patient reached up and put a finger to his lips, gesturing the medical student to be silent. Sam sat down in a visitor's chair next to the bed and for the next ten minutes, the two sat in total silence.

Tony finally looked over at Sam, offered him his hand and said softly, "Thanks." Sam stood up, shook his hand, and walked slowly back to the nursing station. He waited until Mary Ann reappeared, then instructed her to go back and remove Tony's IV.

"No problem. Went real smooth."

Later on, the intern wrote a note in the chart that implied that he had personally given Tony the daunorubicin. The patient was discharged, as was his wish. Absent the effects of the chemotherapy, the stem cells that churned out the leukemia cells in Tony's bone marrow went haywire, disabling his immune system. Within a week the inevitable happened. With no way to fight infection, Tony contracted pneumococcal pneumonia, which progressed in hours to overwhelming respiratory failure. Mercifully, Tony slid into a coma, and after an agonizing conference with his young wife, the faculty oncologist yielded to her wishes to withhold extraordinary life support. He was at a loss to explain to her why the chemotherapy had failed so miserably. Eight days after his prescribed dose of the red death went into the sink, Tony died.

Sam called Lauren. Tony's death had a greater impact on him than he thought it would, and he needed to talk to someone. The pressing demands of caring for the living rarely allowed a young learner time to adequately sort out feelings about death and dying. Tony's passing initiated an intense wave of emotion followed by a blunted, mute sort of mourning. Perhaps old people would be easier, but young Tony was too much like Sam for a simple moment of regret. Sam subconsciously projected Tony's demise upon himself, as he experienced the depression of losing a patient. Lauren came to Sam when he called, and when he told her what he had done, she said she was proud of him. They wept together, and then, for the first time, made love.

CHAPTER 36

Sam had never warmed up to Fred Spencer. The times he had visited Lauren in the lab, Spencer had made him feel uncomfortable in a jealous sort of way. Lauren told Sam repeatedly that it was all his imagination, that Spencer was really a very generous and understanding person. Most of all, he was a good listener. His work was growing more secretive, but he explained that to her as one of the necessary evils of scientific competition in an academic medical center.

So when Lauren suggested to Sam that he confide in Spencer what Sam had done for Tony, he was more than skeptical.

"Lauren, I don't think so. Do you realize how much trouble I could get into? It's nobody else's business."

"Sure it is. You've been moping around for two weeks. It's time to pick your chin up. Look, Spencer's a good head. He sees things that other people don't. Plus, I trust him. Totally. You remember what he did for me. He's never told anyone."

"I feel like an assassin." Sam wasn't convinced, but part of him wanted to confide in another person. He couldn't put his finger on it, but he didn't want it to be Frank. "This is different, Lauren."

"Maybe it is, but I think you're worrying about nothing. I trust Dr. Spencer just like you trust Dr. Klawitter."

"No way."

"Stop being ridiculous. What's making you so distant? You're behaving like you're the only person who ever had to make a tough decision. C'mon, talk to him. Just give it a chance. I know you want to get it off your chest. I know him. He'll be happy to listen."

"He's not interested in *my* boobs."

Lauren struck back. "Chill out. Who do you think you're talking to? I'm not trying to hurt you." Her voice was choked.

Sam felt like an imbecile. What was happening to him? Lauren was right. He didn't trust anybody. Frank's intensity was rubbing off on him. He didn't want Lauren to be angry.

"OK."

"OK what?"

"I apologize. I'll go talk to Spencer." Sam leaned his head into hers. "You know I love you. I don't mean to be this way. It's just that I don't want the whole world to know."

"He's not the whole world. He's special. Go on over." Lauren glanced at her watch. "He'll be there now."

"For you."

"Fine. For me."

"...And so when the nurse left, I squirted the medicine into the sink."

"How did you feel?"

"Scared. Scared and sad. Like I was about to lose my best friend. I know I was doing what he wanted, but I felt like I was letting him down."

"No Sam, you didn't let him down. You set him free. It was the right thing to do. Not many doctors would have had the courage to do what you did. At least not around here."

Spencer drew out Sam's remorse. "I don't know," Sam said. "Right now I feel more like a killer than a healer."

"Don't be so hard on yourself. He was going to die anyway. You let him do it with some dignity. He had more than a horrible disease."

"Sir?"

"More than leukemia, Sam. Let me show you." Spencer manipulated the computer controls and projected a chest x-ray on the screen. "After Lauren told me what you did, I pulled the Albers file and went through all of his studies. I can't believe anybody thought he would have a chance. Look at this. Solid tumors everywhere, scattered throughout his lungs. And here, in the bone."

"He had leukemia. No one said anything about any solid tumors. What were they?"

"Who knows, and to be honest, who cares? It's not unusual to see leukemic infiltrates. The bone mets are probably a second process. I'm sure the oncology boys knew about them. You didn't get the whole story."

"Nobody mentioned anything."

"That's the way they are. Keep everybody in the dark." Spencer flipped the switch to the three-dimensional MRI generator. "Now, watch over there." He pointed to the platform.

"Oh my God." The intersecting beams of light recreated Tony in an image as real as life. It was eerie and made Sam want to run from the room. He looked away.

"C'mon, boy, you were tough enough to let him go. Now look and understand why you did it. You saved him from the people who would have made him suffer. Look back, now." Sam swung his eyes back to the hologram of Tony. Spencer used the computer to peel away the exterior of his head and reveal what was inside his skull. "See that? Hold on, I'll bring it up for you better." He fiddled with a dial and three walnut-sized tumors glowed bright blue suspended in the midst of Tony's brain. "No way he would have gone another week without a seizure. And absolutely no way the chemo would have touched these. They're the worst kind. Tony was doomed."

"I'm not God."

"No, Sam you're not, but now you've come close. Decisions about life and death are why we're here. Doctors exist to alleviate the suffering, and sometimes the only way to do that is to bring people through a different kind of pain. It's the total that counts, not necessarily the component parts. So I ask you again, how did it feel?"

Sam shuddered as he stared at the brain and body that floated in front of him. "Like I was losing a best friend, or a brother. Horrible. Frightening. Please turn that off." This was supposed to make it easier for Sam, but it didn't. "I can't remember. I don't want to. Thank you for trying to help. But please turn that off."

As Spencer shut down the image, Sam saw the reverse sequence in a flash. The tumors disappeared, Tony's cranium and facial features were restored, and he vanished like a puff of smoke.

"Want to see more?"

"No. It's too painful. But look, I appreciate your taking time with me. I know that I don't need to ask, but I hope you won't tell anybody what..."

"Never. Not in a million years. You saved him from iatrogenous torture. Go back to Lauren. She loves you more than you know."

CHAPTER 37

In modern university medical centers, the Chairman of the Department of Surgery was usually more an academic strategist than a clinical surgeon. That wasn't the case at Branscomb. Ray Montague was a brilliant technician, to whom the toughest cases were referred. He operated six days a week, and sometimes seven. When necessary, he would work two rooms back and forth, letting a senior resident manage the mundane parts of an operation in one theatre while he managed a critical maneuver in the other.

Simple cases were performed by him for political reasons. When there was someone important to the medical center, like a trustee, who needed an operation, Montague chose to be involved, even if the problem was minor. The patient before him was such a case. But what had started as a straightforward abdominal exploration to remove some scar tissue was about to turn into a delicate and even life-threatening vascular repair. The patient was very old, so the less that needed be done, the better. Montague talked into the speakerphone on the wall of the operating room.

"Are you positive about this, Fred? I can feel the mass, but it isn't pulsating. If I take it out, there's a good chance it'll have to come with a big piece of him, because it's wrapped around half his insides. Then we've got a real mess on our hands."

Fred Spencer was downstairs in the radiology reading room. He answered without hesitation. "No question about it. It's eaten halfway through his bowel, so if you leave it there, you're just asking for trouble. I'd take my chances. Hate to use the "C" word, but that's what it looks like. What's gonna happen if he springs a leak from his aorta into the great outdoors? He won't last five minutes."

"Damn. He's one of our most famous alumni. If I have to do major plumbing, this could turn into one hell of a mess. Sure hope you're right. Talk to you later."

Montague decided to do the easy part first. He was already inside the abdomen, snipping leathery bands of adhesive scars that had formed in the aftermath of a gall bladder operation performed fifteen years ago.

Loops of intestine had stuck together and twisted on themselves, obstructing the flow of gastrointestinal contents and causing the patient to become severely ill with bloating, pain and incessant vomiting. In his morbid dehydrated state, the Branscomb benefactor was a poor candidate for surgery, but if it could be done quickly and simply, he had at least a small chance to survive. With this new wrinkle, it became a dire situation.

The lattice of adhesions required nearly an hour of careful separation and removal. This part of the operation wasn't difficult, and left Montague with a bare glimpse of the softball-sized agglomeration of fat, bowel and, according to Spencer, blood vessels tucked in behind his patient's pancreas. He ran his fingers over the mass again and again, hoping to feel a telltale thrill of rushing blood. But it was lifeless, spongy and soft, and felt like it would have moved easily, if only it weren't cemented into place on three sides. One of those attachments was embedded in the pancreas itself. To have to remove that organ would be a death sentence.

Spencer had said there was an erosion into the bowel. That was clearly not the case. Maybe he was wrong about the rest of it too. As good as the radiologist was, there was nothing like being there. Everybody did the best that they could.

"Let me have a syringe with a 21 gauge needle." Montague carefully slipped the point into the center of the mass and pulled back on the plunger. Nothing. He redirected the angle and tried again. Same result. He probed twice more.

"That's interesting. I can't get any fluid. It's hard to imagine a blood vessel of any significance that wouldn't give us at least a few drops. Maybe it's clotted off." The Chief lectured his resident assistant as he picked up a scalpel from the tray next to him. "Lets dissect down carefully and see if we can see where this thing goes. Hold that back. Good. There's a tissue plane here." Montague worked around the mass and satisfied himself that it couldn't be easily removed. He removed a few sections the size of peanuts. "Send these for frozen. I've got a hunch."

The surgeons needed to wait fifteen minutes for the surgical pathologist to freeze the tissue samples, look at them under the microscope, and report back. They covered the open abdomen with moistened towels and stood back from the patient, hands clasped and arms folded in front of them. Montague gazed out the O.R. window and watched Elaine Mahnke pass by on her way to observe another case. He had forbidden her to operate. What a disappointment. Montague had held such high expectations for her. It seemed just yesterday that he had announced her recruitment to Branscomb, where she promised to provide an essential balance to the clinical transplant program.

His reflections were interrupted by the pathologist's report. "Avascular lipomatous lipoma with granulomatous nodules. No malignancy seen." Fat, not cancer. There was no indication of extension into the pancreas. It was the wall of a large benign cyst. Fred Spencer had been wrong.

"That's a relief. Well, my friends, you can put this one in your diary. It isn't often that Dr. Spencer confuses fat with cancer. Let's tidy up and close."

"Dr. Montague, I have to admit it still looks like a malignancy to me. What tipped you off?" The resident was awed by his instructor's diagnostic acumen.

The Professor of Surgery had to think. "It was about risk — it was too great. Most surgeons would have taken their chances and cut it out on a recommendation from Spencer. But the stakes were too high. Imagine what would have happened. Keeps you humble. I'm glad we didn't risk this man's life. Call it the caution that comes with experience. Funny though. I wonder what Spencer saw."

In the dressing room, Montague showered and changed back into his white coat. He replayed the afternoon over and over in his mind, and felt a sudden surge of camaraderie for Fred Spencer. It could happen to any of them. A misread x-ray, a sponge left behind, a stitch taken in the wrong place. It was so important to look out for each other, to make the whole better than the sum of the parts.

He thought of Elaine Mahnke. She was brilliant, a world expert in her field. Now the ravages of drug abuse were bringing her down and she was a danger in the operating room. But then, so was he, the moment before he decided against the perilous procedure. There but for the grace of God go I. Montague determined to be softer with Mahnke.

She wouldn't be allowed to operate, of course, but maybe there was something else. He could create a nonoperating consult service, let her teach and focus on her rehabilitation. That would promote her renown and reputation, and she could continue to share her extraordinary knowledge with the residents and students. After all of her years of driven, relentless work, it was worth at least one more good effort.

CHAPTER 38

Lauren was in a playful mood. The big Spring bash, the Medical Student Review, was coming up, and she had volunteered to help write the first-years' skit. It was traditionally a lampoon poking fun at the professors. There were no holds barred and bad taste was encouraged.

"Sam, let's tell 'em what we think about medicine! A stand-up routine. When we're finished, I'll put it to music. They'll love it."

"Will anybody know who wrote it?"

"Not if we're clever."

"I'm not much of a writer. You're the brains of this operation. Besides, I haven't been feeling very funny lately."

"C'mon Sam. Where's your sense of humor? You're getting as bad as Frank. Here, have another beer. Think about what you've seen lately. Surely there's something we can come up with. Take your shoes off. Put your feet up. Relax."

Sam forced a smile and put his arm around her. "OK, I'll give it a shot. We need a title. How about The Art of Doctoring?"

"Yeah. That's great! What Honest Medical Students Know to Be True."

"Let's start with Schmatz."

"Oh no, not that again. Sam, no one will understand. This has to be funny, not miserable."

"OK, OK. Maybe I'm just too hungry to be funny. What've you got to eat?"

Lauren looked in the cupboard. "Nothing." She checked in the refrigerator. "Looks like we're almost out of beer too. I'll run out and pick up some stuff. You can get started without me."

"I'll wait for you."

"All right. But if you get inspired, my name goes on the top."

Sam kept sipping while he began to compose a response to the events of the past few months. The introduction began "Let's face it, most medical students are overworked, owe a lot of money, and have to put up with menial jobs they hate. We get reamed regularly by professors with opinions about what we should do and how we should behave. Too bad they don't play by the same rules. Surgeons are bad, but Deans are the worst." This wasn't so hard.

Sam's mood ran downhill from there. What was supposed to pass for wit came out as pure sour grapes.

"We crave one realistic ordinance. Empathy doesn't seem to have a place in the classroom or on the wards. So here's the real guide to medical student etiquette. Wake up. Even when they pretend to like you, they're sticking a knife in your back."

On an empty stomach, the alcohol affected him. Most of what Sam wrote was true, but none of it was funny. As the grip on his pen loosened, so did his logic. He pictured Waterhouse. "Old deans are obsessed with their health. They love to talk about it. If you're smart, you'll cut off any attempt at a prolonged conversation. If one insists on boring you with sob stories about cataracts, rotten teeth, hemorrhoids and bowel habits, ask whether they've considered euthanasia."

"Are you sure we should leave that in?" Lauren had tiptoed up behind him. "It's gonna rub somebody the wrong way."

"Don't worry, Doop. You know what I say. Better to be rubbed the wrong way than not to be rubbed at all. What can they do? Shoot us? This is America! We have freedom of speech."

Lauren gave Sam the thumbs up. "Keep goin', partner. Get it off your chest. Let 'em have it!"

Sam kept writing until he had four pages of tasteless observations about people with disabilities, security officers, cosmetic surgery, veterans, various forms of gastroenteritis, hospital clergy, and health care financing. He finished with a sheet on billing.

"Doctors love to complain about their income. They think that the world owes them a living. Patients love to gripe about their bills. They think that doctors should work for free. While it may seem contradictory, there are simple religious truths which explain everything:

Catholicism: Patients deserve their bills.
Judaism: Bills are the will of God.
Taoism: Bills just happen.
Hinduism: Bills have always been and always will be.

Fundamentalism: If you don't pay your bill, God will strike you dead.

Jehovah's Witness: If you let me into your house, I can explain your bill.

Atheism: Nobody asked anyone to believe the bill, just to pay it.

Confucianism: Confucius say, "Pay the bill."

Buddhism: What looks like a bill is really an offering.

Islam: A bill is the will of Allah.

Agnosticism: Nobody expects anyone to understand a bill.

Baptist: A person who doesn't pay a bill will burn in Hell.

Rastafarian: Bills are ever living, ever loving.

"Feel better now? This is a masterpiece, but I don't think we can use it like this."

"Why not? The Wall Street Journal publishes editorials that are a whole lot worse. But come to think of it, the only people who ever complain about them are doctors." Sam understood — of course they couldn't.

"Sam, you're a genius and this is gonna blow their socks off, but it's a little too hard. Let me just bring it to the next planning meeting and see what everybody thinks. I'll print it up and hand it out tomorrow morning. With a few modifications, I think we can get it into the show."

The authors gave each other a high five. Then they embraced and kissed. Lauren could sense that a small amount of Sam's tension had just been decompressed.

The next day, Lauren printed a few copies of Sam's creation. She fashioned bright orange covers with a picture of a caduceus and the admonition "Required Reading for Branscomb Medical Students" under the title. She meant for them to be distributed only to the Review committee, but one of her friends left a copy on a counter in the bookstore.

It didn't take long for the document to come to Waterhouse's attention. He received it by courier, along with a note from one of the trustees on the Hospital Board, who wrote, "Have you seen this? It's nice to see where all of our fundraising efforts are going. If the alumni find out about this, they'll probably ask for a lynching party. You better take care of this or you can kiss my money goodbye. What the hell are you people teaching over there, anyway?" The trustee's annual contribution to the medical school put him in the top ten percent of donors. Waterhouse couldn't afford to offend people like him.

When the Dean read the rude satire, he threw his door open and shouted at his secretary, "Find Lauren Doopleheimer. Now!"

"Dr. Waterhouse, do you want me to make her an appointment to see you?"

"No! Find her and bring her to me. I want her in my office this morning! I also want her file. Tell Valerie that I want her here, too."

"If they ask, should I tell them what this is about?"

"Jeanette. For once, please do what I ask. I don't want you to tell them anything. Just find Miss Doopleheimer and make sure that she's in my office as soon as possible. If she asks for a reason, tell her that I've reconsidered our arrangement."

The Dean's secretary pulled out the first-year schedule and located the culprit. Lauren and Sam were sitting together in microanatomy class snoozing through a lecture on mitochondria and the sarcoplasmic reticulum. Jeanette tapped Lauren on the shoulder and curled an index finger for her to follow. Outside the classroom, she transmitted the Dean's message. Lauren hung her head and started to follow like a condemned thief on her way to the gallows. Sam called after her.

"I guess this is it. You don't suppose he's gonna give you an award, do you?"

"Not likely, Roscoe. This is where we part company. Look, save your neck. I'm already on the train out of town, but you still have something important to do. I'll tell him that this was all my doing."

"Lauren, I love you."

"What?"

"You heard me. Telling the truth is noble, but it probably won't work. Besides, Waterhouse'll figure it out sooner or later. I'd just as soon get this over with and start to figure out how to get my real estate license. I'm not so sure that I want to be a doctor, anyway."

"No! Never say that! You want to be a doctor more than anyone I know. You're not coming with me. And you're *not* telling anybody what happened. Besides, it's not over till it's over." She lengthened her drawl. "Even an asshole like Waterhouse might have some sympathy for a poor little ol' woman."

"Not likely. Cobras don't have feelings."

Lauren and the secretary trooped down to the Dean's office. Waterhouse heard them and shouted loudly, "Bring her in. We're ready."

Waterhouse and Snell were faster than a firing squad. Because Lauren was already on probation, the Dean said he had no choice but to put her on disciplinary suspension for an additional quarter. Lauren protested and demanded a hearing. He was enraged by her argument. Waterhouse told her she could have a hearing if she wanted, but then she was vulnerable to outright expulsion. Did she want to take that chance?

Lauren knew she was boxed in. There would be no hearing and no hope for a reprieve. It was clearly stated in the Rules and Regulations of the School of Medicine that the Dean could do this. Furthermore, she was stuck at Branscomb. No recommendation for transfer to another school would be written. She was given one month to finish up her classes and clean out her locker.

CHAPTER 39

"Well, I guess I was wrong. There was no mercy. He was so inappropriate. I told him it was all for the student show."

"Tell me exactly what happened. Don't leave out any details."

"What difference does it make?" Lauren replied. "There's nothing you can do."

"I'll decide about that. Just start from the beginning and tell me everything that happened. I want to know what you said, what he said, and what everybody else said. No detail's too small. C'mon, I want to hear it."

"OK, Sam. I suppose it can't hurt." Lauren explained what had just transpired in the Dean's office. He had Lauren repeat parts of it three times to be certain that he got the details right. When she was finished, he gave her a huge hug.

"What am I gonna do with you? You didn't have to face him all by yourself."

"That was our deal. You can trust me, Sam. What good would it have done to drag you in there? I don't expect anything to change."

"You never know, Doopie. Sometimes a person can push too far."

Lauren had only seen that look one time before. It was after Dr. Ingelhart died. It made her afraid. Lauren reached out and took Sam by the arm. "Be careful. It's a mean world out there."

"Mm-hm."

"Sam, look at me!" Sam made eye contact with Lauren. Now it was her turn to talk tough. "Don't do something stupid. Not for me. If it's one thing you should've learned by now, it's that it's always best to stick to your plan." Her eyes softened quickly. "Thanks for your concern. Anyway, I'm not gone yet. No matter what happens, I'll be around until the end of the quarter. Right?"

"I couldn't imagine having you go anywhere. You know that."

"Hey there, don't look so glum. Let's go have a beer." Lauren squeezed his arm.

"That's what got you into this in the first place, but I suppose it's safe now. Still, I don't think we should write anything afterwards."

"Sam, what's the emergency? The page operator told me that you needed to talk to me right away. What is it? Have you learned something new? Are you sure you want to do this over the phone?"

"No, actually I don't. Frank, I'm sorry, but I need to ask you a big favor. Some things have been bothering me." Sam sounded tired and was more direct than usual. Klawitter was home early for the first time in weeks, and had just sat down to dinner. He wanted to put Sam off, but there was an edge to Sam's voice.

"Come on over. I'll keep a plate warm for you."

"Thanks. This won't take long."

Twenty minutes later, they sat in the study. Sam bypassed the niceties.

"First, I've had my fill of Waterhouse. I want to know exactly how he fits into all this. He just trashed Lauren for no good reason. His power trip here at the medical center is unbelievable. The Dean has to be more than rotten. Sooner or later he tries to get to everybody. You know it won't be long before the son of a bitch is gunning for me, too. I want to understand before we cross paths. Please don't take this the wrong way, but I don't think you've told me everything."

Frank didn't know how much to tell Sam. He wanted to spill his guts about Waterhouse, but he didn't dare to do it at this point. In some respects, the less Sam knew, the better. If he got taken down, it was really important that he not be able to divulge anything.

"Sorry, Sam. I can't comment. You know he's involved, but the details aren't important."

"Frank, for Christ's sake, where've you been? Look at what's happening here. Nobody's on to me. What do you think I'm gonna do, call him up and describe the sounds that Ingelhart made when the weights crashed down on his neck?"

"OK, OK. Let's come back to the Dean. You said you had a request. Was that it?"

"No. My request is that I want to move Waterhouse to the top of the list. I want to be involved. And I want to know how you intend to help me keep Lauren from getting kicked out of here."

Klawitter squeezed his armchair so hard that his knuckles turned white. He wanted to bark an order, but he restrained himself. It wouldn't accomplish anything to have them both angry. He needed to talk Sam down.

"Why?"

"Which one?" Sam replied.

"Why Waterhouse? We've got what we need on him for now. You're still working on the others." Frank hadn't yet shed every doubt about Sam.

"I just told you. Enough is enough. Lauren watches Elaine Mahnke totally fuck up a kidney transplant, does her duty and then Waterhouse thanks her by twisting the story around and putting her on probation. We write something for the student show and he suspends her from medical school. Well it doesn't add up. This has more to it than bad medicine. He's running from someone. Who? There's something you're not telling me."

"No he's not."

Sam was confused. He figured that Frank would say yes, not be so evasive. "Well then, what next?"

"I want you to move on to Mahnke. If Waterhouse went to such an extreme to protect her, there's got to be something there. She was probably going to be the next one. I just wanted to try to avoid it. But after what's happened, we don't have a choice."

"So Frank, why Mahnke?" asked Sam.

"What are you talking about? I just told you why! I'm giving you permission for something I was just about to ask you to do. That's all you need to know."

"Bullshit, Frank! I'm sick and tired of this bullshit! These people don't know we're coming after them. We don't need to run this like Special Ops. Ingelhart was a sitting duck. Mahnke will be, too, and the next one and the next one. I need to know why, Frank. Why Mahnke?"

"Don't push it, Sam. You're on assignment. You don't need to know."

"This isn't the army anymore, Frank. I owe you, but you're asking me to stick my neck out pretty far. Tell me about Mahnke. Maybe it'll make it easier for me to get the information you want. Maybe not. I just want to know enough about her to get inside. Are we partners in this, or am I just a tool to you?"

Sam was wearing Frank down. There was no harm in having him learn a little bit about Mahnke. Klawitter was trying to do what he thought was right, but there were no rules. He decided to take Sam closer into his confidence.

"Here it is. Waterhouse was the Assistant Dean at the University of Pennsylvania when Mahnke was a medical student. She had a nervous breakdown back then and as best we can tell, he cut her a deal to let her off the hook. She started to get shaky at Hopkins, but she stayed clean. Waterhouse helped recruit her here to Branscomb. For reasons unknown, she's still a faculty member, even though she eats Valium and downers like they were M&Ms and can't operate her way out of a paper bag. I don't know the details, but something must have changed, because now she's on the payroll. In some ways, she's different from the others. It seems that she cares about her patients. But that doesn't do them any good, because in one very important respect, she's just like the others. Mahnke knows what she's doing, but she won't quit. I can't figure it. She can't need the money any more. But since she's not talking, we have to assume it's greed. If she won't retire, then we have to convince her to retire. Does that answer your question?"

"That'll do for starters."

"Good. Are we finished now?"

"Almost. Just a few more things. First, I just want you to know that I'm enjoying medical school. I mean, I think I fit in. I think I'm just as smart as most of the people in my class."

"That's good to hear, Sam. I'm glad you're enjoying yourself."

"You don't get the point, Frank. I really want to be a doctor. I want to make sure that when this is all over, that it's all over. No other assignments, no other plans for Sam. We still have a deal, don't we?"

So that was it. Sam was worried about what was going to happen to him when the investigation was finished. Frank could take care of this one easily.

"Sam, I'm not making you do this. When you're finished here, you're free to do whatever you wish. No obligations, ever. That's how we started and that's how we'll finish. OK?"

"OK."

"Is that it?" Frank asked.

"One last thing. Back to topic number one."

"Which was?" Frank said cautiously.

"Waterhouse. Wiley Waterhouse."

"No."

"I'm sorry. I didn't hear you."

Klawitter was done arguing with Sam. "You heard me. I said *no*. After you've learned everything you can about everyone else, then we'll talk about Waterhouse. I know what I'm doing. It's too risky."

"And Lauren?"

"I'll see what I can do about that. Tell her to keep going to classes and to stay out of trouble, for Pete's sake. No promises."

"OK."

"Good luck, Sam. From now on, tell me everything the second you learn it. I have a feeling we're in striking range."

Frank was disturbed by Sam's attitude, but they were too far along to stop now. If Mahnke led them to Waterhouse, perhaps their work would be done.

CHAPTER 40

Sam called to reassure Lauren. He never intended to talk specifics, but when she told him for the third time that she loved him, it poured out of him. The good doctors, the bad doctors, his relationship to Frank, what had happened to Ingelhart, what he knew about Mahnke, and why Lauren had to keep this all to herself. It was overwhelming and she needed to see him right away. He agreed to meet in Spencer's lab, where she would be working when he got out of class. Even though she had been put on probation, Lauren kept on working for Professor Spencer. She had explained what happened with Waterhouse, and his instantaneous response was to tell her that she was welcome to stay as long as she liked. Once again, he came through for her.

When Sam entered the lab, Lauren was completely absorbed at the console. She was sorting cases by organ system, as Spencer had instructed her to do, and filing them by date. He was building a chronology in preparation for a prestigious national meeting. Sam put a hand on Lauren's shoulder and startled her.

"Oh! You frightened me. I didn't hear you come in. Spencer does that sometimes. I can't get used to it."

"You're glued to that thing. What are you doing?" Sam sat down next to Lauren and peered past her shoulder. "Is that what I think it is? You're some artist!"

"What?" Lauren looked back at the screen and faced a perfect rendition of a man's genitals. The superimposed legend read "Case 124-1994: Before Prosthesis." She blushed crimson while she laughed. "I must have done that when you made me jump. I was working on the urology section." Lauren scratched her head. "Might as well see how it looked afterwards. Wanna?"

"Sure."

"OK. Here goes." Lauren moved the cursor on the screen to a special function button, clicked, and then typed in a command. A new image popped up. It was a significantly larger organ. The new legend was "Case 124-1995: Post Prosthesis.

"Where do I sign up?"

"Not necessary." Lauren gave Sam a playful punch. "Hey, I've got a great idea. Let's scan you in. How'd you like to see yourself in 3-D?"

"You know how to do that?"

"It's easy. I've been helping Dr. Spencer scan in the patients. He taught me how to do the basic reconstructions."

"What about the radiation risk?"

"There is none. Go into the dressing room over there and put on a gown. It'll only take fifteen minutes."

"Are you sure Spencer won't be pissed?"

"Of course not. And besides, he'll never know. We won't save you in memory. We'll just savor the moment."

Sam hadn't come to the lab to have fun, but he didn't see any harm in it. He disrobed and stretched out supine on the MRI table. Lauren worked the machine like an old pro. Sam dressed and rejoined her.

"Now, turn around and watch this." Lauren wanted Sam to keep his attention on the stage for the hologram man, but he was more interested in her computer instructions. Enter reconstruction program, double-click on active. Cursor down to whole body. Set automatic reconstruct to 30 seconds, disable error shutdown, maximal contrast internal to external. Set peel mode to manual. He committed the commands to memory. "What do you think?"

Sam was speechless. On the platform behind him was a slowly rotating, perfect image of himself, completely naked. His eyes, and everything else, were perfect. It was as if the hologram were staring at him. "Incredible."

"Well aren't you Mr. Humble."

Sam was confused for a second, and then he understood. Lauren was looking at the holographic groin. "No fair!"

"And, if you need a little help..." Lauren punched a few more buttons and Sam's organ began to glow fluorescent green while it was magnified to twice its original size. Lauren burst into hysterics. "You look like a big pickle!"

Sam laughed too. It felt good. "Enough. C'mon, we have some serious stuff to talk about." They both wiped away the tears.

Lauren had Sam go over the details of what had happened since he had come to Branscomb. He told her everything he knew. When he was finished, she jumped to her feet. "That SOB! I want to help. What can I do?"

"Nothing. Please. If Frank knew that I told you, he'd have me shot. You cannot under any circumstances tell anybody what I've just told you."

"Not even Dr. Spencer?"

"Nobody. Lauren, the only reason I'm telling you any of this is because I can trust you. We're getting close now, I can sense it. Please don't mess it up."

Lauren was frustrated, but she understood. "If you say so. But under one condition. That you keep me posted on what's going on. Now that I know, you can't drop hints and then leave me in the dark. OK?"

"OK."

Suddenly, they were lost for words. For a moment, Sam stared at his glowing gonads and his eyes twinkled as he broke the silence. "All right, what's fair is fair. Now I want to see some of you."

"I beg your pardon?"

"You. Up there." Sam pointed at his image. "Turn me off and let's find a picture of Lauren Doopleheimer. Something good." He grinned.

"Why you dirty dog. And what would that be?"

"Let me think. I'll settle for the waist up. You go get undressed and tell me how to work this thing."

"Don't have to. I've already got what you want in the bank. You can just sit back and enjoy the show."

Lauren evaporated the image of Sam and began to search the computer database for a specific file. Lauren D: Breast Exam. When she located it, she ran through the same set of commands she had used to reconstruct Sam's image. Up popped her nude torso, demurely cut off at the navel.

Sam whistled, then grew inquisitory. "What are you doing in there? A little something special for the professor?"

"Don't sound so hurt. Remember when I had my breast lump? This is the scan from that."

"Nice. Can you make them glow, too?"

"Sam Anderson! Shame on you." Lauren's image disappeared.

"What else is in there?"

"A lot. Look at all these lists." Lauren slid the cursor through a hierarchical maze of file titles, mostly categorized by anatomy. One title caught Sam's eye. Do Not Disturb.

"What's in that one?"

"I have no idea. It's password protected. Spencer has a few files like that. They're for his confidential data. I never go into them."

"You're not allowed to?"

Lauren hadn't given it much thought before. "No, not really. My work's in other files. There's no need to."

"Do you know the password?"

"I'm not supposed to."

"That's not what I asked. Do you know it?" He could tell by her look. "So, you do know it!"

Lauren defended herself. "I couldn't help it. I saw him type it in. Actually, he has two passwords. A main one — he uses it most of the time — and another. I only caught that one once. It looked like DANE."

"So, what's the main one? Have a sense of adventure. Don't you want to know what's in Do Not Disturb?"

"Not really."

"Well, I do. Who knows, it might be somebody famous."

"Do you really want to do this?"

"Of course. Let's go. Type it in."

Lauren acquiesced. She double-clicked on Do Not Disturb and then answered the password request by typing FREEDOM. As soon as she entered the protected file, a new menu appeared.

"It doesn't look like anything special — just a list of names and diagnoses. Let's see — subarachnoid hemorrhage, aortic aneurysm, cervical spine fracture, brain tumor, pancreatic mass, multiple myeloma."

"Pick one."

"Why?"

"I don't know. Just a hunch. Let's see what's there."

"OK." Lauren picked the first one on the list. A black and white brain rolled onto the screen. There was a bright white asymmetric crescent of enhanced blood in the center of the brain. Lauren clicked. In the second image, the crescent was gone. "This isn't too exciting."

"I've gotta agree with you there. Tell you what, Lauren. I'm starved. Want to get something to eat?"

"Sure, but I've got to finish up here. You go on and I'll meet you."

"Burger King?"

"Perfect. Give me a half hour."

Sam walked out and Lauren turned back to the computer. She heard footsteps in the hallway and assumed they were Sam's. Just out of curiosity, she pulled up the next image in the Do Not Disturb file. It was an x-ray of a man's chest, with a wide and displaced aortic shadow. The next film was another chest, but this time it was normal. Before Lauren had a chance to pull up the next view, she was interrupted loudly by Fred Spencer.

"What are you doing?" He pushed in front of Lauren and turned off the computer. "This material is off limits. How did you get in there? You know better than that."

"I...I...it just happened." Lauren was flustered. She didn't mention Sam. "I was just fooling around and the files opened up. I don't know what's in them, really." She couldn't imagine why he would be so upset. "I'm finishing up my work."

"Why don't you call it a night." He saw that she was scared. "I didn't mean to bark at you. There's a lot going on right now. I have to get some images together, so I need to be on the computer tonight. You can do the rest tomorrow. Go on, go home. It's pretty late."

"Thanks, Dr. Spencer. I'm sorry."

"That's all right. I've forgotten about it already."

After Lauren left, Spencer logged onto the computer and retraced her steps for the evening to see which files she had viewed. There was no question about it — she had typed in his main password. There was no telling how many other times she had done that before. Spencer could only assume the worst, which meant that she knew. And if she did, then sooner or later she would tell somebody, unless she already had. As fond as he was of the young woman, he couldn't let that happen.

CHAPTER 41

"Dr. Spencer. I was just picking up the phone to call you. I feel terrible about yesterday. I appreciate what you've done for me."

"Nonsense, Lauren. I should be apologizing to you for the way I reacted. Getting a little tired, I guess. Listen, the reason I called is that I've been reviewing all of the images for my presentation. I don't want you to be concerned, but I may have missed something on your breast scan. It's probably nothing, but I thought I should call you."

Lauren didn't like his tone. He sounded worried. "What did you see?"

"Artifact, most likely. A few small densities that look like fat, but they light up like calcium when I adjust for their depth. That was why I missed them the first time. I forgot to adjust. Somehow the program computed them as if they were on the surface. It's my fault."

Calcium meant calcification. In breast mass lingo, calcification could mean cancer. Lauren sat down. "Are you sure?"

"Oh yes, there's no mistaking them now. Look, I know what you're thinking. But don't jump to any conclusions. You've also got a few cysts, so these could be nothing more than old fluid collections dried up and contracted. You haven't noticed anything new, have you?"

Lauren squeezed herself through her clothing. "No."

"Good."

"What should I do?"

"Well, we'd probably be all right doing nothing, but the safest thing would be to repeat your MRI with contrast, to see if I can get any enhancement around the perimeter. If nothing happens, we're home free. That's fully what I expect to find, but there's only one way to be sure."

"When do I need to see you?"

"There's no rush. A day or two would be fine. Didn't you say you were going out of town?"

"Just a quick trip to the beach."

"Perfect. That matches up with my schedule. I'll be gone for a couple of days to give a paper. We'll do it as soon as you get back. Will you be all right with that?"

Lauren kept her composure. "Yes, I'll be OK. As long as you say so."

Spencer sounded sanguine. "Absolutely. This needs to be done, but nothing'll change in a day or two. Talk to you then. Have a nice trip."

"Thanks Dr. Spencer. You're always there for me."

"That's what advisors are for."

Lauren was more frightened with Spencer's update than she had been by her discovery of the mass. Even though everything he said about alternative explanations made sense, she couldn't get cancer off of her mind. She located Sam at Frank's, who transcribed their conversation to Klawitter. He was concerned, but responded like a doctor.

"Tell her not to worry. Fred Spencer's the best. No, he's better than the best. If he says it's probably not a tumor, then it's not a tumor. I've never seen him blow a study. The only time I've ever seen him change a reading is for a technical error. Misinterpretation isn't in his repertoire. Do you want me to call him?"

"No, Lauren can handle this. She'd ask for help if she needed it."

"Let me know. Now, where were we?"

"You were telling me how the Dean manhandled Elaine Mahnke at Penn..."

CHAPTER 42

The Chief of Surgery was late. He had asked Elaine Mahnke to meet with him at two, and it was already four. His secretary apologized, relaying the message that he got a delayed start on the last case. Did she want to come back later?

Elaine fumed. She wanted to be in the operating room, like him. By the time Montague entered his office, Elaine was in no mood for a philosophical discussion. Montague hurried through the door. When she stood for him, he was reminded of his recent humbling experience in the O.R. and his sudden sympathy for her. Better not to push her to the edge. Instead, he would help her. "Dr. Mahnke — Elaine — I'd like to have a word with you."

Elaine gritted her teeth. Not *again*.

"What about?" Her voice was cold and controlled, even though her hands started to tremble violently. They were in her pockets, thank God.

"Sorry to keep you waiting. I would have handed the case over, but we ran into a few complications. I'm sure you understand."

"Certainly. I didn't have anything important."

Montague let the sarcasm pass. He wanted her to feel good about what he was going to offer, which was the ideal solution to her dilemma.

"I've given it a lot of thought. You're one of the most outstanding teachers we have at Branscomb. Invaluable, really. You know more about transplants than anyone else here. The comments I receive from residents and students always single you out as our best lecturer. That makes us all very proud."

"Thank you. I try as hard as I can to be productive. It isn't always easy, particularly now."

"I know, Elaine. This isn't what we expected, is it?" Montague leaned forward. She didn't know how to answer. "No, of course not. Times were different."

"But I'm not different," Elaine replied.

"Yes, you are. I have to do what's best for everyone concerned, yourself included. Even if you can't see it." Montague had recently assigned her clinical service to someone else, which was the ultimate insult.

Elaine bit her lip and pressed her concealed hands against her sides. "Why did you want to see me?"

Montague didn't intend to play the disciplinarian this time. He wanted her to come to grips with her situation. That was the first step to a true recovery. "We need to decide where it would be best for you to devote your time."

"In the operating room."

"Elaine, please. We've been through that. It isn't possible. I'm prepared to establish a special professorship for you. A full-time opportunity to do what you do best." She didn't react, so he continued. "What do you say to being assigned all the core surgery students? You'll become the Director of Surgical Education. Pass your knowledge to the new generation of doctors who will carry on your work. Make a tremendous contribution to medicine."

"No deals. That's a job for a retiree. I want to operate. You have no right to keep me from being a surgeon."

Montague was trying to be patient. "That's not true. I'm well within my authority. To the hospital, to the patients, and to you. Don't make this more difficult than it has to be. I'm offering you an alternative."

"To what?" The Chief of Surgery looked away. "So that's it!" Elaine glowered. "Why don't you just come out and say it? Say it! You want me to leave. You want me to quit."

"Those are your words. I'm not asking you to quit. This is a chance for you to stay. If you left, that would be your decision. But if you stay, it will be outside the operating room. And we won't discuss this again for at least a year. I'm making you an offer. Those are my conditions."

"Well, here are my conditions. Think about what you promised, and what would happen if I filed a complaint against you for..." Elaine raised a hand to emphasize her point, and watched it sway from side to side, while her fingers twitched out of control. They both stared. Montague slowly shook his head.

"You go to hell!" She ran from the room.

Elaine left the hospital. She needed to walk, to get some air. Away from Montague, she wept with frustration. He was right, but he didn't understand what had driven her to use the drugs. *He treated me like a* common addict. *That arrogant condescending bastard! What does he know about me?* She sneered as she repeated his words to herself. *You'll become the Director of Surgical Education. Pass your knowledge to the new generation of doctors who will carry on your work. Never!*

She worked herself up. *He can't buy me off with a title. I'm a doctor. A surgeon.* Elaine began to mutter aloud. "I'm a healer. I am a *healer*."

The moment she heard herself, Elaine stopped in her tracks, appalled. "But I dropped the kidney!" She thought of her brother and her eyes welled up with tears. *I'll never stop shaking, and he'll never believe me. He said no discussion for a year, but that means forever.*

If I try to operate, I'll end up doing as much damage as Ingelhart, Schmatz, all of them. Montague doesn't even know how bad it is. He thinks it's because I'm an addict. As if I couldn't kick it, if that's all it was! He says no now, what will he say when I get worse?

It would have to be his way or no way. That meant her career was ruined. The finality swept through her like a bitter chill, and she grew numb with depression.

Sam hung out in the clinic for a few days to get a feel for Dr. Mahnke. First-year students were allowed to observe in the outpatient areas, as long as they were properly attired and wore nametags. No one really paid any attention to them, unless they overstepped their bounds and tried to participate in patient care. Sam was the model of propriety.

On Friday morning, he approached Elaine and introduced himself. She was totally disinterested in his conversation and tried to brush him off, until he told her that he hoped he might come to her office the next day after Grand Rounds to discuss a career in transplant surgery. It was the first nice thing anyone had said to her in weeks, but she still tried to refuse him. Sam insisted that he didn't want to talk to a Fellow, because everyone knew that she was the best. Despite her low mood, Elaine said yes. She didn't really feel like talking, but he seemed sincere. Mahnke agreed to meet Sam in her office.

From what Frank had explained, Mahnke wasn't a despicable character like Ingelhart, just a pathetic pawn in the Dean's sordid chess game. With the exception of recent behavior, she evoked more sympathy than animosity. In his head, Sam rehearsed what he was going to say. Lauren's account of the kidney fiasco gave him everything he needed to entice Mahnke to talk.

The case for presentation at Surgery Grand Rounds was one of fulminant hepatic failure in an Asian immigrant who had eaten highly toxic mushrooms because they resembled edible species in the Orient. Since there was no antidote for the toxins, his liver rapidly degenerated and failed. Without a liver transplant, he would have perished. In desperation, he had received a liver from a marginally matched donor, because it was all that was available. Miraculously, it hadn't yet been rejected. This was entirely due to Elaine, who had orchestrated the recipient's immunotherapy behind the scenes. When it came time for questions and answers, Montague gave Elaine full credit for the transplant's brilliant success, but Sam watched her seethe on the opposite side of the auditorium. She stormed out. Elaine wanted to operate, not push chemotherapy. She needed to get to her pills. More and more, it was the only solution.

Sam waited a few minutes, then walked to Elaine's office. He knocked firmly on the door. There was no answer. Sam pushed open the door. Elaine was sitting behind her desk with her head down between her hands. She appeared to be asleep.

"Dr. Mahnke." Sam spoke her name softly. There was no response. "Dr. Mahnke? Dr. Mahnke!" Anderson called her name loudly. Elaine didn't budge. Sam shouted at her. Nothing happened.

"What the hell..." He stepped into the room and locked the door behind him, then moved quickly around behind the desk. Spread out next to Elaine were three fallen pill bottles with tablets and capsules scattered all over the place. Each bottle was half empty. Sam picked them up. Valium. Percodan. Halcion. Sedatives, narcotics and sleeping pills. Sam moved around behind Elaine and slipped his hands under her arms and around across her chest, so that he could pull her upright into a sitting position. As he did, she aroused a bit and opened her eyes to look at him. When she spoke, it startled him.

"Who are you? What are you doing here? Leave me alone." She

waved at him feebly. Sam looked back down at the desk and saw that she had been resting on another bottle of pills. He picked it up and read the label. Elavil, a potent antidepressant. The cap was on the bottle and the container appeared to be full. He put it on the desk.

"Dr. Mahnke, I'm here to see you about being a transplant doctor, remember? I had an appointment." Sam stuck to his charade for no particular reason. Elaine was lethargic from the drugs she had taken. Anyone else who took that amount of medication would be considered to have suffered an overdose. Elaine's endogenous drug metabolism was so juiced up from the constant inflow of pharmaceuticals that she was able to stay awake, but just barely.

"Oh yes, now I remember. Let's see...what did you say your name was? I forget."

"I didn't."

"Look, Mr. I Didn't, I really don't feel so hot. What do you say we postpone our session and you can come back tomorrow. I'm not in the mood to talk right now."

"That really won't be possible. Besides, I came here to talk about something else."

"Something else. Something else." Elaine leaned forward and rested her head on her forearms. She was falling asleep again. Sam put his hand on her shoulder and shook her.

"C'mon now, wake up! I need to talk to you."

Elaine tried to raise her head up, but she only made it halfway. She opened her right eye. "What's so important? Listen, young man, I'm very tired and I'm very cranky and I want you to turn around and march out of here, or you won't have a career in dogcatching, let alone transplant surgery. Now get lost."

"What, like you?"

Elaine opened her other eye. "What?"

"*You're* the one who's lost."

"Are you crazy? Who are you? What are you talking about? Go away. Are you some kind of a lunatic or something? Tell me you're not a medical student."

"And you're not an *addict*."

"You little shit! Who sent you? Waterhouse? Montague? Go tell them to fuck themselves! I'll never give them the pleasure of firing me. The hell with all of you!" She picked up a book and heaved it at him. "Now get out of here!"

"Not yet. Not until you answer some questions." Sam hadn't intended to come on so strong so fast, but it seemed to be working. If Elaine was mad, she might talk.

"Fine. What difference does it make anyway? I'm a woman in medicine. Do you know what happens to women in medicine?" She paused, but Sam didn't say anything. "I'll tell you what happens to women in medicine. Nothing! Nothing happens to women in medicine."

Elaine grabbed the Elavil bottle and flipped off the safety cap. She palmed a fistful of pills. Before Sam could move to stop her, she threw some of them into her mouth.

"Hold on. Don't do that! You don't know what you're doing!"

"The hell I don't." Mahnke opened a small refrigerator next to her desk and pulled out a can of juice, popped the top and used it to wash down the drugs. Sam watched in amazement.

"What are you doing?"

"What does it look like? And why should you care? You were sent here to threaten me, remember? Well, surprise! You don't need to threaten anybody. I'm going to make it easy for you. Actually, I'm glad you showed up or I would have slept through it. Stand on the other side of the room."

Sam looked quickly at how the room was arranged. There was nothing that Elaine could do except scream or pick up the phone. If she attempted to do either of these, Sam could be on her in a second. He decided to go along for the moment. If she tried to swallow any more pills, he'd talk her out of it. Without taking his eyes off her for a second, he backed away from her desk.

"Now, what was your question again? I forgot."

Sam thought quickly. 'Why do they want you to quit?"

"So, someone did send you."

"It's your turn to talk. What did you do?"

"Oh, that's easy. Montague wants me out of here because I'm an embarrassment to him. I shake too much. He isn't into helping disabled women. Sure, he offered to keep me as a teacher, but what's that mean? I'm a surgeon, goddammit! I don't want charity. It's more complicated with Waterhouse. He probably doesn't just want me to quit. I'll bet he'd like to see me dead. So, he wins."

Mahnke picked up the bottle of Elavil again and dumped at least thirty pills into her hand.

"Stop!"

"I'm killing myself and you're my witness."

"I can't let you." Sam started to move towards Elaine.

"Don't take another step. You have no right to stop me. Now, if you want me to tell you anything, you'd better shut up and listen, because I'm starting not to feel too good."

"I don't believe this."

"You don't have to believe it. You just have to remember it. If Waterhouse says he fired me, you go up and grab him by the balls and say, 'That's for Elaine Mahnke. You didn't fire her. You killed her.'"

This was all backwards. Sam was supposed to be intimidating her, and here she was scaring the daylights out of him by threatening to commit suicide with a drug overdose. Ingelhart was one thing, but this was another. He had a chance to help her. Sam took her word for it now, and began to race the effects of the drug.

"Why are you doing this? What did Waterhouse do to you?"

Elaine closed her eyes and leaned back in her chair. She dropped the pills. Everything in the room was spinning, and it was hard to focus. She'd be asleep in a few minutes. The drugs loosened her tongue.

"He was the Assistant Dean. When I came to him in medical school after I had a nervous breakdown, he was going to kick me out. No rest period, no counseling, no second chance, no nothing. Just out the door. Thank you very much. I told him it would be the end of my life, but he didn't care. I was desperate, so I made a bad decision. I let him blackmail me. I'll never forget his words. He said, "Young woman, I've given you a chance."

Sam's loathing for Waterhouse surged with every word Elaine spoke.

"The only thing I had left was money, a lot of it. It was from investments on insurance policies from my mother and brother. I offered it to him and he took it. He wanted more than money. You know what I mean. I refused."

"But he's paying you now. What happened?"

"How did you know that? Oh well, never mind. It doesn't matter what anybody knows now. When I was a resident at Hopkins, Waterhouse flew me out to Washington, D.C. so I could spend a weekend with him at a meeting. He said he'd give me some of the money back. I had temporarily run out of money, so I figured, who has more to lose at this point, a surgery resident or a Dean? You do stupid things when you're broke. I guess I was supposed to act like his mistress."

"Well, were you?"

"No! I wasn't planning to sleep with him, but he took me to a party that turned into an orgy. A bunch of people from Branscomb were there. There was a lot of drinking and drugs. Wiley just stood around watching everybody and taking pictures. He got off that way. Watching."

"Who else was there?"

"What difference does it make?" Elaine was nodding off. Sam ran behind her and shook her shoulders.

"It makes a *lot* of difference! Tell me! Who else was there?"

"Who *are* you?"

"Tell me!"

"Clyde Resnick, Randy Schmatz, Myron Ingelhart. All of the others. I'm sure you know who. Ask Waterhouse."

"You've got to tell me. I can help."

"Don't be ridiculous. This is the only thing that can help me now." Elaine palmed a pill bottle. "Wiley never said no to anything after that. He never resisted. Oh my God, what did we do?" Elaine rested her head on her hands. "I'm tired. Why don't you leave so I can go to sleep?"

"I've only got a couple more questions. Why does he pay you? Who pays *him*?"

"Are you writing a book? He pays us because..."

Elaine slid out of her chair and sat on the floor. She started to lie down, but Sam propped her up. He held out a can of juice.

"Here. Drink this. It'll keep you awake."

"Thanks, but I don't think so. Look, if you don't mind, I've had enough. You should leave now."

Sam saw that Elaine was fading fast. She had to answer one more question. "Why does he pay you now?"

The words were slow in coming. Elaine could barely keep her eyes open. "He's afraid that if he didn't, we'd all go public. He couldn't take a chance we wouldn't. He's the biggest egomaniac of them all. It would destroy him more than anybody if they believed us, which they all would because everybody hates his guts. Besides, the money's nothing to him. He just pulls it out of the practice plan reserve account."

"And?"

"And what?"

"And who pays *him*?"

Elaine forced a weak smile. "That's a good one. The practice plan does. Just like a broker's commission. He takes what he needs. It's been going on for years."

"That can't be all. Dammit, tell me more! An orgy and some payoffs? Everybody does that today. What else is it? What *really* happened in Washington?" Sam clutched Mahnke and shook her violently back and forth. "Tell me!"

Elaine looked up with tears streaming down her face. She spoke with as much hate as a human being could muster. "She never had a chance, and I let them do it. I was so scared. I watched and didn't do a thing to help her."

"Who? Where? In Washington?"

She hung her head. "Yes, in Washington." In her evolving trance, it was as clear as if it had happened yesterday. "She was so beautiful. So young."

"Was she in the pictures?"

"I can't remember the pictures. I threw them out so long ago. I can't talk about this any more."

"You've got to! What happened?"

Elaine fumbled with a pill bottle. "Might as well do this right." She tried to open the safety cap, but it was too much for her. "Damn!" She threw the pill bottle across the room. "Gimme a hand." Sam held a can of juice to her lips and she half swallowed, half choked. "She was a teenager that Schmatz picked up at the meeting. Can you imagine that? Just a kid. Randy ran into a couple of them handing out hors d'eouvres at a reception and invited them to our little party. She didn't know what she was doing. After they got a few drinks into her, none of us could keep up with her. She was so loaded that she could barely stand up. Somebody talked her into doing some drugs. Not party drugs. The real thing. Then she wanted to leave, but they wouldn't let her. The boys needed to make her calm down, to keep her mouth shut. At least, that's what they said. They decided to paralyze her. Completely, like a zombie. They were laughing. Wiley told her to lay back and relax. She was going to have the time of her life."

"And she agreed?"

"She was beyond objecting. They could've just let her sleep it off. But they were too far gone. It was very late. Randy had his doctor bag with him — you know, laryngoscope, tubes, drugs. There was plenty to work with."

"What about you?"

"I sat back and watched with Wiley. He was always watching. Then he got up and helped them. Look, I really need to put my head down."

"Finish first. Don't close your eyes!"

She ignored him and spoke with her eyes closed. She described in anguish the images that projected like a newsreel from her memory. "She was lying flat on the floor. Wiley held her arm while Clyde put the needle into her vein. Randy let Myron inject the succinylcholine. Wiley came back over to me. The girl twitched a few times, then her chest and face began to quiver. The other girl barged into the room. Wiley shoved her out and locked the door. When the girl on the floor stopped breathing, Randy threw in a tube and started to bag her. Something went wrong. Myron lost her pulse. Everybody freaked. She probably had an arrhythmia from all of the drugs and alcohol. We'll never know. Her heart stopped beating. We tried to do CPR, but we couldn't get her back. Nobody called for help. Afterwards, Wiley whimpered like the fucking coward he really is. I was useless. He was useless. We were all useless. And she was dead."

"What did you do with her?"

"They argued for a long time, but there was no bringing her back. It would have ruined everybody. They made it look like an accident. Recreational self-abuse. They dressed her in a black teddy. The coroner called it autoeroticism. Drugged to the brink of death for the purposes of sexual gratification." Elaine spoke so softly that she could barely be heard. "But she went beyond the brink."

"You never spoke up."

"How could I? If I told the truth, it would have been five against one. No one would have believed me. And what if they did? I still would've lost everything. My career. My life."

"And now?"

"And now I've had enough humiliation. I'd like to go to sleep."

"Why don't you help us?"

"It's too late. I want you to leave."

"*Please*."

"What can I tell you. The other girl that Randy brought to the party. You probably know her. She's..." Then she passed out.

Sam shook her again, but this time she wouldn't awaken. Elaine seemed to be in a deep slumber. He couldn't leave her like this, but he also didn't want to be found with her. He turned her on her side and propped up her feet while he decided what to do next. Sam put his ear to her chest. Her breathing was fine for the time being. An anonymous call for help seemed like the most logical thing. He raced to a hall phone and dialed 911. When they asked for his name, he hung up.

Elaine spent four days in intensive care. Montague visited her each day. The Chief Surgeon's former hostility had changed into an empathy that touched Elaine as much as it surprised her. She wasn't used to kindness. His compassion made her cry, unabashed in front of the most important person in her life. Crying seemed to melt something hard within her — something she'd held precious until now.

When it was clear she would recover, Elaine told Montague she accepted his repeated offer of a nonclinical professorship. She was determined to find peace with her decision; she knew Montague was right. She could never again practice surgery. He told her he was pleased, that together they would make this new program work. Finally, she could tell Montague the real reason for the drugs. Oh, the relief of that confession! No more hiding, no more fear. When the Chief of Surgery learned about her illness, he would understand, perhaps even accept, what had driven her behavior. They could even become friends. Maybe they already were. An unfamiliar contentment warmed Elaine. Since her brother had died, she hadn't had a true friend.

The Dean stretched and stood in the window to catch the rays of the afternoon sun. The cumulative stress had etched him noticeably in the past few days. He didn't like being out of control. Malinda had that smug look again. He was impatient with her. "I hope this is important. I'm about to go into a very important meeting now with the Chancellor."

"You can decide. Actually, this'll interest the Chancellor, too. I just heard. Elaine is in the intensive care unit. Overdosed. *Maybe.*" The phone rang.

"Hold on." Waterhouse picked up the receiver. "Hello. Yes, Bob. What? When? Oh my God. I'll talk to you later. I said *later*, goddammit!" He hung up.

All the color had drained from the Dean's face. He rose quickly from his desk and closed the office door.

"I told you. It's all over the hospital. Drugs. Broken career. Pathetic, isn't it? If that's what really happened."

"What do you mean?"

"Think for a second. How much of a coincidence do you think it is that Myron is gone and Elaine is almost dead? Doesn't it strike you the least little bit suspicious? I'd watch my back if I were you." Malinda smiled.

"Who's responsible?"

"I don't know. Looked in the mirror lately?"

"God damn you! Who is it? You *know* — don't you! Tell me."

"What's it worth to you?"

Wiley was in a panic. Something terrible was going on. "Enough. A lot. As much as it takes." He inhaled deeply and asked the question he most dreaded. "Is there a list?"

"Funny you should ask that. I had the same thought. I'm trying to find out. With the right incentive — up front, of course — I can probably find out everything you need to know."

He was resigned to what was coming next. "How much?"

"Two million."

"You're the devil incarnate! I don't need you anymore." It was all falling apart.

"The hell you don't! Who are you gonna ask? I'm sure whoever it is will just tell you everything he knows, give you a big hug and thank you for the opportunity. Let me give you a hint. You just suspended his girlfriend from medical school."

"Sam Anderson."

"You're the biggest asshole on the face of the earth if you expect *him* to confess to one murder and maybe another and then tell you who's behind it all!"

"A million." Waterhouse still had some of Mahnke's money.

"A million it is."

"I want to know *everything*. Who he knows about. Who's in charge. Why they're doing it. What we can do to stop them. And one last thing. This is *it* for you! Not another cent. If you won't agree to that, I'll take my chances and deal with this my own way."

Malinda laughed. "You've got a deal. You're a generous man, Dean Waterhouse. Let me get to work. I'll have some information for you as soon as possible. After you deposit the money in the usual account."

CHAPTER 43

Sam was excited, edgy. Mahnke's story would be the key to the kingdom for Frank. He thought it best to tell him in person.

"She's *what*? She's where? Are you out of your mind?"

"I told you, it was attempted suicide. An accident. By the time I got there, she'd already taken the pills. I called for help. I don't know what happened after that."

"Again! How many times, Sam? How many times am I supposed to believe it could be an accident?" Frank was becoming enraged.

"Frank, she told me everything. About Waterhouse. About Schmatz, Resnick, Ingelhart. She had trouble talking in the end, but she explained about herself. It's a pity. I hope she doesn't die."

"That's right, she better not. You son of a bitch!" Frank grabbed Sam by the collar and slammed him repeatedly into the wall, yelling with each thrust. "Why did you do it? How did you poison her? Why does she have to die?"

"She wanted to kill herself. I tried to stop her." Sam was confused and frightened.

"No she didn't. You tried to kill her!"

"No! I tried to help her!" Frank was possessed. Sam couldn't free himself from the larger man. "I told her to... stop. I...I...tried to get her to...to...trust me. Christ, Frank!"

"You called *too late*! You wanted her to die. You've got to *save* them! Dear God, what have we become? What have *I* become?" He tightened his grip on Sam and bellowed in rage. "They're all so helpless!"

Sam suddenly recognized what was going on. Frank was still blaming himself for his cousin's death, and now he was blaming Sam for Elaine as well.

"Just like the soldier in Kuwait, right Sam?" Frank slapped him.

Sam fought back as he too became angry. He tore Frank's hands off his shoulders. "Listen, you self-righteous bastard. I shot that man in self-defense. But I *didn't* kill Ingelhart. I *didn't* hurt Mahnke. *And I didn't kill your cousin Eleanor!*"

Frank fell back, silent. He stared at Sam, whose chest was heaving.

"Do it. Hit me, you selfish prick." Sam lowered his voice. "But it won't bring her back. She's dead. It's not your fault. Stop doing this to yourself. I'm here to help you. She would have wanted me to help you."

Frank dropped to his knees and began to sob, quietly at first and then without restraint. He groped for a chair and buried his head in his hands. Sam walked over to him and pressed a hand on his back. He kept it there until Frank stopped weeping. Finally able to control himself, Frank looked up at Sam.

"I'm sorry."

"That's OK, Frank. You've needed to get that out for a long time."

Frank nodded. He reached out a hand to Sam and rose to his feet. "Now tell me..."

CHAPTER 44

Sam didn't know exactly what time Lauren would be back from her trip to the coast, but he knew it was supposed to be within the next few hours. He didn't want her to be taken totally by surprise. When he called, he got the tape. "Lauren, I've got to talk to you. Call me as soon as you get back. Mahnke told me about something that happened that's so bad that..." Sam paused in mid sentence. He realized that anyone in the apartment could hear his message. "Call me." He hung up. Maybe she would stop by Spencer's lab on the way back to her apartment. It was worth a try.

The door was locked, but the lights were on. Lauren had given Sam a key to the lab so that he could let himself in to meet her. Someone must have been working and stepped out for a minute, because the MRI data bank was powered up and displayed the menu. It was different from the last time, rearranged somehow. Out of curiosity, Sam perused the table of contents. Why not?

He scrolled down to "thorax" and followed the hierarchical browsers through "female" and "anterior" to "breast." There were case numbers and names. Lauren D: Breast Exam. Sam double-clicked. The flat screen image of Lauren appeared. Sam closed his eyes and pictured the next commands. Enter reconstruction program, double-click on active. Cursor down to whole body. Set automatic reconstruct to 30 seconds, disable error shutdown, maximal contrast internal to external. Set peel mode to manual. There was a faint whirring, and the beams of light began to intersect behind him. He turned around and there she was, absolutely lifelike.

Sam studied her image closely, but could find no flaw. Over the months, he had watched Lauren work these controls, and had learned well. Sam rotated Lauren's image on the pedestal. A new button on the touch screen caught his eye. Auto. He activated it.

In slow motion, Lauren's hologram shed her skin, then her muscles, then her bones. Internal organs vanished to nothingness, then reappeared in reverse. It all happened in the space of a single rotation of the platform. Sam closed the file. He continued to peruse the menu. In between "quadriceps" and "hamstrings," something caught his eye. Do Not Disturb — it disturbed him. What was the password? He typed in FREE-DOM. Nothing happened. He tried it again. Nothing.

Spencer had changed the password. Sam stood up to leave, then remembered what Lauren had said about a second password. DANE. Sam tapped on the keyboard. The screen rejected his attempt with a cursory reply, "Incorrect password. Contact system administrator for instructions on how to proceed." That would be impossible.

DANE. DANE........not DANE! Sam rearranged the letters and entered the word DEAN. The computer clicked and a new menu appeared.

This one had been rearranged as well. There were fifteen titles listed, each with a diagnosis and date, all within the last year. The first five were subarachnoid hemorrhage, atlanto-axial dissociation, aortic aneurysm, pancreatic mass, and breast cancer. A sixth was titled Lauren D: Aux.

Sam pulled up the subarachnoid hemorrhage. It was the same scan he had reviewed with Lauren. One image showed the bleed, and in the next it had disappeared. How was that possible? The scans carried the same date. Atlanto-axial dissociation was a series of tomographic cuts through the cervical spine of an elderly man. In alternating images, there were obvious fractures, then normal, then broken, then perfect. The aortic aneurysm had a name: David Ring. There were only two x-rays. The first showed a clearly widened mediastinum and displaced aorta, while the second was stone cold normal. Identical dates. If the preceding files told a similar story, they were all lies. Spencer was manufacturing his findings, perpetrating a monstrous deceit.

The pancreatic mass melted away with a twist of the dial. Sam was afraid of what he'd find next. He clicked on breast cancer. There it was. The same image of Lauren he had just studied in her other file. Except this time, there were two additional views, both with obvious abnormalities that Sam now knew didn't exist. Imaginary tumors. Like the other films, they were forgeries. But he didn't know the details of the other cases. What was reality, normal or disease?

The final file was Lauren D: Aux. The auxiliary file was something different. There were no preliminary two-dimensional images — just a button that said "dance." Sam held his breath and clicked.

The light generator powered up and projected onto the pedestal behind him. Layer by layer, the image was created. First it appeared as a woman of nameless features, no different than anyone who might pass in front of a mirror. Then it slowly became Lauren Doopleheimer, naked, undulating, seductive. She was even pouting.

"Lauren! What are you doing?" Sam chastised the illuminated vapor. He couldn't believe his eyes. He looked away, then turned back to face Spencer's creation.

It was a program that continued without any further assistance from Sam. The ghost bent over backwards and spread her legs, then leaned forward and leered at Sam. Lauren's image laughed, and then suddenly grew still. She began to dissolve, first without hair, then without a face, and then hideously without skin. All the while, turning, twisting, back to front and front to back. Her natural covering returned while her hands slid suggestively over her thighs and genitalia.

"Damn! You son of a bitch."

It kept repeating. An undulating skeleton, then filled with organs, then muscles, then a face. Teeth, eyes, toenails, pubic hair. Tumors and deformities. Sam spun a dial in the opposite direction and it shifted into reverse. Peeling an onion. Dismantling a human being. Lauren was the woman he loved, and she had been defiled by Spencer's pornographic imagination. It was macabre and obscene. Sam's anger made him shake. He punched off the power and raced from the lab to find Lauren.

CHAPTER 45

"Something that happened that's so bad that..."

Malinda had walked into the apartment to grab her study group notebook and caught the tail end of Sam's message to her roommate through the open door. She moved quickly into Lauren's bedroom and pressed the replay button. After she listened, she erased the tape.

From the sound of it, Frank and Sam were closing in fast. It was only a matter of time before they'd make the link that would ruin everything for her. That couldn't happen. Malinda had come to Branscomb for a single reason. She'd waited too long to give it up without a struggle. Klawitter was going to be a monumental problem, but Sam had to be controlled first. She needed to get to him before he spilled his guts to Lauren.

She would use Sam's discovery to pull in the others. It all had to happen at the same time. It was now or never.

Sam pushed the buzzer three times. Malinda opened the door and took Sam by the arm with a firm grip, pulling him into the apartment. She wore a blue cotton halter-top, black running shorts, and nothing else. Her sandy blonde hair was tied back in a bun and she was wearing lipstick and eye shadow. She was barefoot. Sam didn't believe his eyes. She looked fantastic.

"Help yourself to something to drink. I need to finish getting dressed. I'll be out in a sec."

"Thanks. Don't mind if I do." Sam rummaged and grabbed a dark German beer with a name that he couldn't pronounce. He had to reach past three large bottles of wine. "You planning on having a party?"

"Just you, Sam." Anderson gave a start, because Malinda had sneaked up directly behind him. "I've been looking forward to this for a long time." Malinda had changed into a vivid silk blouse and a wrap-around skirt. She had splashed herself with perfume, but was still barefoot. The skirt highlighted her fabulous legs.

"Excuse me?"

Malinda moved up close to Sam and ran a fingertip down his chest.

"Un-fucking-believable," mumbled Sam. This was all wrong. He was here to find Lauren. He raised his voice to a normal tone. "Why are you doing this?" He pushed back, but she held his waist at arm's length.

"How's this for a surprise? Did you have any idea?"

Sam was flabbergasted. Nothing made any sense. It was all part of some disguise. He had to admit that he was fascinated by this version, but he didn't trust it. And didn't like it.

"No. I would have never expected this in a million years. Look, what are you up to? This isn't right. What's going on with Lauren? She'd wring my neck if she caught me in here with you like this. Where is she?"

"She called to say she'd be late. We've got a couple of hours."

Dwyer carried a beer into the living room and sat down on one end of the couch. She motioned to Sam to join her. He sat at the opposite end of the couch, so she put her feet up. Her skirt fell away and revealed the entire length of one leg.

"Well, 007, tell me what you've discovered. Lauren's told me all about your extracurricular activities here at Branscomb. At least what she knows. You know, your girlfriend doesn't keep a secret very well. She told me all about Waterhouse and how you've been trying to shadow him. What a great story. He's such an asshole. It's too bad that nobody can figure out a way to shut him down."

Sam was furious at the breach. "I can't believe this. She told you all that?"

"Not everything. I'm guessing a little." Sam held a blank expression. "Don't pretend that you don't know. Hasn't Lauren told you?" She needed to goad him if she was going to learn anything. "She also told me about Frank."

Sam jumped up in anger. He needed to call Frank. Malinda pushed him back on the couch. Her voice became softer.

"Don't be in such a hurry. I act the way I do to keep people off me, because most medical students are nosy and uptight. I keep my distance. But it works, you know. They talk to me. Tell me things. Lucky for both of us, I guess."

"Lucky or unlucky, depending on how you look at it," said Sam. "Look, I've got to find her."

"She just called. It's going to be awhile. You shouldn't feel bad. Ingelhart got what he deserved. Sounds like Mahnke did, too. I wonder who's next on your list."

"What do you mean, got what he deserved? He didn't *get* anything. It was an accident."

Malinda's comments didn't make sense to Sam. If Lauren had told her so much, Malinda would never think he was a killer. It was the second time in two minutes that she had tried to pump him for confidential information. He wanted to change the subject. Where was Lauren?

Malinda persisted. "Waterhouse. What a slimeball! C'mon, tell me. Was he doing Elaine Mahnke? How long do you think it'll take her to die? Are you gonna go after Wiley next?"

Christ, I need another drink, thought Sam. *And I need to get out of here. I've got to find Lauren.*

"I'll get us a refill," Malinda said, as if reading Sam's mind.

"Mind if I use the bathroom first?"

Sam went into the bathroom and closed the door. As soon as Malinda heard the latch, she sprang off the couch and raced to the refrigerator. She popped the top on a bottle of the German beer. She looked back to be certain that Sam wasn't coming out of the bathroom. Then she added a healthy squirt of liquid fentanyl from a small glass bottle she'd hidden next to the sink. She swirled the beer gently, then poured it into a frosted mug from the freezer. The colder the beverage, the less likely Sam would be to notice the taste. She poured herself a glass of wine. Before she heard the toilet flush, she had returned the narcotic to its hiding place. She had to grab this chance — Sam's showing up like this when Lauren was out - she might never have another one.

Malinda raised her wineglass to Sam's beer mug. "Here's to your mission." They both took a swig, then Sam downed the remainder of his drink. "Thirsty?" she said.

"Pretty bitter," he commented. "You like this label?"

"Not particularly. That's why I gave it to you. Most people won't drink it. Want another one? I need to use them up on you, because no one else is man enough to drink 'em."

Sam felt a quick rush from the beer, and he liked the feeling. Malinda was beginning to look pretty good.

"Sure, as long as you're still drinking."

Malinda took Sam's glass and went back to the refrigerator. She poured another beer and added nearly all of the remaining narcotic from the hidden container. She held up the drug bottle to see how much was left, shrugged her shoulders and poured it all into the glass. As she handed Sam back his mug, she sat down on the arm of the couch directly behind him. After she put her wineglass on the lamp table, she began to massage his shoulders.

"Man, you're so tight," she crooned into Sam's ear.

The words sounded fuzzy. He was tired. "Don't."

"You need someone to loosen you up a bit. Does Lauren do this for you? If she doesn't, she ought to. How does this feel? Let me know if it's too hard." She ran her hands up the back of his neck and twiddled her fingers through his hair. "How's *this* feel? I think you waited too long to come over here."

"I came to see Lauren. Where is she?"

"Running some errands before she hooks up with her radiologist friend Professor Spencer. She's having an important exam done later. Her breast again. He said it had to be tonight."

"No. No, I've got to talk to her!" Sam tried to get up, but Malinda easily pushed him back down onto the couch.

"That can wait. Do you like this? I can feel you relaxing."

"Aaaahhh," was all that Sam felt like saying. He was beginning to feel weird, as if the beers had been a gallon of rum. He wasn't sick, just incredibly drowsy, and the massage was putting him to sleep. A semi-clad beautiful woman whispering sweet nothings should have had precisely the opposite effect. Sam realized that something was dreadfully wrong. It wasn't that hard to figure it out. As his vision quickly blurred and he began to see double, he knew he'd been drugged, but he was too damn sleepy and weak to do anything about it. The room spun as he slumped down into the couch. His inhibitions left him.

"I've got to go," he slurred.

"Here, let me take this off." As she talked, Malinda removed her blouse. She had beautiful, full breasts. She lifted one and leaned forward. "Would you like to touch it?" Malinda pulled Sam's hand onto her breast and then quickly down her hip. She had to guide his limp fingers. He struggled to keep in focus. All he wanted to do was sleep. "Keep talking and I'll let you feel everything."

She peppered him with questions, and the fentanyl worked like truth serum. Sam told her about his relationship with Frank and how Ingelhart had died. As Sam finished his rendition of Elaine Mahnke's story, he closed his eyes and began to breathe heavy. Malinda wanted to hear more, to learn if they knew *everything*. It was now or never.

Malinda unwrapped her skirt and let it fall around her ankles.

"What do you think, Sam?"

Sam concentrated all his remaining sight on Malinda's undulating pelvis. Just before he lost consciousness, he saw the large brown birthmark extending from the hip bone to just above her thigh, its outline just like the State of Texas.

CHAPTER 46

Sam was comatose on the couch. Malinda stood over him stark naked until she was certain that he wasn't going to wake up. Sam would be out cold for at least the next hour. His relaxation was so complete that his cheek and mouth fell completely away from his face.

Malinda had to move quickly. Knowing that Mahnke had probably explained it all to Sam, she saw one last chance to do what she'd come to Branscomb for. There was no time for an elaborate plan. She'd deal with them however she could. She went to the telephone and called the ER.

"Branscomb ER. Do you want to speak to a doctor or nurse?"

"I'd like to speak with Dr. Resnick. Is he on duty?"

"Yes, I think so. Please hold and let me page him." The clerk put Malinda on hold, while a tape recorder played back a safety advisory. "I have Dr. Resnick now." There was a clicking noise.

"Hello, this is Dr. Resnick. How can I help you?"

"Clyde, this is Theresa Curtis. I'm in medical school here under my new name, Malinda Dwyer. I've got a man unconscious in my apartment who's supposed to kill you and Schmatz. Then he's gonna get Wiley and Bob. He killed Ingelhart. Mahnke's in the ICU. I need to see you. *Now*."

Resnick's jaw dropped. It couldn't be true! Waterhouse had told them all that she'd been paid off, that she'd never show her face again, that they had nothing to worry about. Ingelhart had died in an accident. Oh my God, it *was* her! Even though he'd only been with her for one evening, he'd never forget that voice. That son of a bitch Waterhouse. He'd been lying all along.

It had already occurred to Clyde that what happened to Ingelhart might not have been an accident. So, somebody inside was rotten. One of them had to have had Myron killed. Mahnke was out. It had to be Wiley. He spoke tentatively because he wanted to be certain that this wasn't just a blackmail attempt.

"Tell me why I should believe you. How do I know that you're who you say you are? How do I know that you're not some crazy person who heard a story somewhere and wants to make a little easy money? You haven't told me anything yet that I need to worry about."

"Is that right, you dumb fuck? Clyde, remember how young we were? Remember how embarrassed you were that night? Remember how you couldn't get it up while everybody was watching? Sure. I bet you remember that. Remember how Wiley made you all wear those stupid hats for the pictures? Remember the birthmark on my left hip? Remember how you took me into the other room and begged me to hum the Star Spangled Banner and give you a blowjob? Remember how she died, Clyde? Think hard, because if you don't do what I tell you, we'll both wind up dead."

It was her, all right. "OK, I believe you. Tell me what's going on."

"All right, that's better. We'll have to postpone the formal reunion until later. I've got a man named Sam Anderson with me who's got a load of beer and fentanyl on board. He's the guy who lowered the boom on Ingelhart. He also poisoned Elaine, but that's a story we don't have time for now. I know who he's working with, but that's also not important. The point is, he's on to you and me and everyone else from the party and he won't quit until we're all history. And guess what? You're next. He's supposed to be a medical student, but he's a lot better with his hands than you are with a knife."

Resnick fired back his response. "Is that so? Well, I may not be a surgeon anymore, but maybe it's time for him to have an operation. He can suffer an untimely and tragic death in the O.R. during an emergency appendectomy."

"No! You don't have O.R. privileges. They won't let you in."

"That's *my* problem. This is an emergency. The nurses let the doctors do whatever they want. Who's going to stop me? Besides, at this point it's us or him. Bring him in here... "

"You're no match for this one, Clyde, not by a long shot."

"Then don't bother me, Theresa. Just give him more of the medicine, write a note and make people think he committed suicide. Hell, that would be the easiest thing to do. Then I'll see you. And him, I suppose."

"I want to see you now!" Malinda drew a breath and tried to compose herself. "Besides, I know his boss, and he won't buy that story for a second."

Resnick stood his ground. "Well, Theresa, while Mr. Big's worrying about how to cover for this unusual, but believable complication of surgery, you can be figuring out how to quit medical school and get out of town. Because you're what got us into trouble in the first place. I'll be in the ER waiting for my case. Appendicitis or dead on arrival, either way suits me fine. Better bring him. I'll call Randy. It'll be just like old times."

Malinda didn't see a choice. She raced into her bedroom and threw on a sweatshirt, jeans and basketball sneakers. She wiped off the makeup and lipstick and mussed up her hair. Then she ran out to the apartment complex parking lot, jumped into her car, and drove around to the rear entrance of the building.

After checking to see that no one was watching her, she opened the hatchback and trotted back to the apartment. She rolled Sam over and hoisted him over her shoulder. Grunting and wobbling under the weight, she carried Sam to her car and threw him into the back seat, then sped off to the hospital. It was improvisation time. She'd protect him, if it came to that.

Resnick telephoned up to the O.R. and explained that he expected an emergency appy to come up in about 30 minutes, and to request Randy Schmatz for the anesthesiologist. If he wasn't available, Schmatz was to call Resnick directly. He told the registrar up in the O.R. that the patient was a close family friend of Schmatz and had requested him personally.

Next, he told the charge nurse in the ER, Gloria Koslofsky, that he wanted to pre-register a patient about whom he had just received a call. A first-year student named Sam Anderson had what sounded like appendicitis. From the sound of what he had just heard over the telephone, the boy might have an abscess and be toxic, so he wanted him placed alone in the isolation room where Resnick could evaluate him quickly. The boy was being brought in by another student. He'd taken a lot of pain medicine, so he might be asleep, but that was nothing to worry about. When they arrived, he wanted Gloria to put the student and his friend both in the room together, so he could be sure to get the complete history himself.

The clerk at the main desk called to Resnick, "Dr. Schmatz is on the phone. He wants to talk to you." Resnick walked to a phone out-of-earshot at the other end of the desk and shouted, "I'll take it over here."

The clerk pressed a few buttons and the phone directly in front of Resnick began to ring.

"Hello, Clyde? This is Randy."

"Randy, I need you to come in now to do a case."

"What for, Clyde? Do you know what time it is? What's all this about a friend of the family? I'm not on call. Call someone else. That's why people are on call. Tell the family I was out of town."

Resnick held the receiver close to his mouth and shielded it with his hands. He turned away from everyone. "Randy, you'd best get your butt in here. Somebody knows all about what happened in Washington. I'm pretty sure that Waterhouse is having us picked off one by one."

"What? What in the *hell* are you talking about? Are you smokin' dope on the job again?"

"Randy, you know about Ingelhart. That was no accident. Neither was Elaine. There's a nut on the loose and we're his next targets. I think that Waterhouse sold us down the river, but we don't have time to find out for sure right now. Theresa Curtis is alive and well in Branscomb Medical School. How's that for a bad night?"

"This better be for real, 'cause if it ain't, I'm gonna put *you* to sleep."

"Fuck you, Randy! The whole reason this is happening is because you keep killing people in the O.R. You're incompetent. Well, come on in and show us your stuff. Somehow, Theresa's captured Wiley's man. She's bringing him in for a bogus operation and that's our only chance to straighten this mess out. If you want to leave it to me, fine. But if you do and this doesn't work, I'm serving you up to Wiley any way I can. God, you can be an asshole!"

"Why don't you call me when the case is ready to go? That way, if this whole thing is a fire drill, I don't have to waste my time looking at you."

Resnick needed Schmatz to come in now. "You know what Theresa said? She said that you were the best. That you untied yourself faster than any rube she'd ever shackled. But she wishes you hadn't threatened to inject her if anyone ever found out about the girl. She said that was selfish." It had been a long time ago, but Clyde's memory was suddenly like an elephant's. He and Wiley had watched through the door.

"She said that?"

"Yep. And a few other things. Like that the son of a bitch has a hit list, and your name's at the top. I'm on my way to the O.R. with Theresa and this bastard, and we need an anesthesiologist. Understand?"

"I'll be there right away. Don't tell anyone what you're doing. Damn! I was afraid something like this would happen sooner or later."

"Before you come in, page Bob and Wiley. Get them to meet us upstairs."

Malinda was sitting at the bedside with a look of total concentration on her face, like a prison sentry doing watch duty. Nothing would go wrong if she stayed with him.

"Theresa..." She had aged, but not nearly as much as he.

"Malinda to you now, Clyde. It's been a long time."

"Not long enough. Go into the nurses' locker room and throw on a pair of scrubs. You need to look the part when we go to the O.R. I'll watch the patient."

Malinda walked out of the room. As soon as she left, Clyde picked up the chart and scribbled on it. Then he motioned to Gloria Koslofsky to come into the room.

"Gloria, do me a favor, will you?" Clyde gestured at Sam. "You know who this is. Watch him for me and let me know if he has any trouble or starts to wake up. I might as well keep him asleep, since he'll be in the O.R. soon. His sedation's perfect. Thanks, I'll be right back." Clyde walked out and left Sam alone with Koslofsky.

Gloria looked the young man over. What a mess. Might as well clean him up while they were waiting to go upstairs. Gloria sponged his forehead with a wet cloth and wiped the spittle off his chin and cheeks. There was a sloppy pile of papers lying at the foot of Sam's gurney. She picked them up and started to rearrange them into a semblance of chronological sequence. First came the registration note, then the nursing note, then the doctor's history and physical, then the orders, then the permit.

The permit caught her eye. On top of the disheveled pile of papers was the blue permit for an appendectomy, but it already carried the bold signature of Sam Anderson. That didn't make much sense, since she hadn't seen Sam awake since he'd been wheeled into the department. She flipped through the papers until she found the history and physical. Scanning quickly, she was astounded to read the following: "white male medical student, appears stated age. Pt says he had onset of RLQ pain, N/V/D yesterday PM, worse today. + FH of appendicitis. Pt claims to have self-medicated with fentanyl 1 hr PT visit. PE shows rebound over McBurney's point, absent bowel sounds, no hernia. Rectal neg for heme. Pt informed of need for emergency surgery and gives verbal and written consent."

Gloria knew that Resnick was worthless, but she'd never seen him do anything this blatantly dishonest before. He hadn't spent two minutes with the patient, so he had clearly fabricated the record. Why would he be in such a hurry to whip this medical student into the O.R.? What could possibly be the reason for a falsified medical record?

Sam still had his pants on. Gloria rifled his pockets and found a wallet. She searched through its contents rapidly, but all she found was a driver's license, credit card, student ID and twenty dollars in assorted bills. She started to put the billfold back in his trousers when she had an afterthought. Gloria pulled out Sam's license and held it up against the blue surgery consent form. The signature on the permit didn't match the one on the license. Gloria flipped the license over. There was an orange universal organ donor sticker glued to the license, upon which was written, "In the event of emergency, call 404-854-7642." How convenient, mused Koslofsky. 404 is our area code. 854-7642 is a Branscomb Hospital extension. She turned Sam on his side and replaced his wallet, but kept the license and walked out to the phone at the nurse's station. As she dialed the number on the sticker, Gloria looked over at the observation room and saw Dwyer reenter in a surgical scrub suit. A voice came on the telephone.

"Thank you. Just a minute please. Your call will be answered in the order received."

Resnick walked into the room with Sam. Gloria was about to hang up when a machine picked up and delivered a recorded message.

"Thank you for calling the office of Dr. Franklin Klawitter. Office hours are 8:30 to 4:30 Monday through Friday. If you need a clinic appointment, please call 854-7111. If you are calling for test results, please call 854-9000. If you wish to leave a message, please begin at the sound of the tone, or press 1 for more options."

Gloria hung up. She didn't have time to fool with the answering machine. She dialed the hospital page operator and had Frank Klawitter paged to call the ER. A flurry of commotion distracted Gloria away from the telephone. Clyde was arguing with one of the emergency nurses.

"You people act as if calling report is the same thing as taking care of a patient. I don't care if you haven't called report. I know that the O.R. hasn't called yet, but I'm extremely worried about this patient," insisted Resnick. "I'll finish the blasted paperwork after we take out his appendix. If you're done torturing me, I'll be on my way."

Resnick and Malinda clutched the opposite ends of Sam's gurney and wheeled it out of the isolation room. The nurse who stood in their way turned to Koslofsky with a pleading look as if to say, what do I do now? The charge nurse waved her hand to signal that they be allowed to pass. Regardless of how inappropriate Resnick was, imagine what would happen if the boy ruptured his appendix and the delay to surgery was blamed on the nurses.

Sam had just been wheeled out of the ER when Klawitter answered his page. He was calling on his car phone about ten miles from the hospital.

"Frank, I'm sorry to bother you, but a pretty strange thing just happened. Resnick just examined a medical student and decided he had appendicitis. The problem is that he really didn't examine him, he just took the information over the telephone. Then he filled out the record and forged the op permit. The student's gorked out on something. I think fentanyl. He hasn't budged since he got here. The whole thing's screwy."

"Back up, Gloria," replied Frank. "Why are you calling *me*?"

"Because I'm supposed to."

"Whaddya mean, you're supposed to? Am I responsible for Clyde Resnick now? Did I lose a contest? I don't control Clyde Resnick."

"I'm calling you, Frank, because I pulled this kid's driver's license and it had a phone number to call in the event of an emergency. It was your office phone number."

Frank slammed on the brakes. "What's his name?" He already knew the answer. Frank screeched a U-turn in heavy traffic.

"Samuel P. Anderson. He's out for the count."

"Where is he now?" Frank shouted at Gloria. "Is he still in the ER? Is anybody else with Resnick? Where is he?!"

Gloria assumed that Frank was upset because he was concerned about Sam's medical condition. She did her best to reassure him. "Calm down, Frank, everything's OK. Resnick and a medical student are wheeling him up to the O.R. Schmatz is going to meet them there."

"Oh Jesus."

"I don't know who's gonna do the case, but Resnick said he would arrange for a surgeon. I don't think you need to race in here, but I wanted you to know what's going on since Resnick kind of fudged the paperwork. He probably just wanted to make sure that the kid didn't have to wait a year to get his appendix chopped out."

"Thanks, Gloria. Listen carefully. Call Joe Masterson and tell him I said for him to come to the O.R. right away because our boy is in trouble. I don't have time to explain. Just do it for me. Joe'll understand."

"Frank, is everything OK? Did I do something wrong?"

"No, Gloria. You did something right. Will you call Joe?"

Gloria had never heard Frank this agitated. "Got it. I'll call Joe and let him know what's up."

Frank leaned on the accelerator.

Clyde and Malinda steered the gurney carrying Sam through the main entrance into the operating rooms and directly down the end of the corridor to O.R. 17. This was the most out-of-the-way O.R., usually the site for minor urological procedures. It was one of two rooms that didn't share a scrub sink, so it was even more isolated.

Clyde flipped on the lights and locked the gurney into position next to the fixed table in the center of the room. He checked once again to see that Sam was asleep, then stepped out of the room to change clothes.

There was a knock on the window over the scrub sink. Randy

Schmatz looked through the window and waved to Malinda, who gave him a nod of affirmation. Schmatz was dressed in his operating room garb. Without washing his hands, he stepped into the room.

"Guess we don't need to scrub for this one. Well, well, well. Nice to see you again, Theresa. I never thought that we'd end up on the same operating team. That's quite a change for you."

"Not as much as you think, Randy. Whether you know it or not, I'm a first-year student in med school here. Maybe when this is all over, I'll go into anesthesia and do my residency with you."

Schmatz grimaced. "You've kept your sense of humor. Now, what's going on. This is the assassin? He doesn't look too dangerous."

Malinda stalled with a quick litany of lies. "Waterhouse contacted me about two years ago and said that he wanted me to apply to medical school here, and that I'd have no trouble getting in. At first, he wouldn't tell me why, just that he thought I'd make a good doctor. He wanted me to change my name. He said he had a special job for me. That was, until *this* guy Sam Anderson showed up. Then he told me that I could just be a regular old student. I guess we know now what it was he wanted me to do." An explanation that implicated the Dean kept her out of it for the time being.

"How did you find out who he was?" asked Schmatz as he poked and prodded Sam's arm, looking for a vein. "Who tipped you off that he was working for the Dean?" The anesthesiologist found a good vein on the back of Sam's hand, and inserted an intravenous catheter. He hooked it up to a bag of normal saline.

"What are you doing?" Malinda flashed back.

"Just getting set up. Keep talking."

"I just tripped over him. He was hitting on me, had a few beers and started bragging. When he told me that he was a big friend of Waterhouse and that he'd been brought here for a special reason, I managed to get the rest out of him."

"So, what are we going to do?" asked Schmatz. "Can't we just push him off a cliff or something? Seems pretty crazy to take a chance on getting caught up here."

"I didn't think that staging a stupid accident would work and besides, it's too late for that. We don't have much time. I think that Waterhouse knows that we know, so we have to get in a position to deal with him. This idiot lying here is expendable."

"I don't like this," argued Schmatz. "I've never killed anybody."

"Are you kidding? We're all here. The deal is set up, and I think we should just get it over with." Malinda lowered her voice to barely a whisper. "Besides, we're gonna blame it on Clyde. He's gonna do the surgery. Who would argue if you said that he got confused doing an appendectomy and hacked through the inferior vena cava? Wiley'd have no choice but to cover for you like he's done a million times. Clyde'll take the heat." Malinda studied the room carefully. She was looking for weapons.

Resnick walked back into the O.R. He was fully gowned and gloved, but wasn't wearing a scrub hat or a mask. There was no point, considering that infection wasn't going to be one of Sam's problems. Resnick carried a large multidose vial of potassium chloride, which contained enough of the electrolyte to kill a person easily.

"Hi, Randy. Has Theresa filled you in on our little problem?"

"She certainly has. What are we doing here?"

"Well," said Resnick, "probably the most believable way for him to die would be to have a cardiac arrest during the case and attribute it to an anesthetic error. I brought some potassium with me. All you have to do is squirt this into his IV as fast as you can. We can say that you thought it was a vial of antibiotics and that you grabbed the wrong bottle. Nobody can give you too much grief for that."

"No way," replied Schmatz. "That's the dumbest thing I ever heard in my life. It doesn't make any sense to get me into trouble. I've been up before the QA committee three times in the last six months and I don't think I can bluff my way out of another one. Besides, nobody's stupid enough to give someone a whole bottle of potassium without noticing it. We need another idea."

Malinda grew impatient. "Great, Dr. Schmatz. Why don't you give us one? But I wouldn't take all day."

"Let me think. OK, I've got it!" announced the anesthesiologist. "Here's the plan."

"Let's hear it," said Resnick.

"Clyde, everybody knows that you used to be a surgeon, but that you haven't even carved a roast beef in over a decade. They also think that you have a pretty big ego and are always looking to make an extra buck. Let's just say that you examine this kid and think he has an appy, and that you take him up to the O.R. While you're waiting for the surgeon, you watch him slide into septic shock. The surgeon doesn't answer after three pages. You get anxious, because the boy's turning to stool before your very eyes. You reach back into your glorious surgical past and cut him open, but it's too late. He dies of sepsis and uncontrollable hemorrhage. In the meantime, you toss his appendix into the wrong can, so it goes out with the garbage and nobody can say that he didn't have appendicitis."

Resnick was incredulous. "How do we get all of these terrible things to happen? He's not septic and he ain't bleeding."

"Piece of cake. You cut him open and muck around in his belly. I'll aspirate his colon and inject him with his own bowel contents so the coroner can grow out bugs from his blood. Then I'll blast him with just enough streptokinase so that his blood won't clot for awhile. You get lost in his abdomen and nick his inferior vena cava. We close him up and let him bleed out into his belly. Just to play it safe, we call the coroner and tell him that we're willing to sign the death certificate. You know that goldbrick's always trying to get out of work. No autopsy, so no one's the wiser."

"Boys, boys, *boys!* I can't believe how unimaginative you are." A loud voice resonated from the entryway. Resnick and Schmatz froze. Malinda nearly fell to her knees. It was Frank Klawitter.

"Why don't you try *this?* Sam has an ectopic pregnancy, so you give him the wrong blood. Then he starts to have trouble breathing, so you call from the golf course and tell him to manage his own airway. Then he has a heart attack, so you hand him an aspirin and wish him good luck. Oh, sorry. That wasn't you guys. Despite the fact that Clyde Resnick doesn't know his nuts from his navel and Randy Schmatz is the greediest incompetent son of a bitch to ever call himself a doctor, you both keep trying to save the boy's life. However, it's hard to break old habits. Before Clyde makes the skin incision, he trips over his dick, falls across the operating table and knocks himself out. It's a good thing, because he was gonna cut on the wrong side. Schmatz doesn't actually do a thing, but he manages to send a bill anyway." Frank stopped speaking when he recognized Malinda. "My God. Malinda, what are *you* doing here?"

Everything was coming apart fast. Malinda edged closer to Sam on the table. If push came to shove, she would use Sam as a hostage. She slipped a scalpel into her hand and palmed it against her leg.

"Frank, Sam is in trouble."

"Frank Klawitter. Where did *you* come from?" exclaimed Schmatz. "Theresa, what the hell's going on?"

"Malinda!" Frank spoke again. "I don't get it. Why are these guys here with you? Why did he call you Theresa? What's happened to Sam?" Frank started to walk towards the operating table, but stopped when Malinda hoisted the scalpel and held it to Sam's throat.

"Sorry Frank," said Malinda. "Sam knows something about me that could ruin my life. To help you, he has to make it public. I can't let that happen."

"Malinda, don't be stupid," pleaded Frank. "Hurting Sam's no solution. I'll do what I can to keep your secret, whatever it is, from going anywhere." Frank inched forward slowly.

Malinda pressed the blade against Sam's neck. "Everybody sit down," she ordered.

Schmatz and Resnick went to their knees, but Klawitter gambled that Malinda didn't know what she was doing. There was no other choice. As he started to sink to the ground, he threw the light switch and plunged the room into darkness. Frank had been in this O.R. many times and knew his way around blindfolded. He figured that Malinda didn't. Frank lunged at the table and body-blocked her away from Sam into a bank of instrument trays up against the wall. The scalpel flew out of her hand and she fell under a shower of surgical instruments.

Schmatz also knew his way around in the dark. He jumped up and switched on the largest overhead surgical spotlight. It was pointed directly at Sam, who appeared as a solitary illuminated figure in the middle of the conflict around him. Schmatz slipped back into the periphery of darkness and grabbed a large curved Kelly clamp from an instrument tray. He lifted it high over his head and prepared to plunge it into the patient at center stage.

Frank caught Schmatz's reflection in the shiny steel housing of the spotlight as the anesthesiologist pounced toward his intended victim. Frank jumped directly into his path. Schmatz reared back with his right arm and tried to thrust the clamp into Frank's face. Klawitter countered by reaching straight up with his left hand and grabbing his assailant's right wrist as it came forward. With lightning speed, the ex-army officer slid his right arm under and behind Randy's elbow to lock fingers with his other hand. He held onto Randy's wrist and snapped down hard. There was a sickening crack and then a scream of agony from Schmatz as his humerus shattered into three pieces. Frank shoved Schmatz down onto the floor just as Clyde Resnick began to choke him from behind with the IV tubing that was still connected to Sam's hand.

Meanwhile, Malinda sat on the floor and surveyed the scene with horror. She reached into her scrub shirt pocket underneath her surgical gown and pulled out a vial she'd put there before she left home. Malinda grabbed a syringe with a long needle and drew up all of the liquid. Clyde and Frank continued to struggle furiously. She retrieved the scalpel and slipped it under her belt. No one noticed another doctor enter the room.

Malinda took three steps to the table and emptied the contents of the syringe into Sam's arm. Then a fist struck the side of her head and knocked her violently to the side. The syringe flew from her hand as Joe Masterson pulled her down into a headlock and squeezed until she blacked out. When Malinda went limp, he dropped her to the floor and turned to help Frank, who was being clotheslined by a possessed Clyde Resnick. The IV catheter connected to the tubing had been pulled out of Sam's skin, so blood dripped from the puncture site onto the floor below his hanging arm.

When Masterson saw Resnick choking Frank, he went into a blind rage. He switched on the electrocautery unit, grabbed the handpiece of the bovie, and then stepped on the foot pedal, which made the wire tip of the cutting instrument glow red hot. He jammed the surgical torch into Resnick's left ear as he pushed on the opposite side of Clyde's head with his other hand. The hiss and smell were like a flaming cattle brand as the cautery burned through Clyde's eardrum and wedged into the bones of his middle ear. Resnick roared in agony and dropped the plastic tubing with which he was strangling Frank. Both men fell to the floor, Resnick delirious with pain and Frank semi-conscious from being choked. Joe knelt down to help Frank.

Malinda had come to and picked up another syringe, then crept to the stainless steel cabinets where the emergency drugs were held. She grabbed a bottle of adrenalin and filled the syringe. Someone had opened a thoracotomy set, and a large steel sternotomy chisel was in plain view. Malinda picked it up, then twisted to avoid a punch thrown by Masterson. She took a step backwards and slipped in the puddle of blood that had dripped from Sam's arm. Masterson turned back to Frank.

Malinda fell on the sharp point of the chisel. She was in a pain-driven rage as she watched Resnick flop around on the floor and saw Schmatz cradling his broken arm. They were outgunned. That left her no choice. She crawled over to Resnick, who lay on the floor holding his head, moaning and vomiting from the horrible vertigo he suffered from his tympanic membrane rupture and labyrinthine destruction. Using both hands, Malinda drove the long needle on the syringe into his left breast, aiming for his heart. She was shoving the plunger to inject when Resnick rolled over and snapped off the needle. The adrenaline gave him a blinding headache. He passed out.

Frank shook the cobwebs out. Joe Masterson stood over Malinda, who was clutching Clyde by the back of the neck. Joe picked up the surgical chisel from the floor and put it in the pocket of his long white coat.

"I'm with you, Frank," pleaded Malinda as she withdrew her hand from Resnick's neck. "I'm sorry. I can explain everything."

Frank didn't wait for her next lie. He had a more immediate problem. He felt responsible for this mess, but was losing his inclination to find a solution. He wondered if he should give Schmatz one last chance to disappear forever.

His moment of reflection was interrupted by Masterson. "What do we do?"

"I'll tell you what you do," growled Schmatz, who was cradling his broken arm. "You say goodbye to the civilized world. Who appointed you God? You two are history when everyone finds out what happened here. And this slut, too. I'm gonna bury you. Your careers are over. I'll personally see to that."

Masterson rushed Schmatz, lifted him high up in the air, then threw him to the ground. Schmatz landed on his broken arm and became deranged with pain.

"That looks like it hurts, Randy," said Malinda. "Here's some anesthesia." Before Frank or Joe could react, she grabbed a steel nitrous oxide tank and brought it down on Schmatz's head, gashing his forehead from eyebrow to ear and knocking him unconscious. "See, that wasn't so bad."

Masterson was a step ahead of Frank. He pulled Malinda away from Schmatz. "You're pretty good at hurting people, Malinda. Better start talking. Otherwise, we leave you up here with this mess and let you explain what happened." Malinda was mute. That was what she wanted.

"No, Joe, she's coming with us. Hey, look at Sam shiver. He's coming up fast now. Can you hold the fort for a second? I want to grab a couple of blankets from the warmer outside."

"I think I can manage."

Frank left the room. Just as the door closed behind him, Sam moaned loudly and started to roll off the gurney. Joe turned his back to Malinda and became momentarily preoccupied with Sam.

Malinda reached behind her head and flipped the power switch on the crash cart monitor-defibrillator. After she turned the activating dial, she removed the metal-faced paddles from their stations and gripped the handles tightly, placing her thumbs over the red discharge buttons. Without making a sound, she rose and shuffled into position behind Resnick.

Masterson recognized the high-pitched whine and turned to Malinda just as she thrust the electrified paddles against the sides of Resnick's head. Joe jerked her away at the split second in which she tried to shoot 50 watt-seconds of electricity through Resnick's brain. Malinda slipped on the blood and saline-slickened floor. Her balance completely lost, she spiraled back into the crash cart and reflexly tried to break her fall by holding out the paddles in her hands. The metal cart, machine and Malinda completed a short circuit, releasing a surge of energy through her arms and chest to the ground. Sparks flew as Malinda was shocked senseless.

It was finally over.

The trauma surgeon and gynecologist surveyed the carnage. The operating room looked like a battlefield. Sam was still asleep, but was beginning to move his arms and shift from side to side on the gurney.

"Now what?" asked Masterson. "I don't think they're gonna believe us when we say that this was just a little difference of opinion between surgeons. What are we going to do with these two?" He motioned at Resnick and Schmatz.

"Let me think for a second. First, we need to get Sam out of here. Take him down to your office until he's completely awake. I'll figure out what to do up here."

"Fine," agreed Joe. "Here, give me a hand." The men unlocked the brake on the gurney and began to maneuver through the bodies sprawled around them. They covered Sam with a blanket, then glided him out of the O.R. and down the hall to the elevator. Frank pushed the button.

"Be careful," Frank told Joe. "I'm going back to the O.R. to clean up the others before someone walks in and finds them. Stay with Sam unless I call you. Don't let him out of your sight. Until we know who else besides Malinda is on to us, it's not safe for him to be wandering around. Besides, there's no telling what he might do when he finds out what happened." Frank hung his head. "I can't believe I had any doubts about him. I almost got him killed, bringing him into this mess."

Frank returned to O.R. 17. At first glance, everything was as they had left it. Except that Malinda was gone. Resnick and Schmatz were moaning and nursing their wounds.

"No. That's impossible." Frank ran out of the room and up and down the halls of the operating room complex. He searched quickly in every room, but she had vanished. He alerted Joe, but there wasn't any time now to look for her.

Frank returned to the operating room battleground. He scooped up the instruments that had been flung around the room and tossed them into the "dirty" sink. When everything was tidied up enough to pass for the after-math of a normal operation, Klawitter hoisted Resnick and Schmatz onto a gurney and muscled it out the door. They were too miserable to resist. He rode them down to the basement, and in the gloomy darkness to the exit. Frank pulled the stretcher-on-wheels to the edge of the ramp by the dock, then backed the heavy load down the inclined concrete runway. It nearly tipped over. He tugged and towed, since the gurney was difficult to steer, and headed across campus to the parking lot across from the ER.

"Here we are, boys. Your exit from the practice of medicine as we know it." Frank assisted the injured doctors off the stretcher and pointed them towards the entrance. "Before I let you go, tell me, who was she? Malinda. You called her Theresa. She didn't seem to like you very much."

"She *is* Theresa, or used to be. I haven't seen her in years. I don't know why she was so pissed off. You know, Clyde?"

Resnick was sobbing and clutching the side of his head. "Forget her. She'll never come back. She can't, now. She's got plenty of money. Ask Wiley. He took care of it."

"That's all?"

"That's all I'm saying. Look, Klawitter, just get to the point."

"All right. Here's the point. I never want to see either one of you again, or what happened today'll just be an introduction. Make up any stories you want, but just be sure they end with how you're disabled and can't take care of patients. You can't pass gas with a bum arm, Randy, and Clyde, you sure can't take a patient history if you're deaf in one ear. If that isn't enough, or if I ever see your faces again, you can count on dis-abilities that'll keep you from more than medicine. And if you tell Waterhouse what happened tonight, I'll personally finish what we start-ed." The two pain-wracked men cowered. "Neither of you will ever prac-tice medicine again — anywhere. Eyes will always be on you. I have friends everywhere. And you're not going to retire on the money you stole from Branscomb, either. Each of you will contribute two million dollars anonymously to the scholarship fund. I suspect you'll have plenty left to live on — I know how much you took and exactly how you did it. I'll give you a month to get the cash together or my lawyer and I will go right to the District Attorney. Now get out of my sight."

CHAPTER 47

Sam awoke in the elevator in fits and starts. At first he was completely disoriented, but Joe Masterson kept reassuring him that everything would be all right. By the time they reached the trauma surgeon's office, Sam was lucid. He ached all over as if he had been beaten, but Joe insisted that he had not been harmed. A final wave of dizziness passed as the effects of the narcotic rapidly wore off. Sam interrupted Joe in the middle of his explanation of what had happened.

"I've got to find Lauren."

"Sit down. You need to rest. You've been through a lot."

"No, really. I'm OK." Sam shook out the cobwebs. "I'm not sure, but I think Lauren might be in trouble." He remembered what Malinda had told him. Sam looked at his watch. It was almost eight o' clock. "I've gotta go."

"Frank'll be back in a few minutes. Let's wait for him."

Sam winced as he examined the large bruise where the IV had been ripped out of his hand. "Whew. Bad technique. You do this?" He climbed out of the wheelchair Masterson had used to bring him from the O.R. He didn't feel great, but there wasn't any time to waste. "If I'm not back in a half hour, come looking for me. You might want to bring some help. I'll be down in Dr. Spencer's lab."

"Fred Spencer? What does he have to do with..."

"I can't explain everything yet, but I think he's in it with Waterhouse somehow. You'd better tell Frank where I'm going." Sam staggered out the door.

"Are you sure you're all right?" Joe called after Sam. "Holy shit." Joe raced to the phone to page Frank.

Spencer sounded apologetic. "I'm not trying to be an alarmist, but you can see for yourself, there's probably another mass besides the one we were concerned about before. I don't know how I missed it the first time. It doesn't happen very often."

Lauren was touched by his sincerity. "You're only human. I think it's incredible that you took the time to go back like you did and work on my images. Just for me."

"Yes. Just for you. Now, lay back and relax. I'm going to inject you with the contrast dye and do one last scan. If the tumors don't light up, then they're plain cysts, and we can be done with all the worrying."

"And if they do?"

"We'll cross that bridge when we come to it."

Lauren was lying on the table underneath the MRI magnet. She was dressed in a hospital gown and had a small intravenous catheter inserted in her wrist. Her reconstructed image was projected onto the viewing platform, which rotated slowly. The hologram was naked from the waist up. A new lump was highlighted in her breast, a lump which hadn't been present the first time he had shown her the image. Lauren reached up and took Spencer's closest hand. The other was behind his back, holding an enormous syringe that was supposed to be full of contrast.

"Thank you for being a friend."

"There, there. Look away now." He connected the syringe to the IV and prepared to push the plunger. From the darkness behind him a hand shot out and latched onto his forearm. Sam's fingers gripped like a vise as he twisted the radiologist's arm up behind his back.

"Not as much of a friend as you think, Lauren." Sam grabbed the syringe and yanked it away.

"Sam! Have you lost your mind?"

"I think you're asking the wrong person. Look at this. Empty. Nothing but air. Now Dr. Spencer, can you explain to me why you were going to inject 50 milliliters of air into Lauren? Is this what they call invisible contrast? Or did you have something else in mind?" Sam was squeezing the radiologist's wrist so tightly that Spencer's hand was bloodless and growing numb.

Lauren jumped off the table and inspected the syringe. She was incredulous. "It is empty! Dr. Spencer! All of that air in my veins could have killed me!" Spencer squirmed, but couldn't free himself from Sam. "What were you going to do?"

"Watch this." With his free hand, Sam reached over to the computer controls and entered the hidden programs. A horrified Lauren watched herself dismembered and defiled by the contortions Spencer had fabricated from her data set. After a particularly obscene gyration, she looked away and began to sob.

Sam slapped Spencer and threw him against the wall. The radiologist laughed uncontrollably. "So what? You can beat me, but you can't take away my accomplishments. You understand why I had to do what I did, don't you?" He pleaded with Lauren. "I didn't want to kill you. But you must understand! You could have stopped me and I had to be free to get on with my work. Can't you see that?"

"You're disgusting. What could possibly be your justification for...for...for raping Lauren with this machine."

"Lauren? That was a diversion. *This* was the real raison d' etre." Spencer flicked some switches. Sam had seen what followed. "Look. Now you see it, now you don't. A man has a blood clot on the brain, and then he doesn't. A torn aorta comes and goes. A broken neck heals as if by miracle. A mass in the pancreas is nothing but my imagination. Can you guess why?"

Sam and Lauren were dumbstruck.

Spencer bellowed, "I'll tell you why! To save lives. To purge Branscomb of everything that's evil. To humiliate Wiley Waterhouse by making him bear the wrath of people fed up with his incompetent, disgusting cronies." His audience remained silent. "You still don't get it, do you? Idiots! It was him or me. Us or them. He promised to make me the Dean. That son of a bitch. He lied to me like he always lied to the others. But I was smarter than those fools. I decided to make them look worse than they already were. I changed these results, and a dozen others like them, to lead them into more mistakes, the kind that even *they* couldn't escape. Everybody makes mistakes. I finally figured out that we needed more, not less. The families knew because I let them know. Who would suspect Fred Spencer, the greatest of all radiologists? I fed them bad information, and *they* made all the mistakes. Not Montague, though. He was too smart."

"You intentionally killed people."

"I didn't kill them. *They* did. It was necessary. Klawitter and his team were taking too long. Sometimes a few have to suffer for the greater good. All that matters is that Ingelhart is gone. Mahnke now too, I hear. They were greedy and they were stupid and it all caught up to them. And guess what? Now Waterhouse is desperate, because he's supposed to control this place. It's all the Dean's responsibility. Another sloppy anesthesia and maybe another mishandled stroke or two and he'll be gone. Oh, mark my words. He'll be gone. And then I'll be free."

"What about Tony?"

"Who?"

"Tony Albers."

"Oh, your friend on the cancer word. He had real brain tumors."

"You'll never get away with this."

"Why not? Watch." Before Sam could move to stop him, Spencer lunged at the console and rearranged the toggles and buttons. Lauren's image disappeared and the computer screens went blank. "Poof! Gone forever. Vanished without a trace. What can you prove now?"

Sam grabbed Spencer's lapels. "Why were you going to kill Lauren? What did she have to do with this?"

"Nothing. But she knew. She was in my files. I couldn't take a chance. It seemed a tragedy, but there was too much at stake. I still have so much work to do. It won't be over until they're all gone. Lauren's expendable."

"I'll show you who's expendable." Sam clutched the crazed scientist's shirt and lifted him up against the wall. He dropped his wrist lock and pulled his arm back to throw a punch. His forward motion was halted by four hands that blocked his assault.

"Let him go, Sam." Sam struggled to deliver a blow. "Sam. Sam! Put him down, son. Let him go. This won't solve anything." The hands belonged to Frank Klawitter, Joe Masterson, Jon Herbert and Raymond Montague. "Fred, it's over. We heard everything. Why did you do this?"

Spencer fell to his knees and put his head in his hands. "Our plan was never going to work. I couldn't take a chance that we'd fail. Waterhouse has ruined men tougher than all of you. I had to do this my own way. To save Branscomb. To save myself. He's a monster, and I'm going to destroy him." He leapt to his feet. "And look at what I've done!

For all of you. For all of mankind. I can create or erase disease! Physicians believe everything I tell them. They don't know how to read the images. They trust me. Anything I say is the truth. Look at what I've been able to do. These patients were martyrs. Frank, you of all people should understand. Now, leave me alone. I've still got work to do." Spencer sat down at his desk and stared at the screens.

"Take her home, Sam. We'll finish up here." Lauren gathered her belongings and left with Sam. Frank and the others conferred briefly and then led Spencer away. He was taken to a psychiatrist, who determined that he had become gravely impaired, a schizophrenic. The laboratory was closed, the files were locked away, and Fred Spencer was committed by his family to a posh asylum which would be his residence for the next twenty years. Despite their anguish over genius lost, his colleagues were relieved that he was well taken care of. By the time he was released from the asylum, his greatest scientific achievements had long since been eclipsed.

CHAPTER 48

Wiley Waterhouse lived in constant fear. Fred Spencer was locked in a psychiatric institution. Schmatz and Resnick weren't talking. Malinda had disappeared. Although he no longer had to worry that his scheme would be discovered because of some stunt by his fallen colleagues, Sam Anderson was still roaming in the medical center. Furthermore, until he could get an explanation directly from the medical student, he would never know for certain who had ordered the mayhem. Of course, there was still one person left who had been with them in Washington, but the Dean couldn't figure any reason for him to have acted with such vengeance.

"Jeanette, get me Bob Stoner on the phone. I need to talk to him about the QA meeting that's coming up next week."

"Sure, Dr. Waterhouse. Do you want to take it out here or on the private line in your office?"

"In my office. I don't want any disturbances."

"Of course, Doctor."

Waterhouse walked into his office and latched the door. He went behind his desk and studied the portrait of Pasteur, then sat down at his desk to await Stoner's telephone call.

His private line rang. Wiley picked up the receiver and cradled it against his cheek so that he could keep his hands free. While he spoke to Stoner, he fumbled with the keys in front of him.

"Hello, Wiley? This is Bob. Jeanette said you wanted to talk to me about the QA meeting next week. It doesn't look too exciting. What do you want to talk about?"

"Bob, I didn't call about the QA meeting. I called about you and me. About us. About you and me and Myron and Elaine and Malinda and Clyde and Randy. Remember, you were there, too."

"I know I was there, Wiley. And you know I was there, Wiley. But no one else does. With the others gone, it would seem that it might be easier for you and me now."

Waterhouse found the key he was looking for. He inserted it into the lock of the bottom left hand drawer of his desk. When he turned the key, there was an audible click. He pulled open the drawer.

"Bob, you know it's not a coincidence that everyone got beaten up or thrown out in the last few weeks. Someone is behind all this."

"Why did you call?" There was no hostility in Stoner's voice. He sounded very matter of fact. "To see if I was coming after you?"

"That's enough, Bob."

"Wiley, you don't tell me how much is enough or how much is too much anymore. The others are gone and the nightmare is over. You can't hurt me without hurting yourself."

"So, you're the one!"

"I'm the one what?"

"You set the whole thing up, didn't you? You set them all up. Where did you find him?"

"Find who?"

"Anderson. The medical student. The one who's trying to kill all of us. I mean, the one who's gotten rid of most of us. Did you honestly think that no one would find out?"

The Dean found what he was looking for. In the back of his desk drawer buried in a box of tissues was a .22 caliber Ruger automatic pistol with a silencer. Waterhouse lifted it out of the drawer and checked the clip. It was full. He concealed the gun underneath some papers in the "out" box on his desk.

"Wiley, let's stop dancing. If you're telling the truth, you had nothing to do with the others. I didn't either. And as for anybody else, I don't have a clue. We both know what we did, and neither one of us has any-thing to gain by letting anyone else know. I don't want any more money from you and I suppose you don't want any money from me."

"Bob, that all sounds good, but it doesn't make sense. If we're the only two who know, and I'm not responsible and you're not responsible, then who's behind all this? Have you told *anyone*? Wrack your brain. Anyone at all?"

"No. I haven't."

"Well, neither have I. That can only mean one thing. Someone else knows about us. The problem is, how do we confirm who it is?"

"Sam Anderson knows." Stoner spoke in that matter-of-fact tone of voice again. "The medical student knows. He isn't the mastermind, so somebody above him knows as well. Wiley, you've got to haul him in and get it out of him one way or another."

"You're right. I plan to do just that."

"Then why did you call me? Why didn't you just do it first?"

"Because I had to be certain that you weren't the one."

"And are you certain now?"

"Not completely, but I'm willing to believe that it might not be you. I'll need to hear it from Anderson before I believe it."

"Do it soon, Wiley. Today. We need to know."

"I'll call you later."

"Oh, and Wiley."

"Yes?"

"Show some restraint."

"What?"

"Don't shoot the messenger."

With everybody on the list accounted for, the only person left was the Dean. As much as Sam wanted to go after him, he agreed with Frank that it didn't make much sense now. The point had been to force out Wiley's incompetent associates, not to settle a vendetta. With everyone gone, the assignment was over. Unbelievably, they had finessed their way through this without an investigation, so it was best to call it quits. As despicable a creature as Wiley Waterhouse was, the pleasure of retribution wasn't worth the risk of getting caught. The medical center administration might be willing to smooth over the sudden disappearance of a few faculty members and the truancy of a medical student, but if something happened to the Dean, there was no telling what might happen. If Waterhouse ever got out of line again, Frank had plenty on him.

Frank and Sam shook hands on a job well done. Sam looked forward to getting on with his life. He tried to get back into the normal swing of medical school life.

When Waterhouse sent the message, Sam was filling out his schedule requests for the second year. Sam chose an extra course in anatomical pathology. He could see himself as a cardiac surgeon. That was the most difficult path you could take in medicine, which suited Sam just fine.

The Dean's note was handwritten, which seemed unusual. It was even signed. Why would the Dean send him a handwritten note? He never did anything for himself. Sam deduced that Waterhouse didn't want anyone to know about the note. He asked Frank what he should do. His advisor told him to meet with Waterhouse, but to be careful and above all else, to keep his temper. When Frank left Sam alone in his office briefly to answer a page, the medical student looked quickly through Frank's desk drawers. He found what he was looking for and slipped it into his pocket.

As requested by Waterhouse, Sam came to his office after class. It was late in the day. There were no lights on in the office building except for the one in Waterhouse's office. Sam's knock was answered before he got his arm down to his side.

"Please come in, Mr. Anderson." Sam opened the door and walked into the office. The Dean was sitting in his chair behind the desk with his back to Sam. "Shut the door behind you." Sam closed the door, but he didn't latch it.

"You asked me to come, sir."

"I know. This isn't the first time you've been in this office, is it, Sam?" The Dean swiveled his chair around. "I said, this isn't the first time you've been in this office, is it?"

The loathing welled up uncontrollably. It was agonizing to think that the most despicable creature in the group was going to go unpunished. Still, he had to try to contain himself. He would confront the Dean straight up. Sam reverted to a military style.

"Yes it is, sir."

"Liar! Do you see the picture on the wall behind me? The one with Louis Pasteur?"

"Yes I do, sir."

"Do you know what's behind it? Don't waste our time, boy. Tell me the truth."

"There's a safe behind the picture. It has a standard tumbler that can be opened in less than a minute by any amateur without special instruments. You would do well to replace it."

"Now you tell me. What did you find in the safe, Sam? It was you who broke in, wasn't it?"

Sam felt like a delinquent in the principal's office. This was going to take forever if somebody didn't get to the point. "No, it wasn't me. But I know what was in there. Dr. Waterhouse, you might as well cancel the interrogation. If you ask me anything that I don't feel like answering, there's nothing you can do to get it out of me. As far as you're concerned, I'm a first-year medical student from Rutgers who has above average grades and a clean record. There's nothing you know about me or could ever find out that might be used against me. But again, the answer to your question is no. I didn't break into your safe."

Waterhouse was intimidated for a second by Sam's rapid-fire delivery. "Is that so? Then how the hell do you know so much about it? Who are you protecting?"

"None of your business. Furthermore, given what has happened here in the past few weeks and what you and I both know resides — excuse me, I imagine used to reside — in the safe, I suggest that you make clear to me precisely what it is that you want. Otherwise, I'm requesting permission to leave this office and return to my studies. Also, you'd do well to stay away from Lauren Doopleheimer. Send her a letter of apology and officially let her back into class."

The Dean was fuming. "You don't tell me what to do, you goddamn arrogant son of a bitch. I'm the Dean! I tell *you* what to do. Who put you up to this? Was it Stoner? Tell me! Was it Stoner?"

"Who's Stoner?" Sam meant it. He had no idea who Bob Stoner was.

The Dean reached into his white coat pocket and pulled out the handgun. He held it with both hands and pointed it at Sam's head.

"Sit down. Over here, where I can keep an eye on you." The Dean walked out from behind his desk and waved Sam into the corner. Waterhouse was between Sam and the door.

This was totally unexpected. The last thing that Sam had ever expected was for Waterhouse to threaten him with a weapon. The Dean had to realize that if anything happened to Sam, the entire world would come down on him. Or maybe he didn't.

"Take it easy. Put the gun down. You called me here, remember? I didn't come here to hurt you."

"Just like you didn't hurt the others? Fuck you, Sam Anderson! Or whoever you are. You came here to hurt all of us. Now, I want to know who's behind this. If you don't tell me, I'm gonna blow your brains out."

"I can't tell you that. Not while you're holding a gun to my head. How do I know that you won't blow my brains out after I tell you?"

"You don't. But try this." Wiley lowered the gun and aimed it at Sam's leg. He squeezed the trigger and fired off a shot which hit Anderson in the fleshy part of the inside of his left thigh. The gun barely made a sound, as the silencer registered a soft "ffffssstt," rather than the normal sharp report of an unmuzzled revolver. When the bullet went through his muscle and lodged against the bone, Sam grabbed his leg and spun out of the chair. A small bloodstain marked his pants. He cried out.

"Now, one more time. Who brought you to Branscomb?" Wiley hissed.

"Ingelhart."

"Don't be a wiseass. You killed Ingelhart. I'm not that stupid."

"I didn't kill anybody."

"Sure. Who was it? Fred Spencer?"

"It was Malinda."

"Nope. Won't go for that one, either." Waterhouse walked closer to Sam and aimed the gun at the same leg. "I'm tired of this game." He shot Sam again. The bullet grazed his kneecap, ricocheted off the metal frame of a Waterhouse diploma, and fell to the floor. Sam clutched his leg and retched a few times with the pain.

"Some killer," Wiley scoffed. "I can't believe how easy this is. Maybe they should've hired *me*."

Sam needed to buy time, to figure out a way to subdue the Dean or escape. He squeezed his badly injured leg as tightly as he could.

"OK, OK. I'll give you some information. It was Stoner. He said that the only way to get you to get rid of the others was to take matters into his own hands. He said you'd never figure it out, because he wasn't in the pictures."

"What? He said he wasn't in the pictures? Ha! He was in the pictures, all right. You can't make out his face, but he was in the pictures. That bastard just didn't have the balls to take a chance like the rest of us."

"How did it happen? It was in Washington, wasn't it?" Sam already knew the answer, so it was easy to hit the bull's eye.

"Yeah, it was Washington, all right. Back before anybody gave a damn about drug company handouts and a big night on the town."

"You were at a party."

"We *were* the party. Malinda was just a kid then. It got pretty wild."

Sam thought he could make it out of the room if he could knock the Dean off balance and break through the glass panel on the door. He needed just a moment more. "I've heard about medical conventions."

"The first mistake we made was bringing out that damn Polaroid camera. It was all Myron's idea. He said he wanted a picture so that he could remember how good he looked when he got older. After the others saw the picture, they wanted one too. Asses and elbows. It was a kick at the time. I imagine you already know about our second mistake."

"I do."

"A pity. But that's the way it goes. Happens a thousand times a day on the street, just not to people like us. We couldn't see ruining our careers back then for a little party girl."

"Why the pictures? Why did you keep the proof?"

"I didn't want to, but nobody trusted anybody else to keep their mouth shut. So everybody took home a souvenir. We swore an oath of secrecy. Some oath. As soon as we got home, they all started coming to me for money. They called them loans, but nobody paid them back. I should've stopped the first one, but I didn't. That was my mistake. Blackmail, blackmail and more blackmail. Then Malinda decided she wanted to be more in life than a part-time prostitute. I had to put her through school. It wasn't cheap."

Sam positioned himself to leap.

"So, she blackmailed you too."

"You're pretty smart, Sam. For a long time, she was happy with ten or fifteen thousand here and there. Then she wanted bigger checks. Hundreds of thousands. It got downright expensive."

"What about the others?"

"They were already greedy. And stupid. God, they were stupid! When they started to screw up as doctors, I offered to send them off with more money than any mortal would know what to do with, but that wasn't enough. They always wanted *more*. To tell you the truth, it was kind of nice when you showed up. You solved my problem."

"And Malinda came to Branscomb for what reason? Why would she want to take a chance on being recognized by the others?"

"Because she wanted to be a *doctor*. The blackmailer got bored and wanted to be a doctor. When I said no, she pulled out all the stops and threatened to go to the Hospital Board. I didn't have a choice. She was going to tear up her pictures the day after graduation. That was the deal."

"Fat chance. Did you really think she'd ever tear up the pictures?"

"Actually, no. But that didn't really matter. I was willing to give her a chance. If not, I was going to kill her. Just like I'm going to kill you if you don't tell me who brought you in here. Maybe I should call Stoner. Let's get on with it. I've had enough."

"So have I." As Waterhouse bent over to dial the phone, Sam jumped from the chair, but his injured leg gave out. Instead of tackling the Dean, he fell short and struck his head against the Dean's shoe. Waterhouse kicked him, then stepped back and towered over Sam.

"You bastard! You're going to tell me who sent you here if I have to put all ten of these bullets into you first. How about one in your other leg?" The Dean raised his gun again and started to squeeze the trigger. Sam turned his head away and started to close his eyes, then opened them wide. Lauren had slipped into the office. She seized a large marble mortar bowl from the table near the door and brought it down with all her might on the back of the Dean's head. He fell forward and fired wildly, crashing to the floor face down at Sam's feet.

"Shit! This thing's heavy. Maybe I should have used the smaller piece." Lauren went back to the table and picked up the tiny pestle.

"What the hell are you doing here? Why'd you hit him so hard?"

"He was going to kill you!" Lauren knelt down next to Waterhouse and felt for a pulse. "Still ticking. Guess I hit him harder than I thought."

"Sorry. Thanks. Now, will you please tell me what you're doing?"

"Let me see your leg. Sam, you're slipping." Lauren pulled the knife from the portrait of the French microbiologist and used it to rip Sam's pants and inspect his wounds. "Frank told me."

"Frank? He told you?"

"That's right. OK, where's the Polaroid?"

"What Polaroid?"

"Stop. I know you have it. That's why Frank called me. He's something else, like he's got radar or something. When he realized you borrowed the picture, he figured you'd probably get pissed off and show it to Waterhouse. He was also afraid that Waterhouse might ambush you. Frank thought that with me hanging around, Waterhouse would be afraid to take you on. I just got here a little late, that's all. Wait'll he hears about this. The guy's incredible. He was right again."

Sam looked sheepish as he handed over the photo of the Dean and the others in Washington that he had taken from Frank's desk. Lauren laughed out loud. She nodded at Waterhouse. "We've got to do something with him."

"As far as I'm concerned he's back on the list. Look at my leg." Sam pushed up and tried to struggle to his feet. The pain was too severe and he fell to his knees. "You're gonna have to carry me out. I don't think I can walk."

"It'll be my pleasure."

Sam grabbed the Dean by the hair and pulled his head up. "But I don't think you should have to carry this one. Let's leave him for somebody else."

"You're kidding. He shot you! Aren't you going to do anything? Let's call the police."

"No way! If we do, then I'm afraid that Frank'll get dragged into it. What good would that accomplish? We've gotta let him go again. Next time I won't be so stupid. C'mon. I need a doctor. I'll say I shot myself by accident. Let's get out of here before he wakes up." Sam pulled back the Dean's eyelids and checked his pupils, then looked around the room. "He'll be all right. Let him clean up his own mess." Sam threw his arm around Lauren's neck and she assisted him out the door.

Ten minutes later, the Dean still hadn't aroused. A new visitor looked around the room, remembering this office where Waterhouse had threatened and humiliated. With every other sentence, the Dean had popped a handful of those goddamn jellybeans into his mouth. The jar sat prominently on his desk.

The door closed silently. Waterhouse didn't respond when his face was slapped. The intruder rolled the Dean over onto his back and examined him to see what had happened. His head was bleeding. Waterhouse breathed with the unsettled, snorting respirations of a man who might soon awaken from a deep sleep. There would never be a better opportunity. A gloved hand opened his mouth and poured a hundred jellybeans into the back of Wiley's throat, then pushed his lower jaw up forcefully to hold his mouth shut. The other hand pinched his nostrils. In a few seconds, Waterhouse tried to take a breath, but he couldn't. He began to make violent silent coughing movements, then convulsed. As he seized, his face turned dark blue and he vomited against his closed lips and nose. With his agonizing attempts at respiration, he inhaled a pharynx packed with jellybeans and vomit. He shuddered, then lay still.

The jar on his desk had tipped over and its contents were scattered all over the floor. A fall against the desk corner while choking; that's what it would look like. The assailant picked up the gun, two empty shells, one bullet, and the marble bowl and pestle.

Jeanette discovered the Dean in rigor mortis the next morning. She called the hospital operator, who paged a "code blue" to the Dean's office. When the galloping horde arrived, they weren't able to pass an endotracheal tube beyond his vocal cords because his entire hypopharynx was packed with gastrointestinal mortar studded with jellybeans. It wasn't a straightforward cardiac arrest, so the anesthesiology resident on the code team suggested that the case be referred to the QA Committee.

CHAPTER 49

The QA Committee buried their noses in the folders in front of them. Frank Klawitter and Joe Masterson exchanged a glance. Bob Stoner watched and then nervously began to speak.

"Open your packets to Case 887-A. Dean Wiley Waterhouse. Aspiration and asphyxia, compounded by head injury. This case comes before the QA Committee because there's a regulation in the bylaws that states that any death which has an unusual feature is supposed to be reviewed. Furthermore, I was instructed by the Chancellor to bring it to the committee for discussion." He turned and faced Frank. "Believe me, it wasn't my idea. I've reviewed it carefully and I can't see anything that was done wrong." The Director of Risk Management, Ferdie Gooch, caught Klawitter's eye. The quicker they got through this, the better. But Frank had warned him to expect a curve. "It's hard to find fault with someone who can't get an airway when he has to stick a tube through a wall of jellybeans," concluded the Chairman of the Committee. "God rest his soul."

"What soul?" muttered Joe Masterson under his breath.

"I'll ignore that," answered Stoner. "Does anyone have anything else to say about the intubation?" There was no response. "If not, then I consider the airway management and resuscitation to have met the standard of care. Case closed."

Stoner gathered his papers to leave the room. Before he was able to stand, a solo voice pierced the chatter.

"Not quite yet. I still have a few concerns." Stoner looked up in absolute disbelief. Frank Klawitter was blocking the doorway. He motioned for everyone to keep their seats. "If you don't mind, I'd like to go over a few things that shouldn't be overlooked."

"Come on, Frank. The case is closed. You can't do this." Stoner ignored the rest of the people and pleaded directly with Frank.

"That's right," chimed in Gooch.

"What the hell are you doing?" asked Masterson. He shielded his face from the rest of them and whispered, "Have you lost your mind?"

Frank tilted his head. "Maybe the best thing would be to sweep this whole episode under the rug, but I still have a problem with the cause of death. I mean, he might have choked to death on jellybeans, but I know for a fact that Waterhouse suffered from chest pains. I caught him popping some nitroglycerin a few days before he died. He looked pretty awful. I asked him what was the matter, and he told me it was nothing that his cardiologist couldn't fix."

"Who was his cardiologist?"

"Myron Ingelhart."

"Ingelhart? How could it be Ingelhart? He was dead already," Stoner protested.

"Probably got better advice that way," quipped Masterson.

"Well, that's what he told me." Frank walked over to the group and gripped the tabletop with both hands. "Given the importance of the man, I think it's important to know the exact cause of death. A cafe coronary on jellybeans is kind of an ignominious way to go, don't you think? It might sit better with the alumni and the annals of history if he died of a heart attack."

"OK, Frank. If it's such a big deal, we can say we think he died of a heart attack. The committee can say whatever it wants to say. It doesn't change what happened."

"It sure doesn't, Bob," replied Frank. "But we should do it the proper way. With an inquest."

"What will that accomplish? What difference does it make? Mark my words, I bet he choked to death." Stoner had to scramble. An inquest could prompt an investigation. If anyone developed the least little suspicion that the Dean had been murdered, it could ultimately lead them back to Stoner.

"A bet. I like that. You're on. How much is it worth to you?" Frank suppressed a smile.

"What? What are you talking about?"

"I said, how much is it worth to you? A wager over the cause of death. What would you be willing to put up to find out the precise cause of Dr. Wiley Waterhouse's death? How about a million bucks?"

"Are you serious?"

"A million bucks says he died of a heart attack."

"You're on!" Stoner said.

"And you two are *nuts*. Is the meeting over now, Frank?" Gooch headed for the door.

"Sure, Ferdie. We can finish this discussion by ourselves, can't we, Bob."

"Yes."

"OK, fellas," said Gooch. "The case is closed. It's death by jellybeans."

"I think I'll stick around, just for kicks," said Masterson.

"Suit yourself," responded Frank. "I don't think this'll take very long." He watched Stoner closely while he motioned Joe to stand by the door. "Bob, we have a little business to settle."

"I don't get it, Frank. It's over now. For the love of God, let this be finished."

"What's the bet? A million bucks? I'll tell you, I'm so sure he died of a heart attack, I'm willing to double the bet. Let's make it two million. Two million dollars says that Waterhouse choked to death after he had a heart attack. Are you with me?"

"Frank, this isn't funny anymore. I'm not betting you two million dollars."

"To the contrary," interrupted Frank, "I'd take the bet if I were you. In fact, if you were smart, you'd concede the loss and pay up real quick. Otherwise, we might have to go back to the Practice Plan books and see how a certain bunch of doctors've been making out all these years."

Stoner protested. "The others took money from the Dean, but I never did. There's nothing in the books that would indicate that I did."

"And that horrible accident in Washington?"

"You can't prove anything."

"I didn't think so at first. But you know what that paranoid egomaniac Waterhouse did? He kept a diary. When I found this..." Klawitter held up the Polaroid photograph with Stoner and the other naked men and women. "...I found *this*." He held up a small worn black book. It was closed. "Can you believe it? A diary. Seems like you made a lot of money over the years, Bob. Seems like you were there when the girl died." He paused. "Let me try it another way. What if I told you that there was no way that Waterhouse could have swallowed those jellybeans voluntarily?

Who'd be the logical suspect? Now, let me ask you again. You think you'd be willing to wager two million on the outcome of an autopsy? We could have the body exhumed today."

Stoner gave up any pretense. "I argued with the girl from the very beginning. I told her not to do it. I left the party before it happened. When I came back, she was dead. They threatened me, so I had to help with the cover-up. I may be a lot of things, but I'm not a murderer." Stoner collapsed in a chair. "I would have done anything to save her. I just didn't get there in time." He began to weep, then composed himself. "I don't have two million dollars."

"I'll take what you have." Frank wasn't finished. "And one more thing. You agree to leave this medical center and never come back. If you aren't gone by next week, everything I know — excuse me — *we* know — goes to the Chancellor and to the District Attorney.

"Frank, my entire career has been at Branscomb. You can't..."

"That's the deal. Find another place. Take it or leave it. You won't get another chance. Murder's a pretty serious thing."

"I didn't kill Waterhouse."

"That's the deal."

"All right." Stoner's face fell.

"You can go. *Now* the case is closed."

Masterson waited until Stoner left the room, then ran over and clapped Frank on the back. "You son of a gun! Why didn't you fill me in?"

"It was all a bluff." Klawitter leafed through the empty pages. "He won't bother us any more."

"And the money?"

"Let's set up a scholarship fund for the new blood. Pay for an ethics curriculum, something to try to keep these kids on the straight and narrow so they don't end up getting twisted by slime like Waterhouse and the rest of his murdering tribe. It would be nice for something decent to come out of all this." Frank and Joe shook hands, then left the conference room together.

"Buy you lunch?" Joe asked.

"Not right now. There's something I forgot. I need to visit with Sam."

"Tell him thanks for me."

"I'll do that."

"Sam, you feeling any better?"

"Not too bad, considering that I got shot twice in the leg and just had to have part of my kneecap removed. You'll like it. I got the doc to save it for me. I drilled a hole in it, painted it Branscomb blue and put it on a chain. I'm gonna wear it around my neck."

Klawitter laughed. "Spoken like a true tough guy." He softened his voice and got serious. "Listen, I want you to know that we all owe you a great deal. You saved the medical center. You also saved a lot of people who'll never even know."

"I'm looking forward to the nice peaceful life of a medical student."

"I think that sounds great. But there's something I need to tell you."

"What's that, Frank?"

"Remember how concerned you were that your obligation to me would be over?"

"Yes I do."

"Well, a deal's a deal." Frank took Sam's hand to shake it, then pulled him close and hugged him. "God bless you. That's for my cousin. That's for Ellie." The men straightened up and Sam prepared to leave Frank's office. He turned on his crutches and looked back at Klawitter.

"Any word on Malinda yet? Lauren wanted me to ask again."

"No. I'm sure she doesn't have any reason to come back. The well's dried up."

"I suppose you're right. Oh, and sir?"

"Yes, Sam."

"About that favor I asked you. If it's not too much trouble, she's waiting outside..."

"It's already taken care of. Lauren's been reinstated by Valerie Snell, the new Acting Dean. She can remain at Branscomb as long as she likes. You two will be in the same graduating class." Frank lowered his voice. "Of course, you'll be taking all of your own tests from now on."

"No problem. The ones I got wrong were the ones you answered, I think."

"Go on. Get out of here."

Sam joined Lauren in the hall. She grabbed his arm and started shaking it, nearly knocking him off his crutches.

"Well, what happened? C'mon, tell me what happened."

"Take it easy, Doop. You're in. We're both in."

"Yahoo!" Lauren pinned his arms and kissed him over and over again. "I love you, Sam."

"I love you too, Lauren. Let's go home."

Two weeks later, Frank was settled in his favorite leather recliner in the study when the telephone rang. He thought about letting it go because he was so comfortable, but it wouldn't stop ringing. He lifted the receiver.

"Hello."

"I can see you in there. Is anybody with you?"

"Who is this?" The caller sounded like she was talking through her hands.

"Answer me. Are you alone?"

The attempt at disguise failed. "Malinda! Where are you?"

"Close by. I need to talk to you. Everything isn't what you think. You have to understand what happened."

"You tried to kill Sam. What else is there to talk about?"

"I don't blame you for not wanting anything to do with me, but please let me tell you my side of the story. It's not what you think."

"All right. I'll meet you. Somewhere in public."

"Frank, I didn't want to hurt you. Or Sam. You just got in the way, that's all. Look, they're all gone. You don't have anything to worry about. Can we meet right now?"

"Where are you?"

"Look out your living room window."

She was sitting in the car, holding a cellular phone and poised to make a quick escape if necessary. Frank opened the front door and motioned her over to him. "No one's here, Malinda. Come in. See? No cars but mine."

They sat at the kitchen table. "OK, let's have it. For starters, how did you get away? Where have you been?"

"The electricity just stunned me for a second — most of it went through my hands. I pretended to be unconscious until you and Joe Masterson left the room. I ran out and hid in another O.R. for a few hours. I was surprised that nobody came after me."

"There wasn't time. We had to clean up your mess."

"I'm sorry." She sounded penitent.

"Believe it or not, after all this, Lauren's been worried about you."

"She's a good kid. A real friend. She didn't deserve any of this. None of you did. Neither did I."

Frank was incredulous. "*You* didn't? From what I understand, you're a very wealthy young lady."

Malinda turned red as the tears welled up in her eyes. "No amount of money could ever replace what they took away from me. Of all people, you should understand that."

"Who are you?"

"Malinda Dwyer. Theresa Curtis. Both. I used to be Theresa. I changed my name to come here, so they wouldn't know I was here. I knew they wouldn't recognize me."

"You'll have to forgive me, but right now it's hard to understand how anything could justify murder. Malinda, you were going to kill them in cold blood."

"And I'd do it again."

Frank was astounded. Her eyes were puffy from crying and her attitude was remorseful, but the sentence she had just spoken couldn't have been more heartless. "Why did you come here tonight?" he demanded.

"To set the record straight. And to thank you."

"For what?"

"For trying to help me. For saving my life. I'd be dead or in jail now if it wasn't for you."

That was true. Frank's dilemma was that he couldn't ever go to the police. "Help you? We weren't trying to help you, whatever that means. What do you want from me, Malinda? I'm not Waterhouse. If it's money you're after, you can forget it. You may have been able to blackmail the others, but that won't work with me."

She burst into tears. "You still don't understand. I didn't come here for money. I don't want anything from anybody any more. It was all an excuse, a way to get close to them. I had to pretend to want their money, so I could get them all together in one place and *kill* them. I wanted them dead, like my sister."

"Your *sister*?"

Malinda walked across the room to compose herself. When she turned back to Frank, she was able to speak again.

"She was my sister."

"Your sister.......... Your sister..........*Who was your sister?*" Frank struggled for the connection. Then he saw it. "Oh my God, the girl at the party..."

"That's right. My baby sister. She was just out of high school. She drank like everybody else, but she didn't know anything about drugs. She was so impressed by the doctors, how they came on to her, how they promised her a good time. I knew it was a bad idea to bring her along, but she wouldn't take no for an answer. I'll admit we all got pretty wild, but I never knew what they were doing to her until it was too late." She hung her head and choked up again. "I walked into the room just as they were injecting her. He dragged me out. I begged him to let her go, to let me back in, to let me call for help, but *he* wouldn't let me. That scum-sucking son of a bitch held me so I couldn't leave or use the phone."

"Who?"

"Waterhouse. He was the only one who was sober enough to stop them, and he just let it happen. He kept me from saving her life. He's the one I wanted the most."

Frank bit his lip. "So you came here to kill them."

"You wanted them disgraced. I wanted them to suffer. To pay for all the pain."

"Why didn't you turn them in?"

"They convinced me that it was my fault, too. For bringing her. I was scared. When the police came, everyone was too afraid to tell the truth. They threatened each other, and they threatened me. The death was attributed to alcohol and drugs. They made it sound like she was a whore. Out of deference to the doctors, the whole thing got hushed up. I kept the truth from my parents. They were heartbroken, and I couldn't bring her back. Besides, they were too poor and I was too ashamed to go after that powerful a group. I tried to live with it."

"But you couldn't."

"No, I couldn't. I became obsessed with her death, a wild woman. A crazy woman. I wrote down everything, more than enough to prove what happened, but I didn't *want* to go to the police. Wiley and his boys deserved more than prison. The memories of my sister drove me. I missed her more, not less. Every time I saw a white coat I was reminded. I wanted to rip their hearts out."

"And the money?"

"Most of it's still sitting in a bank account. I needed a reason to stay close. Waterhouse was their leader. The blackmail part was easy. The hardest part was seeing them again. At first I thought the money would help, but it never did. I kept asking for more so they would think that was all I cared about. It took me a long time to work up the nerve. I waited for eighteen years to come to Branscomb. You and I just hap- pened to get to the same people at the same time. I'm sorry I got in your way."

Frank was moved by her fierce motive, her guilt, and the trade-off for what she had done. The bad doctors were gone for all time. He couldn't say it, but they both knew the value. "We were never going to hurt any- one, just expose them and let the system root them out. And you still haven't explained what you were doing with Sam. If we hadn't shown up, he'd be minus more than his appendix."

"I have to admit, you bailed me out on that one. It was all getting away from me. Resnick forced me to bring him. I didn't know what else to do. I needed something dramatic to get them all in the same room. I was hoping for Wiley, too. I would never have hurt Sam. He's doing all right, isn't he?"

"Yes. But you injected him! I thought you were trying to kill him."

For the first time that evening, Malinda flickered a smile. "Hardly. When I found out that you and Sam were closing in on Waterhouse and the others, I panicked. If something blew and the police got into the act, I would never have a chance at them. I drugged Sam just to make him sleep. The medicine in the syringe was to wake him up. The way things were going, I wanted him to be able to take care of himself."

Frank recalled that Sam had aroused soon after the injection, but he was still skeptical. "And your plan?"

Malinda shrugged her shoulders. "At that point, I didn't have one. I was just going to kill them, that's all. Before you showed up, it was three against one. You changed the odds. You're the reason *I'm* still alive. I would have failed. Again."

"Where have you been?"

"In a motel. I can't face Lauren and Sam after all of this. You'll tell them, won't you?"

"Yes, I'll tell them." Frank nodded in understanding. There was one more piece to fit. "So Malinda, Wiley didn't just choke on a mouthful of jellybeans, did he? I figured it for Stoner."

"Wiley was always a sloppy eater." She looked away. "At least I got him."

Frank felt sorry for her. "I suppose it's my turn. Let me tell you about the others." He explained that Resnick and Schmatz were still alive — not dead — but exiled and disgraced. He told her what had happened with Spencer and Stoner. "No one else needs to die."

"Where are they?"

"Gone for good. Stoner left yesterday. He told me there was nothing he could do to save your sister. Was he telling the truth?"

Malinda reached back to a cruel memory. "That's right. He didn't do anything. Where did he go?"

"University of Alabama." Frank put a hand on Malinda's shoulder. "What are you going to do?"

"I can't stay here. I couldn't stand the memories. I haven't done too badly in school though. I suppose I could transfer."

"I have a friend in the Dean's Office at Stanford. He's always very helpful in this kind of situation."

"Stanford. California. That would be nice."

"It is." He shook Malinda's hand. "Put it behind you. They're all gone."

The man sitting next to her on the airplane was bored, so he glanced over at her book. He couldn't pronounce the words, but he recognized the pictures.

"You a doctor?"

"Not yet. Studying to be one."

"Great. Where you headed?"

"Back to school. We start in a week. I'm transferring from Branscomb. Needed a change of scenery. You know, get closer to home."

"Sure know what you mean. I love Alabama, too."